FALLEN QUEEN

MARIPOSA BOOK ONE

Y. R. SHIN

poppypub

Translated by Stephanie Cha
Cover design by Eerilyfair Design

Published by POPPYPUB, Fort Lee
www.poppypub.com
poppypub is a trademark of POPPYPUB LLC.

Library of Congress Control Number: 2020946953

ISBN 978-1-952787-02-7 (hardback)
ISBN 978-1-952787-03-4 (paperback)
ISBN 978-1-952787-01-0 (ebook)

CONTENTS

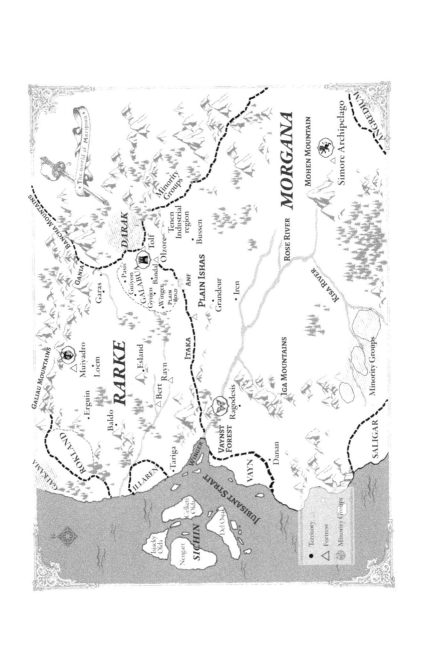

NORTHERN MYTH

Iero, Vineno, Senisa.

The Three Kings, as people called them, were the founders of many kingdoms on the northern continent.

Many myths tell of the birth and fall of the Three Kings. The one closest to the truth is the following:

Legend says that the northern continent became as it is now because of the descendants of the winter god, Kuatra Galiau. He was an ice beast with long black wings that could cover the sky, a mane as red as fire, and a white body. When the ice-covered god settled on the northern tip of the land, an unending winter swallowed the north.

A long time passed and Kuatra Galiau became a mountain range where the snow never melted. Upon learning of his transformation, Nuadga, another god, planted a bay tree next to him as a farewell.

The bay tree bloomed and bore three fruit. East Wind, West Wind, South Wind, and North Wind looked after the fruit with great care, and soon three children tore through the skins of the fruit and came out into the world.

Their names were Iero, Vineno, and Senisa, in order of birth. The three entered adolescence in two weeks and were fully grown in ninety days. They then went their separate ways to found their own countries.

Iero ruled with fear, severely punishing convicts. His strictness bought him both reverence and hatred from his vassals, so he had to constantly be on the watch for their swords.

Vineno poisoned criminals in an effort to give them a clean death. But a vassal who feared his poisoned wine secretly gave his cup to Vineno. Thus, the kingdom lost its king.

Senisa burned his own flesh to absolve all sinners of his land. His vassals were not afraid to sin, so he eventually turned into ash.

Hence, the three kingdoms fell, and the great divide in the north commenced.

Hundreds of years later, the son of Yeigan from Rarke wrote that the Three Kings myth was actually "three roads of a king."

Every so-called king in the north hears this story at least once.

There are three thrones in the world. All those who call themselves kings are forced to choose one of the three.

Which would you choose?

FUNERAL ORATION

Vano oredalak Nuadga, muin janlisas guire Rarkaddanya.
Nuadga of death, lead us to Rarkaddan.
There is a tale of a utopia passed on from the ancient
Rarkalia Dynasty.
When the great ones under the protection of Nuadga draw
their final breath, they go to Rarkaddan.
A land where there is no hunger, disease, or pain, at the cost
of one gold coin.
All the great generals will meet once again past the gate, in
the free land.
So ye who listen, do not fear death.
Love as you will, rejoice as you will, fight as you will.
Rarke in the north did not fear fighting mighty enemies.
The glory of the utopia where all loved ones gather is their
old faith.

PREFACE

This tale begins with a queen from two hundred years ago. A tragedy and a comedy of a queen who madly loved her country, a brother who worshipped her, and a man who loved her as a woman.

> *The time will come for the dance of the swords that could*
> *   not leave the battlefield,*
> *For the arrival of those who come back through the stream*
> *   of time,*
> *And the return of a lost butterfly,*
> *When a blue flower that has not been seen before blooms.*

FALLEN GLORY

It all began two hundred years ago, in a small country in the north.

Rarke was a kingdom on the border between the north and the west of the continent. Dolomete III was the twenty-fourth king of the kingdom, which remained a weak country a quarter of a century since its foundation. He had eleven children: three children from the queen, and eight from two concubines. The eleven children were all intelligent and talented, but the most beloved was the first princess, Swan Sekalrid Rarkalia.

The princess had the king's fiery hair, and she loved Rarke more than anyone else. The soil, the air, and even the grain from Rarke were her source of pride. She shared her bread with the hungry and gave her clothes to the cold. The people widely praised her for the mercy and love she displayed not with her words but with her actions. Hence, the king adored and trusted Swan very much, and the rough-natured nobles admired her as well.

As a merciful ruler to all she decided was hers, Swan was a royal born to reign. The old nobles and the young all agreed about her. "Though she has the body of a woman, she has a better mind and charisma than most men," they would say.

Swan followed the cunning Thick Black Theory, an eastern philosophy that emphasized developing a thick skin and a black mind, encouraging followers to pursue their own benefits while thoroughly hiding themselves behind a thick mask. At a young age, she was sharp-witted and aggressive, believing in the blood-and-iron policy.

She grew up on the rough land, gulling her brothers into thinking of her as a friend by volunteering to train with them and thawing her sisters' cold hearts with calculated generosity and appeasement. Even her natural beauty became a weapon, for the nobles could not resist her smile, which was like a single rose on a rocky land.

Only a couple of years after she first bled, she became the only princess who knew how to utilize her sex, instead of considering it an irreparable weakness.

Though she was beloved by all her blood, she did not truly return their love in the slightest. Her brothers were talented and gifted with the masculinity she was not, but they had no ambition, like satisfied fish in a little pond. The concubines' children who dared to get in line for the throne were imbeciles wrecking Rarke.

Such were her opinions about her siblings, except Peijak Dollehan Rarkalia, the sixth prince of Rarke, five years younger than her.

"Rest assured, brother, I will protect you from now on," she told him.

"And I will protect you, sister, when I am grown. I swear it."

She smiled at him. "You've got a snake's tongue, child."

She took note of her half-brother's potential. She gathered all the love that could have gone to her other brothers and sisters and gave it to Peijak, who looked just like their father and therefore like her.

"I will protect you." As she had spoken, Swan eliminated the remaining supporters of her two brothers, who destroyed each other fighting for the throne. She was soon praised as the sole true heir. Thus, she solidified her road to the throne even before the age of nineteen.

When she reached twenty-one, the king met an untimely death not long after his fortieth birthday.

After the king's funeral, Swan married the margrave from House Brionake, the largest house of warriors, and sat on the coldest and most beautiful throne in the world. In the process of securing her accession, she destroyed her professor, Yeigan, and handed those young sisters who remained in the palace to her supporting houses.

It seemed as if a peaceful era under the rule of a queen was to commence. But alas, her ambitions did not aim at a peaceful reign.

A year after a bitterly cold winter, the most horrifying war since the beginning of time began.

"Until when should the people of Rarke fight over small lands in this cold?" she declared. "Shall we leave the rich, fertile lands with golden crops to the hillbillies in the south and continue to hold our breath for the coming of winter? If you truly are patriots, shed your tears and rise. If you understand the duty of force, follow. Raising my shield and sword for you, even at the risk of my own life, is the future I seek. I will fill your bellies with food and let you strip off your thick coats and run about the fields freely. Prince Consort Margrave Brionake will be given a dukedom and will rule Rarke as regent. Sir Peijak Dollehan will go to war with me as the commander of my army."

Her unexpected ambition thus commenced.

Countless nobles stood by the queen in front of her throne in Norte Hall. In the solemn, suffocating atmosphere, the queen placed her sword on the left shoulder of her red-haired and blue-eyed half-brother, Peijak, who was said to be a superb swordsman. The two, soon to be written as the worst queen and knight in history, swore to each other.

"I, Swan Sekalrid Rarkalia, as the successor of the Bay Tree and the Queen of Rarke, swear to be fair to you. Your life, death, glory, and everything will be as they are done in my hands. All you will achieve from this day on will be in my name."

"As you wish, my queen. *Saturga guire Rarke.*"

Thus, Peijak Dollehan officially became the queen's knight.

No one dared to oppose the twenty-six-year-old queen with the greatest knight in the country, Peijak Dollehan, on her left, and the best margrave in the north, Belbarote Paseid of Brionake, House of Warriors, on her right.

A conquest began that would last eleven years. After five hundred years of peace, neighboring kingdoms fell without even putting up a fight at the sudden invasion. Though Rarke retreated from time to time, they were never defeated.

"All rise and stop the queen of Rarke. Else, you will meet your doom splattered with blood," exclaimed the king of a small kingdom at death's door.

No one could stop the cold-hearted queen, who developed new ways of war, burning castles, changing or blocking water supply routes, and building roads in the mountains instead of declaring a war and then fighting out in the field as the others did. One by one, her enemies succumbed.

Even the nomadic country in the west swore their loyalty to the queen after being chased to the edge of the desert. She finished her preparations to march to the fertile south. This only took her two years.

Swan was like a goddess of war, as good or better than men at sword fighting, archery, horseback riding, spear-throwing, and even hand-to-hand combat. She also had the merciless ghost of war, Sir Peijak Dollehan, by her side. The queen stood at the front of her army and granted love to her soldiers and shameless death to her enemies.

Peijak worshipped his only sister and kissed her blood-soaked hair. "I respect you for your love for Rarke. I love you with all my worthless body and mind."

She reached the age of twenty-eight after two years of war.

She had her first child on the battlefield. It was the child of her half-brother, not her husband, who was ruling back in the palace in her place.

After a small battle, Peijak came back bloodied from destroying a town in the south to find Swan glaring at herself in the mirror.

He fell down and cried. "Sorry. I'm sorry."

"It's my fault for not predicting this. Not yours."

She was pregnant but had not gone back to the palace for two years, because of the war. Things had changed. Instead of wallowing in despair, she sent a letter to her husband.

Duke Brionake replied to her letter and did not blame her for having another man's child. "Even if it is a son, I will keep it a secret if you make our child the heir."

"I will, Belbarote. Belbi, I truly do not know what to say."

Though she did not wallow in despair, she did feel terrible at this moment. The wifeless husband gave a bitter smile.

"But come back to the palace and tend to the affairs of state, Your Majesty," he said.

So, a yearlong truce was pronounced.

The nobles were starting to grow tired of the long war, which they had expected would end in a few years. Those who raised their voices with concern that the queen had no heir held a feast. Small kingdoms in the south who trembled at the news of Rarke's invasion were delighted and sent tribute disguised as gifts. The people prayed the war would end at this.

Seven months later, the queen gave birth to a son. The child looked like his mother, and hence like his father.

Two months later, Swan led her army back onto the battlefield, despite her vassals pleading her to stay and rule.

From then on, Belbarote came to visit her on the battlefield from time to time. She did not blame him for leaving the palace, for she had promised him a child. He implored her to end the war and rule her country whenever he visited.

Peijak, who supported her ambitious plan to conquer the entire continent, opposed Brionake and claimed he was a coward. "You seem to have grown scared even of the littlest things since you got locked up in that castle and started playing with paper instead of a sword, Your Grace."

"Though you may be winning war after war, the people of Rarke are tired," Brionake snapped in reply. "Do you not realize that the number of widows will increase if the drafted men do not come home, and we will soon run out of food because many are taken to forced labor? Not all of that can be replaced with plunder."

"If you mean to stop my sister, I will not just stand aside."

Duke Brionake glared at him, revealing his personal hatred. "The only reason you're still alive after laying your hands on Swan is because you are protecting her."

While her two supporters' animosity toward each other grew day by day, Swan carried another child. It was Belbarote's.

The queen decided to compromise.

She promoted Peijak Dollehan to commander-in-chief. She decided to return to the palace for two years to straighten her country's affairs. Not long after her return, she gave birth to her second child. Another son.

Belbarote pleaded with the queen, who only showed any kind of passion at the continuous reports from the battlefield, even after giving birth. "Your conquest has yielded enough, my queen."

"A little more. We will soon reach Morgana."

In less than eight years, they reached the final border in the far south. With the richest and the most beautiful kingdom, Morgana, left, she ignored her advisors' words.

"A little more, a little more, and the north and the south will unite, and this continent will be named the continent of Rarke," she repeated obsessively.

She was now the age of thirty-four.

She even ignored her husband's pleading and returned to the battlefield, to experience the moment of uniting the country with Peijak, who had been faithfully keeping his place on the battlefield for their grand triumph.

But under the rule of Dernajuke IV, the Blond King, Morgana was an enemy of vast strength that she had not faced yet. The legend of the undefeated army crumbled like a sand castle. The Rarkian army struggled.

And they were defeated.

To Swan, facing defeat was something unforgivable that shook her very core. After repeatedly advancing and then retreating, she roared in rage at the dead bodies of her soldiers. "I will not return before I crush those sons of whores!"

The purpose for her war with Morgana changed from patriotism to merciless hate. More people died, and the war turned into a war of attrition. Even at the cost of countless lives of her soldiers, Swan slowly advanced and reached Olzore at last.

Olzore was a nature's gift of a fort, said to have not once fallen since it was built. There was a narrow valley and rough lands in the front, and a valley with a shallow stream of water behind it.

The queen's army attacked without hesitation, but utterly failed. The fort did not fall to her attempts at infiltration, ambush at night, or battle. It mocked her.

Filled with hatred, the queen ordered a new operation so vast in size that no one had ever dared to think of it.

"We'll tear down that valley, Peijak."

Her generals followed the order with pleasure, for the queen believed that the word "impossible" was a mere assembly of meaningless sounds. They secretly constructed an enormous plan that would take two years to complete, only to satisfy the queen's determination to take down a single fort.

Not knowing that Rarke was in danger of falling apart because of the war that had lasted nearly ten years, Swan focused only on the imminent plan.

The Rarkians continued to fight little battles to fool the enemy, deploying countless soldiers and starting to dig through the valley and build tunnels.

They weren't enough. Swan started to draft workers from the nearby conquered countries. She even brought people from her homeland of Rarke into forced labor.

One day, three months before the end, those who were tired of war rebelled in Rarke. A messenger arrived at the queen's camp.

"I have been ordered to bring Queen Swan Sekalrid Rarkalia back to the palace, Your Majesty. By force, if need be."

She laughed at the messenger. "Who would dare order me to go anywhere? Duke Brionake will suppress the—"

He cut her off. "Duke Regent's orders."

An arrest warrant with Duke Brionake's seal fell near her feet.

Brionake was the head of the rebellion. She lost half of her army and her right wing.

Those who had praised her brought her down, saying that she was mad for war. Her beloved people and the man she trusted with her life turned their backs on her. The shocked queen forced Peijak to flee and returned to the palace alone.

She saw her children at a palace that now felt inexplicably foreign. She couldn't recognize them, for she had abandoned them at birth. She didn't even know their ages.

"You've grown so much," she said. "You must be…"

"It is an honor to finally meet you, Your Majesty," her eldest son said.

It was a hard blow.

Her ears, which had remained deaf to all the people's tearful pleadings, opened at last. She realized her madness at the single uttering of a child.

The nobles forced the befuddled queen to kneel. Some

supported her, saying that she would be a sage queen now. Those who feared she would take revenge on them raised their voices and sentenced her to die for neglecting state affairs.

Her armor, which felt like a second skin after almost half her lifetime, was thrown into the furnace.

Her husband kneeled in front of her. "I loved you."

She chuckled at the paradoxical nature of the first revelation of his true intentions. "I still cannot believe this is my end."

"Forgive me."

"I do not blame you."

"I failed to protect..."

"You protected Rarke."

"You. I failed to protect you."

He had aged quite a bit over the years, but he sobbed like a child in front of her. Time had left its marks on the face of this man who had sworn to belong to the queen.

The war had begun when she was twenty-six.

"It's...how old am I now?" she asked.

She did not even know her own age. What a foolish life it was. The conquest that had started with a loving desire to enrich her people had starved them instead and turned Rarke into a living hell.

"You will soon be thirty-seven."

"Ah...and you will be thirty-nine. No, forty?"

"Forty. It's been a long time."

She could not speak anymore.

Thirty-seven years of ferocious fighting. All she had left was land rotten with blood and the resentment of thousands.

She embraced her destiny without tears, letting her husband's cries pass like the wind, unmoved by them. It was like he was shedding her tears through his eyes.

In ineffable self-loathing, she asked for one last thing. "Belbarote, I ask that you be gentle with Peijak. He...his only fault is that he stayed by me, like a moth drawn to fire. I will pay for everything."

Belbarote's wet lips touched her dirt-covered forehead. She smiled, thinking it was quite warm.

Two weeks later, the sentence was carried out on the scaffold for all to see. It was the end of a twisted patriotism and rancid madness. With the death of the tragic queen, her horrifying conquest disappeared into history.

Thus, the bloody war that left an unhealable wound between Morgana and Rarke ended with Morgana's victory.

Belbarote Paseid Brionake, the first king of the Brionake Dynasty, ordered that Rarke end the war with Morgana under all circumstances, even if it meant they had to sign an unfair treaty. Dernajuke IV, the king of Morgana, and the first emperor (Valarjef I), did not miss the chance to elevate Morgana as the only empire on the continent.

The twenty-fifth Queen of Rarke, Swan Sekalrid Rarkalia's path was recorded in history. She would be remembered as an innovative and ruthless strategic genius, the Iron Queen, a tyrant.

Under the cold dew of the north, all she left behind were resentful cries, seven books of war, and two sons she'd barely even spoken to.

"I'll call for you once everything is taken care of. Trust me and wait, Pei," Swan had told him.

So, he had trusted her.

But not so long after, the news of the queen's imminent execution reached even Peijak, who was hiding in a small town in the fallen Rhine Kingdom. He had faithfully followed her for his entire life, and he could not even imagine losing her. As soon as he heard the news, Peijak took his surviving troops and knights and rode to the palace of Rarke.

Ten days later, the stone wall surrounding Muiyadro greeted him glumly under the gray, drizzly sky. Peijak stared at the severed head hung under the wolf banner on the wall.

Her red hair, as beautiful as twilight, was shorn at the neck and matted with rotting blood.

"A lie..." Peijak murmured.

Her murky blue eyes stared into the southern sky as if to mourn the unfinished deed. The bodies around her reeked of hearts rotten from betrayal. Swarms of maggots and bugs crawled in the pools of blood and rain.

Peijak cut off the rope and held the rotting head of the queen with his shaking hands. He slowly caressed her rotten cheek.

"A lie..." he said through clenched teeth. "She dedicated her life to this country. She was a good queen who didn't hesitate to risk her life to give her people rich land to farm. She was a great queen, the first in the history of Rarke to achieve such magnificent accomplishments of expanding the country's territory and rebranding it as a country with an indestructible army instead of a weak one. Without even thinking twice about it, they betrayed that invaluable leader, who will be incomparable to all those who follow her...

"A lie. This is a lie."

Peijak raised his head. His view was blurred by the rain and his angry tears, but he could still see the white wolf banner on the wall as clear as ever.

"B...Brionake!"

His furious cry spread across the rainy field like thunder.

"Sir Dollehan, the enemies are coming," one of his men told him.

Peijak pierced the ground with his terrifying pitch-black spear. It was a precious gift, with so great a meaning she had not been able to give it a name, so Peijak volunteered to become an actualization of its meaning himself.

He pierced the queen's head on his long spear. Then he turned her head away from the south.

Her blank eyes stared at the palace of Rarke.

"You ungrateful fools of Rarke!"

Peijak fixed his eyes on the Brionake banner following the soldiers running toward him to arrest him and his troops. It was Belbarote Paseid Brionake, the new king of Rarke, and the man who was once the queen's.

"I detest you! Usurper Brionake! I detest Rarke!" Peijak cried out as he glared at Brionake, who was now at the front.

Peijak turned away from the betrayers and spurred his horse. The knights of Rarke who had once worshipped the queen chased after him. Those who followed Peijak until the end rode south without stopping to get away from their pursuers.

Then Peijak and hundreds of knights loyal to him kneeled in front of Fort Olzore, the fort that had defeated the queen after years of war.

"I, the sixth son of the former King Dolomete the third of Rarke, brother of Queen Swan Sekalrid of Rarkalia, request refuge at Morgana."

Creaaaak. The fort's door opened.

Peijak wept at the grand sight of Olzore opening its door after so many days. As he took each step across the border his respected and beloved sister could never cross, Peijak let the rage build inside him.

Morgana was entranced by all the information the man who once fought in the fields with the queen of Rarke had to offer. Pleased with Peijak's loathing for Rarke, the king of Morgana granted him a title and land.

As proof of his loyalty to Morgana, Peijak presented all the original copies of the letters the queen had supposedly written herself and founded a new house. It was the beginning of a new force of power in Morgana, named Mariposa.

Thirty-two years later, as he met an end to his life stained with hatred and madness, Peijak Dollehan Mariposa prophesied, "Tell Rarke. The queen you betrayed will return with me."

And two hundred years passed.

CHAPTER ONE

There was a small town in Galabua of Rarke, near the forests at the southeastern border. Though it was small in size, it was a busy town, full of life, with travelers coming and going. With rundown houses built at an arm's length of each other and the fields spotted with ripening crops, the place looked almost like an undeveloped vacation site.

Its people were peaceful. They didn't even feel that threatened by being not too far from the Gerad border, where there was a war going on. Rather than showing hostility, they mingled like family with the merchants and travelers who came with news from the outside.

It was a serene land where there was no man too rich and no man too poor. Life was easy there.

But there's no place without exceptions. Even in this ordinary town, there was a celebrity whom all the residents found odd. She was the second daughter of the horse dealer, who had recently gotten a very handsome deal with the royal family of Rarke. The girl was a head smaller than a grown man and had dark-red hair that shined even redder under the sun. Her eyes were of the same shade. She was an unusually pretty girl for a small country town.

But the reason for her fame was not her outstanding beauty or virtue. The men in the town were all country bumpkins who did not have eyes for distinguished beauty to begin with, and they had all watched her grow up. There was nothing to marvel at about her appearance.

And her character? The girl, who'd just stepped into her twenties a few years ago, was as fierce as the old man who sold beans, whom all the townspeople agreed was the fiercest of all.

Her reason for fame could be summed up in one word.

Reuyen, the daughter of the only horse dealer, Jess Detua, was a genius.

Though a couple young men had recently gone to war by choice or by force—for even a peaceful town like this could not escape the impact of war—leaving the town quieter than before, Reuyen was at the center of all kinds of trouble. She was both idolized and envied by the local men until fairly recently.

Everyone knew that she was the daughter of a man who raised and sold horses, so her remarkable equitation made sense. What didn't make sense was her swordsmanship and archery, even taking down birds flying in the sky, which no one had taught her.

Young, competitive countrymen challenged her for no apparent reason and tried with all their might, but like the headstrong girl she was, Reuyen beat their pride to the ground without hesitating. Her mother baking bread as an apology to the crying, broken men became an everyday sight in the town.

If that had been all, they would have just thought she was gifted. But it wasn't.

The only place with books in the town was a tiny old bookstore. This meant that the only way to gather any kind of knowledge and information in specific areas was through learning from the town's visitors. Yet Reuyen was erudite enough to teach the outsiders instead.

When it came to the ancient history of Rarke, even the eighty-year-old hunchbacked teacher stopped his lectures when Reuyen was around, for he could not follow her. Though some argued that her words were made up, most of them were true, and there was no way of verifying the rest.

When someone asked, "Where did you learn all that?" she replied, "I don't know," made a sulky face, and changed the subject.

One day, bursting with curiosity, the adults of the town all went up to her father, Jess, and questioned him. The funny thing was, not even the father knew how or why his daughter knew the things she did. What was even funnier was that the so-called genius girl never admitted to being a genius herself. Today, her reaction was the same.

"I understand that I seem smart," Reuyen said to the crowd that had gathered, "but it's not right to say that I'm a genius. So, stop asking."

"Then what are you, I say?" an old man asked.

"I don't know. But you all should be aware, the east wind has turned the other way, so it's going to rain a lot once the sun sets. Why don't you go and bring your laundry inside or something?"

"What? Really?" The old man looked up to the sky, which held not the slightest hint of a cloud, with a curious frown.

"You can doubt me all you want, but do warn Lea. It looked like she was putting out her vegetables to dry."

It would rain if the swallows flew low and the cumulus was high. Her predictions were not one of those hit-or-miss sayings. Just how did she know them, specifically? She was right most of the time, but there was something about her. Everyone thought she must have been hiding something.

"How long are you going to stay huddled there, gentlemen?" she asked.

There wasn't even an inkling of respect in the question she spat out as she held up a bundle of wood. The adults soon started eyeing each other and then they all dispersed. A stranger might have laughed at them for scattering away for shelter from the rain when the sun was still shining strong, but they knew that Reuyen was right seven or eight times out of ten, so they had nothing to lose in believing her this time.

"Thank you, Reuyen! Time to bet if you're right again!"

Reuyen swallowed a sigh as she watched the adults running like children.

She put the bundle of wood down at the doorstep of the smaller room in her father's house. Her little brother, who was resting his head on a hard, wooden pillow and picking at his teeth, looked up with a blank expression on his face.

"What are you up to, sis?"

"Sidan, stop just lying around and help me move the wood. Is that all that's over there?"

"Why are you bringing it inside?"

"We didn't fix the shed leak."

"Rain?"

"Yup."

Sidan tilted his head and looked at the clear sky through the old window. Clear as clear could be. After sulking for a bit, he dropped his toothpick and went out without another question. The Detuas had learned through experience that every one of Reuyen's words and actions had meaning.

Reuyen brushed the dirt off her hands, checking that her easy-going brother, who took after their mother, was heading to the pile of chopped wood and hay under the fence. Sidan's voice came in from the yard.

"Hey, genius sis. Don't you think it's taking too long for our big brother to return? When do you think he'll be back? It's already fall and it's going to get cold soon."

"I wouldn't know."

"Why wouldn't you? You know everything. C'mon, say something smart again. You're good at that stuff."

She scrunched her face and glared at him, but he didn't notice. A sigh escaped her mouth.

Reuyen, the genius of Gyujen. She had heard enough of it. But she felt completely indifferent to being called a genius.

She didn't not know why people called her that. It was true that she was more erudite than anyone else in the town. But a genius had to have an extraordinary ability to accomplish something out of nothing. She was not a genius in that way.

When she was young, Reuyen was as much a troublemaker as any other child. But the year she turned seven, she realized she was different from the others.

~

It was the day her father first gave her a filly as a birthday gift. The filly was only a few years old, and was beloved by the girl for quite a while. The moment she climbed on the saddle with the help of her father, she was elated at getting the horse she loved so much.

The sky felt closer from atop the horse; she could see the world from a higher point, changed. That was the only time Reuyen ever fell off a horse.

Swan Sekalrid Rarkalia.

When she came back to her senses, her surprised mother was clutching her hand and crying, and her father was blaming himself for letting too young a girl to ride a horse. Her older brother was talking to the local doctor, who had come running after hearing the news.

"Why did you let a seven-year-old get on a horse? Are you even thinking or what?" Her parents started arguing louder and louder after the doctor left, and her younger brother started crying. It was total chaos. Reuyen broke into tears in the midst of all the commotion too.

A strange man's voice ringing clearly in her head made her cry even harder.

Swan.

Her mother was surprised by her tears, and rushed to embrace her.

Her trickles of tears turned into weeping, and Reuyen's father stomped out to sell the horse at the market. But for what? She could not stay focused with all the sorrow crashing into her like waves. She stumbled out of the room to stop her father.

"Reuyen!"

"Sweetheart!"

Over the startled voices of her brother and mother, a distant memory appeared.

The world we've longed for is right ahead of us, dear sister.

Before her father could unsaddle the horse, the little girl dragged up a step stool and got on the horse by herself. With tears and snot running down her face, Reuyen screamed at her surprised father and brother, who came running out of the house, almost breaking the door. They awkwardly held out their arms in case she fell again, but dared not put their hands on her or the horse.

Why can you not live outside of here?

The heartbreakingly clear and sorrowful voice clawed at her ears.

Though she knew it was wrong, she tightened her small fists around the reins. Her instincts kicked in. She realized at last that she could ride this horse without learning from anyone.

A higher point of view than ever before.

It was the first moment in her life when she felt her fears extinguished. Her father and mother screamed with fright at the sight of her by on the horse.

The girl precariously held on to the unfamiliar reins and rode on. She only wanted to shake off the scary voices echoing around her.

For our highest honor.

Her hands holding onto the reins of the galloping horse felt empty, like they had just let go of something, and the forest and the field were absent of people who should have been there.

Anything for my dear sister.

The ghastly voice whispering close by her ear unveiled foggy memories.

Carry out the execution.

She shrieked like her own head had just been cut off by the hallucination of a frightening sword. The pampered little girl did not know fear of swords. She should not have known. As if her world had just turned upside down, she kept on screaming like a madwoman and riding on until she lost her grip on the reins, then the mane, and finally fell on the small trail right outside the town. Her beloved horse ran away. She sat on the deserted trail, shaking like a leaf, then dropped her head to the earth.

Swan Sekalrid Rarkalia, you are...

The girl who had been howling fearfully knew who she was.

You are the great queen of Rarkalia.

Not long after darkness fell, her father and older brother, along with the townspeople, found her. The distraught girl was brought back to her home and was looked after with great care.

The filly that dropped her came back after two days.

She gave the horse the name "Dekallia," meaning "of Kalia." She was forbidden to go anywhere near the horses for a while, but that didn't matter. She knew how to ride without being taught, knew how to wield a sword without a teacher, and knew the geography outside the town without a map.

Her memories and knowledge became clearer and clearer as the years passed by, flowing out of her without her wanting it. She was both praised as a genius and misunderstood as a witch, but she was not proud of any of it.

Had the woeful soul of the queen possessed her, or had the unrelenting queen come back from the dead? The girl spent fifteen more winters with the question she could not share with anyone hidden deep in her heart.

Soon after sunset, the dark clouds covering the sky started pouring down streams of rain, thick rain that seemed like it wanted to flood the world. The cool sound of rainfall covered the empty places of the outsiders, who had become harder to spot recently.

It was an evening when even the twilight was fogged by the rain.

Senila, Reuyen's mother, came out into the living room after finishing preparing for dinner and started to put away the leaky flower pots, then suddenly stopped.

"I wonder if he's getting wet at all…"

"Go eat, Mother. I'll put away the pots." Reuyen quickly took over the task.

"Look, Reuyen, honestly… How could your brother not send one letter?"

"These are hard times, Mother."

Her father, Jess, who had extremely good hearing, heard that from the kitchen table and yelled, "Woman! Don't even start about him. He's all grown up anyway!"

"Now I can't even express concern for my own child?"

Jess covered his ears at Senila yelling right back at him. Sidan giggled as he sat down at the dinner table and picked up a nicely roasted chicken leg. The young man quietly put it back down after seeing his father's face.

"But it's already been, let's see…over half a year since he left, right?" Sidan asked. "No wonder you're worried. Dekallia's babe's already..."

"He'll come crawling back when he runs out of money," said Jess.

"But he didn't even bring that much. It's about time he ran out of money, and he's never gone this long without sending a word back home. He seemed quite hurt when he was talking about joining the army before, and with his temperament... You don't think he would have gone to the battlefields, do you?"

"Sidan, what on earth are you talking about?"

"If that's so, will he come back home with a title or something? Will we become nobles then? Hmm..."

Sidan muttered and played with his spoon, and Senila's face turned white. Jess smacked the back of his youngest son's head without a word.

"Ouch!" Sidan moaned and rubbed his head.

"Stop talking nonsense and eat."

With an even more depressed look after Sidan's cheerful words, Senila took the seat to the left of Jess. On his right diagonal side were Sidan and Reuyen's seats. And one last seat. That seat had begun to collect some dust because its owner hadn't returned in a while.

Senila stared at the empty chair and suddenly called out, "Reuyen, just put a bucket under there and come."

"Coming. You can start without me."

Jess glanced at his oldest son's seat and then looked away. "Not an easy one, that one."

For whatever reason, the oldest son of the Detuas, Eivan Detua, had announced that he desired to enlist himself to fight in the Great Battle against Morgana half a year ago. That was around when the royal army, who'd bought nearly sixty horses from the Detuas, was still staying in town.

"I want to fight too," he'd said. "They say that even commoners can receive a title if they distinguish themselves on the field, and I heard a soldier from Deujen actually became a knight."

Eivan's sudden declaration ruined the whole family dinner. It hadn't even been a full day since the Detuas were overjoyed by the big sale to the royal army. Even Sidan was surprised enough to drop the piece of meat he was about to eat. "Eivan…you've really gone mad, haven't you?"

"I'm not as good as Reuyen, but I know how to wield a sword and fistfight."

"A war is no joke, you know. I heard it's absolutely brutal out there. Is it actually a place where everyone and their mother who knows how to use their fists goes and win titles?"

Jess threw his spoon and ended the debate. "No."

"Why, Father? With great risk comes great reward."

"Listen to your father," said Senila sharply. "Eivan, don't even speak of such a horrifying thing. We have a comfortable living… and you're the firstborn, our oldest son."

"I'm sure it will not come to that, but if any accident happens, Reuyen or Sidan will take over the family business. Reuyen is an outstanding individual all around, and Sidan takes great care with the horses, so it really doesn't matter which of us takes over."

Whatever the royal army had told Eivan, it had worked. Eivan had already made up his mind. Jess finally lost control and threw the table on the ground, then struck Eivan across the face. The table crashed with a great racket, and Eivan stumbled for balance. Shocked, Sidan clung onto his father and tried with all his might to calm him down.

"E-Eivan! Why would you bring up weird things like that at the table? Father, calm down!"

Sidan, who especially loved Eivan, tried to change Eivan's mind by shouting at him, persuading him, coaxing him, and telling stories of those who came back from war as a cripple, but to no avail.

After quietly watching him, Reuyen spoke. "Eivan, you can't even stomach that much."

"I'm…"

"A battlefield is a place where you have to march on even if you want to stop and vomit at the dead's guts rolling around, and run straight into your death with oil splashed all over your body if your commander tells you to. It's a place of death where no one cares about ten, twenty foot soldiers dying to save one single knight. You could be one of them. And an edged sword is different than a training sword. Once the battle starts, you have to cut a man's throat like a piece of meat, smash the enemy's face with your shield, open his chest and plunge a dagger into his beating heart, and cut off the legs of those who are chasing you. It's customary to cut an arm or a leg of those who have surrendered if you can't take them as prisoners, so they can never hurt the ones you love again. Reward comes from killing an enemy, not protecting your country. And when the enemy aims for you, they are thinking the same thing. Wouldn't they have the same kind of patriotism as you?"

Sidan shivered at Reuyen continuing without showing any emotion, dabbing her lips with her napkin. Reuyen noticed this and added with a sigh, "...or so I've read somewhere. Anyway, a battlefield is not a place for someone who cries over one dead horse, like you. Trust me."

"Ugh, what on earth was that?" asked Sidan. "Where did you read that? And why the hell were you reading it?"

"None of your business," she snapped. "Maybe you should read some books."

Leaning on the wall where Jess pushed him, Eivan silently listened to his sister. Jess just stared at his daughter, even forgetting that his son had stopped insisting that he would go to war. He looked worried that she had said such unexpected things in such a composed manner.

In the silent dining room, Reuyen looked back at her father and grinned.

Thanks to Reuyen's warning, if one could call it that, Eivan started to give in. After Senila's tearful begging, and Sidan's desperate pestering, he finally took back his announcement.

About two weeks later, Eivan told the family that he was going on a trip with a couple other young men in town to cool off. Senila, who had been nervous the whole time, gave him a bit of pocket money, saying that she'd rather have him be on a vacation. Jess, who was still mad at Eivan, indirectly permitted it by telling him to just get out of his sight.

Early morning in the beginning of winter, Eivan found Reuyen at the door, wanting to say goodbye when everybody else was still asleep. He ruffled her hair and gave her a bitter smile.

"When I think about it, you were always different. Sometimes to the point it became scary. I am relieved to have such a wonderful child as my sister," he said. A quiet utterance.

Reuyen let him ruffle her hair without saying anything, looking at him through the fog made by her breath.

"As the oldest daughter, you have a lot of responsibilities. You know that, right? When I'm not here, you protect the family."

"Sounds like a last word."

With his eyes widened with surprise, Eivan lowered his head and put his forehead against Reuyen's. Not showing any emotion, Reuyen kept her light, cat-like eyes open and stared straight into his. Eivan's low laughter resounded in the morning air.

"Eivan, it's not too late to give up," she said.

"Reuyen." He shook his head. "Listen. We need to fight. I hear Morgana has reinforced their army by tens of thousands."

"It's an exaggeration."

"Exaggeration or not, it's still true that there is a war going on right next to Galabua. We're safe now, but if things go wrong, our town will not be safe anymore. And if the war doesn't end soon, we'll have to pay a lot more taxes."

She set her jaw. "I don't care."

He sighed. "Reuyen, you're smart enough to understand what I'm saying. If Morgana's reinforcements come and start attacking with full force, our border will fall right away. And what would happen if Rarke loses? Even if what I've heard is all just a rumor, nothing changes. It's still true that our enemies are getting closer by the minute. Toby from the fenced house and Hald from the Reeses are joining me. I'm fine with me alone not changing anything and my not being strong enough to do one man's part. It's better than doing nothing. I, someone who cries over one dead horse, might have to kill another man, like you said. I probably will. But I can promise you this. I will never kill for the sake of killing. I am leaving to protect. To protect our town...and to protect our family."

Thinking that Eivan's face suddenly looked sorrowful, Reuyen put an old handkerchief around his wrist without another word.

She could guess what kind of speech the royal army would have given to awaken the patriotism in the young country men. And what kind of hopeful and fearful thoughts the men would have had when they heard that speech.

Reuyen kissed his cheek a little longer than usual. "I wish you good fortune in war."

~

A small figure in a black robe came into Reuyen's sight when she crouched down to organize the flower pots. The man staggering toward the house in the dark and the rain was someone she knew very well.

"Oh..."

A pot slipped through her hands and fell to the floor with a crash.

"Reuyen?" her mother called. "Is everything all right?"

Surprised, Senila came running from the kitchen. Reuyen fixed her eyes on the window, staying completely still. The rain poured even louder.

Knock knock knock.

Her mother went to open the door.

"Toby? Aren't you Toby from the fenced house?"

It was small Toby, who had left with Eivan. The young man had a new deep wound on his left cheek, and he suddenly kneeled on the cold, battered floor.

"Ma...dam Senila...Reuyen..."

"What in good heavens..." began Senila. "Wait, didn't you leave with my son? What happened? Where's Eivan?"

Bloodied armor showed through his sleeves as he lay on the floor. *Clang.* Reuyen saw the moment her mother finally realized the smell of blood was mixed with the smell of rain; Senila froze.

"I'm—I'm so sorry, so, so, sorry..."

"Toby, why are you here alone? Where's Eivan?"

Trying to swallow the hiccupping sobs, Toby handed her an old handkerchief that was now stained a dark red. Sidan, who'd come nonchalantly with a spoon in his mouth, and Jess, who was sulking in the corner with his eyes on Toby, both kept their silence.

"Toby...?"

"Eivan...was trying to save, save me...I was too scared... ran...away..."

"Where is my son...where...?"

Toby's sob burst out, breaking his voice. "I...report."

Stopping herself from covering her ears, Reuyen shut her eyes.

She pictured the man who had left with such a pure desire to protect the ones he loved on the horizon of that beautiful morning where you could see your own white breath. His back had seemed so wide and so dependable.

I wish you good fortune in war.

Good fortune. What a meaningless thing to wish for on a battlefield. From one who knew very well that one could not rely on fortune.

"As a fell...ow in the army of Rarke, third brigade, Ei-Ei-Eivan Detua slew an enemy knight and proudly fell... Forgive me. Please, forgive me. I'm sorry. I'm so...rry... Sorry..."

A teardrop trickled down Reuyen's cheek as she stared at her mother falling to her knees.

"You...bastard..." Father muttered with his head tilted back, crushing her heart.

It was a rainy, dark evening.

CHAPTER TWO

A few years ago, there had been an imperial decree by the emperor of Morgana, a country that was drunk with the title "the only empire on the continent."

"Morgana is upholding the great responsibility of bringing order to this continent. Therefore, the neighboring countries shall double their tributes."

But everyone knew all that gold and treasure would go into building their new palace.

This proclamation provoked Rarke, which had endured all the years of shame since the queen's war from two hundred years ago, just waiting for the right moment to set everything straight again. The vengeful royal family of Rarke not complying with the new order was almost opportunistic.

As always, a war was sparked by a few people's interests disguised as conviction.

Of the three young men in the town who had left saying they were going on a trip, one died, and another came back in bloodied armor.

Those who heard the news started a commotion. Some were even planning on moving away after hearing a rumor that the Morganaans, having won battle after battle, had set foot in Rarke. Some went to visit Toby, half nervous and half excited that they might be able to hear the news of their husband or son who had gone to war as well. But Toby had already left, and an unusual despair and anxiety covered the town.

Reuyen took the anxiety, fear, and sadness with more calmness than anyone else. War was something very familiar to her life.

When she closed her eyes, she could still see and hear her memories of war like it had happened yesterday. Riding in the fog, reeking of blood, passing through horses, enemies, comrades, and corpses. As if guided by instinct, she rode in search of another living enemy among all the dead. She remembered holding all those deaths in her hands like badges of honor and looking down at the enemies pounding their chests with the grief of losing a comrade.

But in this present, she was just the daughter of an ordinary horse dealer. After slowly melting into the country life where nothing special happened, she had put an end to the dichotomy of her identity and let everything from her past life flow away. All she listened to now were stories the visitors told from time to time.

Morgana.

When she heard that name ingrained in her bones, she recalled the memories of the last battle. The abominable sight of the fort she could never conquer flashed in her eyes. But it was all from a far, faraway past. It grieved her, but it did not infuriate her. She simply listened to the stories of Morgana becoming an empire after winning the war, who the current king was, how afraid the other countries were of Morgana, and what other big events had happened since then, like they were unrelated to her.

Looking back at her past self in times of peace, she knew she had been a hypocrite.

She had swept the battlefields with her brother who was called "the ghost of war," stronger than anybody else, proud of not losing one battle. She had later been blinded by her mad ambition to conquer the whole continent. Wearing the disguise of patriotism and shedding countless people's blood as sacrifice, she had not felt any guilt. The queen who had believed madness to be conviction was a fool, not a genius.

Reuyen frowned at the chaos that prevailed in the house when she came inside after cleaning the stable.

"Why don't you go out for a walk or something?"

The news of death had brought its stench from the battlefield.

Her brother, who was three years younger than her, was glaring out the window with red eyes and veins sticking out on his neck, a more miserable expression on his face than ever. Bringing her train of thoughts to an end, she quietly asked, "Did you eat?"

"It's because of what I said. I was the one who said that crap...if he'll receive a title. I...because I blabbered that sort of shit..."

"If you haven't eaten yet, I'll make you something. How's Mother?"

Sidan's head turned like a wooden doll at her excruciatingly serene voice. "How are you this calm?"

Looking back at his eyes full of hatred, she recalled another memory.

There will only be pain beyond this point.

Belbarote Paseid Brionake.

The man praised as the greatest king of the new dynasty of Rarke. She thought of him when she saw the white wolf banner of the royal army that came to buy horses and collect food now and then.

You can stop now. You have already proven yourself enough.

Oh, the wise man of the queen. He knew. The pain, the resentment of those who would have to live on. His advice from two hundred years ago that she'd understood at death's door had become a reality.

She turned away.

"He knew what he was getting into."

"How can you say that kind of crap? He's our brother! Our brother has died... Those bastards of Morgana butchered our brother!"

The most powerful patriotism stemmed from hatred.

She, who had been a tyrant in the far past, knew that as well. So, she understood her brother's fierce aggression. After pointlessly moving her lips, not knowing what to say, she coaxed him. "Let's stop. At least you should come back to your right mind."

"Dear smart sister, please tell me. It's a lie, right? Right? I keep thinking, but it doesn't make sense. He was as good at sword fighting as you. He was good, right? They said that they couldn't find the body, so he must be just missing. That must be it, right?"

Who will retrieve the bodies one by one on the battlefield, where hundreds and thousands die? They had probably been piled up and burned all at once. But her young brother was too unstable to know the truth.

"I'll cook."

Reuyen headed to the kitchen.

Her father hadn't spoken a word since the day they got the news, and her mother hadn't gotten out of bed. Even Sidan was overwhelmed with hatred. She could not figure out where to start, or how to console them.

While organizing the tableware, she suddenly let out a hollow laugh. She kept thinking she was fine, but her hands were shaking. Was her heart paying the price of not stopping her brother, who chose to leave? Was the guilt of ignoring the truth she knew this heavy?

Morgana.

Why is Morgana imposing this shameful pain on me again? The foe from two hundred years ago was merely breathing and living. She shook her head. It was such a self-centered thought. They had only chosen to bloody themselves to clean out years' worth of baggage.

Sidan's enraged voice came flying at the back of her head. "I can't accept this. I can't forgive this!"

"What are you going to do, then?"

"I will fight too."

She snapped back to reality.

You have to look after our family now.

Reuyen dried her hands and turned toward her brother to shake him back to his senses. Her enraged, ready-to-fight brother was standing in the doorway to the kitchen. After a moment of silence at his obvious despair, she walked outside.

"Bring your sword."

Clank.

Sidan took half a step back, shaking his hands. Not losing that opportunity, Reuyen swept in with the back of her sword and threw Sidan's on the ground. Then, the edge of the sword sharp enough to slice through iron, she lunged for Sidan's neck.

The point of her old sword stopped right before reaching his collarbone. While his chest huffed and puffed, Reuyen kept her steady breath. It was an easy victory that came with the cost of a young man's pride.

"Do you think any more would make a difference?"

But even without his sword, Sidan did not give up; he ran into her with a great cry. Reuyen smoothly pivoted around and kicked the side of his knee like she had been expecting it.

Her at-least-a-head-taller brother dropped to the ground with a groan.

"You died twice today. Good thing you have multiple lives, Sidan Detua."

"Ah...Ahhh...! Shut it! You think I'm going to give up here?"

"What if you don't? It all ends once you're dead."

"That's not happening. I'm having my revenge!"

She almost actually slew him in a burst of anger. She held her sword tight to calm down again and glared at her pigheaded brother.

"Stop talking so recklessly. You, who can't even beat me, will go out there in the midst of war and kill enemies for revenge?"

"You're just stronger than normal! You're the strongest in our town! You monstrous woman!"

"So what if I'm the strongest in this tiny town? Not being able to beat a frail woman, someone who's far more inept than the knights fighting out there, just means that you're weak!"

She stared down at the side of his scrunched face that looked like he was about to cry, then kicked his sword lying on the ground far away. After a while of just lying there and fuming, Sidan growled, "Are you not...are you not enraged by this? How can you be so cool?"

"Don't defile the road of patriotism Eivan chose, you fool."

"Youuuu! Ahhhh!"

She bent the arm of her inflamed brother coming at her and knocked him down again. But the obstinate Sidan turned back around and started punching her.

A young man who spends his days riding horses and running errands around the stable is stronger than meets the eye. Feeling the aching pain from her chin like his last blow broke it, Reuyen grabbed his neck, anger flashing in her eyes.

"Ahhh! Let go of me! Let go! So what if he chose it himself? I can't even grieve him since it was his choice? You heartless, inhumane monster!"

"You're the one who's deluded! Do you think a battlefield is an easy place for a soft, weak boy like you to even survive? You think you, a mere boy, can be in the dogfight amongst those who crush their own friends' bodies and live only to take the lives of others, driven by madness?"

"What are you?" His resentful eyes stared straight at hers. "You! You're so great, so gifted that you know everything, don't you? You're not even like a human!"

Tears seeped into the ground his hands were so desperately grasping at. Reuyen slowly loosened her grip on his neck.

"You're not even human."

His cry echoed in her ears. She took her shaking hand off him and stood up.

"You're saying that I'm not even human. You can only say that because you're still blinkered...truly." Everything happening now was rooted in the past. "A battlefield is a place where humans become humans no more." Like the queen, the foolish queen who could not reflect on herself until her love for her country degenerated into madness. "So, come back to your senses. Next time, I'll break your legs for real."

With that, Reuyen threw her sword to the ground. She couldn't stand holding it any longer because its hilt resting in her hand felt freakishly familiar. She turned her back to her brother, who was still on the ground, his eyes furious.

"You cold-blooded monster!"

Ignoring the wretched cry, she walked toward the stable, where the familiar smell of horse manure wafted in the air.

She stopped at the entrance. Her father was tending to the horses as usual, with his back to her.

"Father."

As he fed the horses with slightly shaking hands, his back looked smaller and weaker than ever. She walked to him and put her arms around his waist.

"Let me do it."

"...yelled at him."

At his muttering, Reuyen's head tilted and she touched her father's back.

How could she not feel his heart shattered to bits and pieces? His was that of a parent who recalls how he yelled at and struck his own child to change his stubborn mind, and how that led to Eivan not even being able to say goodbye in the end. She couldn't even begin to imagine how regretful her father must be.

"My son... he was my son," her old father murmured pensively. "Thank the good lord at least you're in your right mind. Yes, now here's a true Detua."

His shoulders started to shake as he continued as if he was consoling himself. A gentle sob followed.

"What was he thinking? I kept telling him not to, but he..."

"Men don't stop running until their whole world falls apart at a glimpse of hope."

He turned his cloudy eyes to her. He wasn't looking at her like she was some monster, as Sidan had. But she could still detect a hint of disappointment in her cold-heartedness in those old eyes of his. A cacophonous sound came from the yard, like someone was breaking things. Jess turned his head away from that piercing noise, brushed off his hands, then turned back around.

"Yes, back to reality. The living must..."

Reuyen silently let go of him. She stood there by herself, looking at the stable that stank of manure.

This prevailing sorrow, yet men still lived on. The grief for someone who was determined to go to war was a grief that would fly by like birds of passage. Even the ordinary ones who could not understand Eivan's intentions would eventually walk their own ways, dragging along baggage rooted in their own reasons.

The death of a son, of a brother. Nothing could be worse to them than that, so all that was left to do was to lick each other's wounds and move on.

～

But five days later, she had no choice but to face her naiveté. Sidan had disappeared.

After Sidan's departure, Senila's sickness worsened. Jess didn't even talk about it or get upset, like he had never had a son at all.

Standing alone in her brother's empty room, Reuyen broke into laughter. It was truly a ridiculous act. Young men who could have lived completely sheltered from war took off for a long journey like moths lured into a fire.

As the oldest daughter, you have a lot of responsibilities. When I'm not here, you protect the family.

She dejectedly leaned against the wall and ruminated on the dead's whispers. An old, lifeless creaking noise, like from an abandoned house, rang in her ears louder than ever.

CHAPTER THREE

Two weeks later, the third young man who had left with Eivan and Toby came back one-legged. After hearing the news of the stagnant state of the war, some residents left to find some other city far away from the border.

With the young man came news of Sidan as well.

"Reuyen," said Eivan's one-legged friend. "Sidan was at the front as a volunteer for the Gerad border. Did you know?"

The front. The hell where blood and despair crashed around like waves.

Senila, who had been trying to collect herself by convincing herself that Sidan had left to cool down, finally had a heart attack and collapsed. She lived, thanks to the doctor who swiftly came and took great care of her, but her last hope had been destroyed.

The next day, Reuyen left the house early in the morning. She walked into the forest, following a small trail until she was alone, and held up the bow she felt as comfortable with as a sword. She aimed at an old tree and fired anything and everything.

She pulled on the string until her lips started bleeding and her fingertips festered, and the arrows drew a circle around the big old tree one by one under the sunlight.

Draw and fire.

Pull like your life depends on it, then let go like nothing matters anymore.

When she ran out of arrows, she plucked the ones out of the tree and shot them again. It was a meaningless repetition of an action, like collecting an abandoned heart and then abandoning it again. But in that meaningless repetition, she started to feel resentful of the countless traitors who disobeyed her orders.

"Fool, fools, imbeciles…!"

But it all meant nothing.

Soon, the thick night fell. After repeated shots, the tips of the arrows became blunt and the string hung lifelessly, frayed like it was about to break. Reuyen lowered the bow.

Her limbs shook, exhausted, and the pain from her skinned lips and fingers came back. After wiping her sweaty chin with her sleeve, Reuyen ripped off a piece of the fabric she had used to wrap the bow with and put it around her bloody hand. Then, she sank to the floor. Everything was a karma from her past self.

You must protect our family. I'm relieved to have you as my sister.

Her pale lips drew a sneer.

How can I, Eivan? They've already left my hands. How?

She had never been more desperate for an answer from someone in her life as she was now.

After the sun set, she fumbled through the darkness on the trail back home. In the quiet nightscape, without even the slightest smell of dinner being cooked, Jess was blankly staring out the window. The same window that Sidan had glared at with hatred.

"Father, you should take Mother and the horses and move away, just in case."

"No."

"Guiyon Fort is known for its impregnable walls, so it should be safe there."

"No."

"We're safe now, but it'll be too late after the war hits here."

His stern, heavy voice echoed in the room. "This is our family's house and town."

With that, the only sound in the house was Senila's mournful cries coming through the closed door to her room. Jess stayed in his seat like a corpse and shut his lips.

Instead of answering, Reuyen looked at the sword that was leaning against the wall in the corner. It was a sword for killing. A tool of murder that sometimes made a hero and sometimes made a slaughterer. A sword, a freakishly familiar piece of metal.

She walked over to the corner and grabbed the cold, cold hilt. Then left the house. She didn't forget to tell Jess, though it was not a goodbye.

"...I'll be back."

Where are you going? Jess did not ask, but she still answered like she was reassuring herself.

"I'll bring Sidan back."

Two hundred years after she had left the battlefield, she was going back of her own free will, though she had believed she never would again.

She took a step into the pitch-dark world, as dark as hell at night. Her father's cry sounded from the house.

She carried those tears on her back, not abandoning a single drop. In the stable, she saddled the six-year-old babe of Dekallia. He was the fastest horse the Detuas had.

Eivan had named him "Den."

Eivan.

Just recalling that name hurt like a well-sharpened spear piercing her throat. She jumped on the saddle. Then she held up a painful whip.

"Let's go."

She didn't wish herself good fortune for the coming journey. She rode through the night, swallowed by grief.

She rode across the flatlands beyond the fields with unripened crops, across a small stream, past a forest she knew well. Every time the night and day switched and the sky changed its color, she rested for a bit and then rode again.

She only thought of one thing on the horse. Where she was headed.

Back...

"Whoa, boy!"

After riding for quite a while, she suddenly felt dizzy and pulled on Den's reins to stop. A dry smell came from across the field. Her heart, which had hardened like a stone, beat harder and harder as she got closer to the battlefield.

Are you going back...again?

Recalling that sincere voice by itself made her heart writhe in pain. She swallowed her mutterings and shook off that voice.

She was after one thing. Bringing Sidan back. But her memories made her recoil from war, like a traumatic wound. All the foolish deeds she had committed with her comrade Peijak, who would have returned to dust by now.

In her childhood, the cool sensation of the blade hit her neck every day, until she let go of all the memories. For a crime she hadn't even committed in this life, she had to be executed every day.

The queen had met such a wretched end. Why was she born again?

She was confused at times, but she considered it a message from God to live a new life this time. So, she lived like a witch in the forests who was content with a life she chose not to see or hear.

But now, she wanted to cut off her legs that desired to go back to the fields. A strange fear grasped at her ankles. She whipped her feet that wanted to stop, trying not to give in.

Coming down after precariously swaying in her seat, she caressed Den's legs.

"Let's take a break, Den."

She leaned against a small tree that had grown in the middle of the road, opened her water bottle, and drank. She then looked across the field full of weeds. A familiar but somehow slightly different horizon came into sight.

She'd been riding for three days straight, leaving only half a day until she'd arrive at the border. A border called Gerad, where there was the Boald Field of Rarke in the north, and Morgana in the south. She didn't know which side Sidan would be on, but it didn't matter. She would search everywhere to bring him back. Then, so he would never do anything stupid like this again...

Her face suddenly stiffened. She realized that she was too carried away in her own thoughts that she had been ignoring a basic error.

Military laws were no joke. If the army was as strict as it was two hundred years ago, those who set foot in it would not be able to leave without a good reason. She wasn't even sure if she could persuade someone who had gone to war with such a strong resolution. How was she going to pull him out without causing a scene?

She couldn't make him become a deserter. She didn't even know how to get into the camp to find him.

She felt utterly helpless.

Had she been mistaking her present self for a queen who could control everything with the wave of a hand, or a single smile?

Feeling her thighs shake from the long ride, she collected her thoughts. *Now is the time to be truly cool,* she told herself over and over to empty her mind.

Perhaps because she had been riding with only a few hours of sleep every now and then, her eyelids kept drooping as she sat there.

When she woke up from a nap she hadn't even noticed she was taking, some knights were riding toward her.

"Who goes there? There has been a strict order not to come near the border during wartime."

Their helmet-covered faces were hard to see because of the sun shining behind them. She instinctively sprang up. They all had triangular brassards around their left arms made from the wolf banner, the symbol of Rarke.

When she turned her head at the rhythmic shaking of the ground, soldiers slowly marching from across the field came into view.

"Is this cavalcade headed to the border?" she asked, her voice still half asleep.

A tall, brawny knight at the front grabbed his sword and said, "Don't you know that those roaming around near the border during wartime can be deemed suspicious and heavily punished? Identify yourself."

"I am Reuyen Detua, the daughter of Jess Detua, the horse dealer of Gyujen about three days' ride from here."

"And what is your business here?"

"I am headed to the Gerad border."

The knights thought she was just walking about the area, not knowing that there was a war going on. They stopped for a moment. They had spotted the long object covered with an old fabric. The moment their eyes landed on the frayed hilt of the sword, they became visibly alarmed.

"Why?" said the brawny knight.

Thousands of soldiers came into Reuyen's sight. The army marched slowly but surely and stopped not far away from the tree she was resting underneath.

She looked back at the knights in bronze armor at the front of the cavalcade. There was a man with a rectangular brassard instead of a triangular one on his left arm. He must have been the commander. The two flag bearers standing next to him bore a wolf banner and a roe deer banner.

Though it was a bit different from her memory, she did remember a yellow roe deer banner. The House of Chesa.

An odd feeling of enervation shot up her spine and pressed on the back of her head.

House Chesa ended up joining forces with the House of Brionake to bring the queen down in her final years, but it was an old house renowned for its loyalty to Rarkalia.

Reuyen forced herself to look away from the flags. She took out an old parchment proving her identity and another piece of parchment that certified the transaction between Detua Stables and the royal family.

"I'm not sure if this will suffice, but here is a receipt from a transaction with the Rarkian royal family. I am one of the war horse providers to the royal family. If you are headed to the border, would it be all right if I joined you?" Reuyen asked, with tentative hope.

Though it was not one of the official trading places, the seal of a northern wolf on the document was not to be ignored. The knight who took hold of the crumpled document next scrutinized it with his sharp eyes hidden in the helmet. All four knights took a look at the document one at a time and then threw it back at her.

"This may be proof of your identity, but you're standing in the way of the cavalcade. That's a serious crime by itself. You most certainly cannot join us, but I will hear the reason you're heading to the border."

"I am on my way to retrieve my brother, who enlisted himself, for he is the heir of our house."

"Move aside. A war is not some kind of a play your little head made up."

The knights scoffed at her and turned their horses around.

Reuyen slowly smiled as she watched them trot away. It was a cold sneer.

She didn't have to make it up. She knew without having to imagine it what lay beyond that horizon in her head. A sudden desire to pull him down from the horse and scream at his face gushed forth. *Do you have any idea who the woman is you're laying eyes on?*

But swallowing all those words, Reuyen quietly led Den and herself out of their way. After all, she was only the daughter of a nameless horse dealer.

CHAPTER FOUR

The wildcat-like eyes, glistening with the kind of energy one feels at the beginning of a new year, era, or time, slowly grew dull with boredom. He was Jacalrin Endo Chesa, the commander of the newly dispatched reinforcements for the rear echelon of the Rarkian army.

Upon hearing the news of Morgana dispatching reinforcements and the scale of the war growing, he had declared an end to his luxurious, comfortable capital life and volunteered himself. The true reason he'd volunteered instead of continuing his war-free, lazy life in the capital was simple.

The division led by Commander Paseid, the current commander-in-chief of the Rarkian army, was winning battle after battle, however small, and his brother, Kalajesh Chesa, was also off subjugating the Galkamas in the northwest.

And Jacalrin had had enough of the uneventful capital life. He was bored. But even this mission was starting to get boring.

To be exact, he was bored of marching.

He was on his way to serve Paseid, his old childhood friend. Now, who was Paseid? He was only the great, sole duke of Rarke, often called the son of the red wolf, the mighty knight who'd spent half his life resolving small and large disputes within Rarke, punishing the greedy Galkamas—who always sought for an opportunity to invade Rarke—and accomplishing a myriad of other majestic deeds.

Though his renown as a knight was overshadowed by his fame as the son of the red wolf, Paseid was praised all throughout the country like none other. Even Kalajesh, who was widely praised for his proficiency in books and swords—not to mention his exceptional beauty that some claimed was the finest in the capital—and who also happened to be Jacalrin's brother, was a step below Paseid.

Jacalrin had left with a spring in his step like a young man in love, excited that he would soon be able to swing his sword to his heart's content with Paseid. But just sitting on his horse and walking for over a month was killing him. Unfortunately, this was the fastest speed ten thousand men could move at once.

Scratching the itchy spot on his cheek hidden under his helmet, Jacalrin unenthusiastically replied to his subordinate's report. "Still following us?"

"Yes, sir."

"Sir Verohan, didn't you say she was the daughter of some war horse merchant nearby? Who is she looking for again?"

A middle-aged knight from House Chesa following on his diagonal, Sir Seisen Verohan, looked back at the woman coming along on her horse behind them at the same speed. It had almost been an hour since she crossed their path.

At this time when the tensions were heightening as they approached the border, she was not a welcome guest. The woman following them, in ragged clothes with a single sword, riding a horse that seemed of extraordinary quality even to a seasoned knight, had an eerie air about her.

"I'll send her away."

Jacalrin murmured, "Do whatever you want," and yawned like he had no care for his dignity.

The woman was persistent.

Whether it was because she had no fear, or she was just a little cuckoo, she stopped only for a moment when the knights and soldiers threatened her and started following again. Her almost obsessive behavior started to make them wonder if she was a

Morganaan assassin with the mission to murder the commander of the Rarkian reinforcements.

Very much unlike the commander of ten thousand soldiers he was, Jacalrin started to lightly pound on his clanging faulds as if he were trying to relieve his lower back, stiffening under the heavy weight of the armor.

Not caring at all about the others glancing at him, Jacalrin looked over at the ridge beyond the vast field, then briefly eyed the band of soldiers following him. They were close enough to the border to be able to feel each other tensing, but the commander looked just as bored as before. Finally, his dull gaze reached the woman's horse, at a bit of a distance from the cavalcade.

Jacalrin's eyes sparkled. He held back the reins with one hand and held up the other in a fist. The army following them soon stopped at his echo of, "Halt!"

Seisen observed the distance left until they reach the ridge with a questioning look on his face. Then, at his commander's sudden orders, he startled and turned his head.

"Sir Verohan, let us stop here and rest for a while. Send a messenger to the border patrol headquarters. And bring that woman to me."

"Sir?"

"We'll have to save up some energy even if we can't join them right away anyway, so it should be fine to stall a little bit until we receive the reply." Jacalrin stated this to put an end to all of Seisen's unspoken questions, and stretched his arms.

Seisen looked like he didn't know how to react to this. But he was apparently unable to think of a reason to persuade him otherwise, as he turned and quietly headed to the rear.

"Here she is, sir. As you commanded."

The woman kneeled in front of Jacalrin, who had dismounted his horse, taken his helmet off, and was wiping his sweaty face.

The woman was younger than he had expected. Twenty-two or twenty-three, at most. Considering that he was twenty-four, one could say she was around his age. Though her appearance suggested she was a northerner, not everyone was convinced she didn't have a secret mission from Morgana to assassinate the commander. Even the knights became more alarmed at her not showing the slightest sign of feeling intimidated.

If they'd been in the midst of battle or a prim commander's army, she would most likely have been taken away and questioned. In that sense, she was certainly lucky she'd run into Jacalrin's army.

After staring at her for a moment, he nodded to the knights, who were keeping a very close watch on her.

"Go about your duties. It's fine. We'll have to move again before nightfall."

When they disappeared at last at his stern orders, Jacalrin scrutinized her.

With reddish brown hair and lighter colored brown eyes, she had the looks of a typical southern Rarkian. Actually, looking into them, Jacalrin thought her eyes had an odd reddish shade to them.

He had seen enough beautiful women in the capital to not feel anything for her, but she did look quite nice despite her modest dress. And yet.

What is up with this woman?

Much to his chagrin, though Jacalrin prided in his ability to read people, he couldn't read anything from her cold, dead eyes. He half expected her to be desperate, since she apparently was looking for someone, but her eyes showed no signs of desperation or any kind of emotion at all. Her steady breath even when facing this powerful knight of Chesa seemed almost stately.

Not being a man of roundabout expression, Jacalrin asked frankly, "What's with you? Why did you risk your life following us?"

At his voice, her stone-cold face faintly gave way. She spoke. Her voice was as unreadable as her eyes. "My name is Reuyen. I was on my way to find my brother."

"Your enlisted brother? For what?"

"I intend to bring him back home, since he is the only male heir to the family."

Losing interest, Jacalrin scoffed at her with disappointment. The House of Chesa was a house of dignity and erudition, but Jacalrin spoke plainly without all the formality. "A house needs a country to exist, and yet here you are trying to smuggle out a soldier to save your own house. This is absurd. I was bored enough to find your absurdity amusing, at least. But come on, don't you think you're being naïve?"

He expected her to have some sort of an emotional response to this degree of sneering, yet she asked a totally different question. "You're from House Chesa, as in the house of Hansen Deuk Chesa, the right-hand man of the duke regent Brionake?"

"Yes, that Chesa... Duke regent? Did you really just say that treacherous word? You just called the founder of the Brionake Dynasty a..."

He stopped mid-sentence. He had realized the oddity in her words.

It had been two hundred years since the foundation of the Brionake Dynasty.

Two hundred years ago, Prince Consort Belbarote Paseid Brionake had overthrown the tyrant and become the first king of the Brionake Dynasty. Some called him the founder. Since then, King Belbarote Paseid Brionake's first son had succeeded the throne and his second son had succeeded to House Brionake, and thus had begun the era of peace in the war-torn country.

No one remembered Belbarote, who'd started a new Rarke, as a regent who had usurped the throne. So, as a descendent of Chesa who was extremely proud of joining the Brionake's revolution and saving Rarke, Jacalrin was not delighted to hear that phrase.

"There's only a certain degree of rudeness I'll let you get away with," he snapped, scowling at her. "Or are you just dumb?"

Reuyen didn't respond at all to the young man's harsh reproach. She was overwhelmed with the familiar smell of metal, and her ears were about to explode just with the sound of her heartbeat and the noise of an army.

Barely coming back to reality, Reuyen looked at the remnants of Hansen Deuk Chesa. With some time, she could almost make out his face in his descendent. The face of Hansen, the man who had once served her but later watched her die at the scaffold with cool eyes. Cool, but with a hint of pity.

Finding herself trying to find the past from a descendent, she unconsciously smiled, her lips shaking.

And… Duke regent, duke regent. It was clearly her mistake. She couldn't think properly.

"My mistake. Forgive me, sir."

Jacalrin squinted at the young woman. His senses became oddly acute.

Forgive me, sir?

Is that something an ordinary woman would say?

Now that he thought of it, there was something oddly formal about the way she spoke to him. He started to wonder if she indeed was an anti-Brionake follower. Outer looks could be disguised. Now he started to doubt the existence of her brother.

But he soon stopped himself. She just must be a little off up there. His intuition was pointing at that. And he knew better than anyone that now wasn't a good time to waste his energy chasing after his own curiosity.

Right then, a rider bearing the red wolf banner of House Brionake came back with the messenger. The knights started going around ordering the soldiers to go back into formation. Jacalrin brushed the dirt off his hands and stood up.

"Stop fooling around here and go home," he told the young woman. "A war's no playground. Don't even think about coming."

Reuyen suddenly raised her head and shouted desperately, "Horses…!"

"What?"

"I'm the daughter of a horse dealer. I could be of use with the horses."

"So? An army this size usually comes with horse handlers."

His face showed discomfort with this rude woman who clearly did not know her place. But even at his obvious derision, she clenched her teeth and didn't back down. Now that she had no other way to get into the camp, this was her only chance.

"A noble knight of House Chesa leading an army of reinforcements must mean that there will be a big battle soon. Though I might be insufficient to fight Morgana, I will be of some help. I may be alone, but one more is better than none."

"I don't know what kind of fake rumor you've heard, but we're going because the damn empire fanatics are starting to make things big, not because we're losing. We have enough men, so commoners like you don't have to—"

She cut him off. "As a worker in the rear, then. I volunteer. I want to."

It was undoubtedly an obsession; she was not even taking a second to think about the consequences.

Amazed at her unbent spirit, but also quite opposed to the words that were coming out of her mouth, Jacalrin silently looked down at her. He started to wonder again if she actually was a spy sent by someone, trying to infiltrate their army.

"Sir Chesa, the supreme command has authorized our approach to the camp beyond the ridge," said a messenger soldier.

Even after his report, Jacalrin stood there like a statue for a while. His wildcat-like eyes narrowed at the woman holding her head up high. "Hmm."

Though it was only for a brief moment, Reuyen had underestimated the young Chesa. The commander still looked a bit like a child and seemed that careless. But the words casually spoken by his slightly arced lips were not what she expected at all. "Still no."

Jacalrin waved away the soldier who'd come to relay the report and squatted in front of Reuyen.

"The receipt with the royal family you showed might be real, but how should I know if your identification isn't forged? We can't even verify if your brother is indeed at the front right now. You should be thankful we didn't arrest you right here and question you. But don't worry. I'm not interested in fooling around with women, so if you just say, 'I am sorry,' and apologize, I'll let this slide. I have a lot to do, you see."

He was thinking that he sounded quite merciful, but on the contrary, her face started to stiffen. Feeling uneasy, he quietly waited for her answer. Something along the lines of an apology or a good old "yes, sir." But her dry lips did not open.

He stayed squatted and rested his face on his hand.

Well, well, well.

Jacalrin was a confident man. Not just because he was the second son of the renowned House Chesa. He truly was a promising, talented young man.

He didn't even consider achieving the same results with half the effort to have something to brag about. He often learned and digested difficult theories in his own, odd way and sometimes even applied those to achieve double the ordinary result.

The same thing had happened when he was learning how to swordfight. His masters had always forced the Chesa's way and told him that he must always keep his sword in hand so he could get used to it, but Jacalrin had found his own way by forgetting everything and swinging the way his body would be most comfortable with. Of course, that had resulted in his rather ignominious style, very much unlike the elegance of House Chesa.

In short, he'd made it a habit to come up with little tricks to find maximum comfort. And he was quick enough to make it work. Some lamented that had Jacalrin not been a childish man who kept saying, "I'm just gonna do as much as everyone else," and "Yeah, whatever," House Chesa could have achieved a greatness unlike ever before.

Though Jacalrin was not quite fond of this, there was a saying about House Chesa: *The world is so fair that Count Chesa fathered the handsomest, most considerate man in the capital, Kalajesh, but he also fathered the cleverest rascal in the capital, Jacalrin.*

"You're going to keep following us, aren't you?" he asked the young woman.

Reuyen remained silent and kept her pale lips shut at Jacalrin's ruthlessly firm question.

He turned to look at the horse she'd ridden here. At that moment, Seisen came and reported to the back of his head.

"Sir Chesa, we are ready for your order to depart."

"Oh, already, huh?" Jacalrin straightened his body, rubbing a spaulder that kept jangling. His eyes were still fixed on the woman's horse. "That horse you brought. Looks like a fine breed."

"Yes, sir. Den is the best from the Detuas."

"His name is Den? The best, huh? If you're patriotic enough to volunteer for war, you should hand him over to the knights."

His words sounded strangely suggestive. Sensing a bad hunch, Reuyen went silent for a moment, then replied, "He's an impatient one, not trained for war yet."

Of course, Jacalrin made a funny face. "That, we can take care of. Sir Verohan, you have some money on you?"

"Sir?"

"I'm taking that horse. Pay her right now so she doesn't say anything later and tie her to that tree."

Seisen looked at the tree he was pointing at. There were some low trees standing in the field. It was still more humane than beating a woman to the point she couldn't follow them anymore, he supposed.

"What are you...?" began Reuyen, looking aghast.

"It's better for the both of us." Jacalrin smiled mischievously, showing his white teeth. "Or is it just better for me? Tie her tightly, sir! Tightly!"

Completely dumbfounded, Reuyen watched the young Chesa walk away as he gave that playful order.

After watching her with cold eyes for a moment, Seisen signaled three soldiers to surround her. "You heard his orders."

"If you mean that preposterous order, yes, I did," said Reuyen.

"Even so, I will comply. You should be grateful to still be alive after daring to block the way of an army."

She glared at the middle-aged knight and gripped the weeds on the ground. Her vicious eyes made Seisen scowl.

"Tie her to the tree and make sure she can't escape. I will send the money for the horse to the Detuas after determining the right price."

But she did not intend to be an easy prey. When the soldier grabbed her wrist and tried to make her stand up, she nimbly shot up from the ground and twisted his arm behind his back. Though the soldier hadn't expected it, her movements were surprisingly fast.

Seisen gazed at her for a moment, his eyebrows lifted in surprise. Then he lowered them and said, quite seriously, "If you don't comply, I will obey the military rules of wartime and cut your legs off, even if the commander does not order so."

He meant it.

She let go of the soldier's arm. She could see Den's black, watery eyes looking back at her as he was taken away by strange hands from afar.

～

Reuyen glared as she watched the army slowly marching to the other side of the ridge, resembling a long snake.

Before she could even react, she had lost Den and gotten tied to a tree. Every time she tried to move, the tight ropes dug into her waist and ankles. She was too flabbergasted to even think. Reuyen swallowed a sigh and started to carefully study the ropes around her.

Jacalrin had underestimated one thing. He probably had thought that an ordinary man's daughter like herself wouldn't be able to move for a while if he did this much, but she was a woman born with the knowledge of how prisoners of war were tied up, and how to loosen those knots.

Reuyen tried flexing her arms. Thankfully, the knots weren't as tight as she had worried they might be. After a quick, deep breath, she twisted her wrists. The pressure, strong enough to cut the circulation in her hands, made her groan. Not giving up, she pressed the long end of the knot tightly against the tree with her thigh and freed her right thumb at the cost of the horrible pain in her wrists, like they were being sawed off. It was a piece of cake from there.

The ropes dropped to the ground, one after another. Her skin burned. She panted. As she caressed her raw wrists and backs of her hands, harsh words escaped her mouth for the first time in a long while. "Damn it, Hansen. You should have seen the babe from your house fooling around like that. No, no, he's your blood, after all."

In Reuyen's eyes, Jacalrin was no knight of a renowned house, but merely a sly fraud.

Of course, it was her fault, loitering around the road to the border with no authorization, but if she were a "real" ordinary woman, she would have stayed tied here indefinitely and starved to death.

She stumbled and dropped to the ground. She couldn't even begin to think of a solution. The ridge was fairly close now, but it would take at least three or four hours to get there, and that was if she were on a horse. She was unsure if she would even get there in a day if she dragged her tired body and forced herself to walk. But she could not walk back the distance she'd come on horseback for three full days.

She'd lost Sidan, and Den as well.

Den was one of the smartest and fastest horses Dekallia had given birth to, but above all, he was a horse she'd raised with Eivan. *He's only a horse,* someone might tell her. But to Reuyen, Den was a remembrance of Eivan, not something to easily give up on.

Reuyen held on to the tree and slowly raised her thin body. She was certainly on the healthier side of the spectrum, and yet, perhaps because she was more tired than she had realized, her body didn't move as well as she wanted.

"Oh, Chesa. That kind of a screw-up's..."

That's one of the commanders? She barely could contain her laughter. *One of the commanders, he is, eh?* Reuyen kept on cussing in her head.

The truth was that she was fine with not being trusted and questioned. She had not done anything illegal in her life, and she was a daughter of Detua for sure, so she'd thought she could clear her name once they took her into the camp. But she was naïve. The last thing she'd expected was that that bastard would just leave her here.

No, wasn't the protocol to arrest suspicious individuals? What a slipshod commander. If all the commanders leading Rarke during this war were like him, the future of Rarke was most certainly bleak.

Looking after the cavalcade that was now far, far away, Reuyen tightened her skinned hands into fists.

You think I'll give up here? You young bastards...!

Instead of discouraging her, Jacalrin's outrage set fire to her stubborn determination. Reuyen raised her exhausted body and took one step, then another.

She could almost feel Hansen hiding somewhere behind those slowly flowing clouds in the blue sky above the ridge, laughing at her like a sly fox.

CHAPTER FIVE

The next day, at sunrise, men who had been busy since early in the morning shouted at the other side of the ridge connected to the Boald Field. The Rarkian camp was set up inside thorn tree fences. The sun hadn't even fully risen yet, but ten thousand reinforcements had arrived from the capital. The council meeting had started earlier than usual that day.

In the headquarters tent, five commanders whose immediate superior was the commander-in-chief of the Rarkian army sat together and conversed.

"Even the food we'd saved in case the war draws out will not feed all the men, including the reinforcements that have just arrived. What if we send a second messenger to Sir Carvein, since he's patrolling the nearby area, and ask if there's some place that could send supplies before the rainy season starts?"

"Haven't we already inspected the nearby towns and lands to secure supply routes? More than that would be exploitation. The lords of Galabua will not agree to that happily, either."

"I agree with you. I think it would be best to wait for Sir Keheif to come back from discussing the situation with the camp on the cliff and decide then..."

"I hear that we have more than ten thousand troops joining us here. There's no downside to preparing for the worst since we don't know how long this war will last, is there? If you have an idea in mind, sir..."

The old knights all turned their attention to the only young man at the table. The black-haired man sat at the finest seat at the table, his head slightly tilted. He had a pensive look on his face. Then, perhaps because he realized that everyone was looking at him, his dark, placid eyes suddenly seemed weary.

Paseid Calandok Brionake.

He was the direct heir to House Brionake, the closest family by blood to the current Brionake Dynasty.

He was young to be a commander-in-chief, but he unquestionably was the most suitable nobleman to lead the war that would rectify the shameful history between Rarke and Morgana. Of course, his blood was not the only reason he had been given the task of victory.

Unlike someone who was born a genius and spent his time lounging around in the capital, Paseid had spent most of his time for the last ten years or so patrolling the outskirts of Rarke and defeating their foes in and out of the country to gain experience on the battlefield.

His teacher was Castro Vander Winford, the knight who was once called the bravest in all of Rarke and still was widely admired by countless numbers of young knights ten years after he retired.

Paseid was also an impeccable knight, so much so that even the experienced old knights who had survived numerous battles acknowledged his expertise. Needless to say, he possessed all the qualities a commander-in-chief must have: patience, generosity, and self-control. Even the oldest and the most seasoned knight, Sir Evinbur, admitted that Paseid had a keen insight that surpassed the older ones' rich experience.

Paseid was known to be quiet, but he was even more taciturn today. He even looked a bit pale, as if he hadn't slept well last night. In truth, he was fatigued from not sleeping well. He had had a nightmare, like he occasionally did when he slept on an uncomfortable bed out at war. He wasn't the type to complain about such a miniscule event, and he wasn't superstitious, either, but he always felt a little off the day after a nightmare.

"Hmm...? Sir Calandok?"

Finally, at the highest-ranking man's silence, the knights started to explain their ideas. Their murmuring complaints filled the tent.

"Those rats are going to start pestering us again soon. They've been quiet for a while, and they've probably learned that we have more men now. I hear their reinforcements number nearly 20,000. Even if it's a bit of a stretch, shouldn't we move before they arrive?"

"Don't you think we'd know that? There's simply no way to drag those shamelessly cowering bastards out. It seemed like they'd arrive right around rainy season. I can almost hear them plotting trickeries from here."

"Stop talking like you're not involved in this, Sir Giotarre. Once the rain starts pouring, we're all going to be stuck right where we are, looking at each other like a bunch of idiots. Wouldn't that be delightful? Like a staring contest."

"You consider that delightful?"

"It's a joke. Who here would enjoy standing face to face with those Morganaan hillbillies?"

The meeting soon became a forum for mocking Morgana, but no one pointed that out.

Then again, there had been only one big battle since the beginning of the war, quite unlike what one would expect after Morgana's conceited declaration of war, when they could not find a solution to Rarke's objections to the increased amount of tribute. The current commander-in-chief of Morgana, Marche Carl Rovantis, was so disappointingly cautious that he only sporadically attacked the Rarkian army with a small number of soldiers. Meanwhile, he was calling for reinforcements and increasing the scale of the war. So, of course the Rarkian knights were disgruntled after they came running to battle, hoping to not miss the chance to rectify their shameful history.

At that moment, light footsteps were suddenly heard from outside, and the drape opened wide without a warning. The unexpected and uninvited guest was a young man wearing comfortable plainclothes, unsuited for a battlefield.

"Hello, my old friend... I mean, Sir Calandok... No, I mean, Commander-in-Chief, sir!"

The knights sitting around the round table all widened their eyes at the young man casually barging into the headquarters. It was Jacalrin. Their contempt for him disappeared as soon as they realized who he was.

Of course. It's that Jacalrin Endo from House Chesa.

Paseid finally broke his silent contemplation and opened his weary mouth. "Did you not receive the message that I will see you after the meeting?"

"I know, I just arrived, but can't I join? The meeting? Oh, Sir Giotarre! Wow, long time, no see, Sir Deusak! And you're looking well, Sir Haldroff! His Majesty gave a letter to give to all you sirs asking how everybody's doing, but I'll bring that later." Jacalrin cheerfully chattered on.

Sir Evinbur Haldroff chuckled. "Did you not wish I were well? Little Sir Chesa."

Jacalrin could not stop with the small talk. "Of course, I did. Oh, Sir Vinsen. Lady Vinsen has asked me to send her greetings to you…"

"How kind of you. Thank you, Sir Chesa," said Sir Vinsen. "It must have been a long journey here. How is everyone back home?"

"My brother is doing well as usual, and Father is at a crossroads because of some ridiculous bet with His Majesty. Seems like our house is about to go bankrupt, but, well, it's not like I'm the next one in line, so I just let Father deal with it and left."

"How's the capital?"

"If there was anything fun going on, I wouldn't be here."

"Of course, of course, hahaha. But there's nothing particularly fun going on here, either."

"You have no idea how many times Father slapped my back for just lying around in the capital."

"Well, sounds like Count Chesa is still the same. Haha."

The glum atmosphere in the tent quickly lightened up with sounds of chatter and laughter like nothing had happened. Paseid wiped off a smile that had snuck its way onto his face and settled everyone down.

"Enough, now. You too, Sir Vinsen. He will never stop if you let him."

Jacalrin clamped his mouth shut for a moment, then grinned like mischievous boy.

Since the newly dispatched young man from "that Chesa" had

wriggled his way in, today's meeting was basically over. The knights chuckled and sided with Jacalrin.

"Wasn't everyone expecting this at the news of Sir Chesa joining us?" said Sir Haldroff. "Haha. You came earlier than I expected."

"I came at full speed," said Jacalrin. "I'm glad to see everyone's doing just fine. Well, not that I thought anything would happen against those morons."

"Well, of course."

The knights guffawed at Jacalrin calling the only empire on the continent a "moron," like he truly could not care less. The guards, who had been nervously pacing outside because they couldn't stop Jacalrin from barging in, appeared between the drapes.

Paseid ended the meeting. "I will most likely report the issue with supplies, but for now, we will discuss it again tomorrow at noon, after general organization of the new men is done. Sir Chesa, follow me."

He grabbed Jacalrin by his collar and led him out. The rest of the knights chuckled and shook their heads at Jacalrin being dragged out by his neck, thrashing about like a fish out of water.

～

One would assume that he would've been tired after such a long trip, but Jacalrin could not contain his excitement. He finally calmed down after Paseid sternly scolded him.

They mounted their horses to check on the newly arrived soldiers building a new fence and setting up tents on the right side of the ridge. As they entered the new camp, Paseid summarized the current situation.

"Their commander, Rovantis, hasn't made any big moves. The big battle will probably happen after the Morganaan reinforcements arrive, considering how Rovantis is buying time with a sporadic invasion of Rarke followed by retreat. This means we have a bit of time to let the soldiers rest. But we can't lower our guards since there still are local wars and ambushes."

"I heard we're the ones on the defense. Wouldn't it be worse for them to drag this out?" Jacalrin asked, rubbing his side. His lower back was hurting from sitting on the horse.

Sir Evinbur Haldroff, the eldest knight in camp, who had come along on their patrol, answered in a languid voice. "The south has supplies they gathered as tribute. They're better off in terms of food too. Maybe that's why they're taking their time with it. Who knows if this war will end before this old man dies?"

"We'll end it as soon as possible, Sir Haldroff," Paseid replied with a faint smile.

Jacalrin wrinkled one eyebrow, then asked, "Oh! Did you see the report I sent? I brought every single gram of military-grade gunpowder I could find!"

"I read it from the last report."

"That should be enough, right?"

"More than enough for those morons."

Jacalrin giggled at Evinbur's joke. He didn't look nervous or tense at all. Jacalrin Endo Chesa was probably the only man who could pull that off at this time.

The whole time they walked on the dry land, all sorts of noises resounded: the clanking sound of hammers beating cleats and posts; the rustling sound the soldiers' armor made as they ran around; people shouting instead of talking. Paseid, who was carefully watching them without saying anything, suddenly came to a halt.

"Hey...I mean, sir?" Quickly correcting himself, because he was still not used to having to address Paseid as his superior, Jacalrin turned his head and looked up at Paseid.

Paseid was squinting one eye. Turning his gaze to follow Paseid's, Jacalrin let out a short exclamation. They were looking at a horse jumping around, tied to the fence, and a group of soldiers struggling to put a suit of armor on him.

"That horse is...?" asked Paseid.

The sturdy horse was clearly well maintained and of a good breed, but too rough to have been trained for the army. No, he was more like a completely untrained, saddled wild horse.

Jacalrin scratched the back of his head. "He's still going at it, huh? What a strong, strong horse."

He'd actually totally forgotten about it until now.

The horse had given Jacalrin's knights trouble the whole march to the ridge. He'd seemed so tame when he was with what's-her-face, but the second he was separated from her, he'd started jumping and thrashing madly.

Jacalrin thought it was a waste to kill or leave such a high-quality horse, so he'd forced the horse to come all the way here. But at this rate, it would take a long time to tame him.

Paseid deemed the horse quite fine too. He turned his horse and walked toward the fence. "Loosen the reins and let go of it."

The soldiers, struggling to not get kicked or bitten, startled at the voice that came out of nowhere.

"Sir! Good, good morning, sir! But this one's so violent he'll kick away the fence and run away if I let go…"

"Fix the post well to the ground and get away from the horse."

A handful of soldiers huddled to fix the post. As soon as they let go of the reins, as Paseid had ordered, the horse started a racket like a mad cow.

Instead of stepping back, Paseid faced the horse head-on. The sight of the animal kicking his hind legs at the posts and aggressively snorting looked so threatening that it even made Jacalrin nervous.

Evinbur expressed concern. "Please do step away from that horse, Sir Calandok. I'll call a trainer."

"Oh, that won't work. Nope, not at all. You can't tame that in a few days." Jacalrin waved his hands like there was nothing else to be said about that, for he had already tried on the way here. The cries and whinnying of the horse pounding the ground with his front legs were so frightening that even those setting up tents nearby flinched.

Nevertheless, Paseid's well-trained black horse held his place and stood there staring at the brown one. The struggling horse seemed to be slowly calming down.

After a while, the brown horse stopped its thrashing. The horse stubbornly glared at Paseid, looking down from a higher and therefore more powerful position for a while, but he dropped his gaze at last and looked straight back at the black horse's eyes instead.

Jacalrin looked back and forth at the two horses glaring at each other. He was witnessing something nonsensical. Mere four-legged beasts were having a silent war. Whether because he realized that the opponent of his own kind was of an innately superior blood, or because he simply gave up, the horse that was causing a racket lowered his head at last.

Jacalrin rubbed his chin and made a sound through his nose, like he hadn't thought of that. "Hmmmm. I've been thinking this for a while, but I guess Rotsa really is an exceptional horse. People kept telling me that Baldoan horses are the finest. Makes me want to stop by at Baldo on the way back to the capital."

"Did he have a rider?" Paseid asked. The discolored, worn-out saddle commoners used seemed to suggest that he was not wild.

Jacalrin suddenly recalled the woman from yesterday and scratched his forehead. *Is she still where we left her?*

He had enough conscience to be concerned.

Though he had completely relied on his intuition, even if he considered all the suspicious aspects of that woman, she probably was a commoner of Rarke who was not going to cause any big trouble. But it was her fault for venturing near the border during wartime, so it ended at that.

"I bought it on the way here, at the field across the ridge," he said.

"Caravans are still travelling in these times?"

"Kind of. You know what, I'll give that to you as a gift, sir. I'm not interested nor good enough to train him. Moreover, my horse isn't as domineering as Rotsa."

Evinbur frowned. That kind of untrained horse was of no use in war. It was better to just let it go. As he expected, as soon as Paseid turned his horse away, the dispirited horse started snorting and stomping the ground with his hooves again. But Paseid seemed to have taken a liking to the ferocious horse.

"Sure," he said.

Jacalrin still didn't think that the horse would really become a problem.

Until the next morning when he found some deranged woman lying unconscious in front of the camp.

CHAPTER SIX

The Hansen Deuk Chesa of Reuyen's memory had a cunning side to him.

By cunning, she didn't mean that he was prone to flattering someone like a conniving snake; she meant that he was by far the best at pranking people behind their backs. He also could not stand defeat. His betrayal at the end of the queen's time had probably been rooted in his personal feelings toward her and her forthcoming end, rather than his loyalty to Belbarote.

She remembered the preposterous sight of him sitting in front of her cell, the night before the execution, facing her, with a chessboard laid before him.

❧

The betrayer with roughly tied sandy hair and eyes twinkling like the fresh meadows asked her to play, as if nothing had happened. Even though he knew she could not move an inch with the chains.

"We should finish what we started before your departure," he said. "Which side would you like, Your Majesty?"

"Black."

"Still?"

Him sitting on his bum on the dirty ground and setting up the chess-

board was not very different from the past. He set up the pieces exactly as he remembered from the game they'd stopped somewhere on the battlefield. It was remarkably exact, but Swan was not surprised.

"You're the one who's still addressing me as 'Your Majesty.' You must not fear those who might listen."

"A majesty once, a majesty forever. But of course, I can't take your side now."

"I'd rather take my own life than take your pity."

"Your Majesty, you're too intimidating. You have to stop being perfect at some point."

"You're now insulting me to my face, are you?"

Hollow laughter echoed in the empty cell.

"Now I can tell you that seeing you galloping across the battlefield with a woman's body was quite astonishing, but it wasn't exemplary. In that sense, you're a failure who could not become a role model to the nobles."

"How sage of you. You're daring to blabber your mouth now only because I've come to this, Hansen."

"What can you ever do to me now, Your Majesty?"

Glancing at the chessboard on the other side of the bars, she suddenly pulled the end of her rough lips into a smile.

"Move the bishop next to the rook on two from the left and three from the bottom two blocks northwest."

"Then I'll move my knight here."

"The queen on the second row to the diagonal of your pawn."

"This? Then I'll..."

Hansen picked up a white bishop with a raised brow, then stopped midway through placing it down. He frowned, gave a little tsk, tsk, then started laughing. He proceeded to put the bishop down and pushed his pure white king, who now had nowhere to go, with his fingertip.

Thump.

The enemy's king rolled across the hard chessboard and fell on the dirty jail floor. His laughter became louder and louder. She was quite satisfied with its strange echoing.

"It was a done deal from the start. It's your mistake for being too blinded by not losing to spot a small victory, Hansen."

"Till the end, really?"

"Ruminate on today's defeat until you die an old man, for there will be no more opportunities."

With a curse-like blessing, the queen was no more the next morning.

~

By the time she reached the bottom of the ridge, Reuyen's cheap leather soles had become completely tattered. Without proper shoes, her feet were suffering their share. But Reuyen kept forcing her blistered and bloodied feet to march on without resting.

She couldn't remember experiencing this kind of hellish pain in all her lives. In her last life, she had occasionally gotten into accidents, such as being slain with a sword, hit by an arrow, or falling off a horse, but those were all passing moments of deliberate hostility, not this kind of pain that tested her endurance.

But this was a fight against herself. Whenever she could not take another step and wanted to rest, she looked up at the sky and muttered, "Look what that babe from your house dared to do to me, Hansen," in a hoarse voice. That made the journey to the camp easier.

Once she found the strength to continue, all the hesitance, fear, and confusion that was holding her back scattered away like a rainbow under the sun. To be honest, she was half-unconscious from the middle.

The only times she was fully awake again were when she was famished or when she spotted traces of wild wolves. Thanks to the young Chesa's despicable kindness of leaving behind the saddlebag, she could drink from the water bottle and eat the snacks that were packed in it.

On the second day, she could feel her consciousness fading away as she went around the ridge. She threw the bag away and kept moving forward with only the small bag of food tied at her waist.

By the end, it almost became a habit.

"Hansen, I do not hate the Chesas, but it is truly hard to let that feeble babe of your house off with mercy."

Her present self was quite pathetic compared to her past self, who would've been full of energy after days of marching, but it was what it was.

When she was starting to sense the imminent danger of extreme thirst, her body threatening to collapse at any moment regardless of her will, a faint smell of metal tickled her nose as she only just pressed her legs, shaking like a crab's, down with her hand. She forced her dropping head up to see a vast field of dry clay behind the ridge. She could barely make out the Rarkian camp with the white wolf banner.

Her heart started to beat fast.

At last.

The smell of torches and dark smoke billowing from the fires reached her nostrils. The familiarity fooled her into thinking for a moment that she had gone back in time.

After only a couple more steps, her body collapsed. Her swollen, wounded feet that had been numb for a while now refused to move at all. Barely awake, she clenched her teeth, but it was no use. She was so close.

"What is that?" said a voice.

"Is that a person?" said another. "Report to the captain. I'll go check it out."

Then, a guard patrolling the area noticed her and cautiously approached. "Identify yourself!"

She was at her limit, just trying not to pass out, and now she saw the shadow of a soldier with his sword against the back of her neck. This was insanity. With all her might, Reuyen stopped herself from groaning and spoke. "...Came...Den..."

"What? Why are you all the way here at..."

"Came to find Den...Hansen's..."

"Hansen?"

She couldn't feel her legs, and now her consciousness was flickering too. Her state was serious enough to make her dry tongue limp and memories muddled. That single word, "Chesa," had gone beyond her reach in her heap of memories, so she could only think of the name she had repeated over and over the whole way here.

"Hansen. That—damn—ho-horse thief...!" She thought she yelled with all the energy she had left in her, because her rational awareness had also escaped her.

Before going completely under, she looked up at the blue sky through her nearly closed eyes and thought, *See, Hansen. After two hundred years...I still can beat you.*

She smiled with victory.

When she opened her eyes again, she found herself inside an old tent in the camp she had so desperately wished for.

When the preparation of the newly dispatched troops was almost done, the leaders gathered at the headquarters one by one. This meeting was not as energetic as yesterday morning's.

In the tent that smelled of dirt, even Paseid, wearing his proper black uniform that came up to his neck, couldn't hide the deep fatigue on his face.

Everyone in the room had a similar worn-out expression after spending a day organizing the new troops. Without any greetings, the discussion resumed.

"You understand?" said Sir Tarayet Vinsen.

Slouching in his seat and looking down at the map laid out on the round table, Jacalrin nodded at the explanation of the knight sitting across from him. Sir Vinsen rubbed the end of his pointy nose and raised his thick eyebrows in disbelief.

"So," Jacalrin said, "the point is that the Rarkian occupation force at the Gerad border of Galabua is a little over forty thousand, including my men who just joined. The Morganaans have a little less than thirty thousand, because their reinforcements haven't arrived yet, so the easiest strategy is to wipe them out before that happens."

There probably—no, certainly—was a more specific explanation, and yet Jacalrin summarized the whole thing in spite of Sir Vinsen's effort. Tarayet agreed by silently rubbing the end of his pointy nose again.

"But what's the problem?" Jacalrin asked. "Weren't we letting them do whatever they wanted until now because we couldn't attack them first?"

After quietly listening to their conversation, Paseid pointed somewhere on the map. "They chose the Anf region south of here for strategic reasons."

Jacalrin looked at the way the black and white chess pieces were positioned there, remembered the rocky geography near the border, and slapped his knee with an, "Aha. But isn't our Jolanta Field right in front of the twin cliffs of Anf and Morgana's Plain Ishas beyond them? Seems large enough for a battle to me."

"In a battle at the beginning of this war, the enemy came gushing through the road between the cliffs into Jolanta and caused mayhem, resulting in thousands of casualties on both sides," said Paseid. "Two weeks later, Rarke won by a very close number of men and the enemy retreated."

"I'm familiar with the victory at the Battle of Jolanta."

"Deducing from the number of weapons we retrieved, about three thousand and eight hundred of the enemy died."

Jacalrin looked surprised. Though not from any official report, from what he had heard, the enemy had suffered a much bigger loss than that at the Battle of Jolanta. He was sure he wasn't mistaken, because he had been there when the nobles in the capital were toasting the great victory that must have crushed Morgana's spirit.

"I heard it was nearly six thousand. Was there an error in the report to the capital?"

Tarayet scoffed at that.

Paseid looked at him for a brief moment and continued explaining. "The number of casualties during the retreat ranged over a thousand."

"What a psychopath. That Rovantis, did he run away as fast as he could to save his own life or something?"

Evinbur stopped listening, his eyes shutting with fatigue. "Perhaps because he got scared he would lose his head after that kind of a result from the first battle, he hid in the Anf twin cliffs and started driving us crazy with his ever-defending tactics. After the first battle, Sir Deusak tried to create additional loss by attacking first, but the geography was too advantageous for those in defense, so he retreated."

"Gosh, that must have been laborious, Sir Deusak." Jacalrin turned around to face Sir Denjak Deusak.

Though there was no hostile intent, Denjak blushed with

humiliation. His slightly hooded eyes narrowed and his thin lips
scrunched up. He then turned back to Paseid.

Paseid finished his explanation regardless of the other men.
"But we can't hide behind the unideal nature of this situation
anymore. Now is the only chance to utilize our greater numbers."

"Umm, what's your plan?"

"We will ambush them and lay siege, as is protocol."

"Do you have any specific plans?"

Ambush and siege were the basics of strategy. But there was a
valid reason they'd dealt with small losses from sporadic battles
until now instead of carrying that into action.

Considering the geography of the Gerad border adjacent to
Morgana, the only way to properly lay siege to the enemy while
avoiding the twin cliffs of Anf was to go around the lowlands of
Itaka in eastern Gerad, surrounding the sides and the rear of the
Rovantis occupation force.

But with the value of Gerad border taken into account, there
was no way they could let the enemy occupy the area by dividing
the Rarkian force in half. Once they got past Gerad, there was a
large road that went through a handful of lands, all the way to the
capital. That probably was the reason Morgana wanted to attack
here first. Though they were not acting that aggressive as of now,
once they learned about the divide in the Rarkian army, they would
think of this as an opportunity.

So, the way to success was to secretly move and aim for the
moment the Morganaans were not expecting any attacks, but there
was nothing in the lowlands of Itaka that would hide the men from
their eyes. Even the sparse trees on Boald Field were rarely found
in Itaka. There apparently were even swamps here and there on the
way across the Morganaan border from the lowlands of Itaka. If
the Rarkians did choose that path, it would be very difficult to
handle emergencies.

In short, it was a flat field where they could not hide from the
enemy and it was very difficult to navigate because of the swamps.

"We will divide our force in three," said Paseid. "Sir Haldroff
and Sir Deusak will be in charge here in my place, and Sir Giotarre
will be in charge of the front of the triangular defense line at Camp
Anf. The rest will follow me to Olzore."

Jacalrin startled at his plain reply and jumped up. Unsettled by this as well, Evinbur clenched and rubbed his chin, and Tarayet and the other knights made odd noises.

"Sir Calandok? Do you mean Fort Olzore?"

"You just described a plan to attack Olzore?"

"Taking Fort Olzore would be a good way to change the current situation, since it practically is the southeastern wall protecting Morgana, but I am here to end the war as soon as possible," said Paseid. "Taking Fort Olzore is not my intent."

The knights' stiffened faces returned to normal.

"Then what is?"

"We will go around the Olzore-Tolf area to infiltrate the Morganaan border and ambush the sides and the rear of Plain Ishas. Using the gunpowder Sir Chesa brought as a signal. When the time comes, Sir Giotarre at the twin cliffs will receive the signal and attack Rovantis's army at the same time as Sir Haldroff. The mission will come to an end when the divided army joins again at the main camp through the road between the cliffs."

So, Paseid's plan was to go around the perilous area of Olzore-Tolf to attack Rovantis's army on the other side of the border. If they were to go that way instead of through the closer lowlands of Itaka, they would have to expect at least twenty days of travel.

"The greatest risk is the timing of the Morganaan reinforcements' arrival, but considering the highest speed twenty thousand men can move at once, I'd say we have a chance. Sir Keheif arrived this morning with information on the occupation force on Plain Ishas and the roads of the twin cliffs."

"Umm...then Sir Keheif will...?"

"At the meeting this evening, he will propose a specific route with the least amount of risk of being noticed by the force on Plain Ishas."

"But if you get caught between the Tolf army and the Olzore army on your way, Gerad will be at risk."

"Tolf has been adjacent to the Daraks for a long time, and as I hear, the situation has worsened between the two. So, the commander of Tolf will not be able to pay attention to Gerad. I am thinking of constructing another plan in case that does happen, but don't worry about that for now."

Paseid seemed like he was determined to end this war in the shortest amount of time possible.

It wasn't like they hadn't had any discussions about Olzore in the past, and it certainly would be possible if they went through Tolf…but it still didn't sound all that appealing. Even the even-tempered Evinbur seemed quite on edge to hear the name "Olzore," like the other knights.

Even to Jacalrin, it was an oddly suffocating thought to have to pass through a valley guarded by an impregnable fort that people said had never allowed any outsiders to step in for seven hundred years or so.

"The initiation of the plan will be after the rear echelon Sir Chesa led here settles down, so in about ten days. A part of them will be assigned to supplies, and Sir Haldroff will be in charge of dividing the rest of the army into three. If this plan succeeds, the issue with the supplies and food until the rainy season will be resolved to a certain extent as well." Though he knew what the complete silence meant, Paseid calmly went on. He seemed to have thought about this for a while now. "Any objections?"

The headquarters were quiet. The knights glanced at each other, unable to think of a more realistic plan to defeat the enemy quickly. Weren't they the ones who had claimed they should spring into action even if it was a stretch, lamenting their having to suffer the enemy fooling around? Of course, had they known the plan Paseid had in mind, they would have refined their expression.

But he had finished his statement, and it would be hard to over-turn his decision unless they thought of a better plan.

The hourglass on the table was as still as a picture. Paseid esti-mated the time spent and ended the meeting. "Then we'll end here tonight. Thank you."

As soon as he finished, the recorder quietly writing everything down in the corner took the record and left the tent silently. When the rest of the knights started to get up, a soldier artfully reported, "Excuse me, sir. I have something to report…"

"Come in."

At Paseid's command, the soldier ran in. He saluted the knights sitting at the table without looking surprised and started his report like he had been waiting for the meeting to be over. "I report, sir, that I found a woman lying unconscious near the camp."

"A woman?"

"Yes, sir. But…Sir Chesa, umm…she says she came here for you, sir."

Everyone who was rustling around stopped at once.

A woman? A woman in the middle of a camp?

The sharp and questioning eyes of the knights simultaneously darted at Jacalrin. But even Jacalrin himself was making a weird face with an open but crumpled mouth, leaving the knights perplexed and their mouths shut. Jacalrin replied, "Hmm? What? Me? Why?"

Paseid slightly frowned, glanced at Jacalrin, and spoke sternly. "Sir Chesa, have you any idea what this is about?" He seemed fairly angry.

Jacalrin shook his head. Had he had some incident with a woman before he joined the army, and someone had sold him out? There was nothing to feel victimized about if he thought about the very free way he'd acted in the capital, but Jacalrin could not think of anything.

"I really have no clue. I'm not crazy enough to bring a woman from the capital. Elhien looked over my preparations very meticulously, as if she already was the Lady of Brionake. Oh, come on, why are you all looking at me like that? Who on earth is looking for me and why?"

Jacalrin's aggressive defense made the middle-aged knights squinting at him clear their throats and turn away.

Frustrated, Jacalrin repeatedly asked the soldier, "So, who is it? Why is she looking for me?"

The expression on the soldier's face was a bit odd. He kept glancing at Jacalrin and moved his lips as if he were trying to decide if he should say it or not. Jacalrin glared at him at last, and the soldier quickly looked down and muttered, "The…woman says she came over the ridge from Boald Field, sir. A guard found her unconscious in front of the camp and took her to the medic. But…"

"Hmm?"

"Umm, she claims that even though she is a civilian, sir, she was mistreated by Sir Chesa, was threatened with death, and was robbed of her personal property ..."

At the completely unanticipated situation, Paseid and the others waited for Jacalrin's explanation. But the man at the center of their attention was shaking his head like he was utterly stunned. "Whaa —what?" He suddenly recalled someone. If that were true, it truly was preposterous.

Paseid asked, "What do you mean by 'threatening with death and robbing of personal property'?"

Jacalrin's fists trembled as chills ran down his spine.

She came all the way here?

His lips twitched. She was crazy. He'd thought she was a little off when she started saying *duke regent,* but she must have been completely cuckoo.

"According to her claims, Sir Chesa seized the civilian's horse and tried to kill her by tying her to a tree..."

"Whoa! I never tried to kill her!"

"...Sir, so...I came to report..."

The soldier shrank into himself at Jacalrin's response. Paseid pressed his left eye for a moment. "Sir Chesa, did you say that you paid for the horse you gave me?"

"Oh, I-I did... Probably? I did tell Sir Verohan to pay her the price, sir. He must...probably...have...paid her?"

Men sighed here and there. They seemed like they'd given up, thinking, *Of course, he is Jacalrin Endo of House Chesa.*

"Then why is she claiming that it was seized from her?"

"I don't know? We're allowed free supply of horses during wartime anyway, sir."

"Seizing from a civilian and receiving free supply are different. Do you not know that seizing of private property without the king's orders is forbidden even during wartime? It's clearly stated in the military law."

"There was a valid excuse, sir. She's a little out of her mind."

Jacalrin decided to calm down and act cool. But the faces looking at him changed in the worst way. *On top of his wicked despotism, he's now framing the woman as insane to save his skin!* he imagined they were thinking. *Wow, he truly fits the bill of Jacalrin Endo!*

Jacalrin jumped up from his seat, feeling extremely victimized. *I am telling the truth!*

But before he could say another word to plead his innocence, Paseid ordered, "Return the horse and send her back with an appropriate compensation." He stepped out of the tent.

Jacalrin froze there for a moment, listening to the older knights clicking their tongues and teasing him almost to the point of scolding, then suddenly came back to his senses and ran out.

CHAPTER SEVEN

A faint moan came from Reuyen's lips as she looked up at the unfamiliar ceiling.

The place they'd left her alone was a small tent for one person, not a military treatment facility for regular injured soldiers. She couldn't tell if it was because she was a woman, or because they thought her suspicious and wanted to isolate her. When she recovered her senses to a certain extent, she started to pick up a strong scent of herbs. It was an unpleasant smell, so she looked around to see where it was coming from. The main source apparently was the mashed-up herbs covering her feet and calves. The bandage wrapping her feet was already yellowed from them. But she did not want to complain about them treating her.

Heavy, bustling footsteps and occasional shouts came through the thin fabric of the tent. "Sir!" someone called out with great urgency, sounding quite comical.

After her body recovered some more, she started thinking like Reuyen again. First of all, she could not tell if she should rejoice or be upset about her numbed senses coming back. With the pain she'd forgotten about, thousands of different unpleasant sensations started pecking at her, from the soles of her feet to the top of her head.

"Is it here? I said, is it here?" An irritated voice sounded out of nowhere, followed by angry stomps, and the tent's drape opened. Reuyen was quite satisfied with Jacalrin's stomping, cross passion.

"Wow, I really was skeptical the whole way here, but I guess I was on to something!"

"I came back...to retrieve my stolen Den, sir." Aside from her hoarse voice, her tongue felt quite unnatural as she tried to address the young Chesa with respect. Though the young Chesa and Hansen looked nothing alike on the outside, for some reason she couldn't help herself from thinking of that cheeky Hansen.

All the same, Jacalrin stood there with a flushed face, trying to catch his breath. Then he saw her feet and looked aghast.

"You're crazy. Is that horse made of gold or something? You really chased me all the way here because you thought a man of House Chesa would 'forget' to pay you back? How did you even get out of the rope?"

She massaged her tingly thigh and muttered as if to herself, "Were you truly trying to starve me to death, sir?"

"No, I never said that."

"Getting out of the rope was not that hard. But there will be serious consequences if you do that to ordinary people, sir."

Jacalrin looked at her like he thought she was a nutcase. He pounded his own chest in frustration.

Reuyen looked askance at him for a while, then changed her expression to a stern one.

"But that's none of my business," she said. "I just want Den back, sir. That's all I ask."

"You'll get him back. You're not trying to sneak into the camp with my name, are you?"

"I'm here for Den only, at least for now...sir."

"Why? Have you got ten lives or something?"

Reuyen's parched lips smiled at that. Her lips tore and started bleeding, but she didn't care. "I looked after that horse since he was a foal, with someone I cared very much about."

"Who? Your dead lover?"

"Dead brother."

Jacalrin hesitated. He couldn't argue her justification that the problem lay with her dead brother, for he also had a brother. He acted a little more somber.

"Oh, umm, umm, yeah? I'm sorry... I mean, how do I know you're not lying?"

"Seven months ago, he volunteered himself to the Rarkian army and fell in a battle. His name was Eivan Detua. If you can't believe me, sir, search the register of volunteered soldiers.

"And I am here now, sir, to retrieve my younger brother who left seeking his own death after being enraged by Eivan's death. The duty of sacrifice as decreed by the royal family of Rarke is one man per family, even if there is a draft, so if he can't be discharged according to regular procedure, I'll request an administrative separation," she continued in a very clear voice, then added with less confidence, "If the military laws remain the same...sir."

Jacalrin made an empty, rather stupid-looking face at the words streaming out of her mouth like she was reading them from a book. He twitched his lips. "Who are you? Where did you say you were from again?"

"Reuyen Detua from Gyujen...sir."

She was quite obviously doing something peculiar at the end of her sentences, but Jacalrin looked very serious. Reuyen read suspicion in his sullen eyes.

"If you're suspicious, my brother will provide an unquestionable proof of my identity. Aside from that, when are you going to give Den back to me, sir?"

"I've sent for him, so he'll be here soon. And..." Jacalrin's voice trailed off as he chewed the inside of his cheek.

She was a really, really strange woman. The reason for her chasing after them here, where a battle might break out any moment, all by herself like she was obsessed was, well, because she was obsessed with her horse and her brother. He could give her that. But that didn't explain how she remained so confident and calm among rough soldiers and knights.

He couldn't smell danger, but it was now pretty hard to ignore the hunch that kept telling him something was up. All would be well if her brother were indeed at the Rarkian camp, but if not, this would become quite a headache for him.

"Your brother...well, all right, I'll at least try looking for your brother. What was his name again?"

"Sidan, son of Detua, sir."

She was surprised by his change of heart. She had a feeling it definitely wasn't because he was impressed by the determination that led her here.

"I'm just looking for him for now, sir."

Reuyen remained calm, not showing even a hint of joy at his generosity. Jacalrin suddenly realized the peculiar impression of a corpse's eyes seemed to be in her light brown eyes too.

Some time passed. A ferocious neighing came from outside, and a soldier peeked in the tent. "Sir, I brought the horse you ordered."

Reuyen's face, until then as pale as a corpse, suddenly brightened. She limped out of the tent, and Jacalrin swaggered after her with quite an uneasy expression on face.

Den was standing in front of the tent, fuming. He started jumping up and down upon finding her. The startled soldiers tried to pull on his reins, but they merely got dragged around like paper dolls.

"Whoa, whoa. Be good, Den," she mumbled in a raspy voice and caressed his cheek.

Den, who had been a complete nightmare to the soldiers the whole way here, suddenly became as tame as a lamb. Then, much to their contempt, he rubbed his cheek against Reuyen's hand, fat tears falling from his eyes.

With a sigh of relief, Reuyen whispered, "You were worried, weren't you?"

Neh-heigh. The horse whinnied as softly as a baby bird. Jacalrin and the soldiers who'd struggled to drag him there looked stunned at his sudden change of attitude, like he was always like this.

That, that, that churlish little donkey!

At that moment, the ground started to vibrate.

Jacalrin noticed and reacted first. Three files of soldiers were marching toward them on the wide road between tents.

He spotted a knight riding a black horse in the front and walked toward them. Following him, Reuyen's eyes widened at the sight of the fine, well-built black horse. The horse had a certain beastly dignity to him.

"Oh, Sir Calandok, where are you headed?"

"A message arrived from Camp Anf, the forward camp near the cliff. I'll be gone for a while, so…" The man had a calm, quiet voice.

He, of course, intrigued Reuyen, but she was too preoccupied with examining the horse. As one would expect, the black horse was a truly impeccable, superior stallion. At the very least, he had to be worth ten young, strong military horses. Even more, if he was of a good bloodline. He seemed just as exceptional as Baldoan horses from great bloodlines.

When the black horse's gaze turned her way all of a sudden, Den slowly lowered his head. Reuyen almost broke out laughing at seeing Den intimidated by another animal for the first time.

Oh heavens, are you intimidated right now?

"Make way."

Make... Oh.

Only then did Reuyen realize Den was blocking their way.

She grabbed his reins and slowly pulled, looking up at the rider on the superb horse as he passed by her: a man with black hair and eyes, wearing a military uniform under a mantle with a red wolf sewn on it.

The color of a raven's coat drew her attention, and she stopped as if her feet were planted in the ground. Her eyes too clearly saw the red wolf of Duke Brionake's rocking on the black horse as it elegantly walked away.

Her pulse and heart rate accelerated, and her chill limbs started to shake.

"Belbarote? Bel...by?"

Belbi.

Though she was muttering to herself, barely moving her lips, her voice sounded bewildered enough to catch the others' ears. The sound of the hooves stopped just like that, and Jacalrin turned from his bow to Paseid to look at the side of her face.

The black-haired man with the red wolf mantle slowly turned his head. The moment they stood face to face, Reuyen felt a shock-like wave and dropped her limp head. Even with a limited field of vision, she could feel his eyes scrutinizing her from top to bottom.

She froze for a moment, until a great shadow cast over her head.

"Just now," said a quiet voice, slipping into her ear, and she quietly laughed at herself. Of course not. The question continued, "What did you say?"

She raised her eyes as if bewitched.

Dark, dark fathomless eyes were looking down at her. She couldn't take her eyes off those straight, black ones. Somewhere between her neck and her chest stung.

Belbi... At that moment, I thought you'd come back to scold me for setting foot on a battlefield again. But he looked much more stubborn than you.

~

The first time the queen saw him was when she was still a young princess of fourteen.

She remembered that rare, hot summer day as clear as crystal. When Margrave Brionake passed away and his son came to Muiyadro to officially succeed his father, she saw the group of people in mourning, wearing black garments that made her sweat just by looking at them, and drew the curtain.

A white wolf banner was laid under the empty coffin.

Dolomete III recited the oration, strongly expressing his regrets. Before him, she recalled memories attached to the name Brionake. She knew the former Margrave Brionake from a few encounters in the past. He was a jovial man, reliable and strong enough to entrust with the country's borders.

But when her eyes reached the Brionake successor, whom she had only heard of, she was quite surprised by his pitch-black hair. It was dark even for Brionakes, who were known to have dark hair. She couldn't find the spirit of the wolf guarding the borders in his calm demeanor, quite unlike his predecessor, to the point that she started to quietly doubt if he indeed deserved to be relied on for the protection of the borders.

After the funeral, the official ceremony of Brionake's succession to the title margrave was administered by Dolomete III. So, the man with eyes as black as his hair was denominated Margrave Brionake.

The eyes are windows to the mind. The princess believed that saying, but she could never figure out what was going on behind his eyes, as if his were painted over with black. Nobles of the capital lined up, hoping to establish a connection with him. But oddly enough, the man refused all the social events and immediately returned to the border.

The princess leaned against the fence on a terrace high in the palace and looked over at the man heading back to his nest. Even in her young eyes, he was quite a ludicrous man. What could his leaving to protect the border mean, when he gave a hollow smile at all the praises people showered him with for his great military force, if it were not a pretense? But she did like him quite a bit, for postulating what his unreadable thoughts were brought her joy in her leisure hours.

He quietly carried on guarding the border until she turned nineteen. Of course, the princess was a cold-blooded woman who thought five years were nothing to prepare oneself for a leap, but even she could have no doubt in Margrave Brionake's unchanging truthfulness.

All this while, there were a couple opportunities for them to meet face-to-face and become a bit closer, since it wasn't like there wasn't any intercourse between the capital and the border.

As there were a lot of belligerent tribes and countries around the small, weak Rarke, conflicts arose frequently. The survivors of the wars all had similar faces of depression or hostility. And the princess was someone who did not hesitate to speak her mind. There were a number of generals who returned in tears at her words, which were as stinging as sandpaper. When that happened, the princess often teased them, saying, "That grotesque face of yours does well with a frown," like she was telling a joke.

But even though he was a warrior just like the others, Brionake's face was quite elegant and soft, and she couldn't mock it as grotesque. The others called Belbarote "black wolf" at times, for Brionake's symbol was a wolf. But.

"How can one be that black? You're just like a raven."

The only sneering word she had for him was probably that.

The princess learned about wars at the border from him. A world beyond the palace walls where conflicts rose incessantly, and blood and flesh splattered. How much damage and pain the enemy soldiers, who thought nothing of Rarke, inflicted on the people of Rarke.

Though he never was the one to reveal his thoughts first, he answered every one of the princess's questions with additional explanations. It was probably more of a method to get away from the bothersome princess than to show obedience.

Then, in the winter before her twenty-first year, the world was covered in white. A common sight, one could say, for it snowed a third of the year in Rarke. The motionless black hair under the high walls of the palace seemed clearer against the white.

"Every time I see you, you remind me of a raven."

The princess silently approached, as if she had blended into the snowy scape, and leaned her head next to his.

An enormous banner of a bay tree, the symbol of Rarkalia, was hanging high atop the wall and looking down at the princess and the margrave.

When he turned to bow, she kept looking up at the tall wall and waved her hand to stop him. He instead nodded to show respect and followed her gaze, as he was doing before.

"What do you see up there that makes you spend all that time standing here whenever you come to the palace?" she asked.

It was just a banner of Rarkalia hung atop a wall tall enough to make the back of her neck ache. And yet, as she remembered, he always stood here before leaving the palace.

"I see a tree."

"And I see a raven who cannot climb the tree."

His lips opened as if he was going to say something, but they soon shut again, and his chin stiffened. The princess slightly smiled, pretending like she didn't catch that. A maid was hurrying their way with an umbrella, finally realizing that the princess had disappeared.

She cast away her eyes from the maid and let her voice resound amongst the fluttering snowflakes.

"I hear ravens like shiny things."

"Apparently so."

"Then, Belbarote, would you like to be the Prince Consort of Rarke? King, the man of a queen."

Instead of a surprised inquiry about the young princess speaking rude, unexpected words, he silently looked at her. She grinned and straightened her body toward him.

"I am a person full of doubt, who values what she has. If you become the Prince Consort of Rarke, I will give you the shiniest, priceless gift of my trust. In turn, will you...become a shield so I can protect my beloved Rarke to my heart's content?"

The playful enticement of her trust rather than power or treasures was perfected by her smile as warm as light.

The red hair shining brightly under the sunlight and the blue eyes completely free of any corruption were more brilliant than the sky pouring down snow. And so, they did not suit the dark man. Slightly tilting his head to look down at the princess who wasn't even blinking, Belbarote asked with a grunt, "Did you just propose to me?"

"I'm sorry I didn't even bring a single flower, but if you want a gift with my proposal, I will gift you the bay tree of Rarkalia you are looking at right now. I will give you the walls of the palace."

The princess's lips drew a smooth arc as she finished her sentence, her face arrogant but serene.

"Princess!"

Then, he saw a maid running toward her and turned away. There was no answer to the princess's proposal.

The black back of the man stood out in the snowfall as he quietly bowed and left. He was beautiful.

Without showing dismay, the princess elegantly walked in the opposite direction. The maid hastily ran after her on the slippery road and held the umbrella over her head. The princess's red hair blew in the snow, which fell as thick as cotton balls.

The next year, on one morning when the short summer was about to end, Dolomete III left on an irreversible journey to the utopia of Rarkalia.

A month after the funeral, Margrave Brionake came to the princess overcome with grief, with a group of riders carrying white wolf banners on their backs.

"Swan Sekalrid Rarkalia."

In front of the stone tomb Dolomete III's ashes were rested, the raven kneeled on one knee. Holding up a single red flower to her.

"I will be your shield."

It was a red, luscious offering.

"You seek to buy a kingdom with a single flower."

The princess gladly sold the kingdom for a single flower.

The present came before Reuyen's mixed memories and pulled her out from her past.

"What did you just say?"

She was too distracted to answer his menacing question. Even without trying, the voice of a man sobbing layered over her ear.

I loved you.

She heard his confession in the far past, right before her death must have made its mark on her heart. The husband she never looked after her whole life, Belbarote. The man she more often called Belbi.

How dare you betray me.

She did resent him so.

I did not look after you.

But she felt guilty at the same time.

Belbarote had that kind of meaning to her, with neither complete hatred nor guilt. A traitor who'd usurped the throne, but someone who'd also thrown his body at the feet of the fallen queen, buried his face in her dirtied dress, and wept like a child.

"Hey, the commander asked you a question," Jacalrin scolded.

Only then did Reuyen wake up from her memories and let out a low grunt. "Oh."

She could not feel her dry lips, as though they had been carved out. She looked at the black eyes looking down at her. Forgetting all about manners, she took her time studying them, as if under a spell.

Then she suddenly realized: he did look like Belbarote at a glance, but there really was no particularly familiar part of his face. Except for those black, raven-like things that caught her eye, neither the shape of the eyes and nose, nor the expressions on his face resembled Belbarote. Somewhere in her gut tickled, and she let out a hollow laugh.

"No... No. Nothing, sir. I made a mistake."

The commander stayed there with Rotsa's reins in his hand, as though her answer was satisfactory enough, but soon erased that expression off his face.

He stretched out his palm, like he was going to leave, and gestured. Then, the soldiers started to move in an orderly fashion again. He turned his black horse when everyone passed him by and unaffectedly ordered, "Sir Chesa, be sure to take this woman back and have her wounds treated."

"Huh? Oh, yes, sir."

He must have seen her feet bleeding again.

With the sound of the black horse's hooves hitting the ground, the red wolf mantle fluttered. The single black horse did not look back even once, followed by nearly a hundred soldiers and knights who all moved away at a steady speed.

Watching them disappear until they were small black dots, Reuyen asked in a faint voice, "Name... What is his name?"

Jacalrin scowled. But Reuyen's eyes were fixated on what she could still see of Paseid.

"For heaven's sake, you don't know Duke Brionake? He is Duke Paseid Calandok Brionake. Hey, what were you saying before? Bel...what?"

Paseid Calandok Brionake.

Paseid. Even his name amazed her. Had someone said this before? Life could amaze you at times.

She lowered her scrunched-up face, somewhere between laughing or crying.

Jacalrin remembered Paseid's orders and looked down at Reuyen's feet. Then, without hesitating, he grabbed her slender waist, picked her up, and put her around his shoulders.

"What are you...!" she cried.

Poof, Den snorted.

Jacalrin tapped on Den's forehead and coaxed him like a sly fox. "Enough. I've been ordered to take care of your master's wound, you cheeky little horse. How come she doesn't even whine until her feet get all bloody like this? Like master, like horse."

"Let me down. I'll walk."

"Don't you think you've been missing a word in your sentences for a while?"

"...Sir. I'm sorry, sir."

Jacalrin mumbled, "It's good to be put on a pedestal," and strode on. He rolled his eyes, suddenly realizing that the woman had become unusually still and quiet.

He felt an odd shaking against his back that could have been laughter or a sob.

CHAPTER EIGHT

Following Jacalrin's decision that it would be best if she went unnoticed by the soldiers, Reuyen was moved to a tent in the far corner at the edge of the camp. On top of ordering her not to move a single hair, he set guards at the entrance to the tent. These, however, were unnecessary measures, for quite a bit of pain followed every little movement when it put pressure on the fresh wound, and she did not think moving a worthy risk.

She sat there like a good girl, just as Jacalrin wished, and continued her train of thought.

All the things she had let go of came flowing back to her with the passing of time. All the memories and sensations from her past life caught between her fingers and clamored for attention. So, as they wished, she unfurled the question she had neatly folded away long ago.

Why was I reborn?

She had been executed by a guillotine on the scaffold on a day that the skies swarmed with dark colors. When she'd woken up, she had found herself continuing her life through an unforeseen reincarnation. Because she still kept all of her memories when others were learning things from point zero, she had learned to adjust her knowledge to the present reality.

She had never met anyone like her. Even when she had tentatively brought it up, thinking that perhaps others were hiding their pasts like she was, they'd treated it like a joke and said, "You really do think differently." So, at a certain point, she'd stopped talking about it too.

Living in a remote town in the forest, she'd had the time to thoroughly organize herself. The isolation gave her a certain answer, that this maybe was a second life given to her, like that given to a butterfly newly emerged from a chrysalis.

But Paseid Calandok Brionake. The shock, the guilt, and all the other confusing emotions that crashed over her the moment she laid eyes on him made her think of another possibility at last. Perhaps this was a punishment to atone for a sin that could not be atoned for with one life.

How was he related to Belbarote? He was called a Brionake. The similarity of their coloring was so dreadfully cruel that it made her squeeze her knees and suppress the bursting laughter inside. Everything she'd tried so hard to cast away clung to her clothes and demanded her attention.

I wonder what happened to you after I died, Belbarote.

The wonder she had ignored all these years planted its roots in her brain. To be honest, it was more that she didn't want to hear those who'd rejoiced after the queen's death than that she wasn't curious. So, she covered her ears, shut her eyes, and soothed herself. Rarke remained strong after nearing collapse under the queen's tyranny, and that was all that mattered.

Another person naturally made his way into her mind. It was no surprise that he did, for she was on a battlefield. He was a part of the battlefield in her past life, and the battlefield was everything to her.

Peijak Dollehan. She believed Belbarote would have tried his best to appease her will, since he was a humble and a generous man. But perhaps under that concrete belief lay a small part of her desire not to hear that Peijak had been executed because Belbarote failed to accept her plea. Probably so. She had avoided it.

That was an indignity she did not want to admit. Like a coward, the queen was unsure she could stand having to bear the sin not even her death could absolve after two hundred years.

Self-deprecation seeped into Reuyen's half-closed eyes.

The smell of night pervaded. The smell of night on the battlefield was different from the ordinary smell of peace. It was the smell of a pitch-black mind muddled with tension, anxiety, and nostalgia.

"Are you asleep?" Jacalrin came into her tent, accompanied by Seisen.

The knight who had ruthlessly threatened her before on the field looked down at her with dissatisfied eyes. Reuyen ignored him and turned her gaze to Jacalrin.

"Your brother," he said, and cut himself off. Reuyen exhaled dryly without realizing it. "Umm, he was there, as you said. He volunteered for the front at Camp Anf, not the main camp."

Jacalrin seemed quite uncomfortable. He scratched the back of his head for a moment, then said to Seisen, "Step outside for a moment, Sir Verohan. Actually, you may be excused. Thank you for today's work."

The middle-aged knight, who looked like he still had suspicious doubts about her, left the tent at his lord's order. But the way Jacalrin was taking a long time to open his mouth again, very much unlike himself, added to her anxiety.

When she could not hold it in any longer, she spoke first. "Did he die?"

"No, no, no, he didn't." He believed honesty was the best policy in all situations, but right now, he was trying to choose his words wisely to explain the situation.

Today, Seisen had run around himself and searched all the registers of volunteers for the main camp and Camp Anf. He found the name Sidan. There was a dead soldier by the name of Eivan Detua as well. At the very least, all of her claims were true.

Once they'd verified that, Jacalrin couldn't deny that he did feel a little bit of sympathy for her. The eldest son of a family had volunteered for war and lost his life. His brother had also volunteered and risked his life on the battlefield, which was...an admirable but pitiful deed.

After checking the dead soldier's name, Eivan, and searching for the whereabouts of Sidan, Jacalrin had sent Sir Seisen Verohan to Camp Anf in person. There, Seisen had verified the woman's features with the young man. And asked if he desired to be discharged at all.

The response, Jacalrin heard, had been quite aggressive. It must have been true that he was enraged by his brother's death.

"First..."

Then again, it made no sense to order administrative separation for a man who offered up his life to save his country with such fierce patriotism, just because his guardian had arrived.

"...I asked him about your features, verified your identity, and asked him about his intentions. Isn't there another son in your family?"

Reuyen gave an empty laugh, for though it was an inconsiderate question, it sounded quite careful and unlike Jacalrin. He didn't explicitly say anything, but she could imagine. It was a relief to hear that Sidan was still alive. But...

Sidan Detua. You little immature baby brother. You clueless bastard. You lunatic.

"He said he'd stay. There's nothing more to be done, so you should go back to your town. A battlefield is not a safe place for a woman to go around as she pleases. It's your fault you came all the way here with your crazy obsession, but I don't want to be hated any more than I am now, so I'll send two knights to escort you back to your town tomorrow."

"I'll go to Sidan myself, sir," Reuyen replied before Jacalrin even finished his sentence. She had left with firm determination. She had turned her back on her anguished parents and born their wails. She couldn't bear another burden when this was already heavy enough.

"How are you going to take him when he doesn't want to go?"

"Well, you can order an administrative separation."

"We don't throw out volunteers by force unless there is a good reason. Haven't you thought about what would happen if their families all came after them and protested for an administrative separation for their sons? I get that you can't understand the inner workings of an army, but this is common sense."

"Say what you desire, sir. But I'm going to see my brother."

Jacalrin's face started to stiffen. Who did she think she was, refusing the orders of the man next in command to the commander-in-chief in the middle of a battlefield without even a hint of concern? It made no sense.

"Orders are orders, and you'll go home if you're told to go home. What on earth are you thinking?"

Reuyen's rounded fists started to shake slightly at his scolding.

Who dares to force an order on me on a battlefield?

A fierce burst of fury flashed in her light brown eyes, then disappeared. Even if she censured this feeling of outrage, if Jacalrin decided so, it would be so.

Outside the tent, she heard the sound of Den tied to the fence, snorting in the night, permeating the camp like a fog. Reuyen calmed her blazing mind with great effort. Then, she looked up at the young Chesa. She, of course, did not miss the pity in his eyes.

Even that annoyingly unperturbable Hansen had seemed a little contrite when she'd climbed the scaffold. He'd most likely thought it frustrating that the queen had been forced to kneel as a loser and let them take away her life in silence, without even a last word. She'd known that, but she'd just looked at them one by one, for she knew that she could not make them understand with all the words in the world. Just like now.

Reuyen silently returned his gaze and slowly cooled down. She had no intentions to obediently comply with his order, but she didn't need to let him know about that. Jacalrin would fulfill his duties, and she hers.

To change the subject, Reuyen asked a question that had been nagging at her. "I understand what you mean, sir. For now. But I had one..." Her voice trailed off. "...Question."

"What?"

"The Royal House Brionake and the Noble House Brionake are..."

There was something about the man she'd seen today that she could not grasp. Paseid Calandok Brionake. It was pathetic of her to look for Belbarote in his looks, but there certainly was a reason for that mistake.

Two hundred years ago, Duke Brionake, Belbarote, in her last memory had overthrown her and taken the throne instead. A king cannot hold a dukedom, so it must have been bestowed on another Brionake. A man similar enough for her to mistake for a man from the past should not have been born in the present. How probable was the spontaneous expression of a blood relative from a long time ago? If this were a coincidence, it certainly was a nasty one.

"Does not the noble House Brionake...have a long history of dukedom?"

A quizzical expression appeared on Jacalrin's face. "They were granted dukedom two hundred years ago, so I'd say it's been a while."

"After the duke re..." She stopped herself right before she pronounced the words *duke regent* in full. "I mean, after the founder Brionake became the king, who succeeded the dukedom?"

Jacalrin frowned slightly, for a different reason. Unlike his expectations that she would insist that she take her brother with her, she'd started asking weird questions.

He had an uneasy hunch about this, but acquiesced.

"Seems like you're not as well-read in the history of the military laws you so like to refer to. Isn't this well known amongst common people too? Of the two sons King Belbarote Paseid had, the first, Prince Peogran, succeeded the throne."

Oh... Oh.

"The second, Prince Tejis, succeeded the dukedom."

She had children she didn't even recognize the names of. Peogran and Tejis. Just hearing the names of those whose faces she didn't know broke her heart.

Suddenly, the memory of the day her wifeless husband had smiled bitterly shattered and pierced her heart.

Even if it's a son, if you name our child the heir...

The mind she was barely holding together collapsed in that one moment.

Her eyes, which had remained dry even in the face of death, started to pour down tears. Something hot boiled in her guts. Belbarote had protected her woman's honor, and now, two hundred years later, it was thrown at her face. Bearing the faults of a wife for a lifetime...

"Wha—what's wrong?" Jacalrin's mouth gaped slightly with surprise.

Not realizing it, Reuyen laughed out loud at the tears flowing out of her open eyes. *Behold the foolishness of bequeathing the finest throne ever in existence to the son of a tyrant, whom he cannot call a son at all.* Until the last of his last moments, Belbarote had still been a humble country man.

Belbarote. Oh, Belbarote.

"There wasn't much atop the bay tree, was there..."

Hollow chuckles escaped her lips. She covered her face with trembling hands at last, unable to control the burst of emotions.

"Belbi..." Her dry lips whispered that name she so dearly longed for.

She knew that caring voice would not return; she knew the smile he smiled in his own kindness, too, remained in the past from two hundred years ago. The image of him kneeling before her was as clear as a framed painting.

Reach him.

Swan Sekalrid Rarkalia.

Reach him.

I loved you.

A foolish woman's forgiveness asked far too late.

Please reach him.

～

Reuyen stayed crouching there for a long while.

What's wrong with this one? Not knowing what to do, Jacalrin stood there and looked down at her. The cries of the woman somehow resonated in him. She had coiled into herself like a porcupine with its quills down. Jacalrin of Chesa was quite talented at joking around and hiding his intentions, but he had no skills in consoling a woman crying like that. His light-green eyes started to look annoyed.

Thankfully, before his worries intensified, Reuyen stopped crying. "What happened to Sir Peijak Dollehan?"

It was quiet and calm, like she hadn't been crying at all.

Not even noticing that she had once again forgotten to add the "sir," Jacalrin stared down at her, then slowly changed his expression. Disdain and hatred flashed in his light-green eyes.

"Dollehan? I do not wish to dirty my tongue by speaking about him, so do not ask. I don't want to lose my dignity with dishonorable words and actions."

Flustered with the plain contempt, Reuyen could not dare to ask any more questions and mumbled in a low voice. "You already don't talk that much like a noble."

"How would a country girl know?"

"I can at least tell that you're not very noble-like."

"Ha. And just what do you know about the duties and virtues of a noble?"

"They think that sophisticated roundabout expressions are virtuous, and they proudly sneer at others as a habit. The young and the old both pretend to be sages and, hence, are headaches."

"Yeah, you're so right. That was so frustrating, so..." Jacalrin cackled at her straightforward answer, waving his hand, then stopped. Realizing the woman had stopped addressing him with respect. But the more shocking thing was that though he had noticed now, she spoke so naturally that it didn't feel strange at all.

Reuyen Detua, the daughter of a horse dealer. Her identity was verified.

Jacalrin felt a chill go down his spine. She was gazing him questioningly, with those light-brown eyes hidden under lashes as long as a camel's.

How dare she not address the second son of Chesa with respect? Her eyes were imposing enough to make him swallow his indignant words.

"Umm..." Jacalrin stared down at her with a dumb expression on his face, then aggressively removed it, turning back to his usual self. "I'm sending the knights at first light tomorrow, and that's that. And for your own good, if you come back again, I will punish you for sure." His stern, coercive voice, unlike his usual tone, resounded.

Reuyen closed her eyes, listening to the sound of his footsteps fade away.

After organizing her thoughts alone for a little bit, she looked at her bandaged feet. She had spent enough time wallowing in sadness, grieving, asking for forgiveness, and crying tears of longing.

Jacalrin had said that Sidan was at the camp near the cliffs, Camp Anf.

She limped across the tent and moved the drape to find that the guard in front of the tent was nodding off. Reuyen stared at the sword lying next to him, then grabbed it, and slunk back inside. She went straight to the back of the tent, stuck the sword under the post holding down the fabric, and used it as a lever to remove the post.

She crawled out of the tent through the narrow opening and limped as silently as she could toward Den.

Poof! Neigh!

Shushing Den to stop him from jumping around with joy, she stepped on the stirrup and mounted with great effort.

"Let's go see Sidan, Den."

There was nothing to be afraid of.

The night on the battlefield, the smell of the battlefield, and the memories on the battlefield were all as soothing as a cradle to her.

She knew the location of the front, Anf. Assuming that the continent had not changed much since her death, she could estimate the direction and distance quite well too. She tiptoed away from the main camp, studied the sky for a while, then carefully led Den in what she hoped was the right direction.

When she was fairly far away from the main camp, she spurred Den to move faster. It would take at least an hour, even on horseback. Her still-ailing body ached, but the most painful of all were her feet, pushing down on the stirrups.

After riding and riding for some time, she suddenly heard horses galloping her way and hurriedly hid herself in the dark. Two riders were coming toward her, most likely sent from Camp Anf. They did not notice her, and flashed by.

A drum pounded somewhere in the distance. When the riders were completely out of sight, Reuyen lashed her whip as hard as she could to get Den moving again.

CHAPTER NINE

"Report, sir!"

At the base at the entrance of the road between the cliffs of Anf, torches lit the dawn and moved around like will-o'-the-wisps. Chaos pervaded as people alternated between shouting and gasping.

Paseid, who had arrived there in the afternoon and stayed to patrol the camp and relay orders related to the new plan, stayed calm amid the sudden ambush and listened to the knight's report.

"There are about a thousand soldiers and regular knights in metal armor, sir! We have verified fifty or so archers in full-plate armor positioned halfway up the cliff."

"Why were the guards and patrols so late with the report?" asked Paseid.

"Seems like they were killed in the night. They were found dead, sir."

The enemy had dared an ambush in the dark of the night and was pushing in from the entrance at the Anf cliffs to the Rarkian camp like a hot knife through butter. Rovantis's cruel trick of placing the archers in heavy armor high up in the middle of the cliffs had already baffled the Rarkian army.

The common soldiers, their shields positioned to defend the soldiers and knights in metal armor, were confused about whether they should block arrows showering down from the sky or the sharp swords pummeling toward them from the front. Even if they tried to shoot the archers in return, if they could not pierce the neck and the face at once, the arrows would just bounce off the thick armor. Of course, there were those who fell because they couldn't hold all the weight of the armor, but that was only a handful.

After the chaos subsided, the disorganized Rarkian defense line started to come back into formation again, but the enemy's goal had already been attained. Reaching the side of the force where the arrows were out of range, Paseid's eyes turned cold.

He was unsure if the enemy had undertaken the ambush because they knew that he, the commander-in-chief, was here, or if they'd simply chosen today out of luck. Considering how they'd attacked about five thousand Rarkians stationed here with only a little more than a thousand, this most likely was another provocation. But that did not mean he could react in a dismissive manner. Defeat was unacceptable, but casualties were inevitable.

Neigh!

Paseid's black horse, Rotsa, who had remained unperturbed at the cries of other excited horses, the clashing of metal swords, the yelling, screaming, and such, snorted at the smell of blood in the passing wind and kicked the ground with his hind leg.

"Place the cavalry in the rear, and order the infantry to drop their swords and hold their shields," the commander ordered. "Two men with shields and one archer as one team. Position the men in the front for defense."

Paseid took out his sword, Rionac, that had been hidden in a snow-white sheath. It had been passed down from one generation of House Brionake to the next; the noble sword made a sharp noise, gleaming silver in the middle of the chaotic battlefield.

"Sir…"

"Follow."

Paseid rode Rotsa to the front. A portion of the knights behind him sheathed their swords, picked up the shields from the rack, and followed him.

The entire area around the entrance to the cliffs was complete mayhem, a battlefield where the only lights shining in the pitch-dark night were torches and fire burning at the points of the arrows.

The soldiers were fighting desperately, barely distinguishing their enemies from friends by the black lion, rose, and wolf ingrained on the armor.

Paseid struck the chest of a knight who had broken through the line of shields and was riding his way, and pierced his neck once he fell on the ground. Blood reeking of metal sprang up, but Paseid remained calm and looked around as soon as he confirmed the enemy's death.

Who is the commander leading them?

An arrow aimed for him hit the shield of a knight following behind and fell. With a *thunk*, the arrow hit Rotsa's chanfron and bounced off.

Unaffected, Paseid swung his sword and cut through a mantle with the figure of a lion holding a rose in his mouth. The knight fell to the ground.

"Aaaaaaaah!"

An enemy soldier was running to attack a Rarkian soldier far away from the defense line. Paseid reared his horse and struck the enemy with Rotsa's hooves. The fierce horseshoe crushed the soldier's face. The Rarkian soldier panted from barely escaping the grasp of death, then shot back up as trained and joined the formation.

A knight was swinging the heavy shield as if it were his own arm at the enemy's helmet. "Sir, perhaps you should stay in the rear..."

"Sir Ranu, find the enemy's commander."

They will soon retreat on their own.

The repeated ambushes at nighttime were exasperatingly cunning. A skirmish with Rovantis was an exhausting battle of attrition. The only difference was that the south had an advantage in reinforcing their losses, for they were more affluent than Rarke.

Amidst all the malicious shouts and exclamations, the particularly vindictive voice of a soldier caught his attention.

"Come at meeeeee! I'll kill you alllllllll! You bastards of Morgana!"

A young man in a tattered armor, covered from his helmet to

breastplate to metal boots in blood, was aimlessly swinging his sword among a group of enemies.

All the malevolence on the battlefield was the bitter grief of those who had lost their human natures.

Paseid's eyes moved in search of a larger, rational malevolence. None of the knights of Rovantis, riding through the chaos, looked like a leader.

With sudden intuition, he directed his eyes upward.

Up there, then.

His black gaze landed on a man in light armor, standing behind the archers on the middle point of the cliff. The banner, bugle, and sword hanging by his waist verified Paseid's suspicion. When their eyes met, the man took the bow from an archer standing next to him and aimed, as though he were laughing at Paseid.

But he was not aiming at Paseid.

As Paseid watched, he shot arrow after arrow at the Rarkians swinging their swords and shields to survive or to kill. Arrows of death rained on the necks and heads of Rarkian soldiers chasing after the retreating ones. In the blink of an eye, a total of four lives crossed the river from which they would not return. At last, the man's arrow pointed at a certain young soldier crazed with the desire to kill.

The black eyes flashed with deep rage, glaring at the man daring to shoot death from over his head. Paseid sheathed the Rionac and grabbed the bow that was hanging at Rotsa's side.

Will it reach?

He nocked an arrow.

The knights protecting Paseid all held their breaths. He aimed in silence. He drew his arm back...

Just then, an object flying at an immense speed passed over his head with a gush of wind.

The startled knights quickly turned their horses and guarded his back, chills running down their spines. Utilizing his sensitive instinct, Paseid turned back as well.

Behind him, a woman stood expressionless, a bow in her hand. Where she had come from, he had no idea. Even after everyone's attention was centered on her, she moved nimbly. The arrows shot from those little hands hit the archers on the cliff one by one.

Paseid followed the arc of the arrow flying over his head. The enemy commander who had been shooting down death from that cliff was now falling down like a dead bird, an arrow piercing his forehead. It was a Rarkian arrow, but the woman who shot it was not a Rarkian soldier.

Paseid recognized the horse standing next to the woman before he recognized her face. He remembered those spots on its forehead. A wild horse like that could not be easily forgotten.

The violent, piercing sound of a gong started to ring, the enemy's retreat signal. The black lions gushing toward them without order slowly went into formation and prepared to retreat.

Rovantis's soldiers gave up as soon as the Rarkians below the cliffs took their leader's body and retreated after the knights like an ebb tide. Rarkian soldiers ran, chasing after them.

Amidst the mayhem and the gong fiercely ringing for retreat, Paseid ordered, "Stop all pursuit. All soldiers back to formation."

A couple of knights, gaping and staring at the woman, snapped back to their senses and left. The rest of the knights kept their eyes fixed on her bow. They had no clue if she was a friend or an enemy. But the mysterious woman dropped the bow and mounted her horse before anyone could grab her. She soon disappeared out of sight.

A few minutes earlier, using the upheaval of the ambush to her advantage, Reuyen had run across the camp and to the entrance to the cliffs without any obstacles. There, she'd searched for the enemy's commander. It was an instinct rooted dreadfully deep within her.

She'd estimated the number of people and the size of the battle from the shouts and the footsteps. Then she'd recalled the geography of the narrow entrance to the Anf cliffs. A large-scale battle was not feasible at this location, so she knew the battle would end if she found the commander and killed him. And her intuition had been pointing directly at a man standing on the midpoint of the cliff.

It's him. It's you.

Finding the commander shooting arrows and Sidan screaming vengefully at him was half coincidental. That coincidence made her heart skip a beat, but she remained cool.

Reuyen had gone straight to the racks that were scattered across the camp and grabbed a bow with the longest shooting range. Then she'd run until the man was in her range and drew as hard as she could. And aimed.

There can be no miscalculations.

Her past self always hit the enemy commander's head. An ordinary, natural deed.

The world dropped to a hum. The screams of metal against metal faded away. All her attention was on the enemy on the cliff. The momentary silence swallowed all the malicious shouts ringing in her ears.

Her arrow pierced the center of the enemy's forehead.

Confirming that the enemy was retreating at the sound of the gong, Reuyen drew one arrow after another and hit three archers aiming at the defense line. And then she ran to Sidan.

"I'm going to kill you alllllllll!"

Though drums were sounding from the Rarkian camp to signal the stop of pursuit, Sidan was jumping over his comrades' bodies and chasing after the enemy. Reuyen pushed through the soldiers and grabbed the tip of her brother's helmet.

"I'm going to kill...!"

"Sidan."

"Those bastards..."

"Sidan Detua. Time to go home."

Sidan stood still at Reuyen's voice and looked up at a crooked angle. His bloodshot eyes were brighter than the blood that dripped down into them. Reuyen bit her lips at the frightening malice and hatred in his eyes.

"Why are you here?" he asked.

"Let's go."

"Why are you here? Let go! Let go, I said!"

"This battle is over. Can't you hear the signal for retreat? More than this is insubordination."

Unruffled by Sidan struggling to get her hand off of him, Reuyen kept her grip on the tip of his helmet and steered Den. As she dragged her brother like a choking dog, Sidan stabbed the air at the Morganaan soldiers running away.

"Those bastards killed them all! My friend! My brother!"

"There's nothing your tantrum can fix."

"Shut...up! Shut up!"

"You foolish halfwit! How dare you speak like that to the one who just saved your life!"

Tears of overwhelming anger dropped from Sidan's eyes. "Let them kill me! You think I'm scared? I'll kill them all and die too!" the young man bellowed, devastated by the fear of war. His sister's heart shattered to bits.

They stood out like sore thumbs, standing on the bodies and having a quarrel in the middle of the soldiers.

Paseid turned Rotsa around, staring at the woman with his quiet black eyes.

"Let me go! Get lost!" cried Sidan.

His shouts alone had enough vigor to squeeze the life out of an enemy's heart. But she read fear underneath all that. He probably witnessed more cruelty in less than a month than he'd seen in his entire life. She understood how frightening that could be, so she suppressed her anger and spoke calmly.

"You have sufficiently proven your grief for Eivan's death. So, let's go back now. Mother and Father are waiting for you."

Mother and Father.

Sidan hesitated for a moment. But soon, he pointed at the body of his friend he stood on, and all the dead bodies of the enemies around them.

"Do you not see that?" he howled. "Do you not see those men? Our brother would have died like that too! Died in agony! They did that!"

"Grieve on your own. Stop bothering others."

"Are you saying that I should just be content with grieving on my own?"

"We can't grieve all these deaths."

"What about our family? Our brother is dead, and you haven't even shed a single tear! How can you call yourself human?"

At that moment, she felt as powerless as she would in front of a vast wall. In the split second her grip loosened, Sidan violently untied his helmet to get away from her, and then drew his sword. It was a ridiculously clumsy stance compared to Eivan, who had trained in sword fighting to become a volunteer guard of their town. *How pathetic.*

"I'm not a child," Sidan said.

"The result of this war will not be determined merely by you. There are people far more adept than you."

"Do you think I'm doing this to become a war hero?"

"Stop being so stubborn! Don't jump in headfirst where your life will only be wasted like a moth in a flame!"

"What do you know? You cold-blooded, apathetic psychopath!"

"Call me a psychopath, a monster, or whatever else you want! But I will bring you back home," Reuyen murmured determinedly, glaring at Sidan. He met Reuyen's ferocious eyes and burst into laughter, almost to himself.

"I thought it was weird when they looked for me to ask how many siblings I have, how many are in my family, and what they all looked like. That was all you? Impressive, Reuyen Detua. How did you even know to find me here? Is there anything that you don't know or can't do? It's so awe-inspiring that it's almost scary."

Reuyen calmly soothed Den, who was trying to back away, startled by Sidan's blatant desire to kill. She tried her best to speak steadily, like nothing was going on. "Have you any idea why they put men like you at the front…"

But for some reason, words refused to come out.

Do you even have the right to say such things? The karma returning to her with the stench of blood ripped her tongue apart. It rushed up to the nape of her neck and whispered: *Do you, you who drove the country into chaos, dare to claim the rights to speak of such things?* She clamped her mouth shut at the nauseating sensation of curdled blood coming up inside her throat. She gazed at Sidan, with his reddish-brown hair like Jess's, and dark-brown eyes like Senila's. He reminded her of Eivan.

You have to look after our family now.

She wanted to follow him to the afterlife, grab him by the collar, and scream at him if she could. *Why did you tell this foolish, self-centered woman that she now bore that responsibility? Do you have any idea who the woman is you just chained down with a couple of words?*

Sidan's shaking legs were threatening to collapse; he struggled to hold up his bloody sword. Reuyen forgot her duties for a moment and stared down at him, at loss.

Why had he come to this? What should she do? Until Eivan's death, Sidan was just a benevolent brother too.

The soldiers clamored as they moved as one at the order to convene. Those being carried off on stretchers moaned and screamed. The cruel side of her that had been sleeping, the nature of a queen who raged at disobedience, started to remind her of its presence.

"Then I will bring you back as a cripple, if need be. You'll know to give up when you learn your own uselessness."

Reuyen grabbed the hilt of the sword hanging at Den's side. Sidan's lips crumpled at her, his face white, and then he fixed his grip on his sword. He didn't show any sign of backing down, but neither did she.

A rhythmic sound of hooves approached her from behind.

"No, we will seize the swords," a stern, apathetic voice ordered.

Reuyen turned her head, suddenly aware.

Before she could even realize what was happening, a knight was standing right behind her with his sword pointed at her lower back, like he would stab her without a second thought. She glanced down at the blade and slowly let go of her sword.

"You two are exempt from the call," said the knight. "The commander-in-chief has ordered you both in his presence. Follow."

CHAPTER TEN

Reuyen stood still and gazed at the man who called her here. Her thoughts were racing a mile a minute because she had not expected to see him again so soon.

But the man with hair as dark and eyes as black as Belbarote was too busy to pay any attention to her. He carefully listened to the post-battle reports and gave an order, then jotted something down on a piece of paper on the table, then listened to the reports again, and so on and so forth. Like he had forgotten he'd called her and Sidan there.

"We have officially verified that the commander who died during this battle was Count Asvar from Rovantis's army, sir. We are currently verifying the number of casualties and the identities of the dead on our side. Also, the scouts have reported that the enemy has completely moved over to Plain Ishas and joined their defense line, sir."

Half-listening to their conversation, Reuyen moved her tranquil gaze across the small tent at Camp Anf, then stopped upon an object.

Rionac.

The snow-white sheath leaned against the table at a slant. She recognized it at first glance.

She, who was a queen of an older time, had once wanted to make an absolutely indomitable weapon like no other in the world, after she was greatly injured when an enemy broke off a shard of her sword.

Narrowly escaping death, she'd searched every single vein located in the northern mountain range of Muiyadro, the capital city of Rarke, gathered all the renowned smiths, and forged the Galian steel, which many renounced as extremely difficult to handle. A set of armor, a shield, and three weapons were made.

Rionac was one of weapons, which she'd given to Belbarote as proof of her noble trust.

"Currently, we have reinforced our defenses and finished the installation of cannons at the entrance to the cliffs, sir. As soon as the dead's identities are verified..."

"The messenger sent to the main camp..."

Their conversation faded away.

Her gaze slowly moved to Paseid. Even now that she recognized he was a completely different person, just recalling the past drowned her in a stinging agony of yearning.

"Tell Sir Ranu to report the rest to me in person when administrations are completed."

"Yes, sir."

With the strange knight's crisp exit, the waiting came to an end.

In contrast to the composed Reuyen, Sidan was still trying to catch his breath. His tired, uneven huffs broke the silence. Paseid, who had been pressing a hand to his forehead like he was lost in thought for a long while after the knight's exit, awakened her sunken senses.

"Did Sir Chesa authorize you to come here?"

Instead of answering, Reuyen quietly looked down.

Paseid didn't ask again, since he did not need a verbal verification to guess the answer to that question. Jacalrin was indeed a free spirit, but he was not a senseless one. In fact, Count Chesa, Rougak, claimed that Jacalrin was a headache because he was a trouble-maker who used his senses. Besides, Paseid had ordered and received a detailed report from the knight who overheard the fight between this young man and woman.

In a battle where even trained war horses threw a fit at the stench of blood, her eyes were clear, an unrevealing shade of mahogany.

"You came in search of your brother," said Paseid.

"Yes, sir. He is a short-tempered boy, unfit for war. His nature will only be a hindrance in your army."

Glaring at his sister, Sidan bowed down as low as he could to the ground and beseeched Paseid. "I won't go, sir. I can't, sir. I will fight for Rarke right here until every single one of those bastards drops down to hell too!"

"The Detuas have already lost their eldest son, Eivan Detua, who volunteered at the Great Battle against Morgana," said the commander. "As I understand it, it's stated in the law to protect the only heir to a family, unless it is at a desperate time of war."

"I would rather end my own life here than be kicked out. Let me fight, sir!"

Paseid swallowed a small sigh at the two obstinate siblings. He looked at the woman. "What did you say your name was?"

"Reuyen Detua from Gyujen, a town in a forest five days away from the border, sir. This boy is Sidan Detua. We are both children of the Detua family, who has been selling war horses to the royal family of Rarke. Please, sir, have mercy on my foolish brother. He ran out to war, not even knowing what war is."

Is she truly just a daughter of a mere horse dealer? Paseid still remembered the speed and murderous aim of the arrow that had passed by his head at a hair's breadth. Her concentration on the top of the cliff. The enemy commander who'd been hit and fallen down like a dead bird. Had the arrow been shot at a slightly lower angle, it would have pierced the back of his head. There was no way this woman was just a lucky shot.

But her fingers were thin, and their tips were covered with scabbed wounds. That actually proved her lack of training.

"It's possible," Paseid answered, suspicion building in his mind. "But as a volunteer, his own will cannot be overlooked. Patriotic motive does not matter on a battlefield."

Reuyen slowly raised her head and gazed into Paseid's pitch-black eyes. Then she pulled up the ends of her trembling lips.

How pathetic is my foolishness in thinking of Belbarote upon seeing him? His unaffectionate eyes and dry, stern voice were nothing like Belbarote. Feeling a burst of anger of which she did not know the origin, she broke her composed demeanor and continued, "Of course it doesn't matter, sir, since luring innocent lads into thinking they'll all become patriotic war heroes and putting them in the front by enticing them with noble titles if they slay an enemy is the cheapest way to go."

Her words started out like a reproach but ended like scorn at herself. Paseid scowled.

"Don't weigh a man's life with such recklessness," he answered with certainty.

"May I say one thing, sir?"

Paseid nodded. "I will allow it."

"I am not unaware of the meaning of the enemy selecting the Anf region as the battlefield, where there is Plain Amarze to the left and Olzore to the right. Defending the border connected directly to the capital is, indeed, important. But is using a boy who cannot even look out for himself to buy time a minimization of damage? If that is not weighing a man's life, then what is?"

"Itaka."

"What?"

"Itaka, not Plain Amarze."

A hundred years ago or so, Plain Amarze had been renamed Itaka, along with the lowlands of Sanka. Paseid pointed that out in an utterly cold tone. Reuyen slightly opened her mouth, thrown a little off guard. She did not care much about the names and geographies of places other than those around Gyujen, so this was the first time she'd heard anything about a renaming of a region.

Paseid's critically sharp eyes studied her from head to toe. He thought she probably was eager to save at least one of her brothers, since the eldest had died and the youngest was blinded by a thirst for revenge and ran out to war, leaving the family utterly devastated. Her effort and courage seemed commendable even to Paseid.

But such commendation was not a valid reason to deny a man begging to serve his country.

"I commend you for your effort in coming all the way to the front for your family, and therefore I will not punish any rude behavior, but I will not turn a blind eye to your obstinacy. I disregarded a woman unaffiliated with the army setting foot on camp by herself because I deemed it Sir Chesa's responsibility, but that is all."

He didn't bother to pronounce it, but on top of that, she had killed an enemy commander. She was probably oblivious to it, but that contribution was important enough not to be overlooked.

"Repulsion and hatred of the enemy can most certainly be patriotism with great destructive power, but a soldier blinded by hatred will kill his own comrade," said Reuyen fiercely.

"The soldiers undergo intense training to avoid that."

Reuyen's lips trembled lightly at his cold answer.

Unable to hold himself back anymore, Sidan shouted in defense, "You kept telling me not to dishonor Eivan's decision like a friggin' know-it-all, yet now you're stopping me. Why?"

At the shriek, Paseid's gaze moved to Sidan's bloodied face.

Malice. Paseid recalled the malice that clearly stood out in the middle of a battlefield, filled with innumerable shouts and cries. A malice beyond fear was this young man's. The fierce willpower of the young, pure, and unrefined rage.

Even if it were an excuse to protect her own brother, the woman's argument was undeniable. A soldier damaged enough to be unable to carry out an order put his own comrades at risk. Paseid was thinking about ordering an administrative separation for the young man; if the situation allowed it, it did not sound like a bad idea, since it was true that his eldest brother had already died. But the woman's next words stopped all his thoughts.

"I will take his place instead, sir."

"Why do you let Eivan…" her brother started, clearly angry she hadn't answered his question. "Wait, what? You're crazy!"

Paseid hesitated for a moment. "We do not accept women below certified knights in the army."

"Is there not an article in the Special Military Laws of Rarke that may be of use in my situation? I believe Article Nine will be enough to grant me the right, sir. Has there been an amendment to the military laws, sir?"

Paseid stopped moving as if in a play. This was a surprise even to him.

After glancing up at his face, Reuyen clearly enunciated her request. "If that article is still in effect, I request the effectuation of Article Nine of the Special Military Laws, based on the contribution of killing an enemy commander. I do not need a title, sir."

In the suddenly glum tent, Sidan blinked his eyes, the only one unaware of what was going on. His sister had known things he did not since they were children, but this time, he did not even have a clue as to what she was talking about.

Paseid's eyes lost their fatigued look and narrowed.

Her poise and skill in archery were quite impressive, and now that he saw her, she indeed was extraordinary. But how in the world did a commoner know an article in the Special Military Laws? Moreover, she knew exactly what her contribution was as well. She knew whom she had killed in that chaos.

"There will be a large battle in mere days," he said. "I do not have the leisure to wait until your wounds heal."

"I am more used to fighting on horseback, so I do not need such consideration, sir. I will be prepared to use whatever weapon the cavalier assigned as my opponent uses. Spears, swords, or whatever else."

Cavaliers. Not regular soldiers, but trained, agile knights. Still not understanding what was going on, Sidan blinked at her, appalled. "What—what are you talking about! Are you out of your mind, Reuyen?"

She ignored Sidan's shouts. Her serene face was enough to perplex Paseid. As someone who recognized her contribution more clearly than anyone, he did not have a reason to deny her request.

After a few moments of silence, Paseid opened his mouth. "Woman or man, we'll treat you all the same."

Reuyen's tense, dry lips drew a warped arc.

After gazing at her with ungenial eyes, Paseid nodded. Without an answer, Reuyen limped out.

When she stepped outside, Paseid coolly looked down at the white-faced young man still sitting there. Snapping back to reality, Sidan stumbled out as well.

"Reuyen!" he cried.

The tent became unbelievably peaceful once again, and Paseid reflected on what had just happened.

Reuyen Detua. Her confident attitude was quite striking. But she'd used a word that was even more striking. A word too odd to be spoken by a young woman who looked like she had just turned twenty.

If that article is still *in effect...*

Paseid raised his body and unraveled the coiled map on the table. Holding down a finger on the Anf region, where they were based, he slowly moved to a certain point in the west.

Finally, his pitch-black eyes gazed at his fingertip.

Plain Itaka.

~

In the dark of the early morning right before daybreak, armed knights stood in a loose circle in front of a tent in Camp Anf. Silence ensued, even swallowing the shadows dancing in the torchlight.

Evinbur, Jacalrin, and Denjak had received Paseid's message and run as fast as they could to the front at Camp Anf. Hearing that Teread, the chief advisor and bodyguard to the commander-in-chief, was also on his way, they assumed there was a good reason they were all called here.

Sir Tabajen Ranu, who had guided them here, broke the silence and simply summarized the situation. He was a knight from a common household, but as the one in charge of Camp Anf, he had a right to speak in the gathering.

"The ambush of about a thousand ended with a retreat as soon as Count Asvar, the enemy's commander, was shot. Damage on our side only amounted to about a hundred casualties and a couple horses. Under the orders of our commander-in-chief, Sir Calandok, we stopped all pursuit and sent scouts. They reported back that the enemy has wholly joined the defense line on Plain Ishas. Hence, last night's battle came to a complete end."

Tabajen's voice was severely hoarse from shouting at the top of his lungs all day and so was quite harsh on the ears. Still, the knights listened without complaining, since this was a matter of great importance. Their facial expressions varied—an oddly crinkled nose, eyes widened with surprise, still lips that had forgotten how to talk—but their thoughts were the same: shocked.

"This man is...?" Evinbur asked.

"The knight who commanded tonight's ambush," said Tabajen.

Their eyes all focused on the enemy lying on the ground.

The corpse's face was mashed up and covered with thick blood and unidentifiable dirty particles. A bone of the arm broken at a strange angle stuck out through the joint of the armor, and a broken arrow pierced his forehead.

"Do you think it hurt?"

"He probably died within a second."

They chatted in front of the body like they had nothing to do with it.

Though he had been laid straight on his back to show a certain degree of respect, the enemy commander was at most a pile of meat in a suit of armor.

Jacalrin squatted next to the body and made a perplexed face as he nudged the broken arrow. "Who shot an arrow in this man's head?"

"The woman you brought."

Hearing Paseid's sunken voice behind him, Jacalrin sprang up to greet him. Evinbur and Denjak also stopped looking down at the arrow impaling the center of the mashed-up head and made way upon seeing their commander.

"She appeared on the battlefield out of nowhere," said Paseid.

"For real, sir? Wha…heaven's sake, I don't understand how that crazy girl got away from my guards and came all the way here. I mean, I'm sorry, sir."

"You will be punished for neglecting your responsibilities at a later time." Paseid approached Jacalrin and looked down at the undignified corpse.

Jacalrin lowered his head, at a loss of words. This really was a mystery. How had she gotten out, and how had she found the right direction to Camp Anf in the dark of night, instead of getting lost? Frowning at the revolting reek of blood, Jacalrin was extremely irritated.

Denjak looked at Jacalrin with disapproving eyes, and asked Paseid, "Was tonight's ambush targeted at you, sir? How dare they?"

"We cannot verify that, but if so, we must be on the search for a swift-footed spy within our ranks. Sir Ranu, has the verification of his identity been completed?"

Paseid looked at the man lying on the cold soil. Tabajen stepped toward Paseid and bowed his head. The large man's armor was tainted with dried blood, but his face hinted at his robust health.

"Yes, it is as I reported, sir. His face is hard to recognize because it has been severely beaten, but I fought him one-on-one at the last battle, sir."

Evinbur had been scrunching up his nose this whole time. "Yes, it seems to me he was the one who followed Rovantis around as well. So, what are you planning on doing with the body now, sir?" he said with a groan.

"If Rovantis does not request a retrieval in three days, we should cut his head off and leave him out to feed the animals."

It was the body of an enemy commander with a title, so a request for retrieval would only be natural. But at this point, with the animosity between the two countries reaching its height, the possibility of Morgana not being willing to bow down to retrieve the body could not be overlooked.

"Hey...I mean, sir, even if he was unlucky enough to get hit by an arrow, wasn't he on top of the cliff, sir?" asked Jacalrin.

"It was not luck," said Paseid.

At his unquestionable voice, the knights surrounding the body, including Jacalrin, stiffened.

"She shot three archers in full-plate armor and the commander behind them from below the cliff without a single miss," Tabajen added in a businesslike tone. "Four knights of Camp Anf who guarded Sir Calandok, myself, and Sir Calandok are witnesses to that."

Jacalrin tensed his jaw to stop his mouth from gaping by itself. Was he supposed to believe that she shot up from below the cliff, and moreover, shot those in full-plate armor without a single miss? Not thinking much differently from Jacalrin, Evinbur and Denjak sullenly frowned.

"This ambush ended with relatively little damage due to the enemy's quick retreat following their commander's death, but I do not welcome battles such as yesterday's," said Paseid. "Sir Haldroff will divide the army as planned within three days, and we will execute the plan to circumvent Olzore-Tolf after six days. I have already finished the explanation about that to Sir Ranu."

Though it was not obvious on the surface, Paseid seemed fairly angry. The knights were seasoned to read the underlying anger in each of his words and simultaneously lowered their eyes. His ire was quite understandable, considering that he wanted to end this war quickly, unlike the other knights, who were excited at the chance to wash away the shame.

It was he, the commander-in-chief, who had to bear the heavy responsibility as the war went on.

"Also, there will be an evaluation of qualification at daybreak," Paseid continued.

"An evaluation, sir?" asked Jacalrin.

"The woman requested an evaluation on the basis of murdering the enemy commander in person to me."

The knights' heads rose, their necks as stiff as wood.

If the murder of a commander was the basis for a Special Military Law, there was only one law that fit this scenario. Article Nine. In effect, it was a law to determine the qualifications of those who had made a significant contribution in war.

It was a custom established to prevent those who were less skilled from killing their comrades in the chaos and then claiming their contributions as their own, and to discern their legal status in case those who were not qualified to receive the title of a guardian from the royal family made a contribution.

The rules were simple. The person in question entered into combat on official ground with one or more knights, and proved their skill by victory. But even if they lost, the witnesses would often grant approval, since the opponent was a knight.

However, this was traditionally executed in the format of a superior recognizing their contribution and offering the trial. Requesting this directly to the commander-in-chief was nearly sacrilegious.

Moreover, a woman from nowhere?

Denjak was outraged. "A woman, not even a soldier, but a woman asked for a title ahead of time, sir?"

"Not a title, just an ordination."

"Even so!"

Paseid completely disregarded Denjak's distress and looked at Jacalrin's still bewildered face. "Sir Chesa, you said she was the daughter of a war horse merchant?"

"Yes, sir. Not a large-scale one, but a small-town horse dealer our soldiers stop by when they are in urgent need of horses, as I'm told, sir. She claimed she came to bring back her younger brother who jumped into war after her older brother died in combat, because he is now the only son left in her family. I have already checked the registry, and on record...she's speaking the truth."

"Are you sure?"

As someone who relied on his intuition to make most of his decisions, Jacalrin was a little apprehensive about assessing the situation based on written information. But Paseid disliked uncertain answers. Jacalrin knew he could not say anything else. "Yes, sir."

Probably? He swallowed the word he almost added like an idiot and gave himself a mental pat on the back.

Paseid looked around at the knights surrounding the corpse. "So, is there a volunteer?"

As if on cue, the knights' gazes all fell to the arrow piercing the dead man's forehead.

CHAPTER ELEVEN

The morning wind carried sandy dust swooping around all of Camp Anf.

As soon as the sun rose and chased away the night, the soldiers stood in formation at one part of the camp, prepared for an atypical event. The fences surrounding the training ground were in turn surrounded by half-jealous and half-thrilled soldiers who were so excited that they'd even forgotten about yesterday's battle.

"I heard he killed the commander yesterday. Does no one know who he is? Which squad's bastard's climbing the damn ladder?"

The news of entertainment excited the soldiers. Many were distraught with the intense training and anxiety of not knowing when they'd die. This event was as welcome as rain during a draught.

Before long, the high-ranking knights of the camp all gathered at the circular training ground as well.

As his comrades' excitement grew with curiosity and interest, Sidan's face grew darker. He kept nervously glancing around at the tough, brawny men, and let out a sigh he could no longer hold. For the reason of their excitement was his sister.

He'd chased after Reuyen last night, but some knight had stopped him and ordered him to go back, so he couldn't talk to her at all. He was skeptical about the sincerity in her words. But the sun rose, and everyone gathered here.

He had had his doubts, but it seemed like his sister was indeed completely nuts. Engaging in combat with a knight. What was she thinking?

A series of brisk clip-clops resounded close by. The soldiers turned to look at the rider on the handsome brown horse who swiftly jumped over the fence, their faces slowly revealing less and less excitement.

The person coming into their sight was not a well-tanned comrade or a muscular knight-in-training, but a woman in light leather armor, with her tightly tied hair shining red under the sun.

A woman? There was a woman like that in their camp?

The soldiers looked at each other with questioning eyes.

The serene woman did not have the air of a soldier at all.

Neighhh!

The soldiers winced at the footsteps of the fierce brown horse walking to the center of the ground. Sidan looked at Reuyen with a stiff, stone-cold face.

Reuyen turned away from him and calmed her coldly rippling mind. Countless pairs of eyes were scrutinizing her and Den, not bothering to conceal their shock. But that was not much of a problem.

She slowly rode inside the fence like she was taking a stroll, then fixed her eyes on the familiar faces outside the fence.

Paseid was wearing what he'd worn yesterday and was standing with Rionac in his hand. The old knight and Jacalrin, glaring at her sullenly, were standing next to him. A knight she hadn't seen before was also standing close by him as a trusted knight would, looking at her.

The young Chesa's eyes revealed a sufficient amount of contempt, but she turned away without a word and gazed at the opposing knight who came over the fence.

"A knight ordained by the royal family of Rarke, Sir Denjak Kalsei Deusak," a voice announced.

Though he looked rather like a weasel with his thin lips and hood, his face as dark as could be, and his figure was not quite small like a typical warrior, he must have been from a noble family. But not one she was familiar with.

"Reuyen Detua," he said.

Reuyen glanced at Denjak's light metal armor and nodded at him. On the left half of the training ground, Reuyen stood; on the right was the imposing Denjak.

Jacalrin obediently looked at the two and mumbled, "For heaven's sake, what a mess this is."

Sir Seisen Verohan, whose loyalties lay with Jacalrin, squinted at the stubborn, familiar woman. He remembered the time at Plain Boald. "She's suspicious," he whispered in Jacalrin's ear.

Jacalrin hesitated. "I know," he agreed.

Upon the order of Sir Tabajen Ranu, a rider on a white horse bearing the banner of the Royal House Brionake galloped around the training ground and exited. Then, as if they were signaled, the excited audience slowly calmed down.

Paseid briskly looked around at the soldiers and knights lined up, and then at Reuyen and Denjak. "As requested by the person of merit, the evaluation will be based on single combat on horseback, and killing is not allowed."

The band waiting outside the fence grabbed their drumsticks.

Bang. Bang. Bang.

Across the empty ground, free of any obstacles or cover, the sound of drums echoed and rang in their hearts.

"Begin. All those present will be witness."

With the conclusion of the drums, a suffocating tension covered the training ground.

Denjak glared at the woman standing across from him. She wore light leather armor. She straightened her back and fixed her grip on the sword. Her relaxed, serene face and fearless eyes were enough to provoke him.

But despite what she presented on the outside, Reuyen was quite nervous. The opposing knight was menacing enough that no one could even joke that he was kind. When was the last time she'd engaged in combat with a knight?

Two hundred years ago.

The twenty-two years she'd spent as the daughter of a horse dealer were far from diligent training. Even if she'd had a not-so-weak stamina from horseback riding or running various errands since she was a child, it was nothing compared to knights who spent their lives swinging swords. The only kind of training she had done was spending time with the local young men who wanted to become volunteer guards, and with Eivan, practicing sword fighting and archery.

Reuyen was resolute to give all she had. At this point, it was irrevocable.

Like the scenes from her past, myriad eyes were looking up at her in silence. Letting go of a short ecstasy, she focused all her attention on the point of the sword in Denjak's hand. Denjak gazed at her staring at his sword, then charged without a warning.

Sidan anxiously watched as his sister stared at the knight charging across the large ground with his sword pointed at her.

"Reuyen!" Sidan shouted in fright.

His shout broke the focus of the soldiers surrounding the fences and caused a commotion.

Reuyen glanced at him for a split second, then tensed her thighs. Fuming ferociously, Den quickly realized her intentions and ran toward the edge of the fence.

Denjak's blade brushed her shoulder ever so slightly. It was an infinitely merciful move compared to his vigor, like he thought all he had to do was to knock her off the horse.

Reuyen glanced at her left pauldron, now marked, and quickly turned her horse. The old sword in her hand flashed as she swung it to smack the left side of Denjak's head. His scoff echoed across the silent ground.

Denjak angled his sword to block and push away Reuyen's with ease. But instead of pushing back, Reuyen's sword changed its track like a stream of water, passing the back of his hand and down to his hip. The blade hit the thin metal armor and made a loud, screaming clang.

Like the seasoned knight he was, Denjak kicked Den's neck without hesitating.

Neighhhh!

Startled from the great shock on his bare neck, Den reared.

"Whoaa!" Reuyen hastily pulled on the reins. While the excited Den shook his head, Denjak's fierce blade flew from above at the left side of Reuyen's head.

She saw the shadow of the blade.

Reuyen looked up at the sword swinging down with such

formidable force. She had no intention of blocking every attack. She instinctively realized that she could not block this one.

Anxious groans sounded from here and there.

Unperturbed, Reuyen lowered her sword and pulled her foot out from the stirrup. Then, she completely leaned her body to Den's right and hung closely on his side. *Bang.* Denjak's sword swung through the air and dug into the left side of Den's saddle.

Denjak scowled at the woman's nimble movement to dodge his attack. He was not the only surprised one.

The eyes of the soldiers were as wide as a walnut shell as they watched the woman balancing on the side of a horse with one foot on the stirrup and one hand holding the harness.

The same went for Sidan. Was that really his sister? This was a whole new level compared to when she was just beating up the local young men.

Den started to jump up and down from the weight focused on one side of him and the shock of the sword digging into his thick saddle. Denjak stumbled and tightened his grip on the stuck sword, trying to pull it out.

Not missing the opportunity, Reuyen used the opposite side of the harness as a handle and swung herself under Den. Without a moment's delay, she stabbed her sword up toward Denjak. The reins Denjak held instantly split in two.

When Denjak stepped aside at the sudden spring of a blade, Reuyen promptly leaped back onto Den's saddle.

Her movements were clean-cut. Without hesitation, she ran over to Denjak, who had stepped to take control over his horse after the reins got cut off, and raised her heavy sword. It plummeted down to the horse's neck, not Denjak.

Neigh!

The scream of the horse stopped.

Brown hair floated through the air. The short hairs drifting on the wind blocked the motionless knight's view. Denjak's surprised horse fumed excitedly.

Reuyen bitterly watched the elegant mane, equable to a fine horse's pride, floating down to the training ground floor. She calmly opened her mouth. "Is that not enough? If we were on a battlefield, your horse would have lost his head. The second you fell on the ground, I would have trampled you to death."

Denjak's eyes flashed with anger as he looked down at the severed reins and the floating hair.

"Damn…" Jacalrin cursed in awe, forgetting that Paseid was standing right next to him. Evinbur, the man in charge of chastising his relentless speech habits, was also flustered and kept his mouth shut.

Denjak was a high-ranking knight with great experience. Even if he was indeed off guard because the opponent was a woman, he was unable to overpower an injured person, and lost. But they couldn't blame him, either. This outcome was due to her unexpectedly exceptional movements, not his lack of skill. Everyone was surprised.

Evinbur carefully opened his mouth. "Sir Calandok, it seems clear enough without Sir Ranu having to step in."

Paseid frowned. He had no retort to Evinbur's statement. The woman was clearly extraordinary, and there was no need to continue the evaluation. Though Denjak had showed mercy in the beginning, considering that his opponent was a woman, he had an apparent desire to dominate. And yet, the result was this. This only added assurance to Paseid's doubts that she was an ordinary woman.

Paseid looked at the woman standing at a distance. Her reddish-brown hair, shining even brighter under the sunlight, naturally swayed with the wind. The light, mahogany-colored eyes flashing under it did not show any signs of joy for her victory, or contentment.

They were serene, as if this was…customary.

Teread, who was standing behind him, automatically clapped a few times as though awestruck, then lowered his hands at Paseid's glance.

"Step aside, Sir Deusak. Sir Ranu," Paseid ordered.

Glaring at the reins that were no longer useful, Denjak finally dismounted his horse and stormed out angrily. Sir Tabajen Ranu grabbed the horse's mane to mount him.

"Wait! Wait. Me, me, me! Me!" Jacalrin's shout echoed over the audience's suppressed excitement.

Reuyen gazed at Denjak stepping back and looked back at Jacalrin with half-open eyes. Jacalrin ran around the fence and stopped in front of Tabajen. "Sir Ranu, allow me."

"Sir Chesa?"

"I'll take your place. Sir Calandok, will you allow it, please, sir!" Jacalrin shouted at Paseid, exhilarated. Tabajen looked back at Paseid, obviously flustered.

"I'll allow it."

As soon as Paseid finished his sentence, Jacalrin swiftly jumped onto the riderless horse without a second thought. Then he jumped over the fence straight into the training ground. Reuyen let out a short laugh at the passion of the young, skinny knight who wasn't even wearing proper armor. The knight's lively eyes and Reuyen's smiling eyes met in the air.

Jacalrin's lips arched. He hadn't jumped in because he was in love with Reuyen's tricks on the horse. And definitely not because he wanted to avenge his fellow knight's defeat. Those eyes, those animated eyes, were what drew him in.

The dead, sunken, light brown eyes were nowhere to be found; all he could see in them now was vibrant life. It was like that from the moment she'd started fighting Denjak. Jacalrin thought her change quite curious.

He went into fighting position at a fair distance from her and yelled, "You're really out of your mind. You know that, right?"

"I do, sir." Reuyen gave a dry smile and fixed her grip on her sword.

"How long have you swung that sword?"

"A while, sir."

"And who taught you those sneaky equestrian skills?"

"My father, sir."

Reuyen glanced at Sidan, standing among the soldiers close to the fence, approximately in the middle between her and Jacalrin. He looked frightened.

A lie...

Sidan had watched his sister defeat a knight without receiving a single wound. He tightened his lips.

A lie. That was a lie.

No one in the Detua family could ride like her. Their father was a mere horse dealer who raised horses and sold them, not a trained, practicing equestrian. In fact, if any of his children had practiced such stunts, he would have scolded them not to do something dangerous.

Jacalrin inattentively nodded and swung his sword over his shoulder. "Shall we?"

"Yes, sir."

Reuyen stopped looking at Sidan and fixed her grip on her sword. Her not-yet-healed thigh muscles were trembling like leaves from having to hang on to the horse for dear life. For that reason alone, she was actually glad Jacalrin of House Chesa had come out.

There was a specific style of sword fighting passed on in each noble house. As the children grew and trained, these styles were completed in different ways, but rooted in the same basic principles. Assuming that the young Chesa's master was not completely unaffiliated with Chesa, if he had learned and trained in the old Chesa style, she wouldn't even have to think that hard to read his moves.

Without the time-consuming act of trying to psychologically dominate each other, Reuyen attacked first. She ran across the wide circle and raised her sword in the air.

As she had expected, Jacalrin lowered his head and tried to dig his sword into her chest. Considering that all she wore was thin leather armor, his move was filled with murderous intent, one that completely disregarded the rule forbidding murder.

Before the audience watching could even let out a grunt, Reuyen turned her body at an angle like she was expecting it. Jacalrin's sword couldn't change its track; Reuyen pressed her arm closely against his level blade.

"Hmm?" she said.

Jacalrin's intention to turn his sword was annulled. But that was the end of her predictions coming true.

With a short nasal sound, Jacalrin took back his sword, throwing the reins aside, and grabbed the hilt with both hands. It was a confident move that didn't even take falling off the horse into consideration.

"I'm not gonna go easy."

With the kind warning, his attack commenced.

Reuyen grimaced, unlike her usual self. It was clear that she couldn't match the force of one of his arms, but now that he was using both, blocking each attack was a risk itself. Alarmed by his storm of attacks, Reuyen arched her back and hurriedly moved backwards.

Clank! Clank! Clank!

His sword swung in from every direction, like he was not about to allow any time for her tricks. This was nothing like the Chesa style of sword fighting. This was no longer a matter of whether she could predict it or not, but whether she could block it or not. She could not help thinking that he was swinging that sword however he wanted.

She could barely contain her anger.

This crazy old bastard! How can a knight of House Chesa swing his sword like a back-alley thug!

He swung at her thigh, her side, her arm, her neck, her chest. Jacalrin was pounding at her so hard, like he had decided to win this by force. She was nearly driven out of her mind just from absorbing the impact shaking her bones. Her arm felt like it was about to shatter to pieces.

But somehow, the more she clenched her teeth and evaded his attacks, the more her movements gained speed. Of course, this was not something that would allow her to overcome her physical limits, but rather a resurrection of her senses.

After a long while, Jacalrin suddenly stopped and made a weird face. "Is it because of your injury?"

Not missing the chance to catch her breath for a second, Reuyen fixed and tightened her shaky grip on the sword.

"Seems like your body and mind are moving separately," he continued.

Reuyen froze. His precise observation had attacked her most vulnerable spot. As he said, even if her mind and instinct intuited the next move a step early, all her relatively untrained body could do was follow their instructions.

She swallowed her voice and panted. Jacalrin had so ruthlessly stormed her with attacks that she was completely out of breath from just blocking and evading. Her throat was dry and she was beginning to feel nauseous.

"Don't just block," he said. "Come at me."

She had defamed him to herself that blood was blood and that he was a cheeky little descendent, but now that she thought of it, he was worse than Hansen when it came to taunting. Reuyen glared at him.

"Or I can go harder."

Like Denjak had done, Jacalrin brought his sword down as hard as he could, aiming for the crown of Reuyen's head. She almost unconsciously reacted to the flow of air caused by the falling sword and slid over to Den's side.

With a huge grin, Jacalrin stopped his sword right before it hit the saddle. He smirked at Reuyen, who was barely hanging by Den's harness.

"Saw that coming. You've pulled that trick on a number of knights, haven't you?"

He pointed his sword at her hiding under Den's belly. Denjak had let his guard down because he hesitated when he was surprised by her nimble move, but Jacalrin had already done his being surprised.

Same old trick. What is she thinking against a Chesa?

But instead of attacking by going around and under Den's belly, Reuyen sprang back up on the saddle as soon as the tip of Jacalrin's sword pointed downward. She was clearly slower, but her movements were still clean and natural. As soon as she found her balance, she kicked Jacalrin's hand without a moment's delay. At the sudden attack, Jacalrin's sword hit his horse's barding and fell on the ground.

Startled by the clang, his horse raised his head and whinnied. Still keeping a level head, Jacalrin immediately reached down to grab the backup sword hanging on the horse's side.

Then, Reuyen threw her sword on the ground.

Is she too tired to go on?

Questioning gazes slid to her.

Then she stepped on the saddle with two feet and jumped onto Jacalrin's horse.

CHAPTER TWELVE

Jacalrin gaped at Reuyen's face nearly running into his before he could even realize what was happening.

Reuyen sat on his saddle and tightly wound the reins around his left wrist. She pulled them behind her waist.

Huh?

Within seconds, Jacalrin was practically holding her by the waist with one arm.

"Did you see this coming too, sir?" Her almost arrogant breath touched his. Lightly smiling eyes stared straight at him. Their foreheads seemed as if they would touch with the slightest tilt. Soon, Jacalrin's face lightened up too. Not because he found it amusing, but because he thought it absurd.

She was exerting this degree of agility with injuries, and without any moans or grunts.

By heavens, this woman…

"Don't your wounds hurt? How's your feet?" he asked.

"Nothing you should worry about, sir." Her nonchalant answer as she caught her breath was even more absurd. Jacalrin's horse let out a small whinny under the sudden additional weight between his neck and back, and flexed his legs.

There were awestruck cries for the woman who'd just exhibited her talent of jumping from horse to horse. Sidan, Paseid, Evinbur, and even Denjak, who had to step aside before he could really do anything, observed in silence. Tabajen, who was originally assigned as her next opponent, seemed quite impressed as well.

Receiving an almost overwhelming amount of attention, Jacalrin twisted his wrist held behind Reuyen's waist. The restraint was pretty tight.

"Is this enough, sir?" she asked quietly.

But instead of surrendering, he blurted out a question. "Are you a spy from Morgana?"

"No, sir."

"Really?"

"I swear it," Reuyen answered without delay. "I have never done anything of the sort, nor will I ever in the future, sir."

Instead of pulling out his held arm, Jacalrin tensed the arm around her waist and pulled her closer to him. "So, the only reason you're going to this extent is your brother, huh?"

Still not entirely convinced, Jacalrin leaned his head toward her and looked straight into her eyes.

The life in the woman's eyes. That was the kind of vitality only possessed by those whose hearts had turned to stone. He did not know why he read that in the eyes of a mere daughter of a horse dealer, but now he was starting to think her shooting the enemy commander was quite plausible.

"I get that your family has a tragic story, and that you have an odd set of skills to do with as you wish," he said. "But this kind of trick doesn't work on the battlefield. Not all knights wield their swords fair and square, either. Why don't you stop causing a havoc and go home like a good girl? Your brother really insists on staying, and respecting that is a way of showing love...I think?"

Reuyen swallowed a laugh down her dry throat. Her muffled laughter resounded in Jacalrin's ears.

"It's too much," he continued. "I mean, who wouldn't worry about their men if they were at the front? But Paseid isn't someone who would sacrifice anything and everything for victory."

"But there is no war without sacrifices."

"There is one with less."

"Even if it ends with a single death, if that death is my brother's, it doesn't make a difference to me now."

"But you said your older brother already died. If things go

wrong, your younger brother will die and so will you. Your parents would prefer to lose one less child than more. If you keep this up, your family will definitely face its doom."

"I'm not here relying on luck."

"Even if you do get ordained, military laws rule over all personal opinions. You don't need me to explain in plain words to understand what that..."

"I understand, sir."

Jacalrin glanced at Reuyen's unwavering stance. That kind of blind drive tickled his senses for some reason. A verified identity according to written records, and yet an uncertain one.

But according to his intuition, she didn't seem like an enemy. "You should be careful, in many ways."

It was a simple warning. He was Jacalrin Endo of House Chesa. Serious, heavy topics were not his specialty. He soon changed the expression on his face, scrunched up his lips, then grabbed Reuyen's waist tightly with his fingers.

Reuyen's eyebrows angled up furiously at the sudden invasion of his hand.

"You should lose some weight, though," Jacalrin said.

"Don't you dare lay your hands on me..."

"Come again?"

"...Sir. Oh, the admired young knight of House Chesa."

Jacalrin chuckled and shook his head. "Oh, well..." He shamelessly rested his chin on her shoulder. "I lost. I, Jacalrin Endo Chesa, owe this woman a life," he shouted lazily.

With his surrender, the evaluation came to an end. Groans resounded around the training ground once more.

Reuyen finally untied the wrist she was holding on to and dismounted. A large hand suddenly appeared in her sight. She let out a short moan at the gushing pain from her feet when they touched the ground. The hand belonged to Jacalrin, who had dismounted after her. Reuyen blinked at the suddenly offered hand, then took it.

"It'll be too late later, even if you cry because you're scared and want to run away."

Hand in hand with a knight on a battlefield. Its firmness

reminded her of the hand of an old comrade. A tender chuckle escaped with her breath.

Applause accompanied by stunned sighs resounded across the grounds, repeatedly quieting down like it would stop, then continuing again.

But Sidan was at a loss, unable to be proud of his sister or simply praise her.

"Hey, Sidan, seems like you know that woman. Who is she?" asked a soldier.

The awestruck soldiers' attention focused on Sidan.

No way.

He'd grown up under the shadows of his so-called genius sister and admired her. Reuyen was indeed admirable. But this was way beyond common expectations. Was she that great? *That's not my sister.* Chills went down his spine. Now that he thought of it, he'd never seen his sister's limit. There was no one in their small village who could match her.

Reuyen's fatigued eyes glanced at Sidan, standing among the soldiers. Unable to handle the overwhelming sensation, Sidan stumbled backwards.

On one side of the fence, Evinbur, who had witnessed everything beside Paseid, opened his prudent mouth. "I do not intend to speak like a schemer, sir, but…"

"Speak, Sir Haldroff."

"I would advise you to keep that woman close by and watch her for a little while, sir. This dying old man's intuition says there's something suspicious going on, sir."

Paseid fixed his eyes on the woman with neither denial nor acceptance. Helping the stumbling Reuyen walk, Jacalrin noticed Paseid's eyes and raised his head.

"Teread," said Paseid, "find the soldier who was responsible for supplying horses by the order of His Majesty and bring him to me."

"Yes, sir."

Teread, who could not keep his gaze off Reuyen, left with Paseid's orders. Evinbur bowed his head at Paseid. "Then I'll be off to chide the soldiers in shock, sir."

The evaluation of qualification was over. Now that the soldiers in the camp had witnessed it, it was impossible to revoke the result.

Evinbur nodded in respect and left. Paseid tightened his fists, his eyes still fixed on Reuyen.

Something was going wrong in the rules he had abided by for nearly twenty-nine years.

Right after the end of the evaluation, Jacalrin helped Reuyen to one of the tents. She looked at her feet revealing their red flesh through the burst, nay, mangled blisters, and clicked her tongue.

It was an ugly sight because the young army doctor, aghast, did not bandage the wounds so they could breathe; moreover, the mashed-up herbs applied on them still smelled horrible.

She carefully looked over her body, trembling from her muscles having worked too hard. The tops of her unpracticed feet were all skinned from straining stunts; there was not a single spot that wasn't red. Her calf muscles were trembling like birds in a storm. Reuyen knew that even small wounds should be dealt with great care on the battlefield, so she was determined to stay still until the wounds scabbed and healed.

As Jacalrin said, this body was far too pathetic.

The queen of the past had been completely fine after marching for a full day or fighting enemy knights for days and nights. Her current body was not that different in size from Swan's, and yet, it was nauseous from fighting only two knights.

At least she could say that she made it through.

She could barely remember combatting a knight in her former life, but the memories left deep inside her mind and the reflexes ingrained in her soul were still quite useful. She looked at the light armor, leather army boots, battle coat, and brassard with a red wolf embroidered on it lying at the entrance of the tent.

Paseid, the man appointed to the position of the commander-in-chief of Rarke, was a man of action. Within half a day since the conclusion of the evaluation, he'd sent some knight and ordained her a knight-in-training. It was surprising that the brassard he'd sent to symbolize the ordination was of the duke's red wolf, not the royal family's white wolf. But she was glad about this, for it did not come with any pressure.

Ordination on the basis of contribution in war required the king's approval. There was a direct road from the Gerad border to the capital, but it would take a month at the very least for them to arrive at the capital, submit it as an administrative task, receive the king's seal, and come back to the border.

So, he'd ordained her a knight-in-training of the Noble House Brionake, not the royal family of Rarke. In truth, it didn't matter which house she belonged to, for all she wanted were the rights that came with the ordination, not the ordination itself.

"You—!" came her brother's voice. Reuyen nonchalantly looked up as at Sidan stomped into the tent. "You went to our commander?!"

"Sir Chesa has approved it, so stay in the main camp's rear echelon to your heart's content," she heedlessly mumbled, ignoring Sidan's heavy breaths. Given that he came after her like this, it seemed as though Jacalrin had properly carried out her favor to him.

She had, in fact, cast away her hope to get Sidan out of the army a long time ago. Instead, she'd decided to reposition him in the rear echelon of the main camp, which was given the utmost priority during an endless war like this. In order to do that, she needed the authority to give orders, or the right to request it. So, she'd gladly participated in the evaluation. And she'd earned it.

Sidan huffed and puffed, glaring at Reuyen like he wanted to eat her alive, then fell silent upon discovering the red wolf brassard lying at the entrance.

"And you—you—what the hell was that? When did you learn all that and—!"

"Oh, come on, are you just now realizing how great your sister is? Please."

"What are you going to do now? Once you're ordained, until this war ends, you're the one who's going to have to—"

"It's not yours to worry about."

"How can I not?!"

Reuyen suddenly turned her head. "Then why did you trample all over our parents' concern for you with your pigheadedness and start this mess!" she reprimanded with a thundering voice. Sidan read the fury lying underneath it and froze instinctively.

A short silence fell between the two siblings. After a while, the frowning Reuyen let go of her anger and added, "Just take care of yourself."

"You—you—you made all that commotion to get knighted…!"

"Why don't you thank your dear sister for extending that life of yours that you don't know how to appreciate?"

"Stop talking like that!"

Reuyen clamped her mouth shut at the nauseating sensation overcoming her innards. This young brother of hers. She wondered if all younger siblings were this hard to control.

She'd had a lot of younger siblings in her former life as well, but the only one she'd had any interest in was Peijak.

But Peijak had been smart and strong. On top of that, he had been loyal enough to his sister that he obeyed anything she said, so she really did not need to take that great a care of him. The Detua brother she was fond of in this life, Eivan, had been mature and generous as an older brother should be. It had been in his nature to be kind and merciful, so they had rarely had a disagreement too. Sidan had also listened to her pretty well before Eivan's death.

So, she had not once encountered any difficulties in engaging with her siblings.

But now she came to this at last because she couldn't control a brother younger by only two years. No, at this point, the pigheadedness of the men in the Detua family must have been genetic. Eivan had run out and gotten himself killed despite everyone trying to stop him; Jess had planted his roots in his hometown even though he was advised to move away; and Sidan was acting foolishly stubborn in spite of his lack of ability to take care of himself.

Sidan glared at her for a while, but soon changed the expression on his face when the drums calling the soldiers started to ring outside the tent.

"Don't you have to go?" Reuyen asked.

"What are you going to do now?"

No clue.

Reuyen grabbed her shaking wrist tight. She had come all the way back here and stepped in the swamp herself, so, what now?

"Who knows what will happen from now on. Brionake might,

though." She was talking almost to herself. She snickered, listening to her voice ringing in her ears like someone else's.

Somewhere deep down in her heart, rage as red and viscous as liquefied metal was boiling. The justification of saving Sidan could not be the target of that rage. The one standing in front of it was herself.

Battlefield.

It was not a place for her now that she had become a mere commoner. But the phrase *it can't be helped* justified everything. Memories entangled, her sight went dark, and her heart beat with anxiety, excitement, or whatever this was.

When the sound of the drums began to reach its climax, Sidan let out a big grunt and went out.

Reuyen lazily lay down on the floor like a cat with her belly up to the sky and looked up at the low ceiling of the tent. The pain would go away soon. Once the wounds healed after a couple days of rest, she'd be fine like nothing had happened.

CHAPTER THIRTEEN

The evaluation ended as Camp Anf's morning event. The soldiers dispersed to train, their individual excitement held in their chests, and the knights returned to their duties. So did Paseid.

Before the afternoon training began, the tent's guards grew nervous at the appearance of a knight from the capital and held their breaths.

"This is a letter from House Laperovahan."

A man wearing a purple coat over a white wolf brassard, the symbol of his belonging to the palace, handed a letter to Paseid. Paseid spoke a few short formal phrases about a personal matter, not an official one, and excused the man.

Then, he worked, and worked without leaving even a short moment to take a look at the letter. Thanks to the supplies Jacalrin's reinforcements brought, there was no shortage as of now, but he thought of a plan in case one occurred in the future. Before going back to the main camp, he spent half a day discussing predicted variables during the final meeting about the mission. He then patrolled Camp Anf, ordered his men to prepare to go back to the main camp, and had a bit of leisure time at last.

By the time the red twilight sank in the navy-blue hue that swallowed the sun, Paseid returned to his personal tent in the main camp, took Rionac in its white sheath off his belt, and laid it neatly on the table. It was the sword of the founder Belbarote, one that was called the treasure of House Brionake. He gazed at it for a moment, then removed his dusty, sweaty armor.

The dry air in the tent dried his eyes out too. His eyelids heavy with fatigue, he left the tent. It was relatively quiet around his tent because Tabajen had called upon the soldiers to prepare for an ambush like the previous morning.

Through the deserted alleyway, Paseid headed straight to the camp's washroom and soon stood on his long shadow in front of a large bucket. He scooped the water and drenched his face.

He leaned over the bucket with his hands on the hard rocks securing it in place and slowly blinked a couple times. The fatigue weighing down on his forehead felt as if it had been washed away. His incessant train of thought seemed to slow down.

Tluck, tlock.

He rubbed his face a couple times at the dripping water, shook off the remaining water in his hair, then looked over at the group of tents, from which wafted the simple smells of food and campfire smoke.

A single doubt that he had cast aside crawled back out at the sounds of leather army boots and metal clanging from afar.

The royal guard Evinbur had brought from the main camp had remembered the daughter of the horse dealer living in a town near the border. Not just the appearance of the woman, but the rest of the family as well, including her brother. Crystal clear. But even after Paseid had officially verified this Reuyen Detua's identity with the royal guard, he still had a dubious hunch. Just as Evinbur had an unpleasant intuition, Paseid had a similar odd feeling in his gut.

Looking back, her complementing her lack of strength with the agility that came with her small figure was more like a habitual reflex, not an inborn talent. Her archery skills were not to be dismissed, either. The result of the battle he'd witnessed was not something he could easily accept.

She was too young to think that her movements were the result of years of training and experience that comes with age. He'd grown up hearing praise for his skills as often as his name in his early twenties, but his skills then were still incomparable to hers.

Though it was an unfair comparison to begin with, frankly; her tricks were something he, a true noble who had trained in the Brionake style and completed the standard process of becoming a knight, could hardly even imitate. That made his heart beat in a different way.

Setting aside his doubts, he'd ordained her a knight-in-training of his house because he thought there wasn't enough time to request an ordination from the royal family of Rarke. But the woman had reacted like she could not care less. That perplexed him even further. Her skills were not those of someone who would just rot away in the countryside. If she had indeed trained in horseback riding, sword fighting, and archery for a purpose, what could that purpose be? But another paradox tailed after that.

The woman did not have that much training. He could tell from the state of her hands and her body. Then what?

Fatigue rose in his thoughts.

At that moment, a soldier found him and quickly ran over to report. He was the soldier who guarded his tent.

"Sir Chesa is here, sir."

Paseid scowled as he followed him and entered the tent.

Jacalrin, who had disappeared after showing up only for a brief moment at the end of the short meeting following the evaluation, was indeed sitting in his personal tent. He was tapping his foot on the ground with half his bum on the wooden table, focused on reading something. He startled at Paseid's sudden entrance and hid whatever it was behind his bum.

Paseid realized what Jacalrin was poring over with his mouth wide open and clamped his lips. The thing in Jacalrin's hand was the letter the knight from the capital had given him in person.

"Why—why didn't you say you were here?" Jacalrin sputtered.

"You're the one who never listens to me telling you to never be off guard."

Seeing that Jacalrin didn't know what to do, Paseid didn't even feel the desire to reprimand him. So, he ignored the young man and put on the black coat he had hung on the chair.

"Did you go for a splash, sir?" After carefully studying him, Jacalrin realized that Paseid didn't look upset at all. He changed his attitude like the flip of a coin and continued, "It was right here, so I skimmed over it for a sec, and, wow. Has Elhien been talking ill of me behind my back like that, sir?"

"Did you have something to report?"

Jacalrin awkwardly scratched the back of his head at Paseid's weary question. "Oh, umm. I took care of the Detua soldier, sir."

"You don't need to report that to me."

"I thought you might be curious."

"Sit," Paseid ordered, then placed two wooden cups on the table and put tea leaves in them. Then he poured cold water.

Jacalrin frowned. "Cold water doesn't look that appealing. Should I tell them to bring some boiling water?"

"Are you planning on staying for long?"

"Oh, come on, I just came. You're already trying to kick me out?"

Despite his complaining, Jacalrin gladly drank the cold water that wasn't even steeped yet. Paseid, however, sat down and pushed the cup in front of him aside.

"Did you intend it?" he asked.

Jacalrin understood what he meant and shook his head. "No. I was fooling around a little, but I didn't particularly intend on losing. That woman… I should have known when she walked here from Plain Boald 'til her feet got destroyed."

"I talked with the soldier. It seems like there is nothing wrong in terms of her identity."

"I humbly conjecture that you're not going to find anything even if you try. Whether she's actually trying to fool us or not. Oh, but the mission should be fine as it is, right? I don't think it'll go wrong, but still." Jacalrin left his sentence unfinished. Paseid's black eyes sunk low with concern.

Soldiers could lightheartedly gossip, gawking at the woman, but things were different for knights who were aware of the situation. From her agility to her fearless attitude, she was almost like an assassin bred from birth.

She was a concerning factor, especially before the commencement of a large-scale mission that needed to be carried out in secret, in case she was in fact a disguised spy infiltrating their army. Banishing her by force wasn't a viable option, either, for Paseid did not know what she could have overheard at the camp already.

Meanwhile, the Morganaan reinforcement was advancing toward the enemy's camp. He couldn't risk losing the extraordinary opportunity to utilize their greater numbers because of an uncertain doubt.

"We'll take her," he said. "Sir Haldroff has volunteered to keep an eye on her."

"Wasn't Sir Haldroff supposed to stay at the main camp to deceive the enemy?"

"We are repositioning. I have already sent a messenger for Sir Carvein."

"You know, you could just leave it to me."

Paseid scoffed and furrowed his brows. "Jacalrin, do you consider yourself fit for such a task?"

Jacalrin had just been caught looking through Paseid's things after barging in without notice, so he shrugged instead of protesting. He agreed that Evinbur was more accurate than him when it came to judging character too. Jacalrin had a certain conviction in his intuitions, but he didn't disregard the ample experience of an old man.

Speaking of which, Evinbur's honest voice resounded from outside, knocking on their ears. "Sir Calandok, are you at leisure, sir?"

"Please come in."

Evinbur was one of the few people Paseid respected and admired. Though there was a rumor that he was at war due to a dishonorable event within House Haldroff, Paseid knew very well how much he actually cared about his soldiers, and how devoted he was to them.

Evinbur pushed the drape aside and stepped in, only to find Jacalrin slouching in his chair. He let out a low chuckle.

"You already have a visitor, I see, sir. Nice to see you, little Sir Chesa. I hope I'm not interrupting anything."

"I'm just here for a brief moment."

"Please take a seat," said Paseid. "We were just chatting."

At Paseid's nod, Evinbur planted himself next to Jacalrin. His deep, aged eyes landed on the letter with the fine seal for a moment, then left.

"Well, I am going to talk about this anyway at tomorrow night's council meeting, but I think you should know beforehand," said Evinbur. "The scouts returned just now. There is still nothing alarming in the lowlands of Itaka, but there seems to be some movement in Olzore."

Jacalrin, who had been resting his sullen face on his hand, let out a small, breathy laugh. Paseid eyed Jacalrin reproachfully and replied, "Movement?"

"I'm sure there's someone with a brain over there too, so they probably have guessed that we will move before the Morganaan reinforcements arrive."

"But the northern gate of Olzore very rarely opens anyway, no?" Jacalrin interrupted.

"There's nothing particularly worrying about their offense, since Olzore is a fort specifically designed for defense, but I've told Sir Deusak to reinforce our guards just in case. It seems like we can move on the route through the valley as we had planned... Except, if they are eyeing Rarkian land, we would have to march only at night once we are near the fort, so it may take a bit longer than we predicted."

"I have considered Olzore realizing our plan as one of the variables, so no need to worry," said Paseid.

Evinbur gave a satisfied smile at the instant, unhesitant answer, almost like that of a proud father looking at his commendable son.

"Then again, even if we divide the army in three, there will be more than twenty thousand men waiting at the main camp. There's nothing to be afraid of, even if those bums who live coiled in their nest take out their swords and spears."

Olzore, the secretive fort on top of the valley, had a long history as the symbol of Morgana's defense line.

The narrow hills and steep valley, which were optimal for defense, made it difficult for a large army to approach, but it also limited the size of the army Morgana could dispatch. But Olzore was also the historical counterevidence of the best defense being a good offense. The best offense Olzore could conduct was inviolable defense, and enemies crumbled before their impregnable fort.

Even the last queen of Rarkalia, the notorious fanatic of war, had met her downfall before Olzore.

Jacalrin rested his chin on his hand and complained irritably,

"I've never seen Fort Olzore, but when I do this time, I'll at the very least spit on it."

"They wouldn't care in the least bit."

"Just thinking about the absurd remark Belrevirehein II dared to make to His Majesty makes my blood boil. How dare those pompous scumbags make such base provocations?"

Displeased at this violent reminder, Evinbur clamped his mouth shut as well.

The story of the letter Belrevirehein II, the emperor of Morgana, had sent to Rarke was well known.

Rarke had been forced to engage in a kind of tributary trade with Morgana ever since the first establishment of the Brionake Dynasty, due to the unfair treaty signed at that time. Then, two years ago, Morgana had unjustly ordered Rarke to double the amount of tribute. Though it was a tributary trade, Rarke was technically not a subject of Morgana's.

King Terendoke of Rarke had sent an enraged refusal, and the emperor of Morgana had declared that he would go to war against Rarke, to show that the empire would not allow resistance from the north. Then he sent a letter insinuating that if they wished to set foot on Morganaan land, they should bow down to Olzore.

Olzore.

That was a weak spot for a Rarkian that nobody should prick. The impact of the letter was quite something, to the extent that even the conservative nobles of Rarke, who weren't so keen on the idea of as war until then, had started an uproar.

Two hundred years ago, Rarke had signed an unfair treaty with Morgana because of the defeat at Fort Olzore. With the submission of Rarke, a rising country equipped with great military power capable of devouring its neighboring countries, Morgana had gained the omnipotent throne of an emperor. In addition to that, the finest knight of Rarke, Peijak Dollehan, who was once loyal to Rarke, had kneeled before the steely gate of Fort Olzore, drunk with Rarkian blood, and betrayed his home country.

Morgana had dug up that shameful history related to Olzore and crushed the pride of Rarke.

Evinbur concluded his ire and changed the subject to break the dishonorable silence. "On a different note, would she be okay with her injuries? Would it not be better to leave her here?"

"It's better to keep her where we can watch her closely," said Paseid.

"So, you have your doubts about her too, Commander?"

"I'm not just sitting back."

"I was visiting her just now, and according to the doctor, it will take a considerable amount of time for the wounds to heal."

Remembering the evaluation, Evinbur could not help but feel stupefied. He could not understand how Reuyen could perform like that, even if the horse was acting as her legs.

"Oh, by the way, where is she right now?" Jacalrin asked out of the blue.

"In her tent. Where else?"

"Which way?"

"Do you want to visit her? Fourth from the east. But there'll be no use if you go now."

Jacalrin blinked.

Evinbur shrugged and explained, "She's out cold. Boy, does she sleep soundly in the middle of this cacophony. I went there to have a little chat and ended up watching her sleep for a long time instead."

"Can't you just wake her up?"

"She's still a lady."

"What lady? What kind of a woman volunteers to be on a battle-field?" He guessed she could if she were extremely fatigued, but where was her sense of danger, sleeping like a sloth in the middle of a camp at the front, where anything could happen at any moment? Jacalrin chuckled at her unchanging preposterousness and sprang up. "Excuse me, sirs."

As Jacalrin rushed out, Evinbur followed him with his eyes and murmured, "It must be hard for old Sir Chesa, with his son still acting like that at his age," and turned to the obviously exhausted Paseid. "By the by, it's quite a concern for us subordinates that our commander-in-chief isn't able to rest properly these days."

"I'm fine."

"I have told the men to light some incense to ease your mind and body."

"I ordered them away. It's not that big a problem for you to be so concerned, Sir Haldroff. I only have bad dreams from time to time."

Evinbur's eyes deepened with affection. Paseid was an extremely trustworthy man, who stayed on the battlefield for a long time, but he was not someone who enjoyed war. He had once asked Paseid, *Why do you not leave the battlefield so?*

To which Paseid answered, *A battlefield is where there is a clear black and white, and I can execute my mission.*

"Well, it's a relief to hear that you are all right, but..." Evinbur scratched his chin, stumbled upon the letter lying on one side of the table, and opened his mouth nonchalantly. "I saw that a rider came from the capital's palace."

"Not for official business."

"It seemed like it. Even if it is just Miss Laperovahan biding her time for Duke Brionake's victorious return, it would be good to end this war soon. Those Morganaan scoundrels are despicable, but the living must live."

Paseid faintly smiled and nodded. "We should indeed, for dear Sir Haldroff's health."

"Wo-hoa, thank you for your consideration, sir, but this old man is still as healthy as a horse," Evinbur smoothly replied. Then he lazily got to his feet. "We should be ready for departure in at least six days, once we finish the last preparations after returning. Please excuse me, then."

"Goodnight, sir."

Evinbur left with the same spirited steps he'd entered with.

Sitting in the silence following Evinbur's exit, Paseid's eyes slid onto the letter with the fine seal. He took it gently and opened it.

My Lord Duke Paseid Calandok Brionake,

How do you do?

Thanks to your industrious work in the place of danger, the people of the capital and I are more peaceful than we could ever hope to be, Your Grace. Thus, I am currently sitting by Lake Ryuga, looking at the boats. I am not sure if I can say this to you, Your Grace, but I am untroubled and have faith that you are protecting the wind, the waves, and the laughs of those enjoying the sun.

I have gratefully put the bouquet of blue flowers from your mansion in a vase. My heart beats with gratitude at their ineffable beauty, and so, I have picked up my pen. I fear you may consider me a woman without patience or virtue for writing to you so first, or that I may be taking your invaluable time in your busy days, but please forgive this silly girl wishing for a word from you.

I was planning on asking little Sir Chesa to deliver this letter upon hearing the news that he was going to war as well, but on second thought, I worried that he might steal a look at my bashful honesty, considering his character, so...I found a knight from the capital's palace heading south and asked a favor.

Also, I have earnestly reminded little Sir Chesa not to trouble you during this war, but I wonder if he is doing so. Old Sir Chesa has asked me to relay to you to please scold little Sir Chesa if he does not listen to you. He has also asked me to bid you to please be strict with him, as Jacalrin must learn to behave a little.

Your Grace, you will return to the capital once this war is over. I am wholeheartedly wishing for your safe return.

Sincerely,
Elhien Devi Laperovahan.

Ingraining the name *Laperovahan* in his eyes, he quietly put down the letter.

The letter that must have ridden all the way from the capital still held the muted fragrance of hydrangea.

CHAPTER FOURTEEN

Jacalrin kept what Evinbur said in mind and walked to the fourth tent from the east with a spring in his step. Evinbur had told him so, but of course.

"Hey." Jacalrin crossed his arms and looked down at the blanket on the bed with a giant bulge in the middle.

"Yo, tomboy," he called louder, but there was still no response. He slowly walked over, looking like a turtle with a sullen face, and snuck a look at the woman's face.

Her face showed through the messy red hair half-covered by the blanket. She was as pale and delicate as a branch of a poplar tree. She was quite an ordinary woman, save for her somewhat intense expression.

Those who had trained a great deal often had rough skin or skin that retained an evidence of exposure to sunlight, but this woman, while she did look healthy, was so pale that she looked like she had nothing to do with weapons or horseback riding. He could understand why Denjak had underestimated her, ultimately leading to quite a shameful result.

Jacalrin studied her for a while, then rubbed his chin, giving a nasal *hmm*. His light-green eyes wandered the tent and landed on the crumbly food she clearly hadn't even touched, and the vegetable soup that was now cold.

"Yo, wake up!"

Jacalrin gave up on waiting until Reuyen woke up on her own and carelessly kicked the leg of the bed with the tip of his hard leather army boot. Seeing that there still was no response, he reached his hand out to just drag the blanket off her. When his inconsiderate hands uncovered her halfway, the woman's pale eyelids opened without a warning. Her brown eyes speckled with red were still half asleep and unfocused when they met Jacalrin's mischievous green eyes.

"Finally…" Just as Jacalrin was about to say something, Reuyen's hand shot up and grabbed his arm. It happened in a flash, before he could even dodge it.

Jacalrin's eyes grew as cold as ice.

Reuyen's slumberous voice slowly let out a sound. "Han…"

Standing awkwardly, Jacalrin snapped out of her hand. She let go of him easier than he'd expected. "What?"

"Oh…"

Reuyen was gazing at Jacalrin with a half-moon face. Looking into her dry eyes, Jacalrin suddenly realized that her focus was somehow off.

Her murky eyes moved from his face to his neck, then to his hands. But her eyes didn't look sleepy; though they were focused on him and were looking at him, they seemed distant, like they were seeing something else.

But, not long after, the wandering eyes started to recover their twinkle again, and soon enough, Reuyen sprang up into an upright position and hurriedly patted her body and hair.

Does she think I did something to her?

He wasn't particularly acting gentleman-like, but he didn't recall doing anything to be treated like a ne'er-do-well, so Jacalrin glared at Reuyen, frowning. "I was just trying to wake you."

Reuyen stopped and tilted her head to look at her legs hidden under the blanket, then sighed like she was breathing out a misty fog. She didn't seem quite right. Once he took the time to scrutinize her, she looked exactly like someone who was still confused from a nightmare, with her face all sweaty, her eyes nervously glancing around.

"Excuse me, sir." She came back to reality and apologized with a still gravelly voice. Jacalrin accepted her apology, for he thought he hadn't done anything particularly commendable as a gentleman when he touched a sleeping patient without her consent.

"I guess you had a bad enough dream to make you look like you just saw a ghost. I was amazed how well you slept in the middle of a battlefield, but I see that's not exactly the case."

At Jacalrin's comment, Reuyen noticed the thick darkness outside her tent for the first time. Her lips scrunched up a little. She must have been asleep for a fairly long time.

"I'm all right, sir. I recall the doctor saying that the prescribed herbs and medicine have a tranquilizing effect, sir. I think it's because of that, sir."

"Why are you trying so hard to seem fine? Just let it be. You're not the only one having nightmares here, you know."

"It wasn't a nightmare, but a—" Reuyen suddenly stopped when she realized that Jacalrin's clear, light-green eyes were looking down at her with pity. She unconsciously brushed her face at the cold air caressing her cheeks and moaned at the feeling of her hair wet with sweat.

She remembered something she had forgotten the moment she was stunned by waking up only to look into those eyes.

When was it? It was when she first encountered the grotesque truth about a battlefield, at the age of twenty-six. A memory as Swan, not Reuyen.

～

Within two months, the queen who had left with thirty thousand men accomplished the deed of eradicating from history a small kingdom adjacent to Rarke's western border.

Revolting fetor drifted from the mountain of bodies revealed through the broken walls across the field ablaze in red. When one tried to draw water from a well in the kingdom's capital city, the bucket filled with water contaminated with blood.

She looked over the enemy soldiers committing suicide before her eyes and the foolish people betraying their own country to beg for their lives. The cries and screams of those running to her feet were as meaningless to her as the passing wind. "Long live King Dorek!" With the last breath of the enemy knight, dying as he praised his king, the kingdom fell.

The first majestic trumpet of victory resounded. But to her, it was a signal of being forced to face an unfamiliar confusion and a kind of fear she hadn't imagined before.

The first time she ordered her army to butcher the innocent, she realized from now on, all the roads she set foot on would be drenched in red.

Passing through mounds of bodies of people she did not recognize, their frightened eyes staring into space, she voiced her fear for the first and last time.

"Hansen, they were people the patriots of this country strived to protect, weren't they?"

Hansen, following her on his horse, vaguely answered, "Probably."

Hansen found Peijak coming back with a group of soldiers, the king's head in his hand. He lowered his voice to a whisper. "Do you pity them, Your Highness?"

"I cannot lie that I rejoice at this sight."

The man was annoyingly relaxed, standing dignified and alone in the midst of hell, as the cries of battle and the smell of blood whirled.

"Then why not turn back, Your Highness? A conquest is...not an easy thing."

The queen was neither enraged nor did she scold the knight for daring to give her uninvited advice.

"I will not eat my words."

This was the path of patriotism she had chosen. The great united under swords and spears.

She slowly closed her eyes, blue as the faraway sky covered by black smoke, and opened them again. The shard of emotion revealed a moment ago disappeared with the blinking of her eyelids.

Hansen gazed at the back of the queen as she let her red hair sway with the wind in the red light that swallowed life, or that spilled life. He turned his head to take in the sight of hell.

"Yes, Your Highness. Do as you wish. The result at the end of this war will tell right or wrong. Once you reach the end of your ambition, all your questions and confusions will be resolved."

"Dear sister." Before she could notice, Peijak came near her and dismounted his horse, holding the head of an old man that was still dripping blood. He sheathed his blood-covered sword and offered the poor king's head up to his queen. "The lives of the people of Rarke you saved."

The queen looked down at the face of the cowardly king who'd left his

body in this world and run away to the other. "Yes, it is so. My people will
live in peace, for this man is now dead." Her lips smiled without her
command.

Why was it? When the queen looked back at Hansen, his deep green
eyes were full of pity, gazing at the undignified head of the enemy king.
When Peijak finally threw the king's head down on the ground, Hansen
looked over at Swan. And smiled a smile as blue as a smile can be.

"Congratulations on your first victory, Your Highness."

Reuyen's dream of her past had ended with her sensing another
person at the far side of her consciousness. Funnily enough, the
first thing she saw as she opened her eyes were Jacalrin's evergreen
eyes, as young as fragile cotyledons.

Now, in the tent filled with the familiar smell of a battlefield,
she was confused if she was Swan or Reuyen. She even struggled to
discern if the eyes that were looking at her were Hansen's or not.
She finally stationed her mind in the present when she noticed her
injured legs.

She was perplexed.

Living as Reuyen, she had never before been influenced by a
dream this clear. She even felt a slight fury at her feeble self who
couldn't distinguish between her past life and her present life.
However, it seemed as though Jacalrin interpreted her perplexity in
a different way.

"What's going on now?"

"It wasn't a nightmare, but a—"

Suddenly, a wooden tray was shoved into her face.

"Yeah, yeah, okay. Eat this first. It was probably disgusting to
begin with, but now that it's gotten cold, it must be even more
disgusting. Do you even know how pale your face is right now?"

Jacalrin was holding up a bowl of cold vegetable soup that had a
layer of oil on the surface, like it had been sitting outside for a long
time, and a loaf of black bread that looked crumbly on the tray.
Reuyen sighed as she took the tray and looked up at Jacalrin. He
was pretty cute when he acted like he was free of the characteristics
of nobles. Probably because he was still young.

"I thank you for your kind gesture, but right now is a little…"

"Oh, please. You think I'm worried about your health?"

At Jacalrin's sneer, Reuyen put the tray down on her lap. Then she silently picked up the bowl and started drinking the murky soup.

"I'm worried you'll drag us down, since you're moving with me."

Reuyen halted in the middle of gulping down the soup.

She put the half-empty bowl down and wiped her mouth. She was preparing herself to train with other knights-in-training and to live according to their schedule once her legs were all healed. But moving already?

"I have been warned by the doctor to rest because my wounds have not healed yet, sir."

"We really can't not fight because of your situation, you see."

"Is the main army moving, sir?"

"No, we're dividing, so just a part of it."

"Dividing…"

"Mhm."

Reuyen's eyes cooled down.

Sidan was to remain in the rear echelon at the main camp. What was happening to him, then? Jacalrin threw a straightforward answer at her voiceless question.

"You won't be able to move with your brother, but that was your condition to begin with, so don't complain."

Reuyen drooped the ends of her lips. She had been given the rights, so she had to fulfill her duties. She especially had to watch herself, since she was under special attention.

Many had come to take a look at her this afternoon too. The doctor had a different assistant following him around every visit, and even the guards glanced at her and tried to strike up a conversation. Someone sneakily approached her and showered her with praise. Of course, there were those who showed great dismay at her entrance itself. These were all results of the duke's brassard now in her possession.

She turned her head and looked at the red wolf brassard neatly folded in the corner of the tent. A sighing laugh escaped her lips. The woman who'd ruled over the wolves now crawled under a wolf and kneeled. How cruel life was.

"When do we leave then, sir?"

"No questions. I came to ask a couple questions of you today, not to answer yours."

Last time, Jacalrin had answered all her questions as she asked them, with additional explanations, like he was bewitched, so he cut her off defensively. But Reuyen simply rubbed her temples, a pensive look on her face.

"Would it not be dangerous to head to Itaka, since there aren't many places to take cover, sir? I don't know for sure about the area right now, but..."

Jacalrin shrugged. "Well, all you have to do is follow as you're told."

But Reuyen was already contemplating the geography of the area and the time of year. Rarkian reinforcements were joining their main force not even two months away from the rainy season. The main camp had remained quiet even without an encounter, except for the Anf region. The enemy's reinforcements were said to not have arrived yet. If they were dividing the army into more than two at this point...

"A feint attack... Are you planning a large battle, sir?"

"Boy, do you have a lot to say."

Jacalrin didn't confirm anything, but Reuyen read a definite confirmation in that. A large battle would be possible in Amarze, the region that Paseid said had been renamed Itaka. But that area was a dry, open lowland. If the Rarkian force was headed there, it would be equivalent to blatantly revealing their plan.

Unable to shake off her vague anxiety, Reuyen said, "If we divide the army to head toward the lowlands, the enemies will deem this an opportunity as well, sir."

"Obviously, Miss Know-it-all," Jacalrin replied irritably at last, like he couldn't keep his mouth shut anymore.

An unidentifiable chill ran down her spine. Her body stiffened as though struck by lightning when a sudden question emerged in her head. When she winced, the tray sitting on her lap tilted and spilled everything on the floor with a clatter. But it didn't matter.

Then where were they headed?

Reuyen barely managed to open her mouth. Her voice was fading away, as though she was speaking to herself. "Ulzore?"

Jacalrin affirmed the question by not denying it. Reuyen's eyes went as cold as ice.

Olzore.

The home of the devilish fort that had destroyed the queen two hundred years ago.

CHAPTER FIFTEEN

The next day, the knights at the main camp and a fraction of the soldiers followed Paseid, the early morning light following them from behind.

The small woman, the only one wearing a red wolf banner among the knights, definitely stood out. Countless men looked at the brassard on her left arm with admiration or question, but none of them were audacious enough to strike up a personal conversation where the high-ranking knights could see. Thanks to that, Reuyen's mind was burning into ashes with frustration.

She had not seen even the shadow of Sidan, now repositioned in the rear echelon after leaving the front, since the violent goodbye the siblings had shared. That was bad enough, but Jacalrin's silence from last night had unintentionally set a painful fire in Reuyen.

She attempted to ask about the details of the plan on multiple occasions, to get some kind of a sure answer, but that was nearly impossible in her situation.

On top of all that, when she returned to the main camp, she was forbidden from leaving her tent due to the order to prioritize treating her wounds above all else. The greeting ceremony with the senior knights she rightfully should have had, as a newly ordained knight, was cancelled, and she was trapped in her small tent, unable to even attend the training session with her fellow knights-in-training. After a couple days, she felt like she was going insane.

At the very least, the blisters and wounds on her feet were getting better day by day. It was a natural and rewarding result for enduring the horrible smell of the herbs. She became very content as walking became less and less of a problem. She tried tentatively suggesting that she could start going around camp now, but everyone was too busy to listen to her. Of course, she did not complain about that. Other than her, all the soldiers and knights were busy as bees because of the upcoming mission.

Fires were built here and there, carts came and went, and the war horses and their barding were prepared. On top of checking the armor and weapons assigned to each, there were training sessions whenever there was time.

Just in time, Jacalrin came into view, busy with moving the carts carrying bamboo boxes.

"Hey, watch it! That's gunpowder. Hey!"

The cry of the soldier startled by the young knight's reproach even reached Reuyen where she sat at a distance.

Watching the familiar scene, Reuyen felt a sudden surge of fatigue and boredom and went back into her tent. It was time to prepare to march to Olzore. Her steps naturally slowed down at that thought pestering her again.

So, the furtive preparation for the mission at the main camp proceeded step by step. The surveillance became stricter with the intensified search for spies, and the knights were busy as beavers.

As Reuyen had observed, Jacalrin was busy carefully packing the gunpowder on the carts so they could signal each other from the other side of the cliffs. He compared every supply item with the lists. Teread and Evinbur, Paseid's most trusted knights, spent the night seriously discussing the feint attack with Tabajen, who would remain at the main camp. On the fourth day, Sir Olbevin Carvein returned from scouting the situation in the lands of Galabua, which included the Gerad border. Paseid delegated him to be the commander of the main camp.

These were days busy enough to completely subdue the heat from the unconventional evaluation that took place at Camp Anf.

Five days later, the council meeting at the headquarters that happened every day finally finished with the discussion of preparations for variables and the repositioning of certain people.

.   .   .

Order of division of the army: Feint attack with circumvention through Olzore-Tolf

Nine thousand men for ambush will carry twenty carriages of gunpowder to signal the arrival at the enemy's rear side, following the circumvention through the Olzore-Tolf region. Two thousand men will remain at the main camp to cause a diversion.

I hereby delegate the authority to report from the main camp and front to Tabajen and Olbevin. When the encircling troops fire a flare after circumventing Olzore-Tolf, all will secure the road between the cliffs and commence the feint attack.

Eighth day of the sixth month in the year 899, in the Dothval Jant Calendar 899.

Commander-in-Chief of the Rarkian defense force, Duke Paseid Calandok Brionake.

After the order of the mission written on fine parchment and two reports to the royal family were sealed with Brionake's wolf seal, all the preparations came to an end.

For various reasons, Reuyen passed her time looking at the familiar campsite and the training ground beyond the fences outside her tent. Whether they were neglecting her because they thought her worthless or because she was a woman, not many people cared about her. There were a couple who looked at her strangely, having heard the rumors of what happened at Camp Anf, but even they often pretended not to see her and hastily walked away.

The sun hung in the middle of the sky, shining on Reuyen's long eyelashes and casting shallow shadows below them. She wasn't unable to understand why the others were nearly abandoning her, but sitting alone amongst all those active people, she started getting wearisome with thoughts from her past infiltrating her mind.

"You were out here, I see," said a stately voice.

It was a man's she'd heard once or twice before. She slowly turned her head to look at the strong-looking old knight.

Evinbur Paldago Haldroff. He was Paseid's most trusted knight, now watching her strangely as they prepared to leave Camp Anf. She couldn't even estimate how mighty of a house he belonged to, for she could barely recall House Haldroff from her memories. But perhaps because of his strong eyes that seemed to gaze through the years, she was oddly uncomfortable when he looked at her.

She rose from her seat on the small chair for guards and greeted him like a knight. Evinbur rubbed his ill-groomed mustache and beard.

"I assumed you would not have learned the code of chivalry and salute of sword yet, but have you?" he asked gently.

"Barely, sir," Reuyen answered vaguely. Evinbur crossed his arms like he didn't care much for Reuyen's answer and looked at the training ground on the other side of the camp.

"Yes, now that you have the brassard, I should address you as Dame Detua. Have you been notified that you are to protect me during the mission commencing tonight?"

Reuyen made a face that clearly conveyed that she hadn't heard of such a thing. Then Evinbur gave a low chuckle. "Of course, you have not. I am here to notify you right now." It was a mischief unexpected from a mature man.

A bitter smile appeared on her lips as she listened to him. A sudden mission to protect a knight. They were taking such an obvious attitude, not even trying to hide their doubts about her, that she didn't even feel like she was being wronged.

In the friendly mutual reciprocation of distrust, Evinbur clicked his tongue with pity. "How are your wounds?"

"Thanks for your concern. They have healed quite a bit, sir."

"That's good to hear. Dame Detua, you were truly astonishing in the last evaluation. The body of the commander you killed in the last battle was traded for twelve prisoners. The other knights are very interested in you as well. I apologize for treating you this way, with the situation being what it is."

"It's all right, sir."

"I can guess about your equestrian skills, but how did you learn archery, sword fighting, and such?"

Feeling uneasy, like she'd just swallowed a bug, Reuyen lowered her head. Back in her town, she could get away with everything by simply saying she didn't know, but a commanding knight of Rarke was asking now, not the resident of a small country town.

"I just played rough with the local young men using swords and bows, sir," she said with a shrug.

"Huh, seems like you are not that good at lying. Don't you try to fool this old man's eyes."

"I had a great master…"

"Tell me his name. If he is a man of that great a talent, I must know of him."

Reuyen bit her lip for a moment at his eagerness. "I stand corrected, sir. In truth…if you are asking how I learned those things, you would not believe me even if I told you the truth."

"Tell me. It becomes easy to consider most things not too unusual at my age."

"I have more talent than many others, sir."

"But you still would have had to practice."

"Though I have not learned much or practiced much, it seems like what I was born with overcomes that, sir."

"Oh, how easy you speak of things that would make several knights cry. That much skill without learning or training, huh."

The old knight's benign, easy-on-the-ears laughter resounded. But the distrust underlying it was so clear that Reuyen laughed awkwardly too. Overcome with concern that he would ask something harder to answer, Reuyen changed the subject. "On a different note, I thought Sir Chesa would be in charge of keeping watch on me, sir."

"Quite direct you are. Little Sir Chesa has no talent in looking after someone. It would be a miracle if he doesn't have a heart attack and faint. Of course, I mean the one being looked after, not Sir Chesa."

"Is that so, sir?"

"I heard you had some trouble on the way here because of Sir Chesa as well, Dame Detua."

"Yes, I did have some trouble, sir." Reuyen didn't even realize the discontent seeping into her words as she spoke.

When she recalled the frustration, fatigue, and the following fury when she'd been abandoned in the middle of a field with even Den confiscated, she became overcome with a desire to grab and twist the neck of that young Chesa right this instant. But instead of slandering Jacalrin along with Evinbur, she asked something she had been wondering about for a while. "You said that the mission will commence tonight, so I wonder if I could hear about the plan a little, sir. It seems like the reason we are headed to Olzore is...not to take the fort. Is that true, sir?"

Evinbur pulled the ends of his tightly shut lips under the white mustache. "Why do you not think so?"

"If the purpose was to take Olzore, I believe an army of less than ten thousand would not suffice at all, sir."

"We cannot take Fort Olzore because we have less than ten thousand men?"

"Thirty thousand soldiers of Dalgdaton could not pass it, and neither could Tetan during Orope's rein with fifty thousand soldiers. To be honest, I do believe that a war is inherently a match of numbers, but there are exceptions. Olzore is one of them. The headcount of soldiers is a number irrelevant before Fort Olzore, so I would think the same even if we had a hundred thousand."

Evinbur had been studying Reuyen's face with his rather sharp eyes that clearly bore the marks of time. "Indeed. This is not something I enjoy talking about, but not only did Dalgdaton and Tetan fall before it, but also the last queen of Rarkalia, who once swept the battlefields, so one could most definitely say that the fort is impregnable. But it is something Sir Calandok knows as well as you, Dame. Taking Fort Olzore is not a part of our strategy in these urgent times, so do not worry, if you were."

Rarkalia.

Looking down at the floor, her face pale, Reuyen pressed on her trembling eyelids. It had been a while since she had heard those syllables. Her stomach churned. She quietly chewed over his words.

Yes, not Olzore. Her throat tingled, as though a piece of bone had slowly made its way up and was pressing down on her uvula.

The devil's fort that no one could dare to covet still stood strong.

Suddenly, the snicker of Guitella, the king of Olzore, who'd ridiculed the queen, echoed in her ear. He had declared to the queen, with derision: *Rarke will never pass Olzore.*

He had kept that damned promise even after his death. That was somewhat impressive. She broke into laughter. Then she suddenly froze.

Lowering your guard.

She sank into self-disgust.

The old knight, full of energy, very much unlike his age, crossed his arms like the upright man he was and snuck a look at Reuyen's face, which was growing pale. He couldn't read what was going on underneath that odd reaction. After gazing at her for a while, he turned his head to watch the soldiers running around the camp. His stoic, dark-brown eyes overflowed with deep affection.

At last, this good-natured old knight clicked his tongue, murmuring, "Oh, dear," upon seeing a young soldier stumbling on a rock and falling. It was like his own kin had fallen.

"By the way, how old are you?" Evinbur asked Reuyen.

"I just reached twenty-two, sir."

"Twenty-two. Best time in one's life, and yet this young lady is spending her days here for a reason only the heavens know."

At a loss of what to say, Reuyen faintly smiled. Evinbur gazed at Reuyen's light mahogany-colored eyes, now dull like they had lost their light, then smiled good-heartedly when their eyes met. He walked away with his hands clasped behind his back.

Using the stars as a compass, the covert movement began. An unprecedented tension overlaid the soldiers as even their lungs filled with resolution.

"Come out," ordered Sir Seisen Verohan, barging into Reuyen's tent without an explanation.

Already dressed in the light armor and brassard she'd received, as though she had been waiting for this, Reuyen quietly followed Seisen outside. Then she mounted Den, who had been tied to the fence, and walked past the silent tents. All around her the camp was quiet and still in the deep night.

"Do you not need to see your brother?"

The distrustful question shook the night air. Reuyen was not unaware of why he was trying to disguise himself in kindness.

"I'm fine, sir," Reuyen calmly answered.

Even if she wasn't fine, nothing good would come out of seeing the fuming Sidan in the near future. She was fairly anxious about not being able to stay back to watch over him, but she was content with him no longer being at the front. She neither had the right nor the intent to complain anymore.

A booming shout pierced the camp. "To formation!"

Reuyen arrived at the point of departure and swallowed a moan as her heart pounded at the sight of the myriad soldiers lined up.

She could feel the bare heat of the night's tension against her skin. There were more soldiers in their formation than she could count. Estimating through the dark, it seemed like a little short of ten thousand. In front of them stood Evinbur, Jacalrin, Paseid, and hundreds of other fierce knights she did not know the names of.

Seeing Seisen take his place in the rear, Reuyen steered Den to the group of knights-in-training, then joined the group of knights in the front at Evinbur's call.

"Forward!"

By the time the moon came from behind the clouds and started to reveal its yellow right cheek, the flag held reverently in both the bannerman's hands stirred the air, slicing through the wind. Thousands of feet aligned in rows and columns hit the ground.

Reuyen slowly spurred Den's steps, matching their speed. In the faraway front of the long parade, a man on a graceful black horse exuded a quiet but pronounced presence and overwhelmed those following him.

A man in pitch black, just like someone in her deep memories.

Brionake's black color blended into the darkness like a shadow on ebony. The only colors visible on the man's reliable back were the red wolf mantle worn over his uniform and…a sword so white it seemed it still kept the day's sunlight the night had held back.

The soldiers lined up long like a snake noiselessly walked, following the white shade.

Booooooo—

Hearing the short but intense cry of the ivory horn encouraging the march, Reuyen moved her unwilling feet into step with the others.

CHAPTER SIXTEEN

The march continued for days.

The first five days of the mission to circumvent Olzore-Tolf were assigned to crossing the flat forests and fields on the edge of Galabua at a facile speed. But when they reached uneven ground on the fourth day, the speed of the nearly ten thousand soldiers started to slowly decrease.

Nevertheless, Reuyen patiently followed Evinbur without a single complaint. The warmhearted Evinbur, much like an old neighbor of a great stature, thought highly of her doing so. Even so, that was not her intention.

But there was a time for everything. Except for the times when he had an occasional meeting with Paseid, meal times, and when she went to the toilet, Evinbur did not allow Reuyen to leave his sight. Though it was quite an inconvenience, Reuyen accepted her lack of freedom without another word.

After two more days, a steep and rocky mountain range revealed itself in the far, far distance. Jacalrin yawned. He was bored after tirelessly running back and forth along the cavalcade and assisting Paseid's command. He stretched uncomfortably in his armor, found Reuyen standing next to Evinbur, and sneakily steered his horse to walk alongside them.

"You're doing pretty well."

Reuyen remembered Evinbur's presence right next to her and

tried to answer as politely as possible. "How hard could being on a horse be for the daughter of a horse dealer, sir?"

"You should be on your guard now. Sir Haldroff, has this girl said anything weird yet?"

"Address her as Dame Detua, Sir Chesa."

"Please, she doesn't even know the code of chivalry. Simply putting on a brassard doesn't make someone a knight."

"Ahem."

"It's all right, sir. Sir Chesa is right."

Reuyen returned all of Jacalrin's dispassionate answers with feigned, formal chuckles.

In truth, she was not in a relaxed enough state to react to all of the young Chesa's benign teasing. So, she ignored the other senior knights who were staring their eyes off at her as well.

She was already doing her very best trying not to let the others know of her stomach churning more and more with each step she took toward Olzore.

Jacalrin leaned his head toward her to stare at her face, which was slowly becoming more dismal, then spurred his horse.

"Sir Haldroff, we'll soon arrive at the rough lands," he said. "There will be another order once the scouts return, so I'll return to my post as well."

"Goodbye, then, sir," said Reuyen.

Jacalrin looked one last time at her oddly scrunched up face, then galloped to the front.

"Do you have a stomachache?" Evinbur asked. "You don't look so well."

Reuyen barely managed to answer. "I'm all right, sir."

As the distance to Olzore shortened, her facial muscles stiffened on their own and her trembling tension intensified. Thousands of thoughts she could not pronounce out loud passed through her mind. She could barely hold herself, to the point that Evinbur noticed it and looked at her with questioning eyes.

A woman who was the daughter of a horse dealer and who performed all kinds of tricks on horseback getting sick while riding a horse must have been an odd sight indeed. But Reuyen didn't even have the energy to explain. She felt a dull pain somewhere inside her lungs, like she was breathing in water. Her heart grew heavier with each step she took, as though she were gathering the memories she had strenuously cast aside and storing them back in her heart.

All the while, the black horse with his rider on his back was standing aloof. Looking so proud, like they had nothing to fear on their way to Olzore.

Myriad sensations that stemmed from the pointless memories tightened their constraints on her wrists, ankles, and the entirety of her back. That strange feeling that slowly fogged her senses as she marched for the past week without resting reached its peak when the clouds started to reveal the shadows of Olzore Valley on the other side.

The valley of the devil showed itself in the distance, stretching its vertical jaws. Its dark eeriness, which had swallowed thousands of Rarkian corpses along with the queen's grudge, revealed itself.

"We'll enter the valley by tomorrow."

Reuyen tightened her hands into a fist at Evinbur's murmur.

Was she frightened, or had her hatred spread its roots and pinned her here? She kept whipping the blameless Den, who kept stopping like he could read his master's mind.

Thankfully, Paseid gave an order not long after.

"We will spend the night here, and tomorrow afternoon, we will pass through the area of Olzore's influence at our maximum speed. Make sure to get enough rest and prepare yourselves."

Reuyen looked at the back of Paseid, who was restlessly looking at the soldiers. Finding her somewhat sharp eyes staring at him, Jacalrin twisted to look at her.

The valley.

Reuyen then saw the image of the steep and rough valley that protected Olzore before her eyes. She pulled down her eyelids.

Still, with the crystal-clear image lingering on the back of her eyelids, she remembered the archenemy she could not defeat.

The tents of the army of nearly fifty thousand standing below the steep hill leading into Olzore Valley were filled with the smell of death and despair.

It had been a year and a half since the queen's army set up a camp there. It had been just about as long since the beacon of the immense fort towering over them started to disrupt their sleep. The valley reeked of blood all the time, and the smell of ashes covered the stench.

The blue butterfly flag hung limp, having lost the help of the wind, over the tent made of hundreds of marten skins in the center of the camp. The knights and soldiers who could not retire to their beds even this late at night lined up in front of the tent and listened to the furious voice coming from inside, not knowing what to do.

"Say that again, Peijak."

"He's dead, Your Highness."

"Dead?"

"Dead."

"Sir Cananso is dead?"

The slim pen the queen was holding broke into pieces.

"We retrieved the body, Your Highness."

"Bring that damned Baganteo this instant."

Her blue eyes flashed with rage, deterring the others from even daring to look into them. His sister, who remained composed at most news, was responding more aggressively than usual. But as the times were what they were, Peijak understood her wrath without being taken aback. A small part of him pitied Sir Baganteo, who most likely would die before the night ended.

Sir Baganteo had lost his men in a shameful way that could not be redeemed at this time, so he would not be able to save himself from the queen's wrath in any shape or form. But Peijak did not like his beloved sister being in a bad mood. He decided to appease the queen's rage for a personal reason.

"But three of our brigades avoided total defeat thanks to him, so soothe your anger a little bit, Your Highness."

"Avoided total defeat? Nothing compares to the degree of shame he has brought by running away and leaving his men to die! He dared to come back alive after letting every single one of the men assigned to him be massacred! If that damn bastard hadn't fled, we wouldn't have had to deal with such preposterous indignity! How those bastards will laugh at me!"

The queen's furious voice shook the tent.

Only for two and a half days. She'd entrusted the strategies to them for merely two days because she was experiencing extreme fatigue during her *monthly bleeding. She had been taking care of the camp not too far away from the valley, leaving them be for only two and a half days, and a commander had panicked when the enemy used that opportunity to ambush. He had haphazardly retreated, leaving his army behind.*

The result were mounds of bodies of her men. Her beloved knight of House Cananso had died at the blow of an enemy's iron mace. Naturally, she was irate.

Peijak's sunken blue eyes looked down at a forty-five-degree angle. The life of a knight hung by a thread at the tips of her trembling fingers.

"As you know, Your Highness, great fury does not aid in uplifting the spirits of the men. Sir Baganteo has taken his armor off and is asking to atone for his wrong, so what do you say to deciding his punishment at daybreak?"

The queen knew that her aggravation was more than necessary. She also knew that the knights were lined up outside her tent, frightened by her fury.

She scrunched her lips as she banged the table with her fist.

"I am stripping away Sir Baganteo's titles. He will be demoted to a laborer come morning."

Baganteo was a knight from a noble house. Becoming a mere laborer in one night without even a proper trial was an absolute absurdity, but no one dared to disobey her on this battlefield.

"Yes, Your Highness."

"Clear all those nauseating things away from my tent."

Though her order was still stern, it was far calmer than before. So Peijak sent the knights outside back to their posts and came back to her. Then, he spoke in a comfortable manner, without any trace of formality.

"You still don't look quite well. Seems like it's getting worse, dear sister."

She remembered the ache below her waist and walked over to her bed covered in blue satin, spitting out foul words. When she lay down on the bed on her back, Peijak sat down next to her.

The queen looked askance at the man, whose strapping figure could not be hidden even under an armor. She did not stop Peijak's impudence of putting his hand on her. He caressed her stomach covered under a thin layer of clothing.

"It hurts a lot this month, huh..."

"You'll know the feeling if someone ever stabs your guts over and over."

"Oh no, should we call a doctor, then?"

"Don't even think about wasting our already short workforce on a trivial matter like this."

"I'm just worried."

"Shut it."

Still lying down, the queen covered her eyes with her arm at Peijak's quiet laughter.

"I already have two sons, damn it. Isn't that enough now? What does this body want more to make it keep inviting the monthly guest back?" she spat out.

Peijak lowered his upper body and kissed her upper abdomen at her ruthless words of self-disgust.

"Now those damned bastards in that fort know my times of bleeding. How shameful it would be to show myself again on the battlefield."

"That's not true."

"I'm fine. Leave."

"I'm too scared you might actually tear up your own belly with a knife to leave."

"If I wanted to do so, I would have done so as soon as I had Tejis. I know enough to value my body. Oh, actually, now that I think of the way things are going right now, that does sound quite intriguing."

"I'll take care of the rest, so take it easy, dear sister," Peijak softly and quietly cajoled her.

"Damn Olzore!"

The frustration piled on top of the hatred pent up for a year and a half came pouring out.

Though she was never deterred by it, a woman's body still was not as free as a man's. Months without pain were fine, but ever since she'd given birth to two children, her premenstrual pain had tortured her more and more frequently. It was solely her responsibility, for it was apparently the price of running out to war without even proper postpartum care, but she could not bear having it be a hindrance at an important time like this.

The only obstacle she, on whom the knights had nothing when it came to sword, spear, bow, or horse, could not overcome with her will was enough of a reason for the enemies to sneer at her.

Even now.

In the short time she was attending to her belly, a shameful defeat knocked at her door again. The skirmishes were supposed to deceive them *anyway. She did not care too much about small defeats. But Baganteo forgoing the control of the soldiers and acting pigheadedly, then fleeing the second his life was in danger was a shame on the Rarkian army, aside from the defeat itself.*

How could the soldiers risk their lives in battle with that kind of commander? Those commanders were the reason Rarke still had not passed Olzore.

"My dear sister...my most respected queen. No one can laugh at you. For I will not let anyone laugh at you."

Peijak moved his lips around her abdomen and waist, blowing his warm breath to pacify her fury. Then his rough, calloused hand caressed the back of her other hand, hanging lifelessly over the edge of the bed. He locked his fingers with hers. He tightened his grip, as if saying, Have faith.

Her fury could not persist any longer. At the sincere effort of her half-brother, who seemed to have been born knowing the way to have all her love to himself, to make her feel better, Swan slowly came back to her composed self.

Someone opened the drape of the tent and came running in. Swan didn't look back.

"Your Highness, a moment of your time, please."

Peijak straightened his back and answered instead. "Sir Volted, Her Highness is resting, so bring all nonurgent matters to my tent."

A rustling noise came from where the man was standing. Peijak suddenly stopped caressing her lower back with the hand that was not locked with hers. The queen slowly lowered her arm and sat up at the sudden pressure on her hand.

"A letter came from the commander of Fort Olzore, Your Highness."

"Guitella Oren Diblis," she spat.

Swan's face slowly became overcome with fury as she took the tattered letter from the knight's hand.

I commend you for your obtuse assiduity, Rarkalia.

I send my humble condolences on the vain deaths of the savages knocking at our walls. Our father of Morgana, Dernajuke IV, expresses his grievance at your selfish foolishness in repeating your defeats. The fort is too high for an immoral woman and her cowardly followers to climb. If you submit your arrogant stubbornness and step back with proper subservience, we will allow it with mercy.

It was an extremely insolent letter without an introduction or the signature of the sender. It lacked even the very minimal amount of decorum a letter to the queen of a country ought to have.

The queen mulled over it.

"Obtuse. Immoral woman. Cowardly followers."

Her fury, which had barely subsided, erupted to the sky. Reading the contents of the letter the queen had crumpled and thrown aside, Peijak scowled at the knight without any trace of the kindness he'd shown before.

"Who brought this letter?"

"A soldier from the second squad who has been held prisoner."

A roaring laughter burst from the queen's lips. She glared at the letter in Peijak's hand.

She sprang up and sat at the table. Then she cleared away the broken pen, spread her finest parchment, and raised a seal submerged in a pool of blue ink on one corner of the table. It was the queen's seal, with the shape of a butterfly engraved on it. She stamped the pale butterfly seal in the middle of the parchment with a loud bang.

"I am the queen of Rarke." The royal blue butterfly displayed its arrogance as it spread its clear wings on the parchment. "Sir Dollehan, tell Sir Baganteo that I will grant him an opportunity to atone for his crime this instant."

The queen threw the parchment at Peijak before the blue ink could even dry. Peijak looked at the blue butterfly in awe.

As she had ordered, Sir Baganteo was sent as an emissary to Fort Olzore that morning, completely unarmed.

A week later, he returned with his head intact, but not in the fine state fit for an emissary.

Two weeks later, the queen mounted her horse once more and charged to Fort Olzore.

"Has that annoying woman come back again?" Guitella, the king of the Fort, played music and sang while the queen's army stood before the fort.

After three days, the queen turned back.

Again, the queen pent up her frustration.

In the heavy darkness of the campsite, Reuyen woke up from her light sleep and sat up, brushing back her flowing hair. She was no longer able to sleep because of the anxiety that made even her fatigue run away. She weakly blinked her eyes. Her heart trembled.

Olzore. The familiar scent surrounded and restrained her.

She slowly raised her body and lowered her anxious eyes away from the tired soldiers lying side by side. A quiet curse escaped her dry lips like a self-deprecation.

"What colossal fuckery this is."

Remember who you are. The wind blowing from the valley seemed to whisper in her ears.

Her zealous eyes looked at the shadows dancing somewhere in the darkness, across the campsite.

CHAPTER SEVENTEEN

The next day, once they reached the entrance to the valley, Paseid gave an order.

"The moment we enter the valley, we will be exposed to the enemy's eyes, and they will enhance their defense and guard. In case of a counterattack, we will reinforce the rear and push out at maximum speed."

The tension prickled everyone's skin.

Jacalrin's green eyes glistened. He took the initiative and moved to the rear with Paseid, with whom he took turns at the front. The front was now left in the hands of Evinbur and the other knights. The soldiers increased their speed and departed to the rock-covered lands with firm determination.

The streams that flowed along the valley had long since dried up into roads of rock and dirt where weeds thrived. Some of them were trails swallowed by the valley to the point that no one could tell where they led.

The soldiers who entered the winding, dreary path increased their speed, following the bannerman's flag guiding them.

Reuyen endeavored to quiet her hands and feet that had started to shake, and tightly held on to Den's reins. When the familiar landscape drew her into her memories and she wanted to hesitate, defying her orders, she scolded herself again and again.

Fort Olzore. The fort atop a valley surrounded by hard stone.

Just taking it in with her eyes seemed to hurt her insides, like someone was scratching them with sandpaper.

Olzore remained solid. No, it was looking down at the Rarkian army with an even more ominous presence than it had in her past memory.

Looking up at the legacy that had survived the passing of time, she sank uncontrollably into the other side of time.

Three months. Had Belbarote given her merely three months more, she would not have had to feel all the hair on her body spike up at this deep remorse.

It was truly a foolish act.

Booooo—

There was no way to hide from the eyes of the towering fort except in the trees, their roots planted in the crevices of the cliff. As expected, the enemy's beacon lit up in red not long after the Rarkians entered the valley. With that, the booming sound of drums and bugles announcing the start of a battle echoed all over the valley. The thundering roar mixed into the Rarkians' signals.

"To defense formation!"

Reuyen held up her shield to cover the sky, like she had been told. Not long after, arrows started to pour down. They sounded like rain hitting a window as they fell upon on the countless Rarkian soldiers' heads, hitting the shields and bouncing off to the ground.

The volley was not too intense, for its purpose was to show the enemy who had suddenly appeared at the valley that they were not asleep. Reuyen unhesitatingly marched on with the army, crossing over the dreary trails, fallen trees, and rough rocks. The deeper they went into the valley, the stronger they could feel the murderous intent of Olzore filling the atmosphere.

And not long after, arrows with fire on their oiled tips started to fall down one by one. The hurrying soldiers blindly marching across the dry, rough land startled at the sudden bursts of fire and tripped over, but soon got back on their feet and persistently walked, protecting each other's heads.

As soon as the fire arrows started falling, Evinbur shouted, "We can't speed up any more than this! Protect the gunpowder carriages! Keep your formation and do not panic!"

Then he hastily looked at the rear, where Paseid was. The front wasn't under any intense attack, but the rear would have to stand firm until the whole army completely evacuated from the valley. Evinbur took the very slightly worried look off his face and turned his horse back around to face the front. It would still take half a day to get past the irregularly wide and narrow pathways and the endless rocks and stones.

"Walk together with your comrades and watch over their heads! If my comrade's head catches on fire, I burn too! Remember that!"

Following Evinbur's thundering commands, Reuyen tightened her grip on the shield. The sound of footsteps before her and behind her hastened as time passed. The screams and shouts did not cease. The weight of the fire arrows and rocks falling from the sky on her shield felt like it could crush her arm. Shields burst into flames, which then subsided.

"Come on, move! Move! Even if they follow us now, if we keep up this speed and get out of the valley and enter Tolf, we can shake them off. You, there! Keep up with your comrades! This isn't a time for a nap!" Evinbur roared at Reuyen.

In the advance, Reuyen closed her watery eyes as hard as she could and opened them. Then she looked ahead.

"The road in the middle is narrowing, sir," someone called. "We need to slow down for a moment, sir!"

"Don't tell me that! Run along and tell Sir Calandok in the rear that! You good-for-nothing, you're more useless than an old man! Sir Eden, watch out so the formation doesn't get disheveled!" Evinbur nimbly blocked a fire arrow with his shield.

It was obvious that Olzore would send a message to the main force of Morgana on Plain Ishas. So, the most important matter was the time it would take for Rovantis of Morgana to hear their report and finish his preparation. Now, everything was dependent on the tick of the time.

"The front will evacuate at maximum speed."

"But the threat to the rear..."

"We still have time. Our commander-in-chief is there as well, so no need to worry," Evinbur assured them.

The reason was quite clear: Olzore was the symbol of Morgana, a fort specifically designed for defense where even the emperor of

Morgana himself overlooked the neglect of duty. It would take at least an hour or two for them to find the Rarkian army, start preparing, and send out their soldiers. Meanwhile, the Rarkian army would evacuate to the other side of the valley, and once they were out of the valley, the soldiers of Olzore surely could not catch up to them.

Even Olzore's miniscule attacks were not unexpected, so the fierce soldiers of Rarke controlled their speed and marched on instead of fearing the arrows they had already calculated.

The only reason the overall formation in the front could stay together while Paseid was guarding the rear was because Evinbur was fiercely ordering the soldiers.

Marching forward like someone was pushing her from behind, Reuyen said to Evinbur, "There is a side path safe from falling objects that way, sir."

Olzore Valley was where the queen had stayed for nearly three years. She'd learned all the geography of the area. In truth, she even had the arrogance to think that she probably knew more about this area than the lord of the fort. But Evinbur scowled at her.

"We cannot risk the danger of going onto an unverified road. Increase your speed and evacuate on the planned path, Dame Detua."

It was a natural answer for someone who was deemed suspicious and was under supervision. And yet, her innards ached at it. After looking like she was half out of her mind for a moment, she whipped Den as ordered at last.

When the wind crashed into her face, the sudden gush of anger subsided like kitchen fire being splashed with water.

I'm Reuyen.

She repeated in her head.

I'm Reuyen.

Her present self was only a daughter of a horse dealer.

"Reuyen."

Her dry lips repeated her name as she rode through the valley.

Her present self was Reuyen. The ordinary woman from Gyujen, daughter of Jess and Senila, Eivan's younger sister, and Sidan's older sister. A woman who only had a set of memories she could not tell anyone, and a nimble body. Reuyen Detua.

The shapeless shadow of the past seemed to be clawing at the back of her neck. Her heart beat like she was being chased.

"Reuyen," she repeated.

"I am Reuyen."

Again.

She needed to get out of here. Or else the begrudging monster inside her would devour Reuyen. She had to bury it. Deep in her heart, she buried the memories of the fort that would never open.

Then.

The rain of arrows suddenly stopped.

"What's going on?"

Reuyen stopped Den, drooling and panting, and instinctively looked up at the sky. Evinbur also realized that the attack had stopped and looked around.

There was silence.

Anxiety, fear, and tension she didn't know the roots of rushed her heart like they were trying to tear it apart.

Creaaaaak.

A scream as chilling as the devil's scratched down the valley and settled eerily.

The thundering sound of a massive pulley turning its wheel resounded from the heavens and washed over the sounds of bugles and drums. Without any orders, all the Rarkian soldiers and knights froze in their steps. A moment of silence began as the valley swallowed all the screams and moans.

Creaaaaaak.

It can't be.

Reuyen's eyes shook. She knew the origin of that sound.

It can't be.

The cries of Guitella as he greeted the queen's army resonated in her ears like a hallucination. Her heart beat like it had gone back in time to the past.

Creaaaaaaak.

The soldiers lowered their shields and raised their heads to the clear sky and the valley high above.

Shards of rock rolled down the valley's cliffs.

Boom.

The inviolable gates of Olzore that boasted seven hundred and fifty years of history opened their jaws with a fierce screech. And from there, fully armed knights and soldiers of the enemy started pouring out.

Even if it were not wartime, horseback riding was a culture of the nobles that was quite useful in revealing elegance and strength at the same time. On top of that, it was the only noble practice Jacalrin, who only ever started things without finishing, had actually taken interest in and learned.

But recently, Jacalrin wanted to throw up when he thought even of the first *ho* of horseback riding. He had run from the capital for nearly a month before he joined the main force of Rarke, and then had to get back on the horse straightaway without any time to rest, so he thought his complaint quite well justified.

Behind him was an endless line of soldiers stretched out like a borderline across the forests and fields. He was sympathetic for them, as they were following the same boring march as him.

It would have been nice if he at least had a talkative friend he could chat with while they marched on, tied to their horses! But Seisen, who was watching his back, was way too polite, and Paseid, who was walking in front of him, was way too proper. Way too polite and way too proper were not that different in the sense that they were both boring. Jacalrin thought it especially a shame that the way Paseid acted in the capital varied greatly from the way he acted on a battlefield. In the capital, he at least pretended to listen to Jacalrin's gossip and stories.

Jacalrin swallowed a yawn and tried to strike up a conversation. "Sir Calandok, it would take more than ten days to get to Ishas, circumventing Tolf, at this speed, right?"

"It will be a flat plain once we get out of the valley, so we'll arrive earlier than that."

Paseid, who was walking in the front, never even looked back. His horse, Rotsa, made sounds as elegant and calm as his master.

A soldier rode up alongside them. "Sir, the scouts have returned. There are no enemies hiding for ambush, sir."

Reports followed at a constant interval from the others.

Not paying that much attention to them, Jacalrin unconsciously turned his head to look at Evinbur, then narrowed his eyes at Reuyen, who followed with a pale face.

He had thought that she was pale, but how did her face just keep getting paler during this arduous march where they couldn't even wash for days? Regardless of Jacalrin's eyes on her, Reuyen's eyes were fixed on the valley beyond his head.

When Jacalrin's head did not come back to face forward for a long time, Seisen coughed at last. "Ahem, hem, Sir Chesa?"

Constantly looking at her was more of an instinctual move; not the masculine instinct of a robust man interested in the opposite sex, but an instinct directly related to survival. It was a keen intuition of discord. Jacalrin grinned mischievously when he locked eyes with Evinbur, and unconsciously tightened and loosened his grip around the hilt of his sword hanging at his side.

There was a trail on a steep hill that led to the fort not far from the entrance to the valley, connecting Rarkian land and Olzore. The known size of the military force in Olzore was about four to five thousand. Even if it were five thousand, it wasn't that much of a threat, since not all five thousand would be able to fight outside.

But Paseid took that into his calculations as well and moved to the rear, leaving the front to Evinbur once they reached the entrance to the valley. Jacalrin, who was assisting Paseid in his command, moved to the rear as well.

"Advance! Keep up the speed!"

While the army advanced into the deep valley where the damp, cold air flowed from, Jacalrin stood aside and looked up at the flag flapping on top of the fort, his hand over his eyes to block out the sun.

"Maniacs, all of them. Building a nest all the way up there."

But of course, that outrageous height was how they never fell to all the tumult over the years. That was why it was considered impregnable. Jacalrin's mood took a turn.

Standing right across from him, a knight reported to Paseid. "Sir, the midsection of the march has completely entered the valley. Another one of the enemy's beacons just lit up, sir."

It seemed like they'd noticed the infiltrators and were getting ready for defense. As he gave his report, another beacon blazed.

"Hold up your shields." As soon as Paseid finished his order, the short, alarming sound of a bugle boomed across the valley. "To defense formation!"

The soldiers immediately followed the order without being flustered, for they had already been warned. Jacalrin changed his grip on the heavy shield and started to become more alert, though lazily.

Though they probably didn't have that many soldiers to come running out, Olzore hid in the shell of the fort and shot arrows at their enemy, as they had done throughout history. Jacalrin evaded the arrows showering down; once he entered the valley, he lost even the slight sense of danger he had been holding on to.

"So, we have to march for hours like this, huh…"

When he was about to start complaining, a knight cut him off with a report. "Sir, the midsection is slowing down due to the narrowing road."

"No need to cause a havoc by hurrying. Follow the speed of those in front of us."

All in the rear, slow! Slow down!

All the ivory horns blowing, the signal flags swishing, and the various gestures from various knights made quite an entertaining sight.

By the time Jacalrin got used to the low temperature inside the valley, the sky started to occasionally spit fire. They were fire arrows. Looking up with disapproval, Jacalrin shouted at Paseid, "The supply unit is pulling the gunpowder carriages, sir. I'll be right back after checking that area."

Paseid followed Jacalrin with his eyes as Jacalrin increased his speed and galloped into the valley. He then carefully scrutinized the area. Paseid scrunched up his nose at the smell of the fire arrows. Then he raised his eyes and glared at the two lit beacons, irritated.

There were three things that irritated him.

First, the smoke from those beacons would reach Rovantis's camp. But there were only two beacons. If they could not relay the specific details by sending a messenger, the main force could not move, either, so it wasn't something to worry too much about at the present moment.

Second, even though this was not an intense battle, only lighting the second stage alarm was as arrogant as the height of the valley.

Third, their attack was suspiciously weak.

A considerable amount of time had passed since the echoes of shouts, the footsteps of the soldiers, the smell of oil and of something burning had covered the insides of the valley. And yet, this was a far weaker response than what he had expected to encounter.

Paseid had even taken the enemy throwing stones with catapults into consideration as a worst-case scenario. Even if they assumed that the Rarkian army had no intentions of taking the fort, they were still passing their range of influence. And this was it?

Evinbur was in charge of commanding the front, and the enemy's attack was negligible. If they marched to the end of the valley, there would barely be any damage on the Rarkians' side. Yet, he could not shake off the odd, uncomfortable feeling. With that eerie feeling, Paseid entered the valley under the knights' protection, away from the falling arrows.

After moving along the winding, rocky trail, Paseid suddenly realized there was an odd vibration. He pulled on the reins to stop Rotsa and closely studied the walls and the floor of the valley.

What is this?

The strange vibration did not originate from the Rarkian army. A small piece of rock rolled down, flew over his head, then bounced off on his shield.

A sudden gush of dirt followed the rock, and Paseid raised his eyes to the sky. The arrows flying across it were nowhere to be found, and there was only clear void without even a single cloud.

Neiiiigh!

The other knights' horses abruptly stomped on the ground.

He could still feel the ground vibrating. It was getting clearer.

Paseid's black eyes slid down from the sky to the tip of the fort. A chill ran down his spine.

His lips opened at long last. "Order Sir Chesa to return to his post."

A knight who heard his order hastily galloped to the midsection of the cavalcade.

And then

Creaaaaaak.

All the Rarkians froze where they were.

A moment of silence passed as the eerie valley swallowed all the screams and moans.

Creaaaaak.

It's opening.

Boom.

Paseid instinctually threw aside his shield and drew his sword, Rionac. The gates of Olzore that should not have opened were now opening.

"All in the rear, lower your shields," Paseid ordered in a low voice.

"Sir?"

His eyes were still fixed on the top of the valley. "They're coming."

He spoke with certainty. Almost simultaneously, thousands of enemy soldiers started to pour out of the massive gates with a thundering roar.

A great sound of *baaaang!* resounded like thunder. At the same time, a fire burst out somewhere in the middle of the Rarkian cavalcade.

Screams and shouts burst out to the sky.

CHAPTER EIGHTEEN

One, two, three...

Innumerable soldiers started to come down the steep hill. The shouts and footsteps of Olzore's soldiers echoed threateningly.

Standing at the bottom of the valley and looking up at the grand sight, Reuyen sank into the sick feeling, like she was sitting on a clock hand retrogressing.

Yes, it looked just like this.

Three years. She'd drunk the air here for the last three years of her life.

～

The queen took the bottom of the valley and the entrance on the hill and looked up at the enemy's fort, and the one on the fort's throne dared to look down at her.

When the enemies bored of looking at the same sight and opened the tightly closed gates, thousands of soldiers poured out just like that.

Guitella was truly a cunning king of the fort.

He stopped the queen's attack and broke her defense by utilizing his geographical advantage. The day those gates opened was the day the entrance on the hill and the outskirts of the valley flooded with blood in the blink of an eye.

Until she set foot in this place, the queen had not stopped even once. Her competitive nature, blind resolution, and ambition were backed up by her remarkable decision-making skills and her innate talent. So, she walked on the carpet of victory drenched in blood.

Until she stood before this great Olzore, she was an arrogant woman who knew not of defeat.

But that arrogance shattered at last.

The enemy's walls wore the God-given geography as their armor and mocked Rarke, and the stones, boiling oil, and steel arrows flying from the skies resulted in ever-growing mounds of Rarkian corpses. The queen stood atop the mountain of the dead rising as high as the valley and repeated to herself.

"This is not a defeat, for this was a small sacrifice for the greater good. Once we climb that place, all the sacrificed of Rarke will find their meaning."

The queen raged, hated, resented, and perhaps came to love Olzore at last. She yearned for the mighty sight as unattainable as the sky.

"If I cannot climb that, what use is all the rich lands of the south?"

Looking up at the silver fort touching the blue sky, she always imagined the grand sight looking down from there in turn. The vision of looking down at all of Morgana atop that place. She filled herself with the selfish determination to undergo anything and everything for that vision.

"You can do whatever you'd like, Your Highness. I will make it so, and I will do so."

So.

"We'll tear down the valley, Peijak."

The queen made a decision with inevitable sacrifices from Rarke.

"We have set aside two years for the operation, Your Highness."

While the furtive operation progressed, bodies piled higher and higher.

"It will be done in half a year."

All those sacrifices and the long wait were for the sweet, sweet fruit to come after the pain.

"It will be finished in three months, Your Highness."

Then.

"I have been ordered to bring Queen Swan Sekalrid Rarkalia back to the palace, Your Majesty," *said the messenger.* "By force, if need be."

The letter with the red wolf seal on it was thrown in front of her.

"Duke regent's orders."

Her trusted husband had betrayed her.
So, she broke down.

Booooo—

The sound of the bugle awakened her. With her back to the icy wind of the valley caressing her cheek, Reuyen looked down at the wolf brassard wrapped around her left arm.

The sigil of a wolf.

She did not resent Brionake, but recalling it was devastating.

She realized her own madness in the face of death. She regretted it. Yet, even so, there was something smeared on her heart like viscid sap. The last deed she had not been able to finish because she was bitten to death by a wolf.

Her past was stirred by the valley's wind. The regrets and the glory from that era, the madness from that time, all came back and cried like a bird fallen out of its nest.

But a long time had passed since then. The fort wearing the armor of the weight of time in layers like strata had become that much harder and looked down upon them with even greater arrogance. Those who followed the queen had all vanished into dirt, and the queen sitting on the footless throne shut her eyes and ears.

The voice repeating by her ear was the voice of the dead that she could never hear again.

I can't even imagine my dear sister losing.

Yes, I once believed so as well. But defeat was something as inevitable as death. You were probably disappointed in me for such defeat.

All the advisors were dead, and the queen was now alone, separated by time.

The crownless queen looked up at the fort and shut her lips with crumpled sadness.

You will climb in the end.

You must be disappointed once again at your sister looking up at that sky.

Peijak.

The scene in the valley broke with the footsteps of the enemy. Reuyen snapped back to reality and grabbed Den's mane as he stepped backward. The soldiers started to get flustered, and groans and confusion broke out sporadically.

"How can this be?" Evinbur lamented.

The response of the enemy was at a speed that made no logical sense. Their sending out armed soldiers who were that prepared meant that they had started preparing five or six hours in advance. It wouldn't be nonsensical to assume that there was a leakage of information. The shouts and stomps of the soldiers echoed through the valley incessantly.

They continued to pour out. Their speed was not very threatening because they were descending a steep hill, but their numbers were—well, they were entirely impossible unless they brought out every single soldier in the fort.

But that was not what was important right now. A forlorn, sunken voice came from between Reuyen's lips. "Order the front and rear to prepare for battle, sir."

Evinbur's deep eyes looked straight at the side of Reuyen's face. But Reuyen wasn't looking at him anymore. She shouted at those who were still frozen.

"If they prepared, knowing that we were coming, we must take an ambush at the exit of the valley into consideration as well. It would not even take half an hour for them to come down the hill from the fort to set foot on the field, sir."

"Dame Detua."

"Also, we must first and foremost move the infantry to a place where they can take cover through that trail there and watch the rear, sir."

The eyes of the knights and soldiers following Evinbur all simultaneously focused on the woman with the red wolf brassard on her left arm.

Evinbur turned around his horse in silence and glared at the rear. Paseid was at the section near the entrance on the hill, but he couldn't not worry at a time like this when at least a couple thousand enemies had suddenly appeared.

Then.

Bang!

Flame burst into the sky with a great thundering noise. It came from somewhere in the middle of the cavalcade and blocked Evinbur's view. Startled by the explosive sound, Reuyen yanked Den's reins. Den raised his front legs and jumped. Had Evinbur not grabbed Den's reins, she would have ended up in a much more embarrassing situation.

A knight opened his mouth, flustered. "The midsection of the cavalcade is where the supply unit is, sir. There must have been an issue with the gunpowder carriages."

"Of course, it never rains, but it pours. Sir Vasar, check what the situation is in the rear immediately."

The fire was great enough for those in the front to see clearly. Before she could even be embarrassed for being so startled, Reuyen was completely absorbed by the fire.

She had heard about the gunpowder from the travelers and merchants passing through her town, but this was the first time she ever saw it bursting into flames. She could almost feel the passage of time with her skin. Judging by the sudden smell of burning flesh, a considerable number of people must have ceased to be in a heartbeat.

Dazed for a moment, she came back to her senses and repeated once more, "We must move this instant, sir. When we do not even know what is happening!"

"If you do not wish to be further distrusted, stop acting on your impulses and wait for an order, Dame Detua."

Evinbur cut her off without even thinking twice about it. Reuyen opened her lips to protest, but chose to remain silent upon looking at his face.

His face was already swallowed by a glum worry. Olzore's army had appeared out of the blue, and Reuyen's claim sounded quite convincing at the unexpected appearance of the enemy, so he couldn't blindly advance forward, either.

Evinbur gave the order. "First, search the exit of the valley and report back."

Two knights galloped ahead at lightning speed. Evinbur's eyes turned back to the rear. The enemies were coming down the hill slowly but surely, causing dirt and bits of rock to crumble down.

Not long after, not-so-delightful news came.

"I cannot confirm the situation in the rear, sir. Two of the gunpowder carriages have caught on fire and exploded."

"I will go there myself and check."

"Sir Haldroff, Sir Chesa has ordered everyone not to approach the area until the fire is under control. Even so, that area is completely in flames right now. Additional damage may occur due to unexploded gunpowder, sir."

"Is Sir Chesa with the supply unit?"

"I heard that he returned to the rear at Sir Calandok's orders right before the gunpowder exploded. I think the only way right now is to wait until the fire is under control, sir."

Evinbur tightened his grip on his sword.

Then, the pale Reuyen standing behind him pushed Den's head in between the knight and Evinbur and blocked them.

"Sir Haldroff."

"What insolence is this?"

"If you would, I can guide you to the rear, sir," Reuyen calmly continued. "Estimating the distance from here to the entrance, it would take over an hour for the scout to return, sir. The most important thing right now is to inspect the enemy's actions, sir. If a battle transpires..."

Evinbur's eyes focused on Reuyen with question, not suspicion.

Why does this woman think and speak like a commander? Why does she not wait for the command of a commander? Such questions arose, then washed away in the crashing waves of urgent situations.

"I do not need your guidance to go through the flames, Dame Detua."

"I know...a safe route through the front, sir."

A short silence fell between them. But she silently looked back at Evinbur's eyes carefully scrutinizing her.

"Is the fire under control now?"

Upon Evinbur and Reuyen's appearance, the extremely tense Jacalrin brightened up and looked back at the valley. But the flames had only diminished by a little, not completely out yet.

"There still has been no encounter?" Evinbur asked. Jacalrin didn't even have time to relay the situation or give his greetings. Paseid was already standing at the entrance to the valley with the knights and soldiers prepared for battle. Without waiting for his answer, Evinbur immediately ran over to Paseid.

"Sir Calandok, what has happened?"

Motionless, Paseid was sitting on Rotsa and gazing at the enemy.

Instead of pressing for an answer, Evinbur stood behind him and looked at the enemy, now at the foot of the hill. There were at least a thousand or so knights and several thousands of soldiers standing proudly.

"The command of the front," said Paseid.

"I left Sir Basan in charge, sir. I deemed it too risky to blindly advance when we have no knowledge of how much of our operation plan the enemies know, so I ordered the men at my own discretion to stay in place...and I ordered a scout to inspect the exit of the valley. What is happening, sir?"

Paseid rubbed the hilt of Rionac instead of answering. He wanted to ask the same question.

It had been nearly half an hour since the enemy came down the hill. The gates of the fort had just closed. But the enemy did not attack. Instead, they stood in formation at the entrance on the hill and slowly but surely increased their size. The chaos on the Rarkians' side slowly subsided as well. Thus, they were standing in an odd confrontational stance.

Why not promptly attack?

A strange sensation unpleasantly pricked Paseid's mind with its thorns.

The actions of the enemy were not appropriate. The Rarkians were in disarray at their quick dispatch. Unless the lord of the fort was an idiot, he would not have missed this boon.

Turning his head, Paseid found Reuyen, who had followed Evinbur, and narrowed his eyes. Reuyen was looking out at the huddled enemy with icy eyes.

Jacalrin passed by Reuyen to approach Paseid and grumbled, "Why on earth are they wasting their time like that?"

Then.

The fort's army split into a small group and a large group, and the larger group turned their backs to the Rarkians.

They're showing their backs?

At the sound of a trumpet, the ones who turned their backs started to march in the opposite direction. And the remaining small group of a hundred or so knights and a couple hundred soldiers all stood horizontally against them to form a defense line. They started to drag thick tree trunks and thorny bushes, and laid them on the road—actions that clearly revealed their intentions to defend.

Paseid scrunched up his brows. In the sunken darkness of the valley, his black eyes followed after them like the currents in a deep ocean.

"Are they... crazy?"

Completely flustered, Jacalrin gaped and walked in front of Paseid. The tensed-up rear soldiers who had remained on guard at the entrance to the valley started to whisper amongst themselves at the enemy's odd behavior.

The geography of the valley was narrow on both the Rarkian army's side and the Olzore army's side, making them pretty much at an equal physical disadvantage, but the psychologically intimidated ones were the Rarkians. Paseid had come to make peace with himself at the bitter thought of losing a part of the rear units if a battle transpired.

A great vibration rang across the valley where the Rarkians had stopped moving. Even after hard blinking, the sight before them did not change. The fort's army was ignoring them and marching away.

"Are they...?"

Evinbur squinted at the tail of the disappearing enemy and groaned. There was no way the soldiers had lost their minds and decided to run out into Rarkian territory and head to the border.

Unless they knew they would have backup.

CHAPTER NINETEEN

Reuyen and Paseid, who were coldly evaluating the situation in silence all along, opened their mouths almost at the same time.

"Did the front of Morgana and Olzore join hands…"

"An already planned feint operation…"

In the surge of attention, Reuyen noticed Paseid's black eyes darting to her and clamped her mouth shut. Before the situation took a stranger turn, Paseid brought it to order. "It most likely is an already planned feint operation. It would be most reasonable to assume that the time aligned like so coincidentally."

"If it is a feint operation, it must be an attack with Rovantis's force in Morgana's front, and shouldn't that happen at the right time as well? Seems like the Olzorean army doesn't have enough men, sir. Something like three thousand? At most," Reuyen answered, as if to herself.

"If they are headed to Camp Anf region, not the main camp."

It was entirely possible, if their purpose lay in easing the way for Rovantis's army to enter by counterattacking Rarke's camp at the Anf cliff road.

After staring at Reuyen like he was uncomfortable about something, Jacalrin moved close to Paseid and whispered, "What should we do, then, sir?"

"Send a messenger to Sir Carvein."

"Should we just leave that, sir?"

Paseid turned his eyes not to the enemy, but to somewhere in the west where Camp Anf would be.

The Rarkians' beacon had not yet been lit. The time left until they reached Camp Anf was about eight days. Though the army was technically divided equally between the main camp and Camp Anf, there still were many more men stationed at Camp Anf than the number of men from Fort Olzore.

If the main camp moved quickly when they receive the message and held back the enemy, this would actually be an opportunity for them. While the Morganaan army completely entered the Anf region and engaged in battle, the Rarkians could go around Ishas to attack them from behind and block both sides of the cliffs. If that happened, they could damage Rovantis's army severely, and possibly even annihilate a part of his army.

Paseid gazed in the direction of the enemy, then turned his horse around.

"At ease. Extinguish the fire in the midsection of the cavalcade as your number one priority. We will continue the operation as planned."

The knights started to move quickly at Paseid's orders.

Evinbur stayed where he was with a pensive look on his face, then turned his horse around without asking any questions. Jacalrin scratched his chin like he wasn't quite satisfied with the situation, but he had no time to ask anything, either, because he was too preoccupied reorganizing the soldiers.

Evinbur found Reuyen standing still like a statue. "Dame Detua, return to the front."

But Reuyen stood motionlessly and kept looking at the disappearing tail of the Olzorean army.

The enemy had not even three or four thousand men, and the Rarkians stationed at the main camp and Camp Anf had nearly twenty thousand. So, she was not completely unaware of what Paseid might be thinking.

But she personally could not just accept that and let it go.

Judging by the current situation, if Olzore had decided to send that large a force, they must have had a good reason. The

Morganaan army on Plain Ishas had to be extremely firm on this plan.

Looking at the long-lost enemy from hundreds of years ago with her own eyes again, Reuyen could feel the mindless monster within her rampaging in fury. *Will you butcher my beloved Rarke's men once more and flood the fields with their blood?*

"Will you truly let them leave, sir?"

Paseid froze in his place as he was about to whip Rotsa back into the valley. His pitch-black eyes turned to the woman standing like a statue.

Reuyen barely managed to speak again with the appropriate respect. "I believe it would be wisest to pursue the enemy and pressure them from front and rear, sir."

"I did not ask for your opinion."

"We can kill every single one of them if we pursue them now, sir. If the knights of Rarke fail to react to their actions at the right time—"

Reuyen's voice was cut off by Paseid's fiery black eyes. "Do not denigrate the bravery of the knights at the main camp. They have been formally trained. Moreover, their experience and years of battle by themselves allow them to obstruct the Olzorean army, so do not speak so presumptuously. Though Olzore's actions were much quicker and greater in size than we had expected, it still is one of the variables we have considered. There will be no changes in the ambush force's planned route."

Evinbur nodded and looked over at Reuyen.

Even upon hearing Paseid's explanation, Reuyen stared at the disappearing enemy like she could not comprehend it. A ringing in her ears distorted into a scream. The enemy from hundreds of years ago was once again escaping through her fingers.

Paseid disregarded her and steered his horse into the valley. Reuyen unconsciously turned her head toward him.

Then, the slowly subsiding fire came into her view.

The flames that licked the high and mighty sky were burning the trees standing at the high points of the valley and finally starting to dwindle. Her ribs winced at another thundering boom of gunpowder exploding. The moment she set her eyes on the explosion, something in her heart twitched.

Twitch. Twitch.

Her obsession flashed like lightning, then started to choke her like a snare. In that short moment, neither Rarke nor Morgana mattered. Only the uncontrollable urge to do something spread its viscid body across her body like sap.

"There is…another way, sir."

But Paseid walked away without even looking back. "Cease your blathering and move with Sir Haldroff. Remember the duty of the brassard I bestowed on you."

The red wolf mantle on his back billowed from the cold wind of the valley.

The queen who'd died in the jaws of that imposing wolf drew back her ambition. She dug a deep and somber cave somewhere in the valley and breathed her last breath after piling all of her desires and wishes there.

The blood-curdling ghost of the queen leapt out of Reuyen's lips. "Take down the fort, and Morgana will face utter defeat, sir."

Paseid halted.

Reuyen's voice started like she was talking to herself and grew clearer with each word she spoke, like she gained confidence each time. "Taking down the fort is much more efficient than demolishing the enemy's army, sir. Then, there will be no need to go all the way around to Tolf. Once the fort collapses, the Olzorean army will return, and their feint operation will fail. Olzore is the symbol of Morgana. The moment their symbol of defense crumbles, Morgana will crack, sir."

"Don't be preposterous. The notoriety of Olzore does not lie in the headcount of soldiers. Do not hold back the march with such unavailing words…"

"The valley." Reuyen took a short moment, wanting to choose her words carefully, then spat out, "Take down the valley, sir."

Everyone fell silent.

Paseid moved only his head to glare at her from out of the corner of his eye. Evinbur, who was gazing at Reuyen in an odd silence, and Jacalrin, who had been running all over the place, both dropped their mouths open, completely caught off guard.

Is this girl crazy?

Everyone, the knights and the soldiers alike, were thinking the same thing. Their evaluation of her was defined by Paseid's single utterance: "Merely a madwoman, after all."

Reuyen could not deny Paseid's statement. He was right, in a sense. She was no longer a queen, but a worthless country woman, and yet...why did she feel such remorse about the past?

All the reasons and excuses flew beyond her consciousness and the blind desire remained like always. She could not stop it.

"Gunpowder, gunpowder. That is an explosive power at your disposal. Then you must..."

Two hundred years. It's been two hundred long years.

The mine that gnawed into the foot of the valley must have weathered in the years and weakened the foundation since then. It was not impossible. She could not care less about all the people surrounding her, looking at her like she was insane. They could even point and sneer at her, for all she cared.

She was not going to waver in her determination when she was standing right before Olzore, with her unresolved grudge. *Perhaps this was the reason I was reborn,* she thought, using that flawed belief to justify her actions.

"There is a mine right below the fort, sir. Where the softest stones and the strongest stream flow...flowed."

With only three months left, she had kneeled, not even able to make the attempt.

"When the confused enemy turns around, we can surround them here and annihilate them. The enemy at the front will bear the penalty of a failed operation, and Olzore will fall, sir."

So, Brionake, at least this time...

"Then, it will be an absolute victory for Rarke." Speaking with great assurance, Reuyen filled her eyes with desperate yearning.

Against the wind blowing from within the valley, Paseid stood there as though deaf. His uniform coat fluttered in the cold stream of air. Reuyen had never been more afraid of those pitch-black eyes she could not read. She bit and bit her lower lip.

"Take down the fort?" said the commander finally.

Paseid could not recall ever encountering a woman speaking of such absurd things in his whole life. The woman with the red brassard around her arm blathered as if she were an official knight of the duke. It was a seriously presumptuous attitude, if not simply dense, such that he was at a loss for words.

But for some reason, the woman was looking up at him, unshaken, even after babbling all that deranged nonsense. Could she not conceive how she would come across?

For a split second, Paseid almost considered her proposal, reading the assurance in her dark-red eyes. Then he suddenly laid his eyes upon the Olzorean army disappearing into a dot on the horizon beyond her shoulder and calmed himself down again.

He sheathed Rionac.

"A waste of time. I overlooked your previous claim, thinking that you were insisting on pursuing them because you were overwhelmed with concern for your brother. But now, I cannot even imagine to what purpose you are confusing our men with such nonsense. But I will question you later."

"It's not…nonsense, sir."

"Do not hold back the army with your meaningless utterances," he snapped.

She could not easily understand the denial. As she slowly pieced together the voice that shattered her hopes, Reuyen's face gradually fell dark with despair. Her lips went numb like they had been severed off, and her throat clumped like she had swallowed a rock.

Brionake, Brionake, why, even now?

Reuyen grew dizzy with the furious urge to shout. "If—if you cannot believe me, please at least see for yourself and decide, sir."

Dismissing her meek voice, Paseid turned his horse around. While the Rarkian army was standing around like this, the enemy was moving. He had no intention of wasting any more time. "Reorganize and depart immediately," he ordered Jacalrin, who was standing still like an idiot, and the knights ahead.

Jacalrin glanced at Reuyen with a bitter face, then ran as swiftly as the wind upon seeing Paseid's stare. The other knights glanced at Reuyen and all left to return to their posts.

"Sir Haldroff, if the scout sent to the exit of the valley returns and verifies that there is no additional ambush, move at your own discretion. I will call for a provisional meeting once we near the exit, before sunset."

In the midst of brisk footsteps of the horses echoing through the cool air, Evinbur rubbed his scruffy beard and nodded. All the while, he still could not take his eyes off Reuyen. He had given her some freedom up until then, since he thought it only right to treat her like a knight because she wore the brassard, at least temporarily, but now that she had said all those things, the situation had taken a turn.

The woman's eyes clung to Paseid's back like the hands of a child reaching for her mother.

Evinbur's stomach was churning. Paseid was right. If she were a spy, she would not have said such nonsense even a three-year-old would scoff at, so she most likely was closer to a mythomaniac than a spy. He still could not fathom how she knew about the small trail in the valley through which she'd led him, but all the other incidents made perfect sense if she were indeed a mythomaniac. If this hadn't happened during the execution of an operation, she could have lost her brassard.

The woman was still staring into the distance, looking like she could break down any minute like the foam on the distant ocean.

"I did warn you not to act on your impulses, Dame Detua."

Reuyen slowly turned her head. Her eyes soon slid away to the fort. They were unfocused, like another layer covered them.

Olzore. The land where she had lost countless generals, spent every last gold coin of Rarkalia as the price for the ferry to the afterworld, and loved and hated. The fort of her yearning she'd let float to a sky she could not reach. The site of the queen's grave.

Though the queen had been taken to Muiyadro and met her end on the scaffold, that had been the death of her body, the life she remorsefully let go. In truth, the queen had died the moment she was betrayed at this place. Thus, the grudges for her unattained deeds remained all over the valley like vines. Her own grudge came back to her in its entirety after two hundred years.

She was Reuyen, not Swan.

Repeating the reminder as if to brainwash herself was no longer effective.

Why had she set foot in Olzore again? Why had she come back to this battlefield? Myriad questions to herself roamed aimlessly in her head and died down without an answer.

Reuyen's eyes followed the man disappearing into a haze. He

was not Belbarote. Even though he was not Belbarote, she could not control and did not know how to handle the surge of viscid resentment and rage running through her. But she just looked at Paseid, internally begging, for she could not even reveal her rage. The noble Rionac swung by his side. The white butterfly in intaglio on the scabbard swallowed the dark shadows.

The soldiers reorganized their formation and started to advance into the valley at the knights' repeated orders. Evinbur finally snapped back to his senses at the sound of the army boots hitting the ground and realized that delaying any longer would anger Paseid.

Paseid was usually a polite and at times generous man outside of the battlefield, but on the battlefield, he was a cold man who did not even smile. Since he had already expressed his determination not to listen, he would not turn back. No matter how much the woman looked at him like that.

The distant flames gradually subsided, emitting black smoke and the smell of something burning. When Evinbur was about to give a stern order to the motionless Reuyen, her self-deprecating muttering mixed in the valley's wind.

"Bearing the proof of your oath on your waist," Reuyen whispered, her lips stiff with writhing rage. "What great loyalty, Brionake."

It wouldn't reach the man who was already in the far distance.

Commander-in-chief. She understood the weight of that title. He had logically kept everything at a distance and chosen not to make any hasty decisions. But now that she was the one being kept at a distance, the only assessment she had of him was that he was truly iron-willed.

How could he, wearing the snow-white sword the queen had granted him as a reward for his loyalty, looking so virtuous... No, who could she blame?

Reuyen placated her desperation and calmly exhaled. This was not the time to get trapped in these thoughts and resentments. If he couldn't believe her words, she would show him. She slowly started to move.

Sensing something strange, Evinbur carefully studied Reuyen. "Dame Detua."

As anticipated, she steered her horse after Paseid like she was bewitched, then suddenly drew the dagger hanging on her lower back for protection. Evinbur's eyes clearly caught the flashing metal. She started to increase her speed at the same time, and soon her horse started to gallop.

The sound of the swift and strong hooves of a fine horse raced ahead and pushed the advancing soldiers aside. Evinbur had an unusual hunch and yelled, "Duke Brionake!"

Evinbur's thundering shout echoed through the valley, urging the knights following Paseid to look back. At that moment, long, reddish-brown hair and the breath of a fierce horse danced before their eyes on the cool streak of wind.

When the knights realized what was happening and drew their swords, Reuyen already had the sharp dagger in her hand pointed toward Paseid's lower back. But not taken aback by this at all, Paseid drew Rionac at lightning speed and blocked her weapon.

Claaaang.

The two blades clashed.

"What is the meaning of this?" His eyes flashed at her.

The end of her dagger held tightly against Rionac and touched Paseid's belt. Reuyen only moved her eyes to take the belt into view, then looked straight into his black eyes with the same expression on her face. She put pressure on the hand holding the dagger.

Snip.

The precious leather belt around Paseid's waist snapped.

"Step back this instant, or you will die!"

The cold blades of the knights' swords touched her neck. After looking at each of them by only moving her eyes, Reuyen smiled faintly and muttered, "I have already put my worthless life in your hands, sir. Can I at least borrow your eyes for that?"

And then.

As soon as the knights reached out to take hold of her, she arched her back in a snap and took the snow-white scabbard tied to Paseid's belt. Before the knights holding their swords toward her could even react, she lowered her body tightly against Den's mane. She swung the white scabbard and struck all the swords pointed toward her away. A loud *clang* echoed in the valley.

The knights were flabbergasted. What she was holding was the scabbard of the historical Rionac, an heirloom and symbol of the Noble House Brionake. In fact, the sword and its scabbard were historical artifacts by themselves. There was no one unaware of their greatness.

The moment the knights hesitated, worried that they might leave a mark if they swung their swords carelessly, Reuyen did not miss the opportunity and ran through the soldiers at a whirlwind speed.

"Sir Calandok! Are you all right, sir?" Evinbur hurriedly came running and examined him.

Instead of answering, Paseid touched his empty waist.

It had all happened within a matter of seconds. The woman had broken the army's formation, holding Rionac. It was clearly a challenge.

A couple knights were running after her, but her horse didn't even have proper barding and was much swifter than the average horse.

"I will ring the alarm to catch—" started Evinbur.

"No."

Anger seeped into Paseid's cool voice. Going around in a large group in a place with rough geography such as this would actually hinder their pursuit. Moreover, it would be impossible to catch up with the woman's horse.

I have already put my worthless life in your hands, sir.

Yes, it seemed so to him as well.

He realized he could no longer disregard her. He had let her be despite all his suspicions, for he recognized her contribution and commended her for valuing her kin like she would herself, but that had turned out to be neglectful and resulted in this. So, this was his own doing.

"Sir Gran, take charge of the rear."

"Sir? Oh, yes, sir!"

Paseid whipped Rotsa. Before Evinbur could even stop worrying, Paseid was running in between the soldiers on the winding, rocky road, following Reuyen.

CHAPTER TWENTY

Disarrayed whispers reached the midsection of the cavalcade and echoed through the valley. Jacalrin, who was looking over those who were injured and counting the number of the dead from the now nearly extinguished fire, turned around at the sudden sound of hooves.

The first thing that came into his sight was Reuyen nimbly moving this way and that, so the soldiers didn't get kicked by her sleek horse. Soon, Paseid appeared with frightening eyes frightening and followed, whipping Rotsa.

It was truly an odd sight.

"What on earth... Hey! Where are you going?" Jacalrin forgot to finish his question.

A giant shadow moved over his head, and he automatically tilted his head back. Reuyen's trick of stepping on a large stone in the middle of the road and jumping over a man sitting on a horse was not even surprising at this point.

But that was not what mattered. Jacalrin took a moment to ruminate on what had just passed by his eyes.

A white stick? A scabbard?

Then Rotsa, who soon followed, did exactly what Den did and stepped on the stone to jump over Jacalrin's head.

"Paseid, what is going on?"

Neigh! Jacalrin winced and ducked at Rotsa's fierce cry coming from right above his head, then saw Paseid's empty waist and gasped. He wanted to stop Paseid and ask something, anything, but Paseid was long gone in the direction Reuyen ran to, completely neglecting Jacalrin.

What's all this about?

Things were going strangely in the rear, starting from the disarrayed formation of the soldiers. *Should I chase after them?* While he was looking around, seriously contemplating this, Evinbur led a couple of knights between the soldiers split on either side of the road. Instead of jumping over Jacalrin's head and making chills run down his spine like Reuyen or Paseid, Evinbur galloped swiftly past.

"Sir Haldroff, what is going on right now...!"

"Stay at your post, sir."

Even Evinbur coldly ran past him without an explanation.

Jacalrin followed the four knights, Evinbur, Paseid, and Reuyen, whom he couldn't even really see now, with his eyes. "Can't you at least tell me what's going on?"

She had lived two childhoods, two adolescences, and two adulthoods. All she did not have was the twilight of old age leading to death, the time when one organizes one's life in preparation for death. She could not enjoy that glorious and monumental time of life because she had been forced to atone in her former life, and because she was not of age yet in her present life. But the reason she did not consider it a shame was that most of her former life was intimate with death, covered in a redder hue than twilight.

She had lived amidst the royal family's covert fights and the nobles' struggle for power as a child, and amidst the battlefield where ruthless swords were swung as an adult. In a life where death was a symbol for weakness, she'd learned how to reflect on her life before a life-and-death crisis, how to let go of those who were leaving, and how to embrace the newcomers in her life.

The only thing she had not learned was how to give up on her hopes.

Men don't stop running until their whole world falls apart at a glimpse of hope.

The words she'd once all-knowingly said to Jess were also a sneer at herself. Those with hope did not allow themselves to give up, running straight into their devastating end. Thus, hope was a hideous, devilish thing. There was a man who once said the humane irony of poison making the drinker writhe in an unending thirst was beautiful, but the queen mocked him. In her life as an heir to the throne, giving up had meant giving up one's life. Hence, it was a beauty that could never be allowed. Even if one was driven to the edge of a cliff because of it.

Once, she had shined purely and innocently. The seven-year-old girl's world had turned upside down the moment she climbed on Dekallia. Since the day her incomplete mind got swallowed in parts by her memories, suspicions followed her around like shadows.

The townspeople had thought her dubious, and at times even her parents had looked at her strangely, like they could not understand her. Eivan had still given her a warm smile and praised her for her excellence, but that was all. She could easily figure out that the attitude Sidan took when he became emotional was the general attitude of the people toward her.

But Reuyen did not blame those suspicious of her. She did not have a way to explain herself, either. It was a time that had passed already. There was neither a way to make them understand her reflection of the past and the impact it had had on her current life, nor a need for that. So, she lived behind a mask, pretending to not notice the doubtful eyes of the world looking at her.

It passed. That's what memories do. Memories cannot overpower oblivion, and oblivion provides space for new experiences and perception, so they will be forgotten in time.

But the moment she was surrounded by the past, Reuyen revisited and repeated her past like a piece of writing. Those memories she had cleared away from her mind exploded like the gunpowder and overturned her reason.

And she realized. Not a single thing had changed.

She'd thought this was a different life. She'd mistaken this as a gift or an opportunity to hold the myriad regrets in her heart and live anew. But her nature remained the same in her new life. Her setting her feet back on the battlefield was the fault of her pride that could not bear the weight of the shackles Eivan had chained on her ankles, and the dichotomy between her past and present crumbling down before Olzore was the fault of a selfishness she could not cast away.

The queen who had dedicated her life to her country had changed the object of her passion and spent her life trying to climb one fort. Two hundred years later, the woman who held up her sword for her young, immature brother was once against risking her life to climb that fort. The consistency was nearly dreadful. And yet, her desperate yearning confirmed it.

This was the reason she went against the natural order of the world.

The reason she was reborn at a time of repeated war and headed to the battlefield like she was enchanted, and the reason these men set their routes around Olzore, were all for this. If this was the place that awakened the obsession of the monster sleeping a death-like sleep inside her, all the chains and shackles would break once she tore this place down. Once the past she regretted disappeared, the only thing left would be the present.

She left the set path and steered Den onto a narrow trail. Studying the trail, so unlike the one from her memory, Reuyen felt her heart beat like the drums.

Tightly grown tall trees angled this way and that, newly flourishing bushes, thickened leaves, stones that somehow moved. There wasn't a single thing that was exactly as it was in her memory. Thus, feeling like she was stranded in the middle of a wide ocean, she moved, using the fort as a reference point.

Even if she could not find the way, even if she forgot the once familiar marks, she could still see the entrance to the mine on the small path right under the fort in her head, as clear as day. That place that drank and swallowed countless people's sweat and blood was her last dream, which she could not let go.

The chilling wind smacked her face and blocked her way, but she did not stop. If she was born again, if she had returned for this, she had to remember. *So, remember.*

Reuyen ceaselessly studied her surroundings. The quickly

passing objects and landmarks had convoluted over the past two hundred years, but she moved her cold eyes without giving up.

The sound of Paseid's horse galloping came from right behind her. She had recognized the horse's fine blood from the get-go, but heavens, he was catching up to her fast. The closer the hooves rang, the harder it was to breathe with all the anxious tension. Feeling like she would be caught if she lessened her concentration, Reuyen couldn't even turn her head.

She just ran forward. She ran until she couldn't keep the fort in view just by looking up. Running around the edge of the valley's path laid out like a spider web, Reuyen sensed an almost murderous fury from Paseid, who was nearing her.

She felt the intaglio on the white scabbard she was barely holding on to.

Are you...going back to the battlefield, Your Majesty?

The voice of the one she longed for hung around her ears and whispered. Reuyen closed her watering eyes tightly, then opened them again.

The last. This is the last, Belbarote. This is the one debt you owed me. This was Rarke's desire. This was the final, lasting grudge of Rarkalia, the country you made to be no more. So... This is the last.

The day that wish comes true, the queen who became a monster driven by madness will disappear into history.

Not caring about the branches scratching her cheeks and her body bleeding from the new wounds, she ran across the trail that changed in its inclination and width. Then, she reached a familiar path and spotted an old sword covered with moss and stuck in a crack of stone. She stopped Den. Paseid, who was following right behind, hurriedly stopped Rotsa as well.

Reuyen jumped off the horse like she was bewitched. She stepped on the slippery moss with her hand on the rough stone for balance and started walking along the wall.

"Stop."

She could hear the armed knight's armor rustling close by.

Dismissing that sound, she looked around. It was here somewhere, but she could not remember where. The aged pebbles, stones, trees, and the bushes sat in the windless silence like they were mocking her.

She felt something hot bubbling inside her. The time that had passed was standing in her way.

As she fumbled along the stone wall covered with softened moss and weed, something violently grabbed her shoulder. Reuyen surrendered the snow-white scabbard she was holding to the force that sprang on her without a warning. She turned her head as weakly as a leaf in a storm and looked up at him. He wasn't even out of breath after chasing her all the way here. His icy eyes flashed with anger.

"I take it you will not object to immediate execution, since you declared your life was in my hands."

He pointed the frighteningly shiny blade against her. Reuyen clenched her teeth and backed away. Her back touched the moss on the wet valley wall. The coldness covered her neck like a snake's scale and froze her in her place.

She was this close, and the man was standing before her like an iron wall.

Den cried and galloped toward them, perhaps sensing the murderous intent of the one pointing the sword at his master. Then, Rotsa raised his front legs and blocked Den, snorting. Paseid glanced at the two horses ferociously confronting one another.

"You wore the brassard, though temporarily, so I will at least hear your last words."

"I will not evade my punishment. But...the mine is here, some-where near here, sir."

The nonsense did not stop even with a sword against her neck. But her voice was so desperate that he looked at the narrow path, then the towering fort, and then forward again.

Suddenly, his pitch-black eyes landed on the valley's wall right behind Reuyen's back. Reuyen gripped her beating heart. "The mine exists for sure, sir. This place is..."

Paseid's eyes were still fixed behind her. His lips opened for a moment. "This place is."

His words ended there. Rionac, pressed against her, did not move, either. Reuyen carefully tried to turn her head to follow his gaze.

Paseid suddenly dragged her away from the wall and pushed her. Reuyen stumbled a couple steps at the unforeseen violence. He stroked the moss on the wall with his palm. After scraping it away with his fingertips, he edged his sword and scratched the wall from top to bottom.

Skreeeeek. The soft stone crumbled down with the moss.

Reuyen's gaze moved to the wall. Before she could even say anything, the sound of hooves rang from not far away.

"Sir Calandok, are you all right...?"

Evinbur and four other knights came running over and stopped before them. They bore open wounds on their faces, like they'd had quite a hard time running along the rough trail. Evinbur approached to find Reuyen struggling to stand and Paseid frozen in his place a couple steps away from her, glaring at the wall. Evinbur hurriedly dismounted his horse. The other knights hastily surrounded her and pointed their swords at her.

Paseid was standing alone like a frozen statue and looking intensely at the valley's wall under the moss. A fuming knight ran over to Reuyen and growled, "Should I execute her, sir?" But there was no reply.

It was an odd silence.

Evinbur realized that Paseid's and Reuyen's eyes were fixed on the same place, and turned around to see what they were seeing. The old knight let out a groan.

"What is this, sir?"

Paseid slowly turned his head and looked down at the valley covered in a dark-green hue. Moss growing in odd shapes popped out. A faint design covered the valley's wall, grown over with moss. It was none other than the numbers and characters of the Royal House of Rarkalia.

Wind carrying a moist scent blew from somewhere. A knight who was patrolling the area in case there was an enemy hiding somewhere shouted, "Sir, there's something here, sir."

"Go and check."

Another knight rode off on his horse.

Twenty steps or so behind Reuyen's back, moist wind was coming out from in between the valley's walls. When two of the tense knights cleared the debris of rotten and broken trees and bushes, a small chasm where four fully grown men could barely stand next to one another revealed itself.

"It appears to be…an entrance to what it seems to be a cave, sir!" the flustered knight shouted.

Paseid's eyes fell on the pale face of the woman.

Only after his eyes were solely on her did Reuyen smile. Her eyes started to water. But this was not the time to shed tears yet. Calming the burst of emotions, she slowly fell to her knees.

"Please, look, sir."

Look with your eyes.

The last struggle of the foolish queen.

CHAPTER TWENTY-ONE

Many knights, including the commanders who were standing by, were called to the entrance to the mine. Jacalrin was among those who'd just arrived. He found Reuyen surrounded by the knights and tilted his head questioningly again.

He was certain some kind of event must have happened, considering how fiercely Paseid chased after her, but their faces and the atmosphere were ever so tranquil. Jacalrin hopped off his horse and wobbled over.

"What is this place, sir? Why did you order us to convene here when we don't have much time…?"

Jacalrin's frustrated voice trailed off as he looked. Something felt oddly artificial. The area was not that different from the other areas in the valley at first glance, but something kept bugging him. If he had to choose the strangest sight of all, it was the knights feeling around the valley's walls.

What's up with them?

Jacalrin thought for a second that the knights who left and arrived before him had all gone mad together. To someone who did not have a clue as to what was going on, the sight was quite peculiar.

"Sir Haldroff? Can't you please tell me what is going on?"

"Look with your own eyes."

Standing firm in his place and gazing at the entrance to the small, dark cave, Evinbur nodded to Jacalrin. Jacalrin looked at the soft walls of the valley. There was nothing special about the wall. Jacalrin approached the wall, put his hands on his back for support, and stretched his neck, cursorily scanning. Then he froze.

Jacalrin quacked like a surprised goose. "Whoa. What are the royal characters doing here?"

Generally, the characters of Rarkalia were used very rarely in letters between high nobles and royals, including royal administrative tasks. Ordinary knights and lower-ranking nobles could not interpret the characters. But Jacalrin was a Chesa.

"Quiet. These are not the royal characters, but the characters of Rarkalia," said Paseid.

"Well, the name really doesn't matter, now, does it? Why are they in Olzore Valley? Technically speaking, this cliff of the valley is all Morganaan territory."

Jacalrin squirmed, then buried his face in the wall with cathartic astonishment. Then he read without even blinking. Those were all numbers, Rarkalia's intaglio characters for counting days: *Janto, ga, beud, teboit, bel, robage...*

It was an assembly of something they were counting.

Why would something like this...?

Then, finally, Jacalrin's eyes landed on Reuyen, standing noiselessly amongst the knights. She looked calm, despite her disheveled appearance, and turned her head toward him like she was drawn to his eyes. Her reddish eyes pierced Jacalrin's. Like someone who had experienced all there was to the world, like she wasn't afraid at all of being surrounded by the knights' swords...

"The scouts came back out, sir!"

Jacalrin turned around at the sudden commotion and looked over at the guard anxiously pacing at the entrance of the cave. A small, dark crevice in the wall came into his view. He recalled the woman claiming that there was a mine and froze like a rod replaced his spine.

The scouting knights who had gone inside with torches to check the narrow mine came back out. As soon as the clamor of their armor could be heard outside the entrance, the anxious tension of those waiting for them subsided.

The scout who came out first ran over to Paseid, standing not far from the entrance. He paused for a moment, but Evinbur urged him on, running out of patience.

"Promptly report to the commander," Evinbur said.

"Oh, oh, yes, sir! First, the cave is narrow at first, but once you move twenty-three steps in, it widens rapidly. And if you walk a bit more along the way—"

"What waits there?"

"I'm not sure if I can say it like this, sir, but there is an empty space as wide as the guard post in the capital."

"Is it naturally made?"

"No, sir. I do not know the specific details of how it came to be, but I can assure you that it is manmade."

Whispers rose. Paseid tightened his hands into fists at the spine-chilling situation. Unless those in Olzore were out of their minds, they would not have dug this kind of a cave right under the valley holding up their fort.

"We could not look around the whole area because the air inside was too damp and the cave itself is quite large, but...there were wooden columns that have rotted away, and the ones holding the ceiling up right now are natural stone columns, sir. And...show it."

One of the other knights who'd gone inside as a scout hurriedly approached and presented a rusty sword, a soiled helmet, and a pauldron tattered with age.

Paseid's lowered eyes closely scanned them. His mouth clamped shut, then faintly trembled.

Jacalrin, who was walking toward them after losing interest in the valley walls, froze upon finding the armor.

At long last, someone's voice as small and faint as a groan said, "Of Rarke."

Evinbur, who was trying to calm himself, took the rusty, delicate sword in his hands, trembling from the shock, not knowing what to do. The sword had withered away with time and no longer held its shape, but they could still discern the curved blade and the shape of the edge, and the bay leaf design ingrained on the helmet. This, in addition to the characters of Rarkalia covering the walls of the valley, led them to a certain conclusion.

Evinbur let out a sigh. "These are in the style of the Rarkian army from at least a hundred and fifty years ago, sir."

All bit their tongues to silence.

Fort Olzore sent out scouts a few times to observe what the Rarkian army was doing. But the Rarkian army simply kept an eye on them, not budging at all from their places.

The soldiers at the fort made their own decision. Since the Rarkian army had witnessed the Olzorean army leaving, they knew they might change their target to the fort. So, the Olzoreans pulled up their drawbridge and sneered at them. Rarke would not pass even the completely emptied Olzore.

But the actual situation was quite different from their expectations.

The Rarkian soldiers were perplexed, just like them. This stall was not due to some great operation, but simply to the commanding knights being summoned elsewhere.

The only cause of this they could think of was the army that had just left the fort. No attack came from the enemy. The soldiers were having a sort of break time, engaging themselves with worries and concerns as varied as those of the fort's mythomaniacs. They blankly stared at the small trail in the valley where all the knights had gone.

Inside the valley, standing at a bit of a distance from the entrance to the mine to look at the valley's wall as a whole, Paseid raised his hand to stop Evinbur from approaching him. He was certain. The entire area where the valley's walls decreased in height was covered with designs of Rarkalia.

He opened his mouth, but instead of making a sound, he glared at Reuyen, kneeling in the center of the circle of knights. She was now sitting still and not causing any more trouble, but she showed no signs of being intimidated. Paseid tightened his fists. He should rightfully threaten her to explain this situation immediately. But Paseid knew there would be no use in that.

"Tear it down, sir," she said. "Then the enemy's operation will crumble from the core, and the glory of Olzore's fall will solely belong to you."

"What are you?"

"You can doubt my identity, sir. If you wish, I will take off this brassard right this second. But as a wise commander, make the right decision, sir. At a time when Morganaan forces are attempting a feint attack to ambush, is it not clear what will be of benefit to Rarke and what of detriment? I swear, sir, I have never in my life thought of bringing harm to Rarke. *Saturga guire Rarke.*"

For Rarke.

Paseid froze at the phrase she nonchalantly added at the end of her argument. *Saturga guire Rarke.* It was an ancient Rarkian phrase dating back to the Rarkalia Dynasty that the modern nobles used as an oath to prove their loyalty.

"How do you know that phrase?"

"Even commoners have ears, sir."

That was hard to believe.

From then on, all she did was diligently give vague answers to his questions that were more like orders. *Was it by chance that you came here? No, sir. How did you know? By chance... I heard from a traveler passing through our town.* Absolutely ridiculous replies. She appeased him with cunningly disguised politeness on important matters, and when he ordered further explanation, she dismissed him by saying that she did not know. There wasn't enough time to properly hold a questioning to make the woman talk, nor did the current situation allow for such luxury.

But from the strange cave came old artifacts of Rarkalia, and the whole wall was covered with Rarkalian characters, so he couldn't just dismiss this, either. In the unexpected situation, the knights fretted when even Paseid went silent, lost in thought.

When they had barely enough time to run out of the valley, a meeting was called. Most of the knights with important duties had already been summoned there, so the meeting ensued right where they were. There were no scribes, tables, or chairs, but the solemnness and the tension were higher than ever.

Jacalrin, who was making a fuss like a calf with his bum on fire, delightedly fidgeted with the old sword and argued like he was actually excited about this. "I think there's a chance. We have eighteen carriages of gunpowder remaining. With that, I could even blow up our mansion."

"But, Sir Chesa, we are in the midst of a joint operation with the main camp."

"Yes, we are, but don't you think it would be better to crush the symbolic meaning of Olzore than to demolish Rovantis's army in the long run?"

"If things go wrong, we will fail in the operation to ambush Ishas, and Olzore will stand as strong as ever. On top of that, we do not even know how this mine came to be…"

"Did she say anything?" Jacalrin nodded at Reuyen, who was closely watched by the knights. A fraction of those present knew that Reuyen had led Rarke to this cave.

Glancing at Reuyen, Evinbur shook his head and continued the discussion. "We have not gone deep enough to know this for sure, but it could be a trap. A beacon does not shine on its own base, true, but Olzore could not have possibly not known about this existing right underneath their fort."

"Who cares? If there are enemies hiding in there, we'll win without having to swing our swords. And think about it! If Olzore collapses, the emperor of Morgana will definitely not have a good night's sleep for days. Then he'll never dare to speak ridiculously again."

The last sentence was more like a grumble to himself. But no one admonished him, for there wasn't a person who did not know what ridiculous thing Jacalrin was referring to.

"May I say a word to you, sirs?" said a knight. "If we do succeed, it will affect the tributaries of Morgana as well."

Evinbur shook his head. "We cannot be sure it will succeed in the current situation."

"I cannot support Sir Newt's statement, either," another knight agreed. "This is neither the time nor the place to be doing this. I do not know how this came to be, but I do not think we should venture into the unknown right now."

"I agree. I believe it's absurd that Olzore is unaware of this kind of cave forming. It's most likely a trap."

Various opinions poured out. Thinking that this wasn't going to end easily, Jacalrin pounded on his lower back, which ached

habitually. His voice diminished to a whisper. "I mean, it's good
to be on guard, but it doesn't make sense that this is a trap,
don't you think? It's been, what, at least a hundred and fifty
years? Two hundred years? Considering that the last battle at
Olzore on record was during the reign of the tyrant of
Rarkalia."

The knights clamped their mouths shut at once at Jacalrin's
simply spoken words.

The last battle at Olzore. There was no one in Rarke who cheerfully talked about that subject, but there barely was anyone who did
not know about it, either.

Since the queen of Rarkalia had met her end after the long
battle against Olzore, no one had dared to covet the fort. The queen
who'd swallowed the entire north and made the rough savages in
the west swear their loyalties to her had fallen to her knees with
tears and blood before Olzore. So, who would ever be brave
enough to aim their sword at the impregnable fort?

To Rarke, Olzore was a shame they wanted to let disappear into
history, and hence they'd never even engaged in a small battle
again. Thus, they knew very well what the meaning of Jacalrin's
question was.

The knights struggled to answer.

It was Evinbur who finally ordered the situation back. He
sternly scolded Jacalrin. "Sir Chesa, please discuss such digressions
at another time. We cannot be sure of anything. Even if we talk the
day away, the final decision will come from our commander-in-
chief."

All eyes were on Paseid now. Seeing his coolly composed face,
they realized how overly excited they were.

Jacalrin opened his mouth. "Sir, don't you think that there's no
way they would dig a trap that basically is like digging their own
graves? Olzore is a fort impeccably defended by this valley alone.
It's preposterous to think that they would create a trap that would
shake their very foundation. Remember what the scouts reported
after examining the area. They said that if there are more areas as
weak as that one, a certain impact will make at least a part of the
valley crumble. Even if only the tip crumbles, half the fort will go
with it, sir."

"But if that were true, we wouldn't have to risk such danger at this moment, would we, Sir Chesa?" said another knight.

"There will be other opportunities in the future, but this is a chance to crush the army that just ran off, don't you think? No damage on our part at all, no need to engage in battle, and Rovantis's army will take the blow and fall apart."

"To be so certain of that, sir, is a bit..."

The longer the knights' discussion continued, the more chaotic and louder it became.

Reuyen, on the other hand, became calmer, like she was sinking into a swamp the more agitated their voices became. She slowly blinked and looked over at those disputing one another.

The knights had already lost their interest in her. Even the ones surrounding her had their eyes fixed on their superiors quarrelling, not knowing what to do.

Reuyen calmed her anxious mind. She wasn't keeping to herself because she wanted to keep to herself. She knew she couldn't force her opinion on the knights when they hadn't withdrawn their suspicions about her, so she pushed down all the things trying to come out and simply waited. Then, Paseid's eyes reached her.

"You are considering my suggestion, right, commander-in-chief, sir?" Jacalrin yelled.

Though all the other knights frowned upon this, Paseid honestly agreed with Jacalrin's proposal. It seemed to him that the mine was a massive secret space someone had created with the intention of undermining the fort. Saying that it was a trap was an assumption without logical proof. But the problem was, he could not figure out the true identity or the intentions of the woman.

Just how did she know?

"Sir Calandok, there may be some damage, but we will be able to reach the exit right after sundown if we move now," a knight reported directly to Paseid.

Paseid still had his eyes fixed on Reuyen.

Reuyen Detua.

The talent of the woman was great enough to overwhelm knights. There was too many a strange thing about her to just overlook that as an inborn talent. Ever since Reuyen barged into the camp, something had gone wrong.

He did intend to ordain her as a temporary knight, not an official one, but it was not conventional to hold an ordination during war in the first place. Having Evinbur keep an eye on her was unconventional too. Even though he'd volunteered for the job, he was one of the commanders in charge of the army, not someone responsible for small matters such as keeping watch on a suspicious individual.

Moreover, the biggest problem caused by Reuyen was military rules. Even now, this woman pointed a sword at him, the commander-in-chief. Motivated by personal and private reasons or not, a woman who had intentionally pointed a sword at his back still lived, and most of the knights did not think this odd. They should have raised their voices to argue why she still lived, but they were all too preoccupied with the sudden appearance of the mine.

But of course, Paseid had terminated that thought for now as well, so he could not blame them. Now that he started thinking back, there were quite a few suspicious things about her. The doubt that was cast aside snowballed until he could not ignore it anymore.

Was killing Count Asvar, one of Rovantis's generals, and requesting a brassard a part of her calculation? Had this woman schemed with Olzore? Was she trying to stall them right now? Finally, reaching that absurd question, Paseid admitted he needed to calm himself down.

She said that it only mattered if someone was an enemy or a friend on a battlefield. And she claimed she was a friend. But she was too strange to be considered a friend. If she were a loyal child of Rarke, she would not have dared to even think about pointing a sword at him. Even if she did not have the intention to murder.

Then was she an enemy? He couldn't consider an enemy that quickly, either. The will to investigate every little thing about her and bring them to light, and the thought that he could not allow her to do as she wished anymore once the operation came to a conclusion, solidified in his head.

"Sir, what should we…"

The spirit of the gathered knights waned at the speed of the setting sun.

The fort was not a severe threat, since most of it had just

dispatched most of its soldiers, but Paseid was not unaware of the reason for their anxiety. He let go of the digressions and organized his thoughts.

His job as the commander-in-chief was to create maximum damage to their enemies with minimal damage on his part.

Regardless of who she really was, and however she'd come to know of the mine, the cave could not be seen as a trap. Even the men who had scouted the area concluded that the mine directly underneath the fort was not that solid. He had enough gunpowder to set a small castle ablaze. If he poured all of that in this to take down Olzore, the fort's army that had left their nest to attempt a feint operation would return, and the damage on his part would amount to zero. He would not be able to enter the fort without shedding blood, but he could take it without shedding blood.

Moreover, if Morgana lost the fort, it would be equal to losing seven hundred and fifty years' worth of history for them. If that could be so, it would surely wash away the shame in Rarkian history and more. The only problem was what would happen if the gunpowder they'd transported here did not have any impact on the valley.

Reuyen's clear, dark-red eyes looked into his black ones. Paseid could easily read the anxiety revealed in them.

"I do not think this is a matter we can suddenly decide upon after a discussion, Sir Ratte," said one of the knights. "No one can take the responsibility of the results if the situation does not turn out as expected."

"This seems to be a waste of time as well," said another. "Why don't we just proceed as planned…"

Reuyen calmed her throat, which was boiling as if she'd just swallowed a flame.

Those country bumpkins.

The discussion that kept digressing continued endlessly. They were trying to spare themselves from the punishment that would follow if the plan failed; it was so plain that it didn't even make Reuyen burst into laughter. If they had brains, they would know how effective giving the fort unredeemable damage at this point would be, and yet they were cowering.

Reuyen started to struggle to hide her anxiety. Why did Paseid remain silent? Even Jacalrin, who was strongly arguing his point, shut his mouth at Evinbur's stern reproach, leaving Reuyen even more nervous.

She'd already done all she could do. She'd run, risking her life, and led them here. And now she was waiting for their decision.

Her eyes landed on Paseid. She did recall Belbarote at the sight of him, but if she actually thought about it, she did not know the nature of that man with the same black hair. She simply assumed he would have the mind and clear vision befitting a man who became a commander-in-chief at such a young age. Hearing that he was Brionake's blood might have heightened her expectation of him as well.

What could she do if he cared about sparing himself like the others? She couldn't read anything in those enigmatic, pitch-black eyes, a still gaze where acceptance, denial, and even flaming fury faded away.

Soon, he averted his eyes from her. Her heart skipped a beat at the anxiety rooted in a clear cause. Reuyen opened her mouth for a moment, feeling a strong urge to say something, anything.

Then, Paseid, who had remained silent all along, opened his mouth first. "Your words bear truth in them, sirs."

It was an unwavering voice, like the anchor of a ship.

Her expectations and wishes shattered to pieces under the weight of his words. What to do now? She dropped her head at last like a reed bent at its waist.

"But...this is also worth attempting."

Reuyen pulled her head up.

"All retreat with the rear as the front."

CHAPTER TWENTY-TWO

Paseid's order was absolute.

The knights shut their mouths and ordered the men to retreat. Naturally, a small battle ensued between the fraction of the Olzorean army standing by in defense formation in front of the valley and the Rarkian army. They fought back the Rarkians coming back out for a short while, then ran off toward the hill, and the Rarkian army stopped the march and assembled where they were stationed.

At last, the sun set when they were at the entrance to the valley. The knights, who were furtively skeptical of Paseid's decision, took off their helmets and gazed at the fort glistening in the last sunlight. This was irrevocable.

"Predicted duration?" asked Paseid.

"Sir Chesa says he can finish all preparations before midnight, sir."

The air surrounding the fort was quite uneasy as well. Their enemy's wondering made sense, since the Rarkian army that had suddenly backed out of the valley were neither pursuing the Morganaan army nor invading the fort, but remaining still. The Rarkians shooed away the fort's scouts a couple times by threatening to shoot.

Paseid stood in the middle of the field blanketed with dry air and gazed at the flag fluttering in the valley's wind, which was starting to change direction.

The dark night crept over the horizon. Confirming that Jacalrin, who was in charge of gunpowder and other military supplies, had evacuated the valley, Paseid ordered the knight standing next to him. "Send a messenger to the general of the fort to come out if he wishes to avoid meaningless losses."

The knight of Rarke ran over to the fort's hill. But the fort sneered at their mercy.

When the moon hung high up in the sky, Paseid's last orders were made.

"Sir Ratte and Sir Evinbur will protect the rear. When the third beacon lights up, they will return. We will not miss that chance and will block their way. Sir Chesa, stand by at the following corps."

The commanders of each corps moved to their posts at once. Then, they relayed the changed plans: the commanders to the colonels, the colonels to the captains, and the captains to the hundreds and thousands of infantrymen. In the situation where the initial plan was stopped, the newly relayed order shook the Rarkian army with clear anxiety and distrust.

Even Jacalrin, who strongly argued his point while not considering failure as an option, swallowed with tension.

"Shall we begin, sir?"

Paseid looked around. "The woman?"

"Over there."

Due to the concern that she would do something unexpected again if she were left with Den, Reuyen was standing at the front of the corps stationed on the field, tied up and looking up at the fort.

The dark and damp entrance to the valley that had held up the fort for hundreds of years threatened them with its chasm darker than ever. The stars and the moon shed pieces of their light onto the night. Like a painting frozen in time, she took the valley and the fort into sight.

"Sound the signal."

The atmosphere, spotted with the suffocating silence and anxiety, tore with a fierce roar at Paseid's gesture.

The blow of the horn went through the field and valley at a chilling speed, like it was going to pierce through the entire world.

When tens of trumpets started to sing at the same time, the fort lit up even more intensely.

Olzore sent out soldiers to the front and the rear of the fort in an effort to prepare for the Rarkians' infiltration, and stationed archers to defend themselves with belligerence. But the Rarkian soldiers did not move. Not long after, a gong started to ring out from inside the valley. The knights who were assigned the final duty of installing and lighting the gunpowder ran out with the gong signaling retreat. The Rarkian soldiers held their breaths.

As the wind slid across the field toward the valley, the night filled with an unidentifiable anxiety. The moment of time when the white flag of the Royal House Brionake fluttered and reflected the starlight. The time when the nearing sound of drums and hooves started to sound of reality.

The valley cried with the tearing wind.

The sound of the creased skies crushing the stones and rocks overwhelmed them.

It was much like the sound of the earth splitting apart, its axis shattering. The pandemonium of the ground sinking down intensified and echoed throughout the valley like the scream of the devil. They couldn't see a single flicker of light or smell a hint of gunpowder, but everyone in the Rarkian army knew.

The carriages and the gunpowder contained in them must have blasted some corner in the valley into bits. That was the reason they'd overturned the entire operation to its core.

Everyone fixed their eyes on the entrance of the valley, where not even the rays of light shining from the dark night sky above, clear without a single cloud, could infiltrate, all thinking the same thing. Paseid sat on Rotsa and waited in silence. Evinbur tightly shut his eyes, and Jacalrin gulped and took in the view that could very well be their last.

Amidst all the stillness, Reuyen slowly stepped forward. Forward, forward, so she could see even the tiniest bit closer. She was stopped by the guards watching her before she could take another step, but even one step felt significant to her.

The gong stopped ringing and the knights stopped galloping to look back. Dearly waiting for the arrogant men looking over them while sitting atop that fort to run out, screaming. Not showing their hearts losing their strength and trembling just from looking at it. *Boo-boom.* The clamor of the valley's body writhing resounded.

Fall. Fall, Reuyen invoked, as the fierce cry of the earth pierced her ears.

But the echo of the explosion disappeared into the night wind. Smoke rose from afar, and flames blazed and faded.

The fort stood as before.

A long time passed, to the point of boredom. Jacalrin's face slowly stiffened at the unchanged majesty of the steadfast valley. Even Evinbur, who did in fact have some expectations, looked around, unable to hide his perplexity.

Did it fail? What happens now?

The soldiers' sharp shock and anxiety became apparent enough to prick one's skin. Evinbur looked back at the valley once more, at a loss for words, and approached Paseid. "Sir Calandok, now what should we do?"

They couldn't go back to the initial operation now, either. There wasn't enough time, and the gunpowder that was to be used as a signal was now all gone.

Paseid cut off the confusion, still standing motionlessly. "We wait."

Even so, the knights started to reveal their frustration. Eighteen carriages of gunpowder. As Jacalrin had so confidently guaranteed, that was enough explosives to shatter a small mansion to bits. Their ears remembered the great, thundering roar that had pierced the valley, and their feet recalled the tremble of the earth.

But at last, the valley boasting its solidity impaled their hearts. Several faces displayed signs of extreme regret as they witnessed this tragic event, but they dared not speak to Paseid and just stomped the ground where they stood.

"Now what do we…"

Stunned, Reuyen tightened her fists and simply watched.

Did something go wrong? Did they not properly carry out their duties? Everything froze like it was turning into stone except her panting lungs.

Indistinct remorse surged.

Alas, was it not meant to be? She had forced hundreds of her people to their deaths, inflicted pain on thousands of them, and devoted years of time only to tear down that one thing. Was her purpose never attainable? Her unending obsession added yet another weight of sin to her shoulders.

Once again, this fool of a woman...

The moonlight cast long shadows beneath her eyelashes, and in those, her bloodshot eyes were looking up at the fort like it had stolen her soul.

The lights on the fort shone brightly as if to mock them.

When the moon started to wane at last, even Jacalrin started to bounce around anxiously. He rebuked and threatened the knights who were assigned the duty of lighting the gunpowder. But before the moon completely disappeared into the horizon, even Jacalrin, who had strongly supported Reuyen, threw in the towel.

It had failed.

Negative sentiment smeared the bitter silence. At last, a knight carefully approached and spoke. "Sir Calandok...it seems as though the best thing to do next is to forego the fort and turn the army back to destroy the Olzorean army heading to the main camp, sir—"

"We wait." Paseid cut him off at once. Then he looked back at the woman standing weakly, like she could crumble away at any second under the moonlight. She was as pale as the skin of a corpse. Her eyes were fixed on the top of the fort, not even moving an inch. Her scrunched-up face seemed to threaten to burst into tears at any moment.

Moments of silence worse than the stench of death passed. The weight of failure, the confusion of the operation that now was all befuddled, and the anxiety that they did not know what was to come in the future overwhelmed the Rarkians to the tips of their hands and feet. But their commander-in-chief ordered silence, so they hid all their emotions inside and dropped their heads.

And when the sun colored the edge of the sky touching the horizon into red, soaring up into the sky once more after going around the earth...

Crack.

A strange sound started to ring from afar. It was a noise like a thick sledge breaking into two.

The Rarkians, feeling miserable as the red light touched their cheeks, raised their tired heads. Jacalrin's voice, spitting out mutters of curses at Olzore, dispirited like a beaten dog, stopped.

And.

It began with a small rock rolling off the edge of the valley holding up the fort.

With a racket of rocks breaking, down came the small debris like waves of sand, then larger rocks tumbled down with the landslide, causing a great tumult.

While everyone held their breaths with shock and expectation, two more beacons suddenly lit up in bright red on top of the fort. The unprecedented, spine-chilling commotion broke the valley in half. Then a massive stone that broke off got trapped between the narrow cliffs of the valley and weighed down the soft stone wall with another great clamor.

The fort tilted like it was being sliced out of the scenery. Soon, parts of the impregnable walls built sturdily around the fort broke off like pieces of paper. The beacon that fell with the walls poured out flames like a waterfall, sending sparks everywhere. Fire started to light up here and there.

The plain red flag signaling an emergency soared up to the tip of the fort, and the gates opened. The people gushing out of them were easily over a thousand. But they were mostly unarmed civilians, for they had sent out most of their soldiers already.

One of the people who ran out, startled by the shaking nest, was the general of the fort.

The Rarkians could neither cheer nor relax. They simply engraved the hundreds of years of history crumbling down like a sandcastle in their trembling hearts. Paseid let out a dry sigh, clamped his lips, and then, with Rionac tightly held in his hands, gave his order.

"Sir Chesa, take Sir Eden and stand by below the hill. Ready for combat to overcome the remaining defense force of Olzore and capture the general of the fort alive."

Jacalrin, who had been as dispirited as a dead weed, ran off in ineffable delight, crying out something unintelligible.

Two hundred years' worth of tears welled up in Reuyen's eyes, reddened with the faint light of dusk.

That day, around sunbreak, Fort Olzore split in half with the collapse of the valley. Without even a proper battle, the Rarkian army captured the general and the high officials of the fort, as well as about five hundred of Morgana's civilian prisoners. But the general of Olzore, who became the last symbol of hundreds of years of history, came down the hill and honorably took his own life.

Fort Olzore.

The unconquerable legend thus met its end.

CHAPTER TWENTY-THREE

Most of the soldiers still could not believe even after witnessing with their own eyes the walls of the impregnable fort bending, snapping, and covering the area with their debris. One of those who quickly came back to his senses cried, deeply affected by seeing the historic event take place before his eyes, and another just rubbed his eyes at this preposterous situation, dumbstruck.

The eminence of the fort that stood strong for over seven hundred and fifty years without even a single crack crumbled like a sandcastle because of a couple carriages of gunpowder. Buzzing engulfed the army. The Rarkian soldiers dared not even move a single step toward the valley as it dropped pieces of its flesh, but merely glanced around.

And time began moving again.

"Do not delay."

At their commander's orders, the soldiers spent the whole day capturing or watching the people of Olzore and organizing all the documents they confiscated from the boxes and shelves in the fort, as well as the top secret Morganaan documents of the high officials of the fort.

"We just sent a second messenger to the main camp, sir."

"We have confiscated the letters to and from the imperial family of Morgana, sir. They are in code, so immediate decrypting seems impossible."

A series of reports from those who had not calmed their excitement yet ensued. There was no sign of fatigue in the faces of those who did not sleep a wink last night. It seemed as though the commanders and the lowest soldiers alike had surrendered themselves to utter delight and excitement. Moreover, they could not even attempt to hide the infinite respect and admiration they had for their commander's wisdom that toppled down the fort without shedding a single drop of blood.

One of them became rather smug at all this. It was Jacalrin. He ran about like a flying squirrel and puffed his chest whenever he locked eyes with another knight, saying, "See? What did I tell you!" Evinbur just smiled awkwardly at him. The old knight hadn't even expected to see such a sight in his life, so he was quite moved as well.

Paseid, on the other hand, looked disgruntled. "Do not relieve yet. Send scouts to the road leading to the main camp and report the enemy's movement."

Many wondered about Paseid not even seeming to take pleasure in this much of a victory, but no one dared to ask aloud.

"The body of the general?"

"I have rested it in the regular army tent with the other bodies. Would you like to see it, sir?"

"Later."

"Sir Calandok, the scouts have returned, sir. They say they just verified the Olzorean army's return. It seems like they will arrive here again by tomorrow at noon."

"Let them know of the general's death and prepare for battle. We will ambush them from three points with the lightly armed cavalry in the front, surround them, and overpower them."

"Yes, sir."

Most of the issues came to a close after sundown.

The busy footsteps and the sound of metal clanging still resounded everywhere, but at least the excited shouts, happy screams, and questioning of their own eyes had ceased. Feeding the tired Rotsa some hay in the little time he had made, Paseid looked once again at the unbelievable sight.

Morganaan prisoners locked up in their camps scattered around the area, terrified. The entrance to the valley was covered with mounds of debris. He had undertaken a risky attempt relying on an uncertain possibility and succeeded. The collapse of Olzore. This was an utter blessing for Rarke. With this, the predicted path of the Great Battle against Morgana would change drastically. They might even have to redraw the map.

Paseid suddenly recalled the presence of the woman, like that of a splinter in the tip of a finger.

The woman who'd stirred his vanity, seducing him, telling that all would be his achievement. That made it even more unpleasant. He simply had forgotten for a brief moment, spending the past day swamped with organizing the aftermath of the event. He looked over at the knights busily running to and fro to reorganize the army, and studied each of them. The woman was not within his view, at least.

Evinbur was off to execute the grave mission of questioning the high officials of Olzore who were now their prisoners, and Jacalrin left to look around the valley that now settled in its new form after the disintegration. Paseid did not know under which knight's supervision she was residing.

After thinking for a bit, he found a knight who followed Evinbur and asked, "Where is Reuyen Detua?"

"She has been sent to a temporary tent because she said she was not feeling well, sir."

"Bring her here."

But the knight who returned after a long while dropped his head, dumbfounded.

It was unbelievable. She was gone.

How, when, and to where had she run off?

Realizing her absence only after the supreme commander's orders, the soldiers started running about and searching every-where. As a nimble woman of petite figure, she should've been easy to spot amongst the muscular men, but she was nowhere to be found. Even by the time their shadows elongated like tall reeds, chased by the sun, no one found her.

The valley shined with the waning red light. Paseid recalled the face of the woman looking up at the fort like she was at death's door.

The knights stood with their backs against a valley as lofty as the arrogance of Guitella, the general of Fort Olzore, and grew glum and dark at the funeral. The tired mourners gathered where the dead of the camp were laid down in peace and revealed the deep pain of the bereaved in their eyes. The torch battling the dark with its sparking flames seemed to weep in the bleak dusk.

The knights that gathered around one corpse among many stood in silence, their hearts heavy with grief.

"Her Majesty has arrived."

"Make way."

Before they could even step aside at the sudden call of a soldier, a small woman, fully armed, walked through the crowd of them and stood in front of the corpse.

"Your Majesty."

Closely following the queen, Peijak stopped the knights who were about to greet her. Looking at her cold, emotionless blue eyes, the knights lowered their heads. A suffocating silence ensued.

Briskly coming to a stop, the queen took off her helmet. The dark-red hair hiding in the rigid helmet flowed down. Brushing her hair that glistened an even redder hue in the torchlight, the queen closed her mouth at a sight she never wished for.

Her clear blue eyes lingered on the deep, punctured wound in the corpse's cheek.

"Have you left this time?"

The voice flowing out of her lips showed no signs of grief. The queen put her hand out at Peijak. Then Peijak quietly placed a gold coin on her palm. She winced at the sensation of the cold coin, then gripped it tightly.

Since her dispatch, the funeral ritual had become not that strange a sight. With her eyes looking at him sunk with grief, the queen wordlessly leaned over. Her hair hanging long touched the cold, stiff cheek of the corpse.

"Dera Notjin Cananso."

The queen caressed the brutishly exposed wound of the corpse, then forced the cold, stiff lips open and carefully pushed in the round gold coin with the intaglio of a bay tree under the tongue. She then quietly uttered her goodbye.

"Nuadga...Muin janlisas guire Rarkaddanya."

Nuadga, guide him to the utopia with this glory as the price.

The simple yet generous funeral ritual and oration continued. Another man who had dedicated himself to royalty had just left on a journey of no return to the eternal land. The queen slowly caressed the corpse's forehead, nose, then either cheek, like she was drawing a cross.

"Forgive me, Your Majesty."

The one knight who'd survived the battle, Sir Cananso, died kneeling with guilt.

The queen raised her body with ice-cold eyes. She had lost many generals at Olzore alone. More than double the number of commoners that had gone on before them to the world of self-annihilation called death. She looked around the knights' lowered heads, then looked down at the knight on all fours with his forehead so low that it seemed like it might touch the ground any minute.

The man's tears of anger were wetting the dirt floor. The infuriated blue eyes flashed through the hair dancing on the cold wind blowing from the valley.

"Who allowed you those tears?"

"It's all my fault, Your Majesty."

"We are carrying burdens of those who have left before us. If you wish to grieve, slay all the enemies who have undone him so first, then grieve. The tears you are daring to shed right now are mere pity. Who allowed you to dare to pity a fierce general of Rarke?"

How could they not know the shame and the sadness and the anger welling up under her cold mask? She was pushing herself with her sternness that did not allow even a single tear.

Hence, she was stronger and more resistant than any other man, and the knights kneeled one by one, feeling a surge of admiration. Peijak solely looked down at the cold corpse with emotionless eyes.

The queen walked past the kneeling knights swallowing their sobs and Peijak silently standing. She put her helmet back on.

"We will mourn them once we tear down that cursed fort. We will not let their sacrifices go to waste."

It was easy to evade the attentions of the soldiers and knights, who were now busy at the sudden turn of events. The red wolf brassard had not yet been taken away from Reuyen and was still a scary thing for the soldiers who didn't know the details. Borrowing a horse and dodging the soldiers guarding the fort's entrance was a simple task for her. She snuck through a side trail.

She climbed the steep hill to find herself in front of the half-opened, unassailable gates when she set foot on flat ground. In the dim light of the night, myriad corpses revealed themselves. They had been trampled or had fallen from a great height near the gates, and were rather more peculiar and pathetic than grand. No enemies came into sight.

Reuyen straightened her back before the gates of the fort and closed her eyes at the sound of the wind. She opened the gates. The excruciatingly dry wind banged its cold body against her skin.

The yellow light of the moon again shone on the fort that had become a castle of the dead. The sight of the desolate fort caressed by the faint moonlight was not a dream. She got off the horse and slowly stepped inside the fort. One step, then another; she left footprints like she was dragging chains behind her.

After a while, Reuyen bent her knees and touched the floor. Then she scooped up a handful of dirt, brought it to her nose, and breathed in, taking in its fragrance. She became hazy with the scent.

The dulled eyes quietly slid across and stopped at the beacon on top of the bent wall. The flames were dying down. Those eyes veiled with a calm light, then lingered on the sight of the fort's insides that had broken and crumbled down.

It didn't feel real. She had walked into the perilous fort that swung its gates open, absent of its owner, and yet, it did not feel real.

Was the fort she'd been determined to climb at the cost of countless lives and countless things this fragile? Was it merely a worthless land surrounded by strong walls made of stone?

Oh, Guitella, were you so smug on this braggadocio's land?

Leaning forward, Reuyen clawed at the dirt floor with her trembling hands. All kinds of smells seeped into the night air and soaked her lungs. Unable to manage the past soaking into her, she curled up and lay facedown on the ground. The unstable surface was still vibrating. This valley that had swallowed whole the resentment and blood of so many, rotting from its roots, was the doing of the ones from two hundred years ago.

The remaining souls of the last moments the queen had left behind, the fossil of sedimentary resentment and yearning so many had been forced to offer their lives for.

"Your..."

She stopped. She had never drunk such refreshing air. Even the smell of gunpowder and burnt ashes smelled as sweet as evergreen trees. Her dry lips moved as her sight fogged.

"Your sacrifices were not...in vain..."

She could not finish. Her throat trembled so much from the surge of emotions that it nearly hurt.

You will climb in the end.

"Yes, Peijak...I..."

Reuyen raised her head, then stopped. Her nose scrunched up; her lips violently clamped shut. Only the dark silence, the trees scattered in the blackness, and the sternly standing stones surrounded her.

How is it this quiet? Olzore has fallen, and yet there is no feast of rejoicing, nor music praising the accomplishment. There is nothing.

Tears dropped down her cheeks before she could notice.

There is no one.

It felt as if she were left alone in a strange world. Her comrades who'd risked their lives with her and should've been here were nowhere to be found. She was sunk so deep in loneliness, she had even forgotten that she was alone.

I can't even imagine my dear sister losing.

Reuyen's lips trembled at that sweet hallucination seeping into her ear, then she broke into tears at last. She pounded the ground and let loose the screams she'd been holding back.

Damn Olzore! Damn Olzore!

She wept like a bird with a twisted neck and cursed the layers of time. Her seething soon came to an end. Then the sobs broke out.

"For this...only...only this..."

Tears welled up and she could not see a thing. She couldn't even move, for her breath was taken over by the sobs.

Olzore had fallen at last, but those who'd fought, risking their lives, for this would never know. Not even praise would reach them. Her quivering hands covered in dirt grabbed at her heart, beating with remorse. The only thing she could do was express her grief for their deaths atop this sole victory.

She looked back, feeling completely empty.

Nothing was left after the storm of that burning desire. Only a single footstep that would also vanish in time was left on the dirt, and no one but the moonlight would see it.

CHAPTER TWENTY-FOUR

Reuyen returned to the camp before the first light broke. Her face was serene, like she had buried all those storming emotions again. The guard patrolling the camp jumped at the sight of her and hastily ran to report to his superior. The person in question who was under surveillance had quietly snuck out, then come back, so his jolting reaction was understandable.

She just stood there for a moment, then walked over to the temporary headquarters tent where she expected Paseid to be, ignoring all the proper procedures. It wasn't hard to guess the location of the commander-in-chief, so she didn't even get lost on the way.

When she arrived in front of the tent, the guard spotted her red wolf brassard and quickly vanished into the tent, then returned.

"Dame Detua, please come in."

She moved the ragged drape over to step inside, then unconsciously stopped at the black hair right in front of her.

Paseid was sitting back in a chair with his eyes closed, like he was extremely tired from last night. It was only natural that he be in his armor since they were at war, but to Reuyen, his fancy armor looked like a sign of heavy fatigue.

Paseid's eyes slowly opened. "You left unnoticed by the soldiers."

"I walked around the collapsed area of the valley, sir."

"I take it you have not been properly trained as a knight, but this is a very rudimentary military law. Did Sir Haldroff, your direct superior, not teach you that moving out of your superior's sight without his command is a violation of the law?"

Reuyen merely lowered her head at Paseid's cold reprimand.

Of course, she was aware of this. That was the reason she'd had to endure all that inconvenience of not being able to leave Evinbur's sight during the days of coming to Olzore. But it wasn't a good idea to remind Paseid of that. She was embarrassed to even count how many violations of military laws she had committed.

Had Paseid not been a man who carefully ruminated on his actions before carrying them out, she would have been treated much worse than she was now.

Paseid gently pressed on his heavy eyelids. Looking at this woman was starting to make his head ache again. Her head was lowered, but her face did not show any signs of fear. Seeing her audacity made his initial thoughts of reprimanding her vanish.

"So, what is the reason you have come directly to me?"

"I have something to ask of you, sir."

Sitting on the tattered wooden table, Paseid cleared the letter he had written to send to the royal court and the daily log on the battlefield away to the side, wiped the ink on his fingertips, then gazed at her.

Reuyen held her breath for a moment.

"You still don't realize your position," he said.

"I do, sir. But I believe the commander-in-chief will show mercy to the provider of the information that was critical to the taking of Olzore, which stood strong for hundreds of years, sir."

Paseid's lips stiffened and shut. He had expected her to use that, and her argument was not even that wrong. "Then first explain how you came to know of that place."

"Among the travelers that passed through our town was a smuggler who traveled across the border, sir. He told me on one of his trips."

"I will verify his identity. His name?"

"I think it might have been Diho, or he might have been called Vera, or it may have been Tatish, but I cannot remember exactly, sir. He would come out of the blue regardless of the time of the year, and leave after a couple days."

"Do not think to move on by giving such vague answers. Do you suppose I will believe that?"

"A smuggler will not go around revealing his identity, sir. I never learned his name, for he never properly told me anything. But I recalled hearing something about the mine under Fort Olzore."

Reuyen's unabashed answer made Paseid glare at her fiercely. "I am not here to play games with you."

"It's hard to explain, sir. But the reason for it being hard to explain is not that I am an enemy of Rarke sharpening my sword. There is no way to explain. Even if I did, you would not believe me."

"I will decide whether I believe or not, not you."

"I knew since the day I was born. Now do you believe me?"

Paseid wanted to shout at her for daring to give such a foolish, fearless answer, then stopped upon seeing her indefinitely dimmed eyes. Her eyes had looked like that when she said, *There is a mine.*

He recalled Evinbur's visit that afternoon.

He had been with Reuyen the whole trip to Olzore as well as the frontline at the valley, and had observed and learned much more about Reuyen than Paseid.

I do not know what it is, sir. But it is certain that she did not learn war written in ink on page, he had said. *She even knew a side trail that the scouts were unaware of. She may be from a country town in Galabua, but she must not have traveled all the way to the Olzore region...*

According to Evinbur, when the showers of arrows started to fall from Fort Olzore, she discussed strategic movements of the Rarkian force before trying to save herself. It was not something a mere country girl could do. It was the commanders' duty to prioritize the lives of the others under the threat of their lives. An extraordinary ability to make a decision that surpassed fear. She had indeed been temporarily ordained as a knight, but that could not have equipped her with chivalry, so it must have been in her nature.

Her sincerity until now must be rewarded, but it would be best to keep her at a distance, sir.

Paseid understood the meaning of that at once. In truth, according to what he had heard, the woman had not lied. At least as far as they knew.

The claim that she was the second child of a war horse dealer in a small town was a verified truth. On top of that, her older brother's death in combat was also a truth, and her younger brother jumping into the front seeking vengeance was a truth as well. Paseid heard that was how the woman inevitably joined the army, and that she guided Evinbur through a side trail. And even the madness that there was a mine right underneath Olzore was true.

The sincerity of a woman whose identity became more and more dubious was quite a burden on their backs.

Paseid asked, "At the battle at Camp Anf, how did you find the enemy commander on the cliff?"

"I do not know, sir."

"A coincidence, then."

"Yes, sir…I was lucky."

Finding that his eyes darkened, Reuyen changed the subject. "I do not know if you will consider this a light matter of a worthless one's devotion and heart, but please think of this as a patriotic act of a lucky woman as well, sir. And I would like to tell you that it is only right for the taking of the fort to be solely known as your accomplishment. It would not be good for outsiders to gossip that the commander-in-chief risked a great danger at a couple words from a woman with an unverifiable identity."

Thinking that he had been insulted, Paseid sprang up and pounded the table. Reuyen took half a step back at the ear-piercing noise. His sharp black eyes shot to the red brassard from the Noble House Brionake, then to Reuyen's face.

"First, do not be aggrieved that I do not address you with respect as a dame. You have never performed a respectable act. All my decisions made thus far were made according to the pros and cons irrelevant to you. I do clearly recognize your contributions to the taking of Olzore. But daring to claim that I risked a great danger at a couple of your words is an extremely presumptuous act."

"I know that the commander-in-chief's decision was for Rarke, sir. But would not the others be confounded by the suddenly changed operation and the suddenly discovered existence of the mine? So, delete everything about me on official records, and leave this as proof of your wisdom on the glorious pages of history, Your Grace."

"Do you mean to insult me? I am not one who cannot discern the difference between true pride and empty vanity."

"I have violated a military law with a crime that not even my death can absolve, sir. Will you officially praise such a woman? Or will you leave all those contributions behind now and punish me?"

Paseid closed his mouth for a moment. He could not find anything to say. Reuyen had expected this and continued with a faint smile. "But, if you feel indebted to me, give me the body of the general. That's all I want, sir."

It was truly ridiculous.

But if he considered the behavior of the woman until now, it really wasn't that surprising a request. "What is the reason you want the corpse of the general?"

Her parched lips clamped shut like those of a doll. Paseid tried to be patient.

He could not ask why she did not act like a knight or a woman who knew the weight of the ordination, even with a red wolf brassard around her arm. But that did not mean he would tolerate everything.

She was a hindrance in the army. He had an intuition, no, a prediction that she would continue to act like this if she stayed. He did admit that his personal feelings had affected his decision, but at the same time, he solidified the decision because of the unbearable feeling of irritation.

"I see very well that you do not value ordination or a title. I will give the order promptly. The temporary brassard I granted you for the contribution of shooting the enemy commander at Camp Anf will be seized, based on the severe crime of pointing a sword at me, the commander-in-chief. But the matter and treatment related to the taking of Olzore will be determined once I return to complete my investigation on you, after I report to His Majesty. Of course, until His Majesty's orders are in effect, I will not speak of the mine."

"I accept, sir. But what about the body?"

Paseid was silent.

"I will take that as your permission, sir."

That was enough for Reuyen. She unwrapped the red triangular cloth around her left arm and put it down on the table. "If I can just see his body, sir, I will never again disturb the discipline of the army with any kind of action."

Was he, the commander-in-chief, to just sit and listen to such things? Paseid opened his mouth, dumbstruck, then clamped it shut.

It really was not that big of a problem to let her see the dead body of the fort's general. Still, he wondered, why did she obsess over his body so?

He scrunched up one eyebrow, then changed his mind and nodded. "In return, I will restrain your freedom until there is an order from His Majesty after the investigation."

"As you wish, sir."

"I also forbid you from holding a weapon."

She lowered her head without protest. "Yes, sir."

But even at Reuyen's humble answer, Paseid's uneasy mind could not come to a rest.

The other knights who were up until early in the morning looked at Reuyen disapprovingly for leaving her post without permission.

Reuyen took in all that without any resistance, sat on a blanket near the water where a campfire had been lit, and looked up at the dark sky littered with lights. She estimated the time until sunbreak. Perhaps around four hours from now. It must have been a short night, and yet the sleepless early morning was long.

The fallen Olzore was far away in the darkness, and here, there was a woman whose joys and delights were burned to white ashes. Only the remorse remained. Her resentment for Olzore collapsing so easily angered her for a moment, but even that dissipated into the night wind. The shattered starlight shone into her eyes.

"Paseid…"

Paseid Calandok Brionake.

Her lips unconsciously repeated his name and drew an arc on

their own. She could not say that they were the same, but she could not deny that his calm face had resembled Belbarote, whose mind was armed with virtuosity, for a moment.

According to her intuition, Paseid was not a man suited for killing another. Not that his talents and skills were unsuited for that, but his nature was.

He claimed he would execute her on the spot, then pushed it back and said he would let her live, though he could take her dubious life even if it were just as a precaution. To be honest, she was quite grateful for it.

Of course, she did not know what calculations were being made in that black head of his, but she wanted to believe he was not the kind of person to scheme, maybe because of his appearance.

That nature was most likely the reason he did not hesitate in protecting the rear and could make the decision everyone had negative responses to. She remembered Jacalrin saying that Paseid wanted to end the war with as little damage as possible.

She recalled being rather proud of piling victory on top of the lives of others. Her fierce nature brought her victories with countless wounds. Her old self, who thought a great victory won with sharp weapons was the only way to achieve glory for Rarke, believed that she alone was the savior of the kingdom.

But in the present day, she now understood that many were doing just fine, living, loving, and cherishing each other. This filled her heart with a bittersweet warmth. Reuyen recalled the time she was surrounded by overflowing love.

She loved, so much. It was a love dear enough to not even resent them for betraying her and taking her life.

She loved the dear people of Rarke who did not stop striving to live on that small strip of land adjacent to the south, in the kingdom of cold winters. She loved those people, the forests and fields, and every single grain of Rarke. She wished they would not be easily dismissed, would not tremble in fear before the break of winter, but would live and love freely in abundant riches. These were wishes that faded away in the lost queen's malice...

She slowly closed her eyes.

Even if the people talked like the world had turned upside down, the unchanged sun would again rise...

Now, there was no grudge to be held.

~

Since early morning, most of the army had been busy reinforcing the defense in preparation for the returning enemy.

Dismissing their business like he did not care at all, Jacalrin trotted apace. He had just run out without even washing his face upon hearing the report that the treatment of the general would take place before the enemy's return. But when he arrived, the ground where the body was laid was empty of all save the corpse. He looked around a couple times, then scrunched up his brows as he pressed down on his unkempt hair.

Darn it, I should have slept in.

He had spent the whole of last night organizing the replacements for those in the supply unit who got injured when the gunpowder exploded. His head felt quite heavy. If he hadn't felt the tension about the battle with the Olzorean army that would take place that afternoon, he would have just plopped down there and fallen asleep.

Feeling rather irritated, Jacalrin tapped on the rigidly stiffened, unsightly body with the tip of his army boot. To be quite honest, when he thought of the unpleasant encounters with Olzore, he wanted to spit on this corpse, at the very least. But now that he was looking at the man who'd witnessed his nest crumbling down in mere seconds and committed suicide in despair, he could not help but think that the man was quite pitiful.

The arrogant, pompous fort that had lived through seven hundred and fifty years had fallen just like that, so the general was going to be mocked for generations. The most incompetent of the era.

"Sir Calandok has arrived, sir."

Jacalrin turned around with his arms still stretched out from trying to wake himself up after yawning. A woman wearing not armor but a set of tattered and glum civilian clothes came into his sight first, followed by Paseid, as calm as always. Evinbur and a couple other knights were trailing behind him.

Jacalrin sprang up and briskly saluted. "Oh, Commander, sir, why is she here?"

Even though Reuyen had put many in a precarious position by disappearing like a silent rat, she looked as proud as ever. That much fearlessness really had no cure.

The knights looked at her disapprovingly.

She followed Evinbur around even though she had no right nor title to do so, and more than a dozen knights had seen her draw out her sword and run to Paseid. They were staying silent simply because they had missed the time to ask for an atonement thanks to the collapse of Olzore, and because Paseid was remaining silent as well.

"I requested it, sir," said Reuyen.

"Yeah?" Just letting it slip, Jacalrin nodded.

Honestly, whatever the other knights thought, Jacalrin had become quite fond of Reuyen since this mine incident. He wondered about her identity, but she probably wasn't an enemy. He could not prove it, for it was an intuition that leaned heavily on his instincts, but after all, he had another thing to brag about thanks to her. So, what was not to like?

The others were doing his share of doubting her and more, even if he didn't chime in. The country would not go down just because he, a single man, did not doubt her.

"But, hey, your brassard's..." he began.

The low-ranking knights wore the triangular brassard, and the high-ranking knights wore a trapezoid brassard. Those were the symbol of one's position that one had to always wear as long as one belonged in the army. It related to hierarchy, so even he, who regarded rules and laws as highly as dog poo, always wore his trapezoid brassard of House Chesa.

Jacalrin unconsciously turned his head to find Paseid quietly gazing at Reuyen, and realized what was going on. He was wondering why she had taken off her armor, but it seemed like even her brassard had been seized.

To be fair, even if she had not been intending to kill him, she had put a blade against the commander-in-chief's back. She should be thankful for him just withdrawing what he had granted and not giving her a worse punishment.

The reason must've been that Paseid took into consideration that she was the one who'd guided him to the mine. Jacalrin clicked his tongue. "I thought you were going overboard. But what did you request, again?"

"I have been given the authority to determine his treatment, sir."

"Hmm?"

Jacalrin made an odd nasal noise and tilted his head to one side. He had expected them to cut the general's head off within the day and show it to the returning Olzorean army, since his corpse had a lot of symbolic meaning. But...

"What treatment? Are you going to cut his head off yourself?" he asked again, but Reuyen did not give an answer he could understand. Guessing that there was an underlying agreement, since Paseid and Evinbur were standing in silence, Jacalrin awkwardly stepped back. It was quite sudden, but considering that truly, Reuyen was the one who had made the biggest contribution to the taking of the fort, they could have made myriad excuses if they wanted to.

But he did wonder if this woman with such slender arms could cleanly cut off a human head. She did have some dazzling skills, but she did not look like someone who had slain another person before.

"If you have a spare gold coin, will you please give it to me, sir?"

Flustered, Jacalrin stopped his train of thought and looked back at Paseid. Paseid was frowning like he had not expected her to request that, either. The woman kneeling respectfully by the corpse with composed, aloof eyes did not seem to want to revoke her request.

Gold coin was valuable in itself as a means of currency, but it had a different meaning to some higher nobles. They said that the gold coin used in a funeral was the rightful price of utopia. But all the other regular soldiers and low-ranking knights present, other than the few knights such as Paseid, Jacalrin, and Evinbur, just tilted their heads at her request.

Reading the disquiet on their faces, Reuyen looked up at Paseid. As he looked back at the woman who showed neither hesitance nor reluctance, his black eyes started to fill with a skeptical doubt.

The eyes looking up at him without even a blink under the

sunlight asked him once more. It was an odd pressure. After standing motionlessly for a long time, Paseid reluctantly nodded. Then, a soldier ran somewhere and soon returned with an old leather bag filled with gold coins issued by the royal house.

Reuyen took out one cold coin from the bag. It was not a gold coin with the intaglio of the bay tree of Rarkalia, but she hoped this would be enough for Nuadga, the guide to utopia. She opened the rigid jaw of the dead enemy commander like she was going to rip it off. Evinbur, who had remained silent the whole time, narrowed his eyes. At the same time, Jacalrin, who was closely observing her, widened his eyes with irrepressible shock.

The royal funeral? For real? She's completely out of her mind!

Paseid, who was looking at her skeptically, took a step forward. "Enough."

"Yeah. Hey, stop that! How dare you do that to some Morganaan swine...!"

Jacalrin tried to approach and grab her. But Reuyen was faster. She shoved the coin into the filthy mouth of the corpse and clamped shut his twisted jaw. Jacalrin awkwardly stopped in the midst of moving.

She lowered her head, then smiled. Her dry lips whispered. That small voice, as faint as a moan, was a secret exchange between her and the dead.

"Guitella."

He probably was named something else, but it didn't matter to her.

To the queen, Olzore was Guitella, and Guitella was Olzore. Looking down at the face of the corpse, she engraved it in her heart. She then muttered the oration of farewell, ingrained in her mind like a fossil.

"Nuadga, muin janlisas guire Rarkaddanya."

Nuadga, guide him to the utopia with this glory as the price.

Her voice was small enough to not be understood even if Jacalrin tried his best, but the sight of her burying her face in the corpse and mumbling something was quite peculiar by itself. Jacalrin stared at her, dumbfounded. The mumbling sounded almost like an oration. No, considering that she'd shoved the gold coin into that repulsive mouth, it probably *was* an oration.

When he looked around to see if he was the only one who was befuddled here, he found Paseid glaring at her with eyes so cold he couldn't even read them. Needless to say, Evinbur's face was as stiff as a rock.

Disregarding their eyes, Reuyen slid her gaze over the corpse. She bit her lip again at her eyes welling up and bent her waist to touch the corpse's cold forehead with her warm one. She could plainly feel the sensation of the dead. A splendid sight of forests and fields and light somewhere in the afterlife appeared in her closed eyelids.

It was the utopia she would never reach.

The other side, where the executed queen and the daughter of a horse dealer would never arrive even at their deaths. Many she missed had to be there. This was the punishment life was giving her.

She hugged the wish she could not say aloud.

So Olzore, tell my countless people there with your shame and resentment and cries. The queen has climbed.

Belbarote, even if you cannot forgive me, I will forgive you. Peijak, we could not be hand in hand, but your sister climbed at last.

Now, all is over.

The woman who hugged the corpse's face with her trembling body and stayed like that for a long while did not even stir. She was like the frozen surface of a lake. No one thought to talk to her or approach her.

The strange silence ended with her raising her body. Snapping back to his senses at the sound of her light inhale and exhale, Jacalrin stumbled out a question. "You...wha, wha, what did you just do?"

Reuyen's eyes looked into Jacalrin's. Instead of giving an answer, she pulled up the ends of her lips into a smile. She looked over at Paseid with softer eyes than ever, then slowly bent her torso. "I thank you for your generosity, sir."

Paseid looked at her. The clenched mouth of the dead, the gold coin, the oration. In contrast to the soldiers who'd just exchanged gazes, still not knowing what had just happened, the woman sounded refreshed, like she had just been relieved of a great burden.

"Are you aware of the meaning of placing a gold coin in the

dead's mouth?"

"Do you not think the ancestors of Rarke resenting Olzore would rejoice, sir?"

"Where did you learn it?"

"I read it in a book, sir."

He did not believe her answer, but he didn't show it. He had a hunch that he would not get the honest answer he desired even if he asked again. Maybe a part of him was getting used to her strangeness.

She was not a pressing matter in this present moment. Paseid raised his head and estimated the time by the position of the white sun soaring through the sky. Then, instead of a series of reprimands and questions, he ordered the knight standing across from him:

"Cut the head and hang it up."

Soon, Reuyen was dragged off by the soldiers like a criminal. That noon, the severed head of the fort's general was hung at the front of the Rarkian army.

The returned soldiers of Olzore erupted in a chaos at the sight of their crushed nest. The shocked men lost the will to fight after a short battle, resulting in about a thousand of the four thousand or so running away or surrendering. The remaining three thousand or so of the Olzorean soldiers who fought until the end were overcome by the nine thousand or so soldiers of Rarke, who took over the entire field.

After defeating every enemy in the fort, the Rarkians returned to their main camp after eight restless days of marching.

Rovantis's army, which did not hear about the Olzorean army's retreat and was still moving according to their feint operation, pushed into the Anf region and tried with all their might, but retreated after thousands of casualties when the Rarkian army standing by at the main camp joined forces with the army at Camp Anf. The tragic news that Olzore had fallen soon circulated, and the Morganaans' spirit dropped down and down into the deep earth. The Rarkian army used that momentum to raid Rovantis's army along the cliff road, and took the entrance to Plain Ishas.

As the queen had done, Olzore fell without leaving anything behind. Thus began the great war that shook the continent.

CHAPTER TWENTY-FIVE

The soldiers were full of energy on the road back to the Gerad border in the aftermath of Olzore, unlike when they had come. Their excitement was hotter than the dry sunlight.

At Paseid's orders to move with the Olzorean people who had now become prisoners, Reuyen came to be treated not quite differently from a mere criminal. She felt nervous, as though she were naked, in the unfamiliar situation of having to bear the soldiers' eyes pricking at her bare body uncovered by armor. She could imagine how the soldiers viewed the strange woman who had been granted a red brassard and was now treated like a guarded prisoner. But she did not make a single sound of complaint.

She had let go of the obsessive grudge when Olzore fell, and that was enough. She did not even care about how many of the enemy returned, how many died, or how many surrendered.

After enduring a long period of inconvenience for days on the road, she arrived at the main camp. The place felt rather empty. As she overheard from the knights who came out to greet the returning force, most of the soldiers still standing joined forces in the fierce attack at Camp Anf and left to pursue and destroy the Morganaan army.

"Make a list of prisoners from Olzore who may be useful in negotiating with Morgana and report back," said the knight who was guarding her. "And Reuyen Detua, you follow me. Sir Calandok has ordered us to temporarily seize your horse and have you reside in the central tent."

Leaving the lines of Morganaan prisoners, she followed the knight.

The central tent...

Reuyen swallowed a sigh. It was the safest place in the camp, a location permitted only for high-ranking nobles or knights of such families who had not yet found a place to stay. In short, it was not a place for Reuyen at all. She could easily guess Paseid's intentions. It being the safest place meant that it was the most heavily guarded and the farthest away from the outside, so he clearly intended to nip any escape plan she might have in the bud. Still, she could not care less.

The atmosphere in the main camp was heavy.

The smell of dry dirt coupled with the smell of sweat and tension wafted in the air with a hint of metal. She stopped her thoughts and calmly took in the scene. Greetings of those returning at the change of plans resounded from here and there, and fires lit up to prepare for an untimely meal.

Seeing a familiar man running through the scene of soldiers and knights, Reuyen froze her face, feeling uneasy.

"Where is my sister...? Reuyen, hey, hey!"

It was Sidan, running through the crowd of soldiers like someone who had just spotted a ghost. With his eyes as red as a rabbit's, he charged at her like a bull. He frowned at her tattered look, being dragged off like a prisoner, then hugged her without a word.

The knights frowned at the sudden reunion of the brother and sister, exchanged gazes, then ignored them. They had families as well, and this considerate move was for the soldier rejoicing at his sister's safe return, not for Reuyen.

Reuyen smiled faintly, then tapped on her brother's large arm wrapped around her. "Enough, you're embarrassing me. You didn't leave your post without permission, did you?"

"I got the captain's permission. Are you...are you okay?"

He must have been startled at the news of Olzorean army's dispatch not long after Paseid's army went east. The size of their army was not that small, either, so the main camp would have been engulfed in extreme anxiety. Her younger brother's breath, uneven with relief, rang in her ear. Perhaps because of that, the small amount of contempt for Sidan that had remained in her disappeared into thin air.

"I heard the crazy bastards of Olzore came all the way over there, so I was thinking that maybe something had happened... I was so, so..."

In the rusted sorrow, Reuyen suddenly recalled something that she had let sink down deep in her mind.

The warmth from another body pressed against her skin in the present, filled with worry and fervor. Finally, she felt like she had actually returned. Yes, she was here for this child.

The beginning was for this child.

"You know better than anyone how amazing your sister is," she told him. "Don't worry."

"You really are stubborn, you know that?"

"Do you want to give up, then? Since you're so worried?"

Reuyen lightly patted Sidan's back.

Suddenly coming to his senses, Sidan pushed her away, his face flushed. "Shut up! I'm—I'm still mad at you!"

"All right. It doesn't even seem like it would be possible right now, so let's talk about that later."

Instead of insisting, Reuyen gently let the subject go. Sidan narrowed his light-brown eyes at the unusual response from his sister, then stared at her empty left arm. "By the way, why aren't you wearing anything?"

"Oh."

"What's going on?"

"They took it."

"Took it? Your ordination..."

"Duke Brionake did it."

As soon as she gave him her answer, Sidan clamped his mouth shut. His eyes darkened with anxiety. *Did you...did you do something bad?* He was unable to ask that question because of the knights standing near them.

Then, the knight who had given them a bit of time walked in

between them. "Enough now. Return to your post, soldier. Woman, follow me."

"Whe—where...?"

Unable to find something to say, Reuyen simply smiled. Stunned, Sidan looked at her walking away surrounded by knights, and scrunched up his face, heartbroken. She became rather sorry at the sight of Sidan's pale face appearing in her periphery. She supposed she didn't have the right to be mad at the Detua men anymore, for Sidan would be watched with suspicion because of her actions.

But even if Paseid thoroughly investigated her and Sidan, the children of Detua were not the type of people he would find any dirt on. She was relieved. So, she followed the knight in peace.

The rainy season was extremely humid and sticky. The rain poured for over ten days straight, sometimes stopping for a moment, only to start pouring again. The army greeted the dark clouds covering the sky like they were their old friends for the first couple days, but as the rain continued on for nearly two weeks, complaints arose.

The courageous soldiers of Rarke were busy with training and missions even during the bad weather. Reuyen's days were infinitely fixed compared to theirs. At first, she was so preoccupied with the people busily walking around her that she didn't have the time to feel bored. The days would just pass by as she did nothing but sit around and watch what they were up to. But now, she was reaching her limit.

She heard from Sidan that Paseid asked around about her. He apparently even sent someone to their town. But seeing that he still had her locked up in the tent, it was certain that he hadn't found anything satisfying enough.

Tap, tap, tap. The sound of the rain was overpowering. Reuyen sat on the damp bed that was growing fungi in the humidity. It seemed like it had been over a month and a half since she'd come back here. It had been around two months since Olzore fell.

Olzore.

When she felt like that damn thing crumbling down in mere

seconds didn't actually happen, those chatting about the collapse of Olzore outside her tent reminded her of the reality.

She might have looked like a lucky woman who was provided with room, one whole tent for herself, and board, but she was under extremely strict surveillance, such that even just asking where Den was caused them to reinforce the guards. It was truly boring. There had been a fair number of people who took an interest in the woman who was temporarily ordained, and wanted to start a conversation with her; now, there were none at all.

The only people who did have a meaningful encounter with her were Sidan, who visited under strict permission when he had some free time, and Jacalrin, who strutted around like the world belonged to him.

Sidan was still holding a grudge against her for sending him away to the rear echelon. As he was a man honest about his own feelings, he didn't hesitate to blame her, either. But it was apparent that most of the grudges had disappeared since she came back from Olzore, so Reuyen took all his complaints quietly. When she thought of this deeply affectionate child pacing about, consumed with worry upon hearing the news of the fort's army, her heart grew heavy with the thought of their parents who were still waiting for them back in the town.

Sometimes, she found herself not able to overcome the boredom, and she glanced outside the drape, waiting for Jacalrin's visits. Seeing someone who did not care about strict manners or suspected her was quite delightful.

The recent news was that Jacalrin was extremely busy setting up more camps around Camp Anf and on Plain Ishas in Morgana, which explained why he didn't visit her as often. But alas, he was a man who could not be trusted to not turn up out of the blue and start talking about something odd.

The funniest of them was when he poked her side, asking her to whisper into his ear her secrets as if he were her old friend. *How did you know? Who told you? I won't tell anyone! Come on, don't you remember me taking your side?* After pestering her several times that amounted to nothing, he finally stopped protesting and gave up when she said, *I know you will go straight to Duke Brionake and report every single thing I say the second I tell you, sir.*

But his abandoning his stateliness as a knight, needless to say his dignity as a noble, and looking at her with puppy dog eyes and puffed-up cheeks was honestly kind of cute.

Everywhere was getting humid with the intensifying rainfall. At the time when even the shouts of the soldiers got swallowed and suffocated in the rain, Reuyen stretched her body after trying to beat the boredom with a nap.

Jacalrin wasn't coming, and neither was Sidan. In the midst of stretching like a cat, she blinked at the appearance of an unexpected guest.

"May I come in for a moment?"

"Yes, sir."

It was Evinbur. The drape opened and the cool sound of rain rushed in. Reuyen gazed at the drops of rain falling from the wet raincoat Evinbur was wearing, then lowered her eyes.

It just happened to be that the one person she found most difficult to face at this moment was Evinbur. The old knight's wisdom and insight had followed her the whole trip back from Olzore. Unlike the others' suspicion, his watch was persistent. Their doubts were valid, and she had no complaints about her treatment, but his gaze made her uneasy.

"You seem to be doing just fine. I thought I would pay you a visit."

"It's all thanks to you, sir." Reuyen didn't know what else to say.

"Is everything all right?"

"Yes, sir."

"It will get better soon."

Evinbur studied her stolid face, then rubbed his wet chin. "Once the reply comes from the royal road and your rewards are determined, you may be able to be officially ordained and receive a title to negotiate your position, or even leave with your brother with an honorable discharge. But I hear you are not interested in titles at all."

Unable to think of an appropriate answer to the question, Reuyen remained silent. It was not like she could tell him that titles meant nothing to the woman who had once been a queen, when no one stood above her. She would much rather live as a lowly commoner than feed her greed with their meaningless praise. That was most likely her pride.

"Who are you, if I may ask?" he said after a moment.

Realizing that he was speaking with respect to her, Reuyen raised her gaze to him.

She had heard that there was a reason for the saying that with age comes wisdom, and indeed, Evinbur's intense gaze made her sigh. "Who do you suppose I am?"

"It has been over twenty years since I first set foot on the battlefield. I have never seen someone like you. You are not just an ordinary country woman. Of course, I do not suspect you are a spy. I do not know if you simply recited the oration, or if you can read and write the ancient language, but…it seemed to this old man that the characters of Rarkalia engraved on the valley wall were to count the days. Did you know that too?"

The tips of her fingers flinched. Evinbur's speculation was precise. But it was a bit more than that. The characters not only counted the days but also the number of the dead.

Many had died there, and many days had been spent there. That wall in the valley covered with characters was the register of all the days and the dead. Even that was no doubt buried under the erupted earth now, so that no one would pay tribute to their deaths.

She lowered her eyes halfway and carefully chose her words. "Did it seem so, sir?"

"Why do you not wish for the suspicions against you to be lifted?"

Trying not to reveal anything personal to Evinbur, who was speaking like he was speaking to a pitiful child, Reuyen politely answered, "I believe you, Sir Haldroff, must possess eyes that look upon the world differently from the young, for you are a fierce general with age and wisdom. Who in this world would wish to live with suspicions? Of course, I want to be trusted, sir."

"Well?"

"I believe there are matters one can only keep silent about, for there is no other way. Like you devoted yourself to war for various reasons, consider my silence rooted in such reasons, sir."

"Why not try, at least?"

"I have already told you my honest situation, sir. But I have not gained your trust."

Evinbur's eyes grew rather serious. Reuyen waited for his answer for a moment, then continued like she was defending herself. "Do people not live hearing fictional tales of double rainbows appearing in the sky, three-headed horses being born, and a snowstorm engulfing the south, sir?"

"Do you mean to say you are as fictitious as those?"

"I do not mean to say that I am fictitious, sir. It's different from a secret. Truly, I swear that I…I can only tell you that I knew such things by coincidence."

"Quite a mysterious woman you are…"

Reuyen smiled at Evinbur's muttering. He looked into her deep, deep eyes for a long time, then fixed his raincoat. He shook his head.

Reuyen looked up at him. "Rarke will win, right, sir?"

"So it shall be."

Reuyen saw him off through the small gap between the drape and the wall. The old knight walked away through the heavy rain, not even looking back. She looked at his strong back for a while, then crouched down like a turtle retreating into its shell.

Had Guitella relayed her wish on his way to utopia? She would never know. Afraid the part of her she let go of would come back, she buried her face between her knees. It would all be fine if she left this all-too-familiar battlefield without any delay. Then, all would be well. All had to be well.

Reuyen waited for the royal messenger with a longing as dire as someone being chased.

CHAPTER TWENTY-SIX

I t had been about a year and a half since the outbreak of the Great Battle against Morgana. At the beginning of the last summer, Fort Olzore, often called Morgana's best defensive military base, had fallen, and Rovantis's force had retreated following a battle over the Anf region of the Gerad border. Thus, the Rarkian army had achieved the splendid feat of winning the entrance to Ishas.

Messengers and pigeons carrying the news of the collapse of Olzore swept every region of Rarke. In less than a month, the entire country of Rarke rejoiced as if a festival had commenced. Even the incessant rain could not put out the fire of joy.

Jacalrin had gone to Plain Ishas with Tabajen and busied himself with the duties of a director who oversaw the establishment and maintenance of the new camp. Preparing for the main army's moving fell to the other knights as well as Paseid. In accordance with Paseid's will that there was no need to shed blood within Rarkian territory, the large army bustled to move over to Plain Ishas. Jacalrin had to stay there for days, since he had to establish a big enough camp for that large an army.

But, for some reason, that man who should've been across the cliffs suddenly appeared, covered in blood, and barged into Paseid's tent.

"Sir—Sir Chesa!" cried Paseid's guard. "You cannot…"

"Oh, even if he yells at someone, I'll be that someone, so don't worry!" Jacalrin waved away the guard trying to stop him. Paseid's personal tent had withstood the year of time since the beginning of the war and looked rather finely equipped, unlike the barren headquarters tent or the equally barren ordinary tents for soldiers.

There were no fancy decorations, since Paseid had a rather simple taste, but the tent had an elegant, light-brown table, a small desk, and a bookshelf, even. There were even books on that massive bookshelf. Most of them were journals containing information on strategy and tactics, but some of them were empty diaries. Jacalrin stared at the red wolf banner hung on one side of the tent, unintimidated by the furniture's grace or the feeling of distance they somehow gave to the spectator, then inhaled.

"Sir Calandoooooook!" he shouted.

There was no answer.

Instead, a small noise came out from behind the bookshelf that was completely silent, as if no one was there. Jacalrin stomped in, leaving wet, bloody footprints on the antique carpet.

"Paseid, Paseid—I mean, Commander, sir!"

"What is the meaning of all this?"

Paseid was standing as straight as a pin behind the bookshelf with a book opened on his palms, not even looking at Jacalrin. The familiar design engraved on the side of the old, tattered book was something Jacalrin knew as well. Jacalrin squirmed restlessly with his eyes on the side of Paseid's face buried in the book.

"I would just wait if this were any other day. But I barged in here looking like this because it really is a pressing matter. Can you just, for a moment, listen please?"

Paseid finally looked up to find Jacalrin dripping bloody water everywhere. He walked over, suppressing a sigh. He put a string between the pages of the book and put the book down on the table. Then he threw a training towel at Jacalrin.

"Do you not know swords and armor will rust if you do not take care of them?"

Jacalrin took the towel and dabbed it on his armor.

Paseid pressed on his forehead at the sight, then gazed at Jacalrin with his fatigued eyes. Jacalrin slowly put down the bloodied towel.

"We had some conflict with the enemy scouts wandering about the Ishas region, sir. I didn't send a messenger to report because it really wasn't a battle."

"What is this pressing matter?"

"Oh, the—that woman, Reuyen. What's she doing now?"

Paseid's face scrunched into a frown.

"What are you going to do with her?" asked Jacalrin.

"I will soon report to His Majesty following the proper procedure and reward her."

"You're going to send her out of the army, right?"

Sensing a certain anxiety on Jacalrin's face that was quite unusual, Paseid quietly said,

"I would need to hear what this is about first."

Jacalrin's eyes suddenly landed on Paseid's snow-white sword, Rionac, leaning against the table. He made a complicated face that Paseid could not make out the meaning of, then searched for something in his clothes.

A dagger tightly wrapped in fine red satin was neatly placed on the table. Paseid moved only his eyes to look down at the arm-length dagger Jacalrin unwrapped. The blue hilt and the design engraved on the scabbard stood out.

"It's a dagger one of the Morganaan knights rammed into the ground near our camp, sir."

Jacalrin waited for Paseid's response with a mixed expression of anxiety and excitement. Paseid took the sword Jacalrin presented and held it in his hand.

His eyes flashed at the familiar intaglio he could feel with his fingertips. Disconcerted, Jacalrin pushed the soft, tightly weaved satin toward Paseid.

It was a message from Morgana.

A gift to my great sister, the conqueror of Olzore.

The conqueror of Olzore.

For no reason in particular, he thought of a woman.

~

"Just leave us."

The frightened soldier who had just received Paseid's fierce energy in its entirety was quite unfortunate. It was a sharp retort to an obligatory report. But no one could speak for the soldier.

Evinbur crossed his arms and looked down as he sat across from Paseid. It was an emergency. Tabajen and Denjak had also been ordered to drop whatever they were doing.

"So just what is this, sir?"

The knights had heard about the blue dagger and the message from Morgana written on the satin wrapping the dagger. They were all dumbfounded. Among them was someone who became extremely tense and argued that they should eradicate the root of all suspicions.

What was this dagger? There was no answer, but no one asked for it again. In truth, they knew as well that there was no one who could give a proper answer.

Sensing something, Evinbur subtly started the conversation. "Do you deem this is related to the woman, sir?"

"It sure is suspicious."

"Sir Chesa, has she not said anything to you, either?"

"Nothing. But isn't it possible that the dagger is unrelated to Reuyen?"

"There are more than just a few suspicious things about her to conclude that it's unrelated. The more we investigate, the more suspicious she becomes."

The soldier they ordered to investigate looked into every little detail about the town she lived in and all of her movements and reported back. But alas, they found nothing they didn't already know about, such as her being born the second child of three of a war horse dealer in a town near the border, her older brother dying in combat, and the youngest in the family being here. All things she had said herself. The only new piece of information they learned from a resident of her town was that she'd lived there twenty-two years with the nickname *genius*.

The woman had grown up in a small town where the only ones who knew how to swordfight were volunteer guards. She was without a proper master, but apparently there was not a single weapon, whether it be bow or sword or whatever else, she could not wield.

A woman who had a far vaster knowledge than any other person of her age. A woman who had never lost a single fight with the local young men. A genius.

But that couldn't justify all the actions she had displayed. The obsession and the unhesitant attitude, and the confidence she had shown that allowed her to be certain about something no one else knew about. And the presence of this dagger was added to the list now.

"I do not understand what this is all about," said Paseid, shaking his head. "What did the enemy mean when they…?"

His eyes sank coldly.

Had they slandered Rarke, that took Olzore, by claiming it was like a female? No, no. If so, they would have been so polite. Incidentally, it was hard to think that the message from Morgana was intended to mock them. If it were, the Morganaans would have realized very soon that their intentions had failed.

Did he have to question the woman himself to make her talk, even though she had no Morganaan connections? But Paseid stopped that thought. Though they hadn't explicitly announced it, due to the gag order, the biggest contributor to the taking of Olzore was that woman.

It was enough to be criticized for not treating the biggest contributor, who'd risked her life for the deed that would be talked about for generations to come, with utmost respect. Torture and questioning were unimaginable.

"But are you, Sir Calandok, not the taker of Olzore?" asked Denjak.

He did not want to hear it. "That's no question. What is the reason you are even bothering to bring this up?"

"It's written right here, 'the conqueror of Olzore.' I was not there in the valley at the time, but I am not unaware of what happened. But all the decisions and orders were made by our commander-in-chief, so it rightfully is your achievement, sir. If this dagger was gifted to you…"

"Enough." Paseid cut him off.

Denjak lowered his gaze to hide his embarrassment. The atmosphere grew colder and colder.

Evinbur, who had remained silent, slowly opened his eyes. He could guess what Paseid was thinking, as he did not greatly rejoice at the victory over Olzore. Thousands of soldiers had all gathered to praise him as the great and wise commander-in-chief who made the decision that destroyed Olzore, but they were all hollow words to Paseid. Pursuing military contributions could be a great motivation out on the battlefield, but they were nothing to be proud of. Paseid was someone who was in charge of the battlefield with that already in mind.

As someone who was more conscious of the unidentifiable woman like a splinter than anyone, Paseid had to be extremely uncomfortable with the fact that she was the reason he'd overturned the whole operation. He was that kind of a man. And now, that decision was suspected as being in relation to Morgana. This was no longer an honor, but a disgrace.

Evinbur opened his heavy lips. "Sir Calandok."

Paseid raised his eyes taciturnly. Evinbur paused for a moment and chose his words. Those eyes conveyed a certain conviction as unbending as Paseid's nature. Then Evinbur changed the atmosphere by chuckling.

"Whatever happened, your decision led to the present victory and saved countless lives, sir, and there is no shame in being proud of that."

"No more of that, sir. Back to the present matter."

Jacalrin studied each knight, rolling around his light-green eyes like he couldn't handle the awkward atmosphere anymore, and massaged on his temples. "By the way. The thing engraved on the dagger. I keep thinking...the...doesn't it look the same? Er...am I the only who thinks that?"

Everyone's eyes turned to one spot at Jacalrin's mumbling.

Rionac. They blankly stared at the white scabbard as if they were suddenly knocked out, then looked back at the blue scabbard.

Paseid grabbed the hilt of the sword. Finally, the knights snapped back to their senses and lowered their heads, like they had just committed some great crime. The heirloom had been passed on from generation to generation in House Brionake. The intaglio of a butterfly was inscribed on Rionac's white scabbard, and the design of a butterfly with its wings spread out was engraved on the royal blue dagger. It was an unconscious comparison, between the great heirloom of the Noble House Brionake and some dagger from Morgana of which they did not know the origins.

An uneasy hunch hit them.

"Who was the commander of Morgana's front? Was it Count Servantes?"

"I received a report last time that the head of the eastern region, Margrave Zars, is in charge of it, sir. In the latest report, they said that Count Servantes from the middle region might be appointed, but it seems as though he has been eliminated."

Paseid glared at the dagger laid on the table, then reluctantly gave his order. Further discussion was unnecessary.

"Bring me Reuyen Detua."

CHAPTER TWENTY-SEVEN

I t was the end of the rainy season.

The Morganaan camp was truly engulfed in a turmoil of horrendous rage. Marche Carl Rovantis, the man appointed as the commander-in-chief of Morgana, could not draw a faint smile at the news that the reinforcements were at an arm's distance now. He couldn't even swallow a sip of water down his throat. Needless to say, his sleep was dreadful. Had he had two lives, he would have given one up already.

There had been no tragedy like this before. About a thousand of his soldiers had already died or were missing, and more than twice of that were injured. If it hadn't been for the timely beginning of the rainy season and hence a short armistice, he couldn't imagine how much worse the situation would have been by now.

All of these consequences became a responsibility weighing down on his shoulders. He had had a bad hunch from the silence of the Olzorean army that had promised a joint attack at the last battle, but that was days after a skirmish commenced on Rarkian territory across the cliffs. At first, he'd thought there was a misunderstanding about the timing between them and Olzore when they previously discussed the operation. But the news he'd heard when he was about to order a retreat to reorganize his soldiers was absolutely unexpected.

Olzore had fallen.

Bullshit. It had seemed like a foolish, ridiculous rumor even a three-year-old child would scoff at. But he had still dispatched a group of soldiers, for he couldn't just ignore a report he had already received. The report was enough to put the Morganaan army in complete mayhem.

They didn't even know how it had collapsed. They had simply heard the report that the collapse seemed to have started from the bottom section of the valley.

The reality that the entire valley had collapsed, taking with it their historic pride, had been so infuriating that he'd thought he might pass out. The news had reached the imperial palace like a swift-footed horse and enraged the emperor. The whole empire of Morgana was grief stricken.

The original plan to wear the enemy out with wars of attrition and skirmishes had gone to waste. With the Rarkian army taking even the large campsite for the Morganaan army and the Morganaan army fleeing to the southern part of Plain Ishas, he had to think of some way to turn this back around. His parched throat felt sandy. He gave a fierce cry.

"What are the enemy's movements now? Bring Margrave Zars to me as soon as his reinforcements arrive..."

The voice drenched in desperation trailed off before he could finish his sentence. There was a sudden commotion outside his tent as busy footsteps and voices of a couple knights overlapped. Marche grew extremely on edge. It was hard to forgive those daring to ruffle his feathers when he was already so tense. But before he could order his aide-de-camp to see what was going on, the drape swung open without a warning.

"What—how dare you...?"

Marche frowned at the group of armed knights who barged in. He fixed his eyes on the knight standing in the front.

To his surprise, the knight was a woman. Even the ponderousness of the blue armor dripping water on the floor could not hide her slender figure.

Her cold turquoise eyes, revealed between the raindrops dripping down from the helmet covering her forehead, looked straight at him. Marche's eyes carefully scanned the woman from head to toe, then stopped at the design engraved on her pauldron. He scrunched up his face.

"Hello, Marquis Rovantis. I am Eila Sinis, the Grand Master of the Order of Mariposa."

"I did not hear that the Order of Mariposa had dispatched reinforcements. Have they arrived yet? Count Zars—"

She cut him off before he could finish his sentence.

"Count Zars is not coming."

"What do you mean by that?"

"Count Zars has returned."

"Then who led the reinforcements here..."

Instead of a proper answer, Eila coldly but respectfully nodded, then put down a letter from the imperial family in front of him, almost like she meant to throw it.

"What impudence is this?" he sputtered.

"Please rise, sir. My lord has ordered to finish all preparations before he arrives here. From this moment on, all the corps of the main force and the reinforcements of Morgana come under the jurisdiction of the Order of Mariposa as a temporary measure, as ordered by His Imperial Majesty. Thank you for your service, sir."

Eila's words were simple and clear. So much so that the aide-de-camp watching them winced and moaned.

But Marche had to put all his efforts into figuring out just what was going on. The object his eyes was fixed on was most definitely a letter with the almighty imperial family's seal. A foreboding grasped at his wrist, but he suppressed his reluctance the best he could and opened the letter. His eyes moved from side to side a couple times, then froze. The script from the emperor clearly stated his eviction.

His rough, thick fingers started to tremble like leaves. His voice that had been full of ferocious energy until just now trembled like his fingers.

"Balroid...is he dispatched too? Where is he right now?" he asked, his voice rising.

"Please rise."

"How insolently arrogant you are, you mere wench of a knight! I have no business with you. Where is he? Is he standing by outside? Mariposaaaa!" Marche sprang up like he would run out any second.

Unflustered, Eila replied, "My lord has gone directly to the border to take care of other business."

"I will hear from his own mouth why his subordinates are barging in and committing such insolence!"

Eila's eyes cooled as Marche fiercely shouted at the top of his lungs. She glanced at him with indifferent eyes, then ordered the knights standing behind her.

"Prepare to greet the lord."

The men in blue armor behind her briskly moved at Eila's order and violently ripped off the Rovantis banner covering one side of the tent. Then one of them took out a large, neatly folded blue fabric from his armor, laid it out, and hung it on the wall. Marche tightly closed his eyes at the clear blue hue engulfing the tent, then opened them again.

The Rovantis banner of a lion holding a rose in his mouth dropped down like a piece of trash, and the bewildering sight of a blue butterfly spreading out its graceful wings hung in its place.

The flag of a wolf hung heavy with water atop the headquarters tent in the center of the Rarkian camp.

In the headquarters tent, on the map laid out for the discussion of strategy, a strange object wrapped in shiny red fabric was placed down.

"What do you know of this?"

An angry voice resounded. The knights standing on either side of the round table held their breaths and waited for the woman's answer.

Reuyen just blinked at the unexpected situation. They'd told her to stay low, so she'd stayed low. They'd said they would even consider an honorary dispatch, depending on his majesty's reply, so she'd waited for that. And now, they had suddenly called her here, sat her down, and pressured her with such a fierce atmosphere.

"Speak."

Reuyen frowned at the abrupt, accusatory questions, then reluctantly unwrapped the satin. A blue dagger, cold to the touch, rolled out. Her eyes slid along the dagger.

A butterfly, so clearly embroidered it looked like taxidermy, lay on the satin as soft as silk. And another intaglio of a butterfly on the blue scabbard seemed almost obsessive now.

Her movements stopped at once.

"We should question her this instant instead of dilly-dallying. Make her start talking."

Jacalrin stepped in at the protest from Denjak, who was standing on Reuyen's right side. "Isn't that a bit rash when nothing is certain yet, Sir Deusak?"

"Sir Chesa, you should learn when to step in or not," Evinbur fiercely reproached. "There is a war going on, so we must follow the wartime laws. I believe we have already tolerated enough of Miss Detua's silence. We must not let this simply pass by this time."

Reuyen pushed all their trifling voices out of her ears. Only Jacalrin pounded his chest in frustration, clearly showing that he had had enough of her silence.

Oh, come on!

Reuyen's eyes were still fixed on the blue dagger. She did not know the butterfly spreading out its wings. Although, it looked quite similar to something she had seen often. The man questioning her was probably aware of that too. This butterfly and the one engraved on his white sword were, even with the consideration of the miniscule differences, extremely similar.

Then, a soldier rushed into the headquarters tent. "A—an urgent report, sir!"

Jacalrin stopped pounding his breastplate and spat back at him with pent-up frustration.

"Did the order not to let anyone in go in one of your ears and out the other? Hmm?"

"A man who claims he is the commander-in-chief of Morgana just ca—came himself, sir! He said he had a business with the taker of Olzore..."

"Rovantis?"

"No, sir. Uh, a man I have never seen..."

What on earth was this about? The knights' faces turned to frowns.

Fort Olzore.

Considering the renown of the impregnable fort that had finally fallen, and that Morgana was quite severely damaged with the fort disassembled, it wasn't odd to hear they'd replaced their commander-in-chief. This must have been the reason Rovantis had stayed quiet when he was pushed down to the south.

But a visit? This was something no one had expected.

Paseid, who was looking at the light-brown eyes of the woman, asked, "How many men has he brought?"

"Thirty-four knights in blue armor and one knight in black armor, sir."

"How was there no report on this until he arrived at our doorstep?"

"I do not know, sir. He just appeared out of the blue…"

The air in the headquarters became cold and tense.

The blue dagger with the clear intaglio of a butterfly had been enough to put everyone on edge. Now an enemy commander was visiting their camp with only thirty knights in blue armor, volunteering as an ambassador. The Rarkian knights' murderous intentions pointed at Reuyen instantly changed their target.

"Prepare for battle," commanded Paseid. "Sir Chesa, bring her out just in case. Sir Giotarre, send a scout to inspect the surrounding area of the camp, and Sir Haldroff, call the soldiers to form a defense line."

When Paseid left after giving the orders, Jacalrin hesitantly stepped toward Reuyen and stood beside her, his face dumbstruck. He would have made some silly joke had it been any other day, but he couldn't even think of one right now.

Her mouth slightly opened. Reuyen blankly stared at the dagger in her hands and muttered in despair.

It can't be.

Clear letters were written on the blood-red cloth wrapped around the dagger.

A gift to my great sister, the conqueror of Olzore.

. . .

It can't be.

~

The southern border between Rarke and Morgana had been drawn
anew.

The rainy season was just coming to an end, and the whole
world was filled with humid air. Raindrops fell on the armor and
made a *tap, tap,* noise, filling the area with extreme tension where
not even the silence could sneak in.

The cold air flowed through the occasional drops of rain. Only
the barely breathing torchfire and black smoke rising were seen
under the dark-faced, scowling sky. At the far edge of the plain
across the Rarkian camp, the enemy's flag fluttered above the
knights in blue armor. The rain wetting the flag made it hard to
make out the sigil, but everyone could see the flag's royal blue hue.

Paseid stepped in front of the convoy, sitting on Rotsa with
tightly fastened barding and saddle. Behind him stood archers,
spearmen, and knights in horizontal lines.

"Did they make any movement?" he asked.

"They kept their places since the request to see the contributor
to the fall of Olzore, sir."

Jacalrin tightened his fist at the knight's report. "That bastard
is..."

Soon, the order in blue armor started to move.

When Paseid raised his left hand, the archers who were lined up
took aim. In the extreme tension where everyone felt as though
they were walking on thin ice, the enemy formation moving in
exact precision split in the middle. Soon, a man armed from head
to toe in black armor walked out through the gap, riding a pitch-
black horse.

Exclamations broke out.

Paseid was instantly certain of his identity.

The shame of Rarke.

A refined animosity flashed in his eyes as black as night. By
appointing this man as the new commander-in-chief, the empire's
mockery had reached its peak. The man who appeared with the
blue butterfly banner was the same man who had caused a sensa-

tion among the central nobles of Rarke by taking the middle name *Peijak* a couple years ago for whatever reason: Balroid Peijak Mariposa.

Now that he was out on the battlefield, the war would not end anytime soon. This was an unavoidable matter of the country's pride.

The knight on the black horse approached without any guards and stopped about thirty paces away. A slick voice came out from under his helmet. It was a relaxed but excited voice.

"I will forego the unnecessarily time-consuming greetings since you all seem to know very well who I am. Where is the person who devised the plan to take Fort Olzore?" The man sitting high atop his arrogant horse scanned the soldiers who stood ready for defense.

"I am the commander-in-chief of Rarke," said Paseid sternly.

"I heard today's son of the red wolf is quite virtuous and honorable, so I did not expect him to be a man who proudly claims another's contribution as his. I am not here to see the enemy commander who bears a false fame rooted in another's contribution. Bring me to the one who reported the location of the mine in Olzore Valley."

The mine in Olzore Valley. How did this man know about that? Despite the man's insults, Paseid stiffened with surprise.

"How dare you, you shameless kin of a traitor!" Jacalrin shouted, his face flushing. He drew his sword. *Clang!* The silver blade flashed in the light from the setting sun. Almost at the same time, the order standing across the plain all started to move in preparation for a battle.

But in the intensifying tension, they snapped back to their former formation when the knight dressed in black raised a hand.

Paseid glared at Jacalrin. "Sheathe your sword."

"Yes, do not complicate things, for I am not here to fight right now," said Balroid. "Not being able to control your young, feisty self is understandable, but do watch your neck. I repeat. I am here to see the one who took the impregnable Fort Olzore that has never fallen in seven hundred and fifty years of history. I take it you have properly relayed my gift."

Was that truly the reason he'd come all the way here, right in front of the enemy's camp? Denjak and a couple other knights looked back at Reuyen, standing at a diagonal angle from Jacalrin.

She was looking up at the knight in black like it was all she could do, even with the fierce men's eyes all locked on her. The eyes of the enemy commander naturally moved to her as well. Even the sound of meek rainfall faded away in the tension that could break into a great chaos any moment.

A short silence. Then, an ecstatic voice came out from under the man's helmet. "Finally."

As the woman's frozen face cracked, the knight in black thrashed his reins. Jacalrin tried to block her from the front upon seeing the black horse charging and leaping like he was determined to trample the target. But the massive black horse sprang up surprisingly nimbly and landed between the woman and Jacalrin instead.

Neigh! Jacalrin's swift horse raised his front legs to dodge the horse jumping in.

"What are you thinking?" Jacalrin cried. "You can't possibly be stupid enough to forget that you have come right in front of the Rarkian camp all by yourself. Do you not even know that the border has changed since the Battle at Olzore?"

The blue eyes shining in the black helmet looked straight at Reuyen. She was frozen, the back of her neck stiffly held up like she had just seen a ghost. Her eyes spotted the intaglio of the Morganaan lion on the horse's saddle.

It can't be.

The man's sleek voice resounded faintly in her ears.

"Move aside. I only intend to congratulate her for the taking of Olzore."

As if I'd believe that. Jacalrin waited for Paseid's order, not hiding his blatant hatred. But Paseid's tightly shut lips did not open. At last, Jacalrin, who was narrowing his eyes like a wildcat, stepped back. The knight in black gave a satisfied smile and tilted his face down to look at the woman.

The blue dagger was in the hand of the woman who wore a tattered top and pants. He opened his mouth, free of even a single drop of doubt.

"I have waited for a long time." He spoke in a gravelly voice, full of emotion. "I believed…my dear sister would return."

What did that bastard just say? Jacalrin, who had stepped aside, grew still like he'd seen a ghost.

"I knew it was you as soon as I heard about Olzore. I truly admire your realizing that wish, even after all this time. Only…"

The knight in black bent down on the horse and carefully caressed her cheek. Only then did the woman faintly raise her chin to look at his face. She gave a moan full of despair.

This can't be…

The familiar clear blue eyes shattered her hope to bits.

"It was a shame I could not be there with you. Let's go. You do know this is not your rightful place, dear sister."

"Are you…are you right now…"

She stumbled a couple steps in his direction as he pulled on her arm. A fierce voice that could be concealed even with affection spoke. "Yes, I knew there was no way my sister would not recognize me. Let's talk more afterward. There is no need to mix with these revolting sorts anymore. For I have come here to take you, dear sister."

Paseid, who was standing at the front at a small distance from them, opened his mouth. "Sir Chesa."

Jacalrin sprang forward like lightning and grabbed the man's arm holding the woman. The eyes in the black helmet overflowing with infinite affection flashed viciously and glared at him.

"I have no clue what kind of dogshit you're talking about, but what remorse does the head of the traitors have left in Rarke to do this?" Jacalrin shouted.

"Chesa. Are you that Chesa? Kalajesh Ransen? Or his younger brother? Anyway, step aside, young knight."

"His younger brother. Don't you see those archers over there? That's a warning. Next, a sword just might spring out. Seems like Morgana realized its ass is on fire and decided to switch its head, and if you don't want to be known as the commander-in-chief who lost his head as soon as he was appointed, move back."

In a dreamlike situation she could not comprehend, Reuyen called him in the haze of the bubbling feeling of betrayal. Though she didn't know how it could be, she instinctually knew.

"Peijak."

"Yes." His white breath dissipated in the falling rain. "Swan."

That one word swept away the last doubt.

Is this a dream? Is this, a dream?

A moment passed when everyone held their breath at the tension, and then the woman's shout drenched with fury rang out through the rain like thunder. "How...how...how can you wear their armor, sit on their saddle, and point your sword at Rarke...!"

The eyes in the black helmet seemed flustered for a moment, then started to shine with murderous intent. A completely different atmosphere now surrounded him. He glared at her with widened eyes, then stepped back upon realizing the arrows were aimed at him.

"No, what are you speaking of right now...?" he said.

"You...!"

"It's a wish that has been waiting for hundreds of years. Have you forgotten their brutality? Or are you mistaking something? Surrounded by the kin of Hansen, who betrayed you, and Brionake, who repaid your generosity with betrayal. Dear sister."

Jacalrin could not follow their conversation for his life. He was dumbfounded. Had he already been hit in the head with an arrow? The words coming from the man who called himself the newly appointed commander-in-chief of Morgana all sounded completely bonkers.

Reuyen, who was standing like she was just as bonkers as him, stumbled back, then suddenly drew the sword hung at the side of Jacalrin's horse. The horse fumed, startled by the sharp, piercing noise of metal. The enemy looked down at the sword pointed at him at a couple steps' distance, then suddenly took off his helmet.

Weak raindrops fell on his face. The reddish-brown hair revealed under the almost set sun and the blue eyes were so familiar, like she had seen them in a distant memory. They flashed fiercely. *Why do you point your sword at me?* His eyes were asking so. Reuyen froze.

"Go back to your land," Paseid asserted. The voice she had heard over and over suddenly sounded strange. All the sounds in the world just faded away. Like a dead tree, Reuyen stood without moving, silent. The knight in black, who was pinning Reuyen down in her spot without a single word, realized Paseid's intent to murder and clenched his teeth.

The knight ferociously turned around his horse. The dark-gray mane of the horse swung right before Reuyen's eyes and sent the smell of an old battlefield into her nostrils.

"If you need more time, dear sister, I will wait a bit longer. This will be all for today. Treat my sister with the utmost respect until then."

He pulled his reins and glared at Paseid. "And…Paseid Calandok Brionake…a word to you. There is no need to be fair and just with me. I will not be as dumb as Rovantis, the idiotic former comman-der-in-chief."

The agile black horse started to gallop to the other side of the plain.

The blue mantle swaying on the back of the man disappearing across the falling rain jumped out at Reuyen's eyes. It was a recog-nizable sight, as hazy as a blue butterfly landing on earth. Within a short time, the enemy's order disappeared into a dot across the plain.

Only after they completely disappeared did Reuyen begin to come back to her senses. *Is this possible? What absurdity is this?* Jacal-rin's sword escaped her uncontrollably trembling hands and fell on the ground with a loud clang.

As everyone glared at her warily, Paseid gave his order: "Follow."

It was an unexpected meeting on a day at the end of the rainy season.

CHAPTER TWENTY-EIGHT

The place Reuyen was almost forcibly taken to was not the headquarters tent, or a cell for an interrogation or questioning, but Paseid's personal tent. Once he entered the tent, he excused all the other knights who followed them in and stood in silence for a long time, leaning on a corner of the table where paper, pens, books, and such were neatly organized.

The sound of people bustling about nervously came in from outside the tent. Paseid turned his body and glared at the woman, whose face had turned pale. She still seemed like she was not her usual self.

Balroid Peijak Mariposa. He was the madman of Mariposa, the shame passed down from Rarke's bowing down to Morgana.

The animosity Paseid felt toward Count Mariposa, who'd barged in like he thought himself an ambassador, was as strong as his deep loyalty for the Royal House Brionake. But he didn't have the time to wallow in that animosity. For he could not understand a thing Balroid had babbled, nor the woman's attitude toward him.

The man who was said to have even changed his name with a deep, deep animosity toward Rarke, to the woman who led the collapse of Fort Olzore, the symbol of Morganaan legacy.

If Mariposa's true purpose was to throw the Rarkian camp into confusion, he'd succeeded.

Paseid suppressed the strong urge to slay Reuyen right then and there. He swore he'd never, even for a single moment, trusted her, but he could not deny he'd subconsciously determined that she was not an enemy, either. He believed the affection she displayed for Rarke, so he let her be, taking many possibilities into consideration. Thus, he looked away from all suspicions. But what if that assurance was his mistake and her scheme?

A rage surging in him like it intended to rip away his reason made him tightly clench his jaws.

Blue veins bulged out on the back of Paseid's hand as it gripped Rionac. Reuyen was still blankly staring down with moony eyes.

"I will not forgive your silence anymore. Explain." His voice was as edged as a blade.

Reuyen raised her head at last. Her parched lips moved hesitantly, then closed again.

It's a wish that has been waiting for hundreds of years. Have you forgotten their brutality? Or are you mistaking something? Surrounded by the kin of Hansen, who betrayed you, and Brionake, who repaid your generosity with betrayal.

His voice once again rang in her mind. Reuyen dropped her gaze to Paseid's feet, unable to bear those familiar black eyes staring at her.

"How are you related?"

"Not...at all..."

Reuyen's trembling voice dissipated in the fierce atmosphere in the tent. *It can't be*, she repeated in her mind, but she was already listening to the whispers of her instinct.

There was nothing different in his familiar way of speaking, the blue eyes she remembered well, or anything else. It was deluded to claim that it was impossible. That there could be another in this whole wide world who was given a new life with a strange birth, just like her. It was something she'd often imagined since she was a child. But...

It can't be.

She started to feel nauseous, as if she were being dragged away in a strong current. Her fingers curled in, as if to grasp at straws. It was a desperate wish. *It can't be.* Peijak was her only blood, with whom she'd roamed the battlefield in the past. She was not unaware of how much he detested and hated Morgana, and how he'd slain Rarke's enemy with so powerful a loyalty.

So, it was apparent.

The enemy commander of Morgana could not possibly be Peijak. Even though he had a similar way of talking, those lips that called her name that had become an antiquity, and the familiar butterfly sigil.

Something pierced through her brain. She froze like she was struck by lightning.

What happened to Sir Peijak Dollehan? she had asked Jacalrin.

Dollehan? he'd replied. *I do not wish to dirty my tongue by speaking about him, so do not ask. I don't want to lose my dignity with dishonorable words and actions.*

She had dismissed their conversation some time ago. Her face grew pale, like a field covered with the deadly snow. An insuppressible moan came out of her tightly shut lips. Why had he reacted so strongly at the mere mention of the name?

It was a costly price she had to pay for living as a blind and deaf country girl.

How dare you, you shameless kin of a traitor!

Why had Jacalrin shouted to the *Morganaan enemy* that he was a shameless traitor?

"What happened to Peijak...Peijak Dollehan...?" Her voice, precarious like the moans of a choked animal, slowly became clearer. "What—what happened to Sir Peijak Dollehan after Queen Rarkalia's death?"

"I did not say you could ask questions," replied Paseid angrily. "Explain why that man acted affectionately with you, and how he knew about the existence of the mine not even the soldiers of this camp know about because of the gag order—"

"What happened to him?" she demanded. "How—how is it that there are those in Morgana wearing a mantle with the queen's symbol? I am asking how this came to be!" Reuyen's voice ripped in a thousand different ways.

Paseid stopped talking. The eyes of the woman, who had surprised many people with a courage quite unlike other docile northern women, were frozen, as though frightened.

Peijak Dollehan Rarkalia. The tale of the man who had betrayed

Rarke two hundred years ago and defected to Morgana was a tale that appeared within a couple pages of a history book. For a woman who apparently read books of military laws and orations not to know that famous story was paradoxical. Even the fact that she was bringing him up at this moment.

"Do you not know?"

"Why, just why would he be…of Morgana…? Why—what…?"

The woman was stuttering, unable to continue, and she looked like she had lost her mind. Paseid glared at her, then suddenly sprang up to bring back a book from the bookshelf positioned at the side of the tent.

It was an illustrated book that contained the houses, sigils, and symbols of each country. He opened one section, put it down on the table, and slammed his hand down on it with a loud bang.

A threatening warning ensued. "Do not pretend like you do not know that the man you kept in contact with in secret is the descendent of Peijak Dollehan Rarkalia, the ignominious betrayer of the north."

Reuyen's distraught eyes were fixed on one side of the tattered book Paseid pressed down on. She could see the clear butterfly design covered under the inside of his palm. She stumbled to the table and pushed his hand like she was trying to rip it away. The chillingly beautiful creature landed on the dead tree smelling of old leather, the design that should've been recorded as the queen's symbol, was…

Her eyes slid down bit by bit.

Betrayer Peijak Dollehan founds:
Mariposa – of Morgana

Her eyes stopped on the writing she could not understand.

"This…"

This is not your rightful place, dear sister.

The memory wretchedly echoed in her ear. Reuyen barely regained her balance. She leaned on the table with one hand. Her limbs trembled, and her spine felt fuzzy with chills.

Traitor.

She engraved the unbelievable word on her mind. Like someone who thought staring at it so would change the word itself.

"This cannot...this..."

Her voice repeated it over and over. Her throat ached like she had swallowed a blade, and her tongue shivered like it had been touched by fire. Then, she suddenly stopped. Her oft-tranquil face distorted like that day when she turned seven.

Reuyen lost the grip of her body at the rush of stupefaction and slipped down to the floor with her hand still on the table.

How?

She finally regretted neglecting Peijak because she'd been afraid of those who would rejoice at her death.

How?

But it was already too late.

"This is the end of your absurd behavior," said Paseid. "If you do not explain your acquaintance with Balroid Peijak of Mariposa, I will arrest your brother and the rest of your family this instant to closely interrogate and punish them. Keeping contact with an enemy during wartime by itself signifies treason. The punishment will be execution."

Sss. Following the sound of the swiftly drawn metal, Paseid's unforgiving blade touched her neck. Reuyen felt goosebumps run along her body at the cold metal touching her skin. She clenched her teeth. The eyes shining through her hair revealed a disordered resignation.

"Sidan—Sidan doesn't know anything. My parents do not know anything either," she stammered.

"Then state what you know and who you are."

A tsunami of reality that she could no longer laugh off or give excuses for crashed over her.

"I am...I am."

She raised her head.

As she did, the tattered strategy book neatly laid on the table caught her eye. The book that carried the dullness of years seemed like it had already been sewn back together several times. The shadow of an already faded design on the cover jumped out at her.

The shock from the appearance of an odd order of knights was not just applicable to the Rarkians. The Morganaan army also wondered who these knights were who appeared and shook the entire military system.

Many witnessed the thousands of knights in blue armor standing in formation, with over ten thousand soldiers standing behind them. There were those who excitedly chattered that *the ones* looked like a great wave crashing on the plain.

No one could deny that the situation had taken a sharp turn in an unexpected direction, starting with the collapse of Olzore. The rumor that the commander-in-chief of the black lion army, Marche Carl Rovantis, might resign had become a fait accompli within half a day.

Then there was the appearance of the murderous knights who carried a blue banner, Mariposa. They were the object of fear for those who were honest, and the object of detestation and disdain for those who were ashamed to admit their fears. Is a friend who frightens their friends truly a friend? They could not help but ask that question when it came to Mariposa.

Regardless of the soldiers' initial impression of them, the knights in blue armor moved in an orderly fashion and occupied various sections of the camp bit by bit. The heads of the black lion army could not hide their confusion.

"Sir Visevar, this does not make any sense."

The question was pointed at the banner bearer, Sir Visevar, who was also the second-in-command of the black lion's army. He was a middle-aged man of great stature, especially among the small but stoutly built southerners.

Marquis Rovantis, the commander-in-chief, was not in his right mind at the moment, so the fact the knights were visiting the second-in-command instead to seek a solution to the situation was not an odd event.

About three months ago, they had received the notice that Count Zars from the east would lead the reinforcements, after rumors circulated that Count Servantes from the middle of the country or the knight from House Loweia who led Ebloom's mercenary company would be dispatched.

But the one who arrived at the Morganaan camp was not Count Zars; he was Count Mariposa. And he carried a royal document stating that he had been appointed as the new commander-in-chief.

"Do not display disloyalty," Visevar coldly answered and threw the fabric he'd just torn apart into the fire. It was a letter from his family on the archipelago a knight of House Mariposa had brought. It was not filled with greetings or how-do-you-dos. It was a simple summary of the current situations on the archipelago and at Angredium.

There were three main topics: a question about whether his house should dispatch at least a little bit of its men; the current, urgent situation in Simore Archipelago spurred by the collapse of Olzore; and the news of the Angredium Kingdom, which was not too far away from the archipelago. The most infuriating thing in the letter for him was that King Ionin of Angredium had given a public speech about the fall of the impregnable fort.

"Even so, Mariposa? It's too much, sir. If it were someone like Sir Loweia...no, you, Sir Visevar."

Visevar turned his attention from the lamenting knight to his now tattered sword.

Too much.

Could the talk of too much or too little even exist under absolute imperial orders? It was a significant insolence to even dare to judge such a thing.

The soldiers of the black lion already knew that Belrevirehein II was that kind of an emperor. He didn't think much of life and dictated the decisions on most of the matters outside of the archipelago. The south pretended to be proud of this by justifying its subordination with the phrase *dictation is the pride of the southern imperial house,* but there were times when one could not help but ask if that were right or not.

A couple years ago, Belrevirehein II had put Mariposa on the list of the central nobles who could freely enter the imperial palace. Since then, the people knew that Belrevirehein II had his eyes on the current Count Mariposa, Balroid.

Still, they could not have been able to anticipate that he would think to put Mariposa and Rarke against each other. Did the emperor think this war was some children's game? Unless that was so, he would not have appointed Count Mariposa as not even the second-in-command, but the commander-in-chief, knowing that either side would be emotionally involved in this war.

The reason dictation is not right is clear. It is the fisherman's duty to catch fish and pick clams, and it is the huntsman's duty to hunt or raise animals for food. Selling satin and utensils is a merchant's job, and raising crops is a farmer's job. One man cannot be proficient in every field. We have forgotten that. I do not mean to praise the way the northern royal court is run. But they have nobles who can officially oppose the king to direct the king in a sensible way. We are no more than hundreds of different countries tied together under the name of an empire with the oppression of building private armies and the emperor's right to appoint whomever he wants. This is on a different subject than the claims that we should strictly apply our laws on the descendent of the black lion. But at times, we must raise our voices.

The one who'd said those words to Visevar was Duke Zordia, who incessantly opposed the war against Rarke. Duke Zordia was once one of the closest advisors of Belrevirehein II, but he turned his back on the imperial house when the issue of his duchess and Belrevirehein II's affair had surfaced.

About two years ago, Visevar had considered those the words of a petty man holding a grudge for having his wife stolen away. But now, he couldn't help but think that Duke Zordia was right.

The emperor did not know war. He was an almighty being who could not see every soldier's face, and hence could not know how each of his decisions caused such varying results.

"Have they not reported Count Mariposa's arrival yet?" asked Visevar.

"No, sir. Marquis Rovantis is waiting only for him right now."

A sigh escaped his mouth at the thought of their commander-in-chief restlessly waiting for Balroid. The more he breathed in to resolve and let it out, the more his lungs filled up with muggy frustration.

Visevar knew that he was not a perfectly innocent person, but he believed a fight was only cleanly resolved when it was fairly executed and there were no personal feelings involved.

That's the end of that, then. Now, the scale of this war will become even larger than it already was.

The main cause of the current racket in the Morganaan camp, House Mariposa, had had an idiosyncratic beginning.

It had begun two hundred years ago, when the last prince of the Rarkalia Dynasty, who'd left the north seeking asylum, had been granted a land west of the Iga Mountains by Dernajuke IV (the first emperor, Valarjeff I), who was the king of Morgana at the time. The land beyond the mountain range in the southern continent was a barren land, and there, Peijak Dollehan Rarkalia had founded his house, Mariposa, and devoted his whole life to Morgana.

It was right after Rarke's conquest had ended. The southerners had detested House Mariposa as much as the northerners did. Amidst the countless prejudices and various practical issues, House Mariposa had established a unique system to survive. They'd volunteered to become the dogs of the Morganaan imperial family, paid their taxes with blood, and trained mercenaries for their army instead of strictly regulated private soldiers. It was quite a famous tale.

Of their recent achievements, the ones people still remembered were how they'd crushed the outskirts of Angredium, massacred minority groups, and greatly contributed in blocking the Daraks, who were marching south to invade Tolf.

They were also the pendulum that balanced the relationships among two kingdoms and over twenty lands west of the Iga Mountains, where their home, Ragodesis, was located. They were the ones who had saved the empire's border when the king of Vayn, who died ten years ago or so, attempted to undertake an invasion of the west. In short, they already exercised quite an influence when it came to brute force. Visevar would not have had to think this deeply if ability to influence and honor held the same meaning.

On top of these, they'd gained the notoriety of being an invincible order of knights who had not once lost since the current head, Balroid Peijak Mariposa, was delegated all powers.

Sure, it was reassuring to have strong soldiers during wartime, but a massacre was not all there was to a war. Rather, it was a great fight where rules and morality needed to be adhered to more than anywhere else.

Visevar turned his back to the knight and walked out of the tent, trying to hide his complicated feelings. He looked up at the dark midday sky. It seemed like the rain was not going to stop.

"I'm sure His Imperial Majesty had his reasons."

Even while saying so, he was certain of the darkness already above them.

The appearance of Mariposa was a clear trigger for war.

CHAPTER TWENTY-NINE

The rain poured hard.

By the time Balroid returned to the Morganaan camp, it was already early night, with the sun below the horizon.

"My lord."

The former commander-in-chief, Marche Carl Rovantis, who had been biting his nails and waiting for Balroid to show his face, ran out from under the awning of his tent and shouted at the top of his lungs.

"Mariposa! Explain the meaning of this!"

The knight on a completely soaked black horse turned his head to look down at Marche. The night's shadow cast upon his helmet hid his face. Marche was overcome with the terrifying feeling of being chased to the edge of a cliff as he stared into the undistinguishable face.

"Explain to me this very moment how this—!"

"Bring me a negotiator who is skillful enough to discuss the prisoners with Rarke." With that, Balroid turned all of his attention away from Marche. One of the knights who was standing nearby quickly ran off to carry out the order.

"How dare you—how dare you ignore me!" Marche screamed, which sounded more like a reproach to his insipid attitude. "What are you doing right now, Mariposa? How dare you insult me like this! I do not know how you inveigled His Imperial Majesty with that snake of a tongue of yours this time, but…!"

His pitifully cracking scream carried a mixture of desperation and rage. It was because he knew what would happen if he simply stepped back, after spending the whole year infuriating the emperor by emptying the exchequer for provisions for the army.

Balroid, who was remaining silent like he could not hear, slowly dismounted his horse. He took off the helmet that was dripping water and blocking his sight and threw it aside.

The thoroughly wet reddish-brown hair and the blue eyes as clear as the midwinter sky were revealed at last. Upon seeing him eye to eye, Marche winced and instinctively lowered his gaze and followed the black helmet that had been thrown down. With an irritating clang, the helmet rolled through a puddle and stopped by Marche's feet.

"The emperor's orders have already been decreed."

"This—this—this is a preposterous measure. The last defeat was due to the idiotic general of Fort Olzore!"

A numbing silence covered the area.

"Do you, Marquis Rovantis, know why Olzore collapsed?" The chillingly low voice pierced through the pouring rain and reached Marche's ears.

Marche recalled the fallen Olzore, then recalled the emperor's fury and let out a dreadful moan. On top of everything, he didn't know much about the fort's collapse. A blush rose in Marche's cheeks.

But like he didn't even remember asking the question, Balroid turned his back to Marche and fixed his eyes on the black horse he'd ridden here. He held the hilt of his sword in his hand.

"Oh, the general deserved to die as well," Balroid muttered, and gave a cynical smile.

Another legend of the undefeatable had crumbled on that revolting land, Olzore.

Pitch-black eyes. The horse he was on fluttered his long eyelashes in his barding. He was shivering, wet from the rain. Balroid quietly gazed into the black eyes in the barding, then scrunched his lips. They suddenly reminded him of someone. The remnants of the fury that had subsided at last during the ride back suddenly sprang up to the surface again.

"That will all be revealed through an investigation!" cried the Marche. "Balroid, it seems like your arrogance is soaring through the sky because of the single fact that your house has entered the fifteen central nobles! But, His Imperial Majesty will soon know of your filthy blood—!"

"You do not even know who stands there."

"Who doesn't know the Rarkian army is ther—"

Laughter broke out through Balroid's wet lips, which had stayed motionless. The frighteningly sharp-edged sword hanging by his side swung out without a warning. *Neighhhh...* The horse's whinny ceased. The fierce cry of the blade resounded, and hot streams of blood gushed out and up through the rain. Steam flowed through the air with the revolting smell.

Startled, Marche gaped and ungracefully stumbled back. But not paying any attention to him, Balroid just stared down at the black horse's head rolling around on the ground. Like his eyes were fixed, or taken hold of.

At last, the headless body of the horse splashed blood as it crumbled down. A couple knights stepped back at the massive body falling. Only then did Balroid look back at Marche, shaking the blood off the sword.

"Take it away."

It was extremely ambiguous. *Take it away? Who? Me?* Marche winced and made a squeak, then came back to his senses. The female knight who was standing like a wooden doll the whole time started to move at Balroid's order.

At his single, cold word, and Eila's single movement of the eyes, four knights wearing the blue armor disassembled the dead horse's massive body lying limp on the ground. Blood splattered everywhere, and the sounds of flesh being torn apart and bones being ground echoed. They dismantled the horse into bits, then threw the horse's body onto a small wagon without much care. The head of the poor dead horse was carelessly thrown onto the wagon, as well, and soon disappeared out of sight.

Balroid wiped his bloody lips with his thumb and continued, "If you intend to appeal to the imperial decree, I will not stop you. But first, you will have to visit the archipelago. Is there anything else you'd like to say?"

Marche fumed like he would stop breathing altogether, then turned around. *Stomp, stomp, stomp.* He intentionally walked away rougher, tougher, and faster.

Once Marche disappeared, the tension lessened a bit. Balroid raised his head and gazed in the direction he had ridden this whole afternoon.

Eila approached and spoke. "My lord."

"The preparations?"

"I completed most of the transfer in your place before you arrived, my lord." Eila's straight gaze went down to the bloodied ground. "I will prepare a new horse, my lord."

"Good."

Eila turned around at the nonchalant reply. But she stopped after taking only a couple steps away. Eila carefully turned back around and asked, "Have you, by any chance, not met the one you sought, my lord?"

Balroid's furious eyes looked straight at Eila's calm ones.

Rather than getting flustered or showing signs of being frightened, she kneeled down. "If you were offended, my lord, please punish my insolence for daring to be presumptuous in your presence."

He gazed at the northern sky. He once again sank into the feeling of dreaming.

It had been a long, long time. Long enough to churn his innards by just trying to count those years.

He'd met her. After two hundred years, he'd met her once more. It didn't matter if her looks were different. The eyes that were looking at him, the lips that called him, they all were...

Peijak.

Swan.

His eyes trembled with excitement. Ecstatic joy rushed through his lower abdomen, tensing it.

He'd once again met Swan, his only world.

At last, time started to flow again. At last, he saw the light outside the hell. But all he could enjoy was the delight of a reunion. In desperate anxiety, like he was standing at the edge of a cliff, he slowly gazed across his sight fogged by the rainfall. He saw the blue butterfly flag he had ordered to hang in places across the camp. That much was clear.

How...how...how can you wear their armor, sit on their saddle, and point your sword at Rarke...!

Balroid calmed his breath.

He was already certain about meeting her; he had no doubts about that. This was the reward of those atrocious times from two hundred years ago. But it could have been something unexpected that required a bit of time to think about for her. For now, her recognizing him was enough. Seeing with his eyes that she had returned was enough. He had already waited more than two hundred years in hell and had no reason not to spend a bit more time there.

"As of now...I can be patient for a bit longer."

He tilted his chin and looked up, mumbling like he was trying to brainwash himself. The black night looked over him.

Under the darkness that swallowed the entire sky, Swan was still with Brionake. Rage boiling like a furnace surged and made his throat feel like it was melting down from the inside. The starlight embedded in the night's layers was as bright as the eyes of the man atop a pitch-black horse who had looked down at him.

Balroid looked up at the sky for a while, then moved his fatigued feet. Fierce hatred and delight entwined and filled up his footsteps like rainwater.

Faint steam escaped his mouth, flowed through the waning rainfall, then dissipated.

Under the night on a battlefield where even the smoke rising from the fire disappeared into the darkness covering the sky.

When was it?

She was sitting on the throne of a small kingdom somewhere west of Rarke, in the empty throne room of the king where there was no one to harm her even when she took off her helmet and armor. The air was depressed with the smell of blood. Dismissing the familiar stench and the slowly ceasing screams as though they were air, she lowered her dry lids.

The scene clearly drawn on her closed eyelids and her blackened eyes was the same as always.

All the people of all the countries worshipped and feared Rarke. They offered flowers of admiration. Some were wary of her rather romantic wish, saying that it was an uncontrollable idealism, but no matter. She was certain all would become Rarke's glory in the end, so she did not care about their words. All the kingdoms on this continent would lose the masters of their thrones and submit to Rarke.

She sat there, enjoying the silence and drunk with victory, until the horrendously broken door to the throne room opened with an uncanny sound. She glanced at the group of knights coming into the room. A man covered in blood was at the front. She waved her hand while still leaning on the remnants of the throne.

"What majesty you bring with you, Sir Dollehan."

The knight at the front nodded at her sharp, cold voice. Then, the knights following behind turned around at once and exited the room, like they had been rehearsing it. When the scattered echoes of their armor clanging at the joints and their army boots hitting the floor subsided, the knight in a black suit of armor approached her, a bloodied sword in his hand. Her eyes narrowed, and his immediate reply followed.

"Seems like my sister is unhappy."

"Peijak."

"Forgive me for unpleasantly carrying my sword around like this. My scabbard has broken. Sir Chesa and Sir Belakish have completed their missions as well. We killed every single one of them, including the queen who had run away, so all the troublesome buds have been nipped. So, let us leave now, Your Majesty."

The queen listened to the tragic news without changing her facial expression at all. The deaths of those she did not love never stirred even an inkling of pity or guilt in her. She listened to Peijak's sweetly spoken report and caressed the throne of the small country she had taken apart to bits with her fingertips. It felt cold and hollow.

"How long did it take until we got here?"

"Four months?"

"If those who attempt meaningless strife block our way everywhere we go, it will take quite a while."

She sounded as if she were dissatisfied with destroying a kingdom with two hundred years of history in only four months, even if it was a small kingdom in the middle of nowhere where not even maps clearly stated its name. Peijak, who was still standing, smoothly bent one knee to sit down.

The queen nonchalantly tossed a question. "The body of the queen?"

"I have thrown the body aside and brought only her head. Would you like to go see it?"

The queen's detached blue eyes landed on the knight's sword soaked in blood. His sword looked grotesque stained with the blood of a noble queen of a worthless kingdom who had looked down on Rarke. The curdled, dripping blood on that blade would have been the fear and regret of the end of a life shed.

She pushed down on the armrest and rose.

"I should not be satisfied with this little a victory to make Belbarote understand."

"Why do you care about the duke regent? Though he is taking care of the stately matters, the throne is yours, dear sister. You are Rarke as you are."

Peijak bent down toward her to look into her eyes and whispered, "If you wish to unite the continent, do so. If it is your wish to crush your enemies below your feet, do so. If you wish to burn the world, do so. If the battlefield is a shelter for you, I will make the entire world one, wherever that may be."

Instead of just passing by like she was going to, she stopped to caress Peijak's cheek. "Now, the battlefield is more comfortable than the palace." She recalled saying so before. Her lips lightly touched Peijak's cheek, then separated. "It is a reward for your commendable behavior."

"Dear sister."

Peijak reached his hand behind her neck. Then he pulled the butterfly mantle hanging on her back. He pressed the noble fabric to his lips, then raised his cool eyelids to longingly gaze into her eyes. The pitiable admiration surging inside of him whispered. "I do not know the reason you chose this, but flying freely suits you in its own way."

The layers of his faint, low voice echoed and lifted the light movements of the wings.

"Fly, without a single worry. Do not care about the duke regent, nor Cratoia, Ardonis, nor Roinsa, nor Enhoza of Sichin. I will make bloom a flower you can sit on, sit and rest on, wherever it may be."

The queen just scoffed. "What a poem you are reciting."

The war continued for years.

Everywhere she set foot on became an offering for Rarke, and every-where she laid her eyes upon, blood-soaked earth like red flowers bloomed. And behind that queen always followed the best knight of Rarke, Peijak Dollehan Rarkalia, his clear presence like a shadow under the sunlight.

Something that could not be explained by any word, whether it be friendship, love, or admiration, existed between them.

Thus, in the present after two hundred years, another story began.

-To be continued-

THE HYDRANGEA GARDEN

"May I ask why you made a butterfly yourself?"

"You never ask about such things."

"I thought women liked to compare themselves to a beautiful flower."

"A flower...oh, a flower."

"Do you dislike them?"

"Flowers?"

"Yes."

"I do like flowers as well. I simply do not receive them, since no one gifts them to me."

"I will procure some on my way back, once official business is completed, and send them here."

The queen stopped on the marble floor covered by a red carpet. Then slowly turned back and smiled.

"It's a joke, so no need to answer so seriously. Of course, I like flowers, but I did so because I liked blue things more."

What was she trying to say?

Her tranquil voice resounded like a lullaby.

"But I have never in my entire life seen a blue flower. I have seen butterflies, though. Everywhere I set foot on is covered in red, so why shouldn't the thing I like be blue?"

〜

Spring had sprung. The fierce winter stuck its tail between its legs and ran off. But the capital city of Rarke, Muiyadro, still suffered the fool's spring the winter had left behind. In the season when the persistent sprout that sprang on the infertile land reached its young leaves toward the sunlight, Muiyadro of the northern country was still cold.

A girl stretched out her neck like a deer and scanned the low walls of a mansion. The tip of the short girl's nose was frozen in a red hue in the chilly spring wind. The eyes moving restlessly were a clear pumpkin color.

The overseer of the duke's mansion in the heart of Muiyadro, Halman, found the girl and noiselessly went outside the walls of the mansion.

"His Grace has not arrived yet."

Elhien, who had been sneaking a peek inside, winced at the stately voice coming from right next to her, then changed her attitude into a prouder one and raised her chin.

"Long time, no see."

"Yes, my lady. I hope you were doing well. Where are your guards and maids?"

Elhien gave a quizzical smile instead of answering. Halman, the overseer of the masterless mansion, shook his head like he understood the meaning of that smile and handed her the flower he held. It was the famous blue hydrangea that was said to only grow in the greenhouse at Duke Brionake's mansion.

"I heard he is arriving sometime this morning…"

"A message came stating that he will be a day or two late because of the snowfall in the area, my lady."

Elhien took the flower. "I see."

Elhien just stared at the fragile but rough-feeling flower enwrapped by her hand. Then, with clearly disappointed eyes, she looked up at the massive mansion across the low walls. The red wolf banner was fluttering with dignity, regardless of the cold wind.

Achoo! Once her excited anticipation subsided, she started to suddenly feel the cold. When she sneezed, Halman offered, with a smile, "Would you like to warm yourself inside, my lady?"

Elhien scrunched up her pretty forehead, then shook her head, smiling brightly. "No. I'd better get going. My carriage is right over there, so no need to worry."

"Have a safe trip back home, then, my lady."

Elhien looked back at the banner of Brionake once more, unable to cast her regret away, then grinned. She held the flower lightly and gracefully turned around. It was clearly a well-thought-out movement to look more like an adult than anyone watching would have realized. Thinking the child was quite adorable, Halman smiled on the inside and bowed.

After a couple brisk steps, she suddenly came to a stop. Then she slowly looked around and smiled. "Can you keep my visit today as a secret?"

Halman finally made a sound like he was swallowing laughter when her heavy skirt was far out of sight. She was such a pure girl, just like one should be at her age. She was also a noble lady he would have to obey as his mistress before long, but simply watching her brought him joy.

Elhien Devi Laperovahan was loved by all. She was Paseid's betrothed.

In the early morning, children wearing thick coats ran around on the dirt roads in the capital and merchants waited in line for the morning market to open. Even in the welcomed cold of the spring that tickled their noses, the people started their days with a prayer as always.

May today be as usual.

But a sight quite different from what was usual arrived, despite the prayers. There were knights that had come out in groups and were standing in front of the firmly shut gates of the castle like statues since early in the day.

The knights wore white royal mantles draped over their backs and trapezoid armbands, brassards of their respective noble houses on their arms. They were standing in formation motionlessly. At their formidable presence, the people wondered if some serious event had occurred. But the knights did not budge. The spectators grew bored, and the people's curious eyes slowly turned away.

When the sun reached the highest point in the sky, a flag signaling to open the gates fluttered on the bridgehead. The ear-piercing sound of the pulley echoed. A group of knights and a cavalcade following them appeared on the other side of the slowly opening gates.

A red wolf banner fluttering in the spring breeze grew larger and larger. The royal knights started to move. Those who were quick enough clapped their hands.

"His Grace, the duke of the northwest, has come."

The people lost their interest and went back to their chores.

Paseid walked through the gates with many knights and nearly double the number of servants. He scanned the scenery of Muiyadro in the cool spring. It had been nearly four months since he'd last come here. Paseid spent more time in his land, Rokland, than in the capital, unlike the other central nobles. Even so, he was too busy going back and forth between the barren lands in the west and the coastal region in the southwest for the last couple years to visit often.

The lower city of Muiyadro did not look that different from his last visit. The roads had become a bit sleeker and the houses were cleaner and taller. The reason he was filled with tranquil serenity and affectionate emotions at the common, ordinary sight was probably because this was the home of his childhood. If the times were peaceful, he would have been able to enjoy those emotions a bit more. It was a shame he couldn't.

Paseid turned his eyes away from the miniscule things to look at the massive white castle boasting its overpowering presence at the end of the crossroad. The walls of the palace, with its back to the Galiau Mountains from the northern legends, were laid out like ever-present snow. Beyond the walls, he saw towers standing tall like straight trees and a round roof hung like a rainbow connecting the sky and the earth.

The sight of the capital's palace standing in harmony with the mountain range was blinding, like a large sepulcher of snow.

A knight wearing a white wolf mantle on his back sped up to ride alongside Paseid, who was riding in front of everyone else.

"His Majesty is waiting for you, my lord duke. The prime minister and the other noblemen have already gathered at Norte

Hall. Please allow me to accompany you until you enter the palace."

Only then did Paseid turn his head. "All of them?"

"Yes, my lord duke. So, the sooner, the better."

Paseid gazed at the royal knights' glum faces.

If it was a council meeting with all the central nobles and high officials at a time like this, it must not be about something good. He turned his horse away from the mansion.

"Sir Keheif, move first and lead the others to the mansion. I will first head to the palace."

"Yes, sir." A knight of the duke raised his flag high up at his orders. "Follow me!"

With the thundering shout, the cavalcade of the people with the red wolf banner broke off in the opposite direction at the crossroad.

Paseid watched the slowly disappearing tail of the cavalcade and gazed in the direction of Brionake's central mansion, then turned his eyes to the grand palace on the other side of the road.

Paseid untied the tattered, dusty mantle once he arrived at the palace. He put on a new red wolf mantle over the back of his dress suit, which was a handsome navy uniform, the symbol of a soldier, with layers of silver embroidery.

A royal servant in charge of his wardrobe carefully wrapped a rope made of golden strings around his waist to fix the straightened pleats of the outer layer of his dress suit. Once his clothes were set, Paseid snatched the mantle before the servant could even drape it over his back.

Even though he only intended to wash up and dress in the simplest form that was still respectable, for he could not show the evidence of the days of journey in the presence of the king, a fair amount of time had passed.

His feet maneuvered through the complicated corridors of the palace and the roads stretched out like a maze, then came to a stop. The guards before the massive door to the throne room of Norte Hall, the place that was said to have the coldest throne in the world, recognized Paseid, blew their horns, and opened the door.

"Paseid Calandok Brionake, the son of the red wolf, the head of Palan Sholgo, and His Grace the only duke."

The throne room that was buzzing with the already arrived guests' discussions fell silent at once as he entered. Paseid's black eyes grew calm at the cool air of the throne room rushing toward him.

King Terendoke was sitting at the end of the seemingly infinite red carpet, and Prime Minister Laperovahan and Marquis Toulsio from the east were standing on either side of him. Paneche, a well-known scholar of diplomatic science with a skilled tongue, also from the east, and Count Chesa, the commander of the knights of the capital, were standing opposite them.

"The wolf of the northwest has arrived."

Terendoke's clearly irritated voice greeted him. Paseid briefly gazed at the man with dark-brown hair wearing a pure white garment, then walked along the carpet. Once he reached the first step leading to the throne, he bent his left knee.

"Greetings, Your Majesty. Paseid Calandok Brionake, the lord duke, has come at Your Majesty's calling."

"Yes. First, rise."

"Yes, Your Majesty."

"Thank you for coming at such short notice. It is only right that you be greeted with a feast after this long a time, but we will first start with the meeting, as this is a pressing time."

Terendoke's voice became a bit calmer. But his eyes, as blue as Sichin's ocean, still flashed with complicated displeasure.

Paseid stood up and stood at the left of the lowest step. Prime Minister Laperovahan, who was standing on the right, made a light gesture to say hello when their eyes met. Paseid reluctantly responded with a nod.

The discussion that had been briefly cut off because of Paseid's entrance started again.

"I hear the Galkamas' invasion has become more vigorous and that you are hard at work. I hope I have not inconvenienced you at a busy time."

"No, Your Majesty."

"Well, I am not unaware that you are doing well on your own."

Terendoke seemed more displeased than usual. He scrunched up his lips, then made a flicking movement with his fingers above the armrest. "This summoning was rather abrupt because I determined that discussing the diplomatic discord within the empire with you was necessary. To the point, then. I'm sure you have heard about the empire's perverse acts. What exactly do you know?"

"Only what I heard from the night wolf you sent me and the contents of your letter, Your Majesty."

"Gilloheim, explain."

"Yes, Your Majesty."

Gilloheim was the name of Prime Minister Laperovahan. He bowed his head and ensued with his explanation.

"Half a year ago, the empire demanded tributes, tributary women, and laborers from Rarke and the neighboring kingdoms. It was not just Rarke. According to the rumors, they have relayed that imperial order to the minorities living within the empire by borrowing land—Angredium, Saligar, the principality of Illaren in the north, and even Vayn. Most of the southern countries have an intimate relationship with the empire, so it makes sense, but it is preposterous to take such an oppressive attitude toward Rarke. So, we sent ambassadors to express this injustice and request a remodification."

Paseid locked eyes with Prime Minister Laperovahan for a moment, then nodded. "Yes, Prime Minister. I have heard that you went yourself with Paneche and Marquis Toulsio to rectify the inappropriate demand."

Paseid had left the capital at the time to stop the frequent invasions of outside tribes in his land in the countryside in the northwest, but that didn't mean he had gone deaf. The reports from Brionake's spies scattered all over the continent allowed him to have a rough estimation of the current situation.

"Then is this due to the empire's demands still not being rectified?"

Marquis Toulsio, who was standing glumly with a pale face, nodded at Paseid's question. Terendoke raised the hand not being used to support his chin. "Belja, show the lord duke."

The servant who was standing by handed Paseid an extremely crumpled letter. The letter with the roaring lion seal was from Morgana.

Paseid could feel Terendoke's rage at his fingertips.

Brionake, Terendoke Ranfel.

Forgetting the mercy the empire has shown you thus far is truly unfortunate. A dog daring to bite a lion will be killed by the lion, so beware. The empire's magnanimity of striving to guard the laws of the continent will show one final mercy. The crime of disobeying will be punished by expulsion of the name of your country. If you mean to atone for your crimes, bow down. Olzore is always open to you. If not, only the sharp blade will be aimed at you.

Belrevirehein II Rahdos Sharl Loare Mohgan Morgania.

Veins bulged out from the back of Paseid's hands as he read the letter from introduction to conclusion. Not a single section was not a provocation. All but Terendoke looked down.

"Expulsion of the name of our country does not quite make sense," Prime Minister Laperovahan muttered.

It was absolutely preposterous. Though it was indeed the only empire on the continent, the north and the south had clearly distinct roots. From Rarke's point of view, it did not matter what Morgana did to countries of the south like Saligar, Vayn, and Angredium. But if they meant to rule as the suzerain of Rarke as well, that changed things.

"Not only that, but Marquis Toulsio and Paneche have also said that they have met the descendent of the traitor. Tell us that story, Marquis."

Marquis Toulsio stepped forward, rubbing his long, braided beard. He was a man from Gania, a place known to still be retaining most of the customs of Gideraka of the east.

"Yes, we have met him. Though we only saw his face from afar."

Marquis Toulsio's brusque answer was followed by the explanation from Paneche, a man who had sharp, narrow eyes and a rather fierce-looking, protruding nose. "As I heard while we were staying at Thrush Street, where the administrative matters of Morgana are said to be processed, he is encouraging the emperor and influencing him by supporting the construction to extend the imperial palace. I do not know how much Belrevirehein II trusts that man, but even so, there is talk that he has had a blatant dispute with

Duke Zordia, the man known to be the most reasonable in the southern empire, over a related topic."

House Zordia was one of the greatest powers existing in the southern empire. And the current Duke Zordia was a cousin of Belrevirehein II and was once famous for being one of his close advisors, but he was now showing skepticism of the southern empire's dictatorial government, or something like that. Though there was not much exchange, Paseid had heard the name once or twice.

Count Rougak Chesa, who was quietly staying in his place and twitching his graying eyebrows, pounded his chest once like he was frustrated. "I am sure he is the cause."

Not daring to throw the letter addressed to the king on the ground, Paseid handed it back to the servant. His voice was rigid, like he was spitting out something bitter. "Mariposa."

When he spoke the name they had been furtively avoiding, the faces of those listening grew glum.

"Do you mean that man, Balroid Iserse, Peijak Mariposa?"

Mariposa. It was an unwelcomed and shameful name.

The house of a traitor who deserted his duties and kneeled before Morgana to officially throw Rarke's dignity in the dirt. It had happened two hundred years ago and now that house had completely made its place in Morgana as one of the fifteen central houses, but Rarke did not forget.

Especially when they thought of today's Count Mariposa. Whatever their lives in the south were like, it hadn't been even ten years since he'd started to be talked about. Balroid Iserse Mariposa, who had purged all the moderate relatives related to his house as soon as the former Count Mariposa died and become the head of the house at a young age, had taken the name of *Peijak*, and made himself known in Rarke.

When they first heard the news, the Rarkians had gnashed their teeth. He should've known to be ashamed of himself for running away to the south. How dare he give himself the name of the traitor? The name *Peijak* could not welcomed by Morgana, either. It was a name of the northern prince who had once tried to destroy them.

As the south was massive, it was inundated with various nobilities, and the imperial family of Morgana had a duty to be responsible for the south's disorder to effectively reign under the title of an empire. This was the reason the south had strict prohibitions on establishing private armies, unlike the north, where the establishment of private armies was relatively accepted.

Among them, the Mariposas had been an exception because they used a loophole in the laws and identified themselves as a mercenary company rather than a private army. They subsisted for two hundred years as a house of brute force that volunteered to take care of the imperial family's dirty business. It was only a matter of course for the Morganaan imperial family to regulate Mariposa.

According to the rumors, the north had also been thrown into a racket when Balroid first announced the change to his name, and even the current emperor, Belrevirehein II, had summoned him by force.

But instead of a reflection and a rectification of his action, Count Balroid Mariposa had compared Belrevirehein II to Valarjeff I, the greatest man in the history of the continent, who had elevated Morgana to an empire and confused the world once more by officially pledging his loyalty.

Whether it was because he was satisfied with Mariposa or because there was some deal happening under the table, the incident of Count Mariposa's changing of his name had petered out. Belrevirehein II had even officially approved his new name after publicly announcing that he had an upright will and firm loyalty. Even if one tried to think kindly, it was a blatant mockery directed at Rarke.

The Rarkians had not stayed quiet at the time. When the name they had shamefully buried came back alive, a fraction of the Rarkians who were in Morgana drew their swords in rage. A couple secret agents were discovered in the process and were executed.

Now that Paseid thought about it, it had probably started then. The beginning of the tension and tightly packed away animosity between Morgana and Rarke spilling over the edges.

Paseid suppressed his surging enmity. "We cannot respond to them. Rarke is not a subject of Morgana."

"He is right," Count Rougak Chesa agreed. "There is no reason for us to suffer the tyranny of the empire that even Vayn escaped."

"Lord Duke, that is why we have invited you here," Prime Minister Laperovahan answered Rougak.

"Do you not think that we cannot turn a blind eye to them anymore, since their intentions are obvious? We hastily invited you to ask for Palan Sholgo's agreement."

Palan Sholgo. That was the title of the head of the royalist Palan party.

Paseid raised his head to study Terendoke's face. He had an overwhelming hunch.

Prime Minister Laperovahan drove the nail into the coffin. "Why else would Count Chesa and Marquis Toulsio be here?"

Count Chesa and the old Marquis Toulsio, who had been remaining silent all the while, bowed their heads.

Paseid fixed his eyes on Terendoke. The four elements required to form the atmosphere of a war were all already established. Morgana's threat was underlined by their soldiers, the Rarkians' by their will to resist enemies. And the hope and expectant uncertainty that they might win this time, washing away the shame from the past, and the incendiary will that encouraged conflict.

"Have you decided so already, Your Majesty?"

"We are only waiting for your decision, Lord Duke."

Terendoke glared at the letter from Morgana in the servant's hands like he was about to rip it apart, then answered Paseid's gaze in a more relaxed tone than expected. "The time has come to pay them back. What do you say, Lord Duke?"

Jacalrin's brisk footsteps echoed in the hallway. Realizing that the walls of the mansion were now painted over with dark murals, he whistled.

The painting was in a dark and glum style, not at all aligned with the sight of warm sunlight filling the hallway. It was probably according to the prime minister's taste. As this was the mansion of an overwhelmingly rich prime minister's house, it was quite an entertainment to just look at the decorations and carpets and such that changed every time he visited.

His speed of walking was rather inconsiderate to the maid of the Laperovahans following him, and he slowed down by a wink when he reached the hallway on the third floor, then finally came to a stop in front of a door in the center of the hall. Jacalrin carelessly knocked on the door.

"Yo, I'm coming in!"

Innocently glancing at the out-of-breath maid panting and running after him, Jacalrin swung open the door without even waiting for an answer.

"Elhien, did you hear? Today ..."

The room suddenly became chaotic. The very first greeting he received was a clamor of a group of women nearly screaming.

"Er..."

Jacalrin was just as flustered at the sight that revealed itself behind the door.

"Sir Chesa, you cannot just barge in like that!" The maids let out flurried grunts.

Elhien, who was still in her underwear while getting the help of the wardrobe maids to put on a heavy dress, saw him and turned white.

"You, you, you...!"

The startled maid hastily covered her.

Jacalrin soon changed his flustered expression and rubbed his chin. He scanned Elhien, standing behind the maid from head to toe, with his light-green eyes. Then, he saw the various dresses laid out on the bed and the wardrobe maid's arms and grinned innocently.

"How much are you planning on wearing this time?"

"Get out!"

Jacalrin quickly closed the door when a hair accessory suddenly flew at him. Right after the door closed with a loud bang, he heard the sound of something hitting the door with great force.

After a short while, Jacalrin looked down at Elhien, who was refusing to even look at him like she was still angry. He scratched the back of his head.

"You should've locked the door properly."

"Do I have to lock the door of my own home now?"

"I'm sorry. But it didn't even occur to me that you might be getting up now and changing when it's already midday. I forgot you're lazy."

"It's not that I'm lazy...! Wait, are you saying that you haven't done anything wrong?"

Elhien blushed like she was about to explode. Realizing that her mistress was in a particularly bad mood right now, the maid who was straightening the lace flowing on the purple silk dress quickly stepped back.

But Jacalrin, the one who'd actually made her mad, sat at the table without even asking for permission and sneered. "So, you're not lazy, but you were just changing into different dresses all day, hmm? You did hear that he's coming, didn't you? Gosh, women."

Elhien ignored him and answered in a calmer tone. "I knew way before you did. It's only right to be properly dressed when I'm seeing him after such a long time.'

"You don't look good in purple. No matter how many times you change, you just look like a kid!"

"Jacalrin!"

"Wouldn't it be proper to address me as 'sir,' since I've been ordained?"

"I'll treat you like a knight when you act like one. I can almost hear Count Chesa sighing because of you. I feel sorry for him."

Jacalrin, who was sitting with his arm hanging limp like a sloth's, glared at Elhien fiercely. Elhien held her chin up and smiled, like she was quite happy with that response.

"Right at my weak spot. If only I could just smack that little thing," Jacalrin said, shaking his head.

"Even if I weren't a little thing, you can't lay a single hand on me."

He rolled his eyes. "Please, the daughter of a prime minister is not all that fancy-schmancy."

"It is fancy-schmancy, thank you. Where did you even learn to speak like a good-for-nothing?"

Reading a sign of excitement in her eyes, Jacalrin gave up on responding and rested his chin on his hand. "Are you that happy?"

"Are you going to stay in my room? Shouldn't you be somewhere?"

Cheeky girl.

She might not have been that excited about having Jacalrin around because she already had a male sibling who was more than twenty years older than her and hence had already moved out, but Jacalrin was quite fond of her, since he only had Kalajesh as a sibling.

On top of that, because House Chesa had a more frequent exchange with House Laperovahan, for they were neutral, Elhien and Jacalrin were like friends. Having a father as great as the prime minister of a country, Elhien held her chin high and acted rather childishly with him at times, but that was not that big a problem for Jacalrin, who was very generous to "insolence."

"Did he contact you to meet some time?" he asked her. "Seemed like he was already in the palace."

"No, he didn't, but he's a busy man."

Jacalrin shook his head.

Elhien had been arranged to be Paseid's wife ever since she started to walk properly. So, it might be only right for her to love Paseid. But to think that she had been doing this since early morning was…what was the word?

"You poor thing."

"Me? Why?"

"You try so hard, but for what? A woman is most attractive when she is hard to get, you know. A man burns with love when a woman turns him down at least ten times when he tries to court her. But you're just putting yourself on a silver platter for him to take at his disposal. No wonder he doesn't see you as a woman."

Whether or not Elhien's face stiffened, Jacalrin mumbled with his chin on his hand like he didn't have a single care in the world. "Wait, isn't that the fundamental problem? His taste is…"

"I don't want to hear it. To be frank, Jacalrin, you're just aging without even a proper woman to marry. Why don't you worry about yourself before you start worrying about me? And start acting like an adult a little."

"It's not that I can't get married; I just don't want to."

"Huh?"

"I have someone I like."

"Who?"

"She has hair as black as a raven…and a killer body. Her breasts are so big that I just feel like I'm going to suffocate when I bury my head in them…and you don't even know how sexy she is…when she's nakey-nakey…I just melt…"

"Jacalrin! Stop saying such vulgar things!"

Elhien plainly revealed how flustered she was. She regretted giving him any attention at all much too late. But Jacalrin started guffawing at Elhien's cheeks that were as red as red could be. She was only sixteen, so no wonder she was so innocent.

"That's your problem right there. Of course, Paseid thinks you're just a child. You'll probably call the guards in shock when he unbuttons your top."

"Paseid is not some scoundrel and strumpet like you."

"I honestly cannot deny that I'm a scoundrel, but I'm not a strumpet, thank you very much. Oh, poor Paseid. How hard it would be to lead his house all by himself for years because he's bound to some silly child like you."

For she was still young, despite her acting like an adult. Elhien pretended to be just fine but failed to hide her sneaking sadness; it was written all over her face, as her cheeks scrunched up a bit and her eyes looked like they might be about to water.

Jacalrin didn't feel all that guilty, even though he'd just spewed out cruel stings. They were true. And it wasn't like a couple of his words were going to destroy their relationship.

One thing even Jacalrin, who was not interested in politics at all, knew was the balance between Prime Minister Laperovahan, the head of the Bant party, and Duke Brionake, the head of the Palan party. Elhien and Paseid's arranged marriage in the midst of the polarity between the two parties was, in short, a symbol of the firm political union of the royalists and the nobilities.

Paseid might be the object of love for Elhien, but at least to Paseid, this most likely held more of a meaning as a political relationship than anything else. Because she was not unaware of this, Elhien was fussing around and trying to get his attention. Well, if this was her effort to live at least a little more happily when her life was already all set for her, then it sure was commendable.

"You, you, you…"

But once Elhien's face went beyond becoming stiff and started to contort, he started to feel uneasy. Jacalrin tried to amend all the things he'd said. "Well, the fact that he won't care at all about you no matter how hard you try won't change, but you're still getting married to him, right? I mean…I should probably try harder to seem likable to the noble lady who will be a duchess in the future."

Her eyes welled up with tears at last.

Jacalrin stood up. "Hey…hey…?"

"You'll be doomed because of that mouth of yours. You will be doomed!" she cried.

"Come on, what did I say that was so bad? If you cry, all your powder's going to be ruined and you'll look like a monster."

Elhien clamped her lips shut. "Jacalrin…I never want to see you again!"

"Hey, that's too harsh to someone who doesn't have anyone else to play with but you. All right, I'll speak to Paseid on your behalf. Hmm? So, don't get mad at me. You're not going to cry, are you?"

But Elhien's face didn't seem to brighten up at all. Jacalrin twitched his fingers.

He didn't know what to do, for he'd only hung out with male siblings and women who were rough tomboys at best since he was a child. Jacalrin was a man who had learned by experience that it was easier to skedaddle as fast as he could with the excuse that he was giving them time to be alone than to carefully caress them, like caressing a glass that could shatter at any moment. But he couldn't just abandon someone of such importance and run away.

"I take it back! I take it back! You're perfectly his type! Yup! His type indeed!"

"Are you kidding me right now…?" Elhien's voice trailed off and her head dropped. Her tears dropped as well. It seemed like she was ailing on the inside even though she was pretending not to. To be fair, though, people said they were the perfect groom and bride, short of nothing, but those were just words. Their relationship was only a relationship tied by an arrangement in a stranger's eyes, nothing more.

"Pa—Paseid should be coming soon. If your eyes look like the carps' eyes in Lake Ryuga, he's gonna completely stop liking…"

Jacalrin stopped vomiting out any words that came to mind at last and tussled his hair. He didn't mean to make her cry like this, but alas, his filterless mouth had to go rogue and ruin everything.

Jacalrin contemplated whether he should wipe Elhien's tears or not. But that only ended as a thought. Instead, he felt an overwhelming surge of the desire to flee and started to back away.

"Why on earth do you just say whatever...!"

"I'm sorry, I'm sorry."

"What's saying sorry going to do? Why can't you stand not irritating me for a second?"

"It's not that I'm trying to irritate you; it's just true... Oh, I take that back. I take that back too!"

Jacalrin slapped his own mouth with his hand. Finding that Elhien's eyes were becoming vicious, he glanced at the closed door.

Then, a savior appeared.

"Little Sir Chesa, are you here? Big Sir Chesa is looking for you, sir."

"Kalajesh?"

"Yes, sir. He is at the entrance of the Laperovahan mansion right now."

Darn it. Jacalrin pouted at the pressure. He was supposed to participate in a guard training with Kalajesh. He had snuck out, and he wondered how Kalajesh knew that he was headed here. If he was seen wandering about like a lazy ne'er-do-well, Kalajesh would give him a lecture again.

Jacalrin contemplated for a minute, then sharply inhaled when he locked eyes with Elhien, who'd stopped crying at once and was glaring at him. The look of struggle soon changed to that of relief.

Before Elhien could reproach him again, he shouted, "Sorry! Kalajesh is looking for me, so I'd better go!" and ran out like the wind.

Paseid finally returned to his mansion at sundown.

The large, elegant mansion had been neatly cleaned and was in good order, despite withstanding years without its master. He looked at his mansion with tired eyes and moved his feet forward.

He didn't even have the energy to individually respond to all those who'd rushed out to greet their master who had suddenly returned. He went straight to his bedchamber to change out of his uncomfortable clothes, then listened to Halman's report of what had happened at the mansion since he'd been gone.

"Master, I have assigned the recently arrived knights and the servants in the east wing and the west wing, respectively. I will organize the list of guests who visited the mansion during your absence and present it as well. I have not changed anything while you were not here, Master, but if there are any grievances, please tell me straight away. You must have not eaten yet. I will prepare your dinner first."

"No need for a meal."

Halman looked disappointed for a moment at his stern answer, then bowed his head. "Also, I sent the document about the budget for the mansion to Rokland five days ago. Forgive me for not anticipating your visit and properly preparing for it."

"Halman, you have done well."

Halman's face soon brightened up by his expression of appreciation. But Paseid was not in a state of mind to engage in a conversation, for he was overwhelmed by complicated thoughts.

Now that Terendoke was firm on starting a war with Morgana, he blamed himself for not gladly agreeing, even though he was just as furious as him. They must have reached a decision on that matter far before his arrival. What Rarke needed to justify this war was royal blood, a chess piece with a considerable amount of experience that would increase the likelihood of winning.

The grudge between Rarke and Morgana had never changed since the old days. The animosity between them had existed since the foundation of the Brionake Dynasty, and every patriot of Rarke did not forget the shame.

But a war.

He had to spend his days with his sword never out of reach due to the frequent breakouts of fights at Rokland, the land of the Brionakes, and had inevitably grown up seeing more blood than anyone else in the capital, but that word was a word he'd never liked nor gotten used to. The people of the border had already bled enough.

The nobles of Muiyadro wanted a Brionake to be dispatched. Since Terendoke couldn't fight himself, their expectations naturally directed toward the Noble House Brionake.

If one tried to give an excuse to justify it, one could come up with hundreds of them. Paseid thought about his deceased father for the first time in a while.

The man who was called Palan Sholgo was someone who had devoted his life to the Royal House Brionake by establishing a sharp opposition against the Bant party with the help of Marquis Jafein. He had not been wise, as everyone knew, but he had been a good man at heart.

Son. You may consider yourself rather wise in worldly matters. I will not deny that. I should rather be proud of you, for you have grown up just the way your grandfather wished you would. But I do have one concern. Your clear understanding of good and bad will easily turn others into enemies, no matter your convictions or desires. If you cannot tame that nature, do not set foot in the mud.

The father who spoke so had established his legacy of a half-completed union of the two parties by arranging a marriage between Paseid and Elhien. He had passed away when Paseid was around seventeen years of age. It was right after Paseid returned from Sichin.

Though it was not entirely because of his last words, Paseid had slowly stepped back from politics as his father had wished. Paseid protected Rarke not with tongue and pen like the politicians, but with a sword at the borders. Though he had not intended this, Muiyadro naturally became a distant name to him, and the title *Palan Sholgo,* his by inheritance, became only a name. The ring of the Brionake and the ring of a Palan Sholgo had both become keepsakes in the drawer because he often had to wield a sword, but now the time had come when he needed them both.

Paseid gathered his disordered thoughts and stood by the bedchamber window with his back turned to Halman. Then, he opened the window. The fresh fragrance of the plants flowed in through the northern window. Paseid's seething mind naturally calmed down the moment he smelled that dizzying aroma.

"If there is anything else you need…"

"How are you maintaining the place?"

Halman stopped at his sudden voice. The *place* was the second-most beautiful in the capital city, but also the most secretive. "The gardeners have taken great care to organize it. Should I prepare it for you?"

The only place more beautiful than there in the barren north was the rose garden in the palace.

"Yes."

Halman, who had been longing for his master's return while he kept the empty house in order, bowed his head down deep and went outside.

There were two strict rules regarding the only house of their dukedom in Muiyadro.

First, the title of the duke. Since the first King Brionake had founded a new dynasty in Rarke, the royal family and the noble family had come to share one root. And yet, the difference between the royal family and the noble family was very apparent even today. So, at least in the capital where the king's ears were everywhere, addressing Duke Brionake as lord duke was to show respect to the royal family.

The second rule was to not rashly set foot in the secret garden in Brionake's mansion. It was not known why finding the entrance to the garden was difficult. But many had learned from hearsay that there remained an inheritance from the first king.

There was an old wall covered in winter ivy if one followed it along the road leading behind the mansion. If one did not stop and kept walking in on the path, a sight of the utmost artificial beauty revealed itself beyond the glass greenhouse surrounded by countless bushes and flowers.

People called the glass greenhouse behind the north wing of the mansion the Garden of Hydrangea. After a long time, that name had become its own idiom and settled as a sort of a pronoun of Muiyadro. The Garden of Hydrangea was also known as a place where only those of the direct bloodline of the Noble House Brionake could enter.

But now, the only direct bloodline of the Noble House Brionake was Paseid Calandok Brionake, the current duke. Even so, he spent more time in the country, essentially leaving the mansion's hydrangea garden only to the butler and gardeners of House Brionake. So, the ones who were hoarding the beautiful sight they could not show to anyone else, much to their shame, were extremely delighted by its owner's return.

Halman reported the preparations were finished. Paseid passed the north wing of the mansion and headed to the hydrangea garden located behind the wall. The sight of the hydrangea that bloomed in blue all year long was dizzying from the entrance. Coarse plants that had withstood the cold winter were spreading their roots outside the greenhouse, but inside there were only a white wall, a platform, and true-blue hydrangeas.

The lonely flowers of the garden that bloomed regardless of the season wafted in their fragrance like they were excited to see a visitor at long last.

The greenhouse was completely silent, without even a slight breeze. It was peaceful, cut off from the rest of the world. Feeling more at ease, Paseid sat down at the table. He pushed the tea Halman had already poured to one side. There was not only tea, but also a couple books on a subject he might like. Ignoring the books as well, Paseid lowered his head and closed his eyes.

After meditating to calm his mind, Paseid raised his head by the time the tea had cooled to room temperature. Then, he gazed at the snow-white wall standing straight on the flat, low platform located in a more inner part of the greenhouse.

Its white shine that the tattered years polished elegantly lingered in his sight. It was a sight he had not seen in a long while, and yet it was familiar, as though it were something he saw every day. It was more disparate because it was in the middle of a garden where nature of a truer blue than the sky bloomed. The shine felt more like something foreign.

Paseid gazed at the solitary frame hung on the wall, covered with a clean fabric.

The hydrangea garden had been founded by the first Brionake, so its preservation was the descendants' responsibility. But that painting that had been passed down was something Paseid could not accept, so covering it with a fabric was sort of a compromise.

After spending some time gazing at the wall, Paseid turned his head and opened a book.

Darkness soon veiled the garden to the point that he could no longer make out the letters without a lamp. The candle on the table melted down to a thin, flat shape and shined its last light. When he was about to close the book, Halman carefully came into the garden.

"Master, the lady of House Laperovahan has come to visit."

Laperovahan.

He recalled the girl.

The small girl who still somewhat looked like a child was standing quietly by the entrance to the greenhouse and waiting for him. She frowned every passing moment, then brightened up once Paseid came out of the greenhouse. Spring in Muiyadro was always bleakly chilly like this, most likely because of the north wind from the Galiau Mountains where the snow never melted.

"How is it that you have come all the way here without even a notice?" Paseid asked.

"It's not odd for me to come see you, now, is it, Your Grace?" Her voice sank down dejectedly toward the end, disheartened by Paseid's reproach.

"That was not how I meant it. How have you been, my lady?" Paseid gave a soft smile without looking like he was annoyed and looked into her eyes.

Elhien rolled her eyes, trying to figure out what he was thinking, then changed the subject. "Oh, oh, I forgot to say hello. I'm glad to see you after such a long time. I know you may not be delighted by me visiting you first like this, but…I was afraid you might return only for a short while this time too."

"I am planning on staying for a longer time. I should have contacted you beforehand."

"I know very well that you are a busy person."

Paseid's lips arched spontaneously into a smile at the small, mumbling voice. Elhien soon blushed and lowered her head.

The feathered fedora pulled down over the flowing brown hair was loose and crooked on one side. Paseid wordlessly looked down at that, then reached out to fix it. He gazed at Elhien's dress that exposed half of her shoulders despite the cold weather and took off his coat to put it around her shoulders. Elhien's round, orange-coral eyes widened, then fell to her feet.

"Is there time for me in your planned schedule during your stay here, this time?"

It seemed as though she was rather disappointed by him coming without saying so and leaving without saying goodbye whenever he visited Muiyadro.

Instead of an answer, Paseid looked around at the scenery after the sun set. "I did not know you would visit at such a late hour."

"The thing is, I did get permission. I actually planned on coming a little earlier, but something happened in the morning..."

She rubbed her eyes. Paseid slowly put his arm around her shoulders and started walking. "The hour is very late today, so I will take you back for now."

She walked a couple steps, following his lead, then suddenly raised her head like she'd just snapped to reality and looked up at him. "But I just came."

"It's late."

She blinked like she was flustered at the imminent danger of being ejected as soon as she met him, then soon calmed down her breath. "I want to stay a bit longer."

"My lady, the hour is late."

"I will be an adult soon too."

She was sixteen now, so she would have a coming-of-age celebration soon. Paseid slightly nodded.

"I will be an adult soon, so..." Elhien repeated.

She rubbed the stone floor with the tip of her shoe and pouted when the expected answer did not come out of Paseid's mouth.

Paseid didn't not know what the answer she wanted was, but he swallowed his breath and buttoned his lips. In truth, Paseid never knew what to say when he was facing Elhien. It was not that he did not know the set answers, but he did not want to treat her with falseness that did not come from his heart. When it seemed like he was not going to answer at last, shame started to cover the young girl's cheeks, and her eyes welled with tears.

Finally, Paseid reluctantly opened his mouth. "Did we not agree that we will discuss the matter regarding marriage once you have come of age?"

"The lady of Deliad and the lady of Pesikio, who are even two years younger than I am, officially married the esteemed sons of Grinsa not too long ago."

"My lady."

"It's Elhien. I don't understand why it feels more and more like there is a wall between us. You used to call my name without any hesitation before, and you used to come visit me first no matter how busy you were before…"

Looking down at Elhien whining like a child, Paseid swallowed a sigh and smiled. This girl had been kindhearted since she was a child. She was a lovely girl, regardless of her father. He could not help but be soft to Elhien. But his assessment of Elhien and his feelings for her were two different matters.

"I have said so before, but…"

"I know what you are going to say, Your Grace. But I know a girl who got married to a forty-year-old old man."

Paseid showed a bit of dismay. "An old man. That's not a good way to talk."

"Oh, I'm sorry. I've been spending time with Ja—Jacalrin, little Sir Chesa…"

Realizing that she'd just said something flippant, Elhien shook her head, embarrassed. Paseid gazed at her with benevolent eyes, then went back to the previous subject. He spoke with a kind tone, like he was cajoling her. "If you mean the second daughter of House Vintraki, I heard she was much past the right age, as she was twenty-four at the time. Though the age difference was great, the marriage ensued with the determination that there would be no problem in carrying out the marital duties on either side, so it would be best not to compare with such a thing. Do you understand?"

"I do not. I don't think it's a problem that there is an age gap. Rather, it's a good thing."

Paseid was quite surprised at her having a firmer stance in her opinions since he'd last seen her.

He was twenty-seven, and Elhien had just turned sixteen. In truth, age was not that big of a problem when it came to noble marriage, just as she said. But Elhien was someone Paseid, at the very least, wanted to be careful with. His deceased father and the prime minister had set their arranged marriage in stone for the union of the two parties, but he still remembered her as an infant, which Elhien couldn't even remember herself.

He of course knew that he would someday marry her, but he could not set his mind on that yet. It was hard to treat a girl who still looked like a child, and he thought of more as a sister, like a woman. Maybe, if he didn't have any feelings at all. But for now, it was a tragedy that made him extremely uneasy just in imagining it.

"Really, it disheartens me to see you keep distancing yourself..." she said softly.

But regardless of Paseid's feelings, Elhien was determined not to just return home like this today. It was a great shock to see Paseid, whom she hadn't seen in more than two years, try to eject her as soon as he saw her. Of course, it was not proper for a woman to just barge in early in the evening instead of waiting, but she did not have the time to consider such things. She longed for him that much.

"Am I being too harsh?"

She was plagued with worry that Paseid might get mad at her for being too presumptuous, though she didn't show it. But when Paseid didn't seem offended like she had expected, she swallowed her embarrassment and gathered up her courage.

"If you are saying that you are being considerate of me, I can tell you that I am just fine."

"Elhien, I must apologize if my inattentive attitude has hurt you."

"I'm not trying to make you apologize. You are a busy man, Your Grace. I know going back and forth between Rokland and the capital must be hard by itself. I have heard about the Galkamas as well. How tired you must be. But I'm not certain if that is a valid reason to postpone the wedding. It has already been decided, and it would be more beneficial for you to do it earlier than..."

Paseid remained silent for a while, then tiredly smiled. "It's difficult for me...if you keep asking like that."

Elhien dropped her head like a scorned child. Sixteen was an old enough age to get married, and yet Paseid seemed like he was not going to give in, using the age gap as an excuse. If only she'd been born ten years earlier.

"I really…" Her voice trailed off before she could finish. All the nobles had been jealous of her arranged marriage with Paseid at first, but now, it was only a relationship for the sake of itself.

The young girl was not foolish enough to think that they were in love. Even though he was unusually kind to her because he was fond of her, she knew very well that he did not see and treat her like a woman, as Jacalrin said.

Paseid probably was unaware of this because he was always busy going back and forth between Rokland and Muiyadro, but she stayed in the capital and heard all sorts of rumors. When the plan for the wedding kept getting pushed back and back, a rumor about the dukedom and House Laperovahan being at a discord had started to spread. Some were even deluded enough to make up that Paseid actually had a mistress and that he was considering breaking off the engagement with House Laperovahan.

Since this was the case, their jealousy and envy inevitably subsided as time passed. The vain sons and daughters of the nobles truly pitied her.

Paseid had shaken off the hounds by declaring at last that they would get married once Elhien came of age, but that was long after the anxious girl's heart had turned to ashes. And Jacalrin stirring the pot this morning played a big part too.

"I am aware of the matters regarding the marital duties and procreation of an heir too. I would be…"

"I do not want it," Paseid firmly stated.

"I really am not attractive because I'm too young, aren't I?" Elhien asked in an extremely discouraged voice.

"It's not like that."

"Little Sir Chesa said that men like mature women. I'm too short, and my breasts are still too small…"

"My lady. That's not what I meant."

"Of course, I don't expect you to be a ne'er-do-well like little Sir Chesa, but if it is because I am deficient in terms of appearance…"

Paseid could guess what sort of hogwash Jacalrin, that uncontrollable good-for-nothing boy, had blabbered to Elhien. He sighed, quite unlike his usual self, and lowered his voice to a kinder tone. It was true that Paseid didn't have any sexual desire for Elhien, but that was certainly not to do with her appearance. "That is not at all what I meant."

"I know you still think that I am young, but I have started to bleed as well, so I can bear your…"

Where is she going with this?

Thinking he had no way out, Paseid put his hand on Elhien's head. She was surprised and stopped midsentence.

"Elhien Devi."

Thanks to him, the fedora that was prettily placed on her head got squashed down to right above her eyelids. It was one of his duties to comfort his betrothed as well. Paseid slowly pulled the girl that barely reached his chest into his arms.

"There is no need to be anxious, for you are beautiful enough and lovable enough. Also, if we proceeded with our wedding this moment, you would have to conclude your life in the capital and move to Rokland. I will try my best to give you a satisfying life in Rokland, but you will be lonely without any friends or family. Getting married early and leaving is not the only solution. Do not be disheartened."

He realized that the girl was slightly shivering. "We should first head inside, for it is still chilly outside."

The small girl's sigh blew against him. "Then can I go in there?" She looked up at him.

Realizing what she was talking about, Paseid turned his head to look at the glass greenhouse. She had indirectly expressed the desire to go in the greenhouse a couple times in the past, but he'd always declined. It was a place one could only enter with the permission of a direct bloodline of House Brionake. He felt a bit uneasy about letting Elhien in.

Overwhelmed with the anxiety that he still might decline, even though she'd just outright asked him, Elhien mumbled, "Are you going to refuse this too? Can't you say yes to this at the very least?"

Letting out a small sigh, Paseid gestured to Halman, standing silently with his head down a couple steps away from them. Suppressing his fatigue, he nodded. Elhien grinned, like that alone was enough to make her happy.

It had truly been a long time since an outsider had set foot in the hydrangea garden. At a time when its owner only visited on a yearly basis, no wonder there were no outside visitors. Hence, her visit was a very meaningful thing. To her, and to the garden.

They took a small lamp and walked side by side along the blue path of flowers melted into the dim evening.

With her dejected air completely gone, Elhien's footsteps were light and brisk, like she was about to fly away. Seeing that her childish face blushed with excitement, Paseid laughed. "There's not much."

"Still, I'm happy. This is a place only a Brionake can enter."

"Not necessarily, but it is customary that outsiders usually do not enter."

Regardless of that, Elhien smiled innocently and breathed in the sweet smell of the flowers.

Paseid guided her to the table on the low patch of grass. Elhien carefully sat across from him.

"Oh, you must have seen my father at the palace today. You must be exhausted since you just arrived. I'm sorry if I'm..."

"It's all right. I rested enough on the way here."

She stared at Paseid, then fanned herself with her hand like she was suddenly shy. "It really is beautiful. I heard hydrangeas bloom all year long like this at your mansion. It's really warm here. If I become a duchess in the future, can I come in here every day?"

Paseid pulled his lips into a smile. "It's a similar structure to the palace's rose garden."

"But, wow, it really is just hydrangeas. May I ask why there are no other flowers?"

Her surprise made sense, but Paseid stayed silent, unable to find an appropriate answer.

Elhien looked around, then was completely absorbed by an unfamiliar sight. She saw a white wall standing a little deeper in the garden.

"Is there something else over there?" she asked.

"It's the same. And to answer your previous question, I am not quite sure, since this place has been merely preserved without touching the bushes and flowers that were planted a long time ago."

"Haven't you thought of planting something else?"

"There is a reason for that." Paseid grinned.

"I heard the first king of Rarke took care of this place himself.

He must have really liked this flower. Why else? Do you like them too, Paseid?"

Paseid's eyes slowly darkened. Elhien continued, unable to notice him because she was too excited. "But there are much prettier and fancier flowers. Of course, I do not mean that hydrangeas aren't lovely."

She noticed the frame covered with fabric and asked, "Is that a painting over there? Oh, is it perhaps...?"

Before Paseid could say anything in return, she rose from her seat. She trotted over to the portrait, her eyes filled with curiosity. Paseid stood up and reflexively took her by the wrist. She blinked in confusion.

"Paseid?"

"Better not."

"What?"

"It would be better not to see it. It's not something I am too proud about."

Startled by her arm aching with pain in his grip, Elhien stopped.

That evening, Elhien returned home looking quite depressed, but Paseid couldn't even walk her out.

Terendoke's cold voice shot at Paseid. "Paseid, I will not order you. All decisions are yours to make. Of course, I will not simply sit back and let Morgana be, even if you refuse."

"Your Majesty."

"Lord Duke, I know that a war at this time is dangerous as well. However, it is our true duty to remind the enemy who claims to be the empire of the south that Rarke has not bowed down to them because we are weak."

"You are always right, Your Majesty."

"If you consent, Ransen of House Chesa will step in to complete the transfer of Rokland and the cessation of hostilities and foreign invasion."

Paseid stayed silent with his mouth shut tight, then asked, "Excuse me, Your Majesty, but I must ask one thing before I can answer. Until which point do you intend to continue this war?"

"Until the doom of Morgana. That is a wish of Rarke that is hundreds of years old. What kind of a ruler would deny that?"

"It is."

"But a wish is only a wish. I will not require a conquest of Morgana. The purpose of the war is to repay Rarke's shame that we have experienced for hundreds of years and to remind the enemy of their arrogance. If this cannot be so, I will not be able to even show my face with shame."

Paseid's face seemed calmer than before.

"So, will you bring back victory for your wronged king?"

"Give me the order, Your Majesty." Paseid bowed his head even deeper.

"My brother, Brionake. Go crush the enemy's arrogance to bits and return."

Terendoke's blue eyes flashed.

"Yes, Your Majesty," Paseid's flat voice answered.

Paseid Calandok Brionake, the current head of the Noble House Brionake, was appointed as the commander-in-chief of the entire Rarkian defense force with the king's decree. No one dared to declare that they disagreed that he was fit to be a commander of the Great Battle against Morgana, the war between the north and the south claiming itself as a holy war to wash away the disgrace in history.

Before even a month passed by, Muiyadro was flooded with soldiers and armies from each noble house. Soon after, the eldest son of House Chesa, Kalajesh Ransen, was ordered by the king to stop by to see him on his way out of Muiyadro to receive some instructions for Rokland.

While the tension heightened, Paseid stayed in the outskirts of Muiyadro and had an introductory meeting with the called soldiers and the dispatched knights.

There was no declaration of war from either of the countries, but Morganaan moles must have reported on the odd state of the Rarkian army, and so the war became a fait accompli.

And today, the official appointment ceremony was finished.

"I name Duke Paseid Calandok Brionake the commander-in-chief of all the Rarkian forces for the Great Battle against Morgana."

Terendoke's shining silver sword silently pressed its weight on Paseid's shoulders.

~

Paseid returned to his mansion after almost two weeks to find Kalajesh, whom he had met on a couple of occasions at official gatherings during the preparation for the reorganization of the army. Kalajesh was leaning against the wall at the entrance of the mansion and chatting with Halman, like he had been there for a while.

"Kalajesh."

When Paseid let his presence be known, Halman walked away quickly.

Kalajesh came straight to Paseid and greeted him with a hug. Kalajesh Ransen Chesa was Jacalrin's brother and Paseid's close friend, a year older than him. The man with sandy-blond hair, like their mother, and green eyes was a good-looking man, as his nickname, *the most handsome man in Muiyadro,* suggested. He looked clean and neat, like he'd just taken a bath before coming, and smelled of something easy on the nose but fragrant.

Paseid hugged back the lean man who seemed toned and almost as tall as Paseid but not all that muscular, and greeted him. "I was so busy that I didn't even properly say hello."

"Jacalrin came and chattered away about everything, so no worries."

"Where is he?"

"He's grounded. He was found gambling on this war's results at a gambling den in the outskirts of the city a couple days ago, and Father was furious."

It was quite an unfair punishment, considering how Count Rougak Chesa liked to gamble just as much as his little son. But it was their family's business.

"Which side did he bet on?" Paseid's simple question came with a slight laugh. Kalajesh faintly smiled as well.

"Chesa's patriotism is no less than Brionake's."

"That makes me feel a little better. Anyway, what brings you here?"

"I've carved out some time because I was sad I was too busy to really talk to you after such a long time. What do you think, Commander-in-Chief?" Kalajesh said jokingly.

Kalajesh was far more mature and tamer than Jacalrin, but blood was blood, and he seemed to be Jacalrin's future when he talked so mischievously.

Though he was extremely tired, Paseid's excitement exceeded his fatigue as well. So, he kept his smile. "Sounds good. Would you like to go for a walk?"

The knights and the workers of the mansion following him couldn't move and were just standing by, because Paseid was standing at the entrance to the mansion. Kalajesh made an apologetic face at last, like he'd done something very inconsiderate, and nodded, then started walking.

"You might be over thirty by the time you return from this war, you know."

"It might end earlier than you think."

"I hope so. I have been transferred to the west in your place. I prefer this peaceful place to the battlefield. I finally got a nice position out of Chief Manager Rijeyes, and look what it amounted to. I'll just have to quickly finish everything before they take away my spot at the administrative office. You should come back safe and sound as well."

Kalajesh was a man with talent, good with swords and well read, and hence was recognized as a government official and as a knight. But he himself wanted to take an assistant administrative position and become a high official rather than spreading his name as a knight who wielded a sword. To Paseid, who knew this about Kalajesh very well, his friend's disappointment could be clearly felt.

In addition to that, the reason Kalajesh was dispatched this time was that they needed someone to take Paseid's place while he was gone, and mediate the disputes with the Galkamas near Rokland.

This war could very well become a war where no one could make any predictions even by the day, but Paseid mostly wanted to end it as soon as possible and return. There was enough war just with the daily disputes happening on the northwestern border. And the fact that Kalajesh had to leave west in his place was uncomfortable for both Kalajesh and Paseid, even if it was indeed the king's decree.

"Was it six years ago that I last visited Rokland? A lot of fun things happened then."

"It has changed a lot," said Paseid. "Commander Tur will provide you with all the information regarding the region. I have sent a messenger to him last night in advance, so he will be of good use if you take him as your advisor."

"Yes, well. I've already heard that much, but I'll keep it in mind. And Sichin started acting amicably recently. If they join forces with us, it shouldn't be too hard. By the way, is it true that Count Haldroff volunteered for the Great Battle against Morgana? Seems like it will be a big one, considering that Vinsen, who was on bad terms with him, is also joining. Oh, have you sent a message to Sir Winford?"

Castro Vander Winford was a Rarkian knight who was once widely known as a master-like figure for Kalajesh and Paseid when they were boys. Terendoke held the symbolic title of the best knight in Rarke, but in reality, the best knight in Rarke was him until ten years ago.

Paseid gave a genuine answer from his heart. "Sir Winford has already retired, so I cannot dare bother him too. He's not someone who would gladly come back because someone called him, either."

"Well, that is true. He must be old now. I haven't even properly sent my greetings in a while. I've been too busy. Have you talked to him at all?"

Paseid shook his head. "It's been a while since I've heard from him as well."

"Maybe it would be good to pay him a visit next time." Kalajesh ended the topic with a comment that sounded like something said for the sake of formality, even though he knew that he would not have time for that, then suddenly changed the subject. "By the way, what's happening with the wedding?"

Paseid, who was walking a little ahead of Kalajesh, slowed down, then came to a complete stop.

Kalajesh was looking at him with a comfortable smile just like usual. But Paseid could easily read the complex thoughts embedded in that smile. Paseid pretended not to know that the reason Kalajesh visited him was not just to say hello.

"It will have to happen after this war's ended."

"Elhien came last night and bawled her eyes out. She was truly disheartened that you do not visit her, not even once. Take some care."

Paseid let out a light sigh instead of an answer. Kalajesh was one of the many nobles in the capital who adored Elhien. If Kalajesh hadn't said the next thing so firmly, Paseid would not have answered at all.

"Paseid, you have a lot of things I do not have."

"Kalajesh."

"Unlike me, who has not succeeded the house yet, you are already a lord who leads a house and a land, a knight, and the guardian of the borders. Yes, you must be busy. But it's not just because you're busy. I know you're still pondering and just indefinitely pushing it back. I know why as well. Laperovahan is a name we both are inevitably averse to. But that's not Elhien's fault. Eslan..."

"Enough."

"I know better than anyone that you're not as cold as you seem on the outside, no matter how you act. Don't do this to me too. You're honestly uncomfortable with leaving Elhien like that too, aren't you?"

Kalajesh sounded like he meant it as a joke. But Paseid lowered his gaze, feeling like he didn't want to hear what was to come next.

"I know that you're making sacrifices. I know that very well. But you should accept it if it's not something you can avoid. And stop torturing the people around you. Elhien only has eyes for you." Kalajesh ended in the lightest tone possible. But he could still not stop the air growing heavier.

To be honest, Kalajesh didn't feel all that comfortable about urging him like this. It was true that he cared about Elhien like he would a sister, but Paseid was his old friend too. Kalajesh was one of the few people who knew the true reason Paseid kept pushing back the wedding regardless of his age, which he did not reveal to anyone.

But wouldn't it be better to get it done and over with if it was inevitable? That was all he thought. Elhien was a girl worthy of a better treatment. Not just because she was of a high, noble birth. She was beautiful, indeed, but she was surprisingly mature and wise for her age. Of course, she would revert to a child of her age when she was with Jacalrin and would sometimes cry and say something spiteful, but that was because Jacalrin acted so imprudently. It was quite surprising how Jacalrin had a peculiar talent in undoing the reins of patience with everyone he engaged with.

What Kalajesh felt the most as he watched Elhien grow more mature by the year was sympathy. Because she loved her betrothed, who was far older than her, she'd given up on the behavior that she could indulge in at her age.

Of course, it could be that she was intentionally acting mature because she was aware that she was the daughter of the prime minister, that she held the name Laperovahan, and that she was certain she would become a duchess in the future. Since people had their own complicated reasons, regardless of their age.

Because of the destiny the adults had decided upon when she was very young, Elhien's life inevitably revolved around becoming Paseid's wife. So, who could blame her? It was only a matter of course, since she lived her life looking only at one person.

It was truly a hard thing to watch Paseid slink away into a deeper place by his side as Elhien's heart grew fonder. He would much rather have them get married as soon as possible and settle down with each other.

Knowing that repeating the same thing would be of no use, Kalajesh still couldn't stop trying to persuade him.

"I don't know how much longer you're planning on making her wait with this excuse and that, but I don't want to see Elhien with her heart aching because of you anymore. And...I do not think there is a reason for Elhien to take responsibility for the faults of Laperovahan and Bant."

Recognizing a reproach hiding at the end, Paseid felt a surge of anger. "Kalajesh, I don't think that's something you need to interfere with."

Kalajesh's green eyes looking deep into Paseid's dimmed with resignation. "You may think I have no right to say such things, but that kind of attitude still affects me in a negative way. We Chesa do just watch from the side, as we are neutral, but we are still affected, since the nobles in the capital sway spinelessly whenever a rumor of discord comes from Bant of Palan."

He couldn't not know what the meaning of that was.

Feeling drained, Paseid covered his forehead with one hand and slightly turned his head away. "I will make certain of my attitude once this war ends. I promise you."

Kalajesh grinned and shook his head. "You should say that to Elhien, not me."

Even after hearing what he wanted to hear, he still felt uncomfortable. Not many eldest sons of high noble families married out of love, true, but the burden Paseid had to take on was a particularly heavy one. He felt a little indebted to Paseid.

Kalajesh and Paseid concluded the topic and had a bit more small talk about Morgana, planned movements, predictions, things about Galkama, and about southern tributary countries. Though they were simply exchanging opinions in an informal setting, the time flew by just by listening to Kalajesh's various opinions, for he was as well versed as Paseid, or perhaps even more so, in facts based in theoretical principles.

Kalajesh soon left because of an urgent message regarding the work related to the organization of the army that was to depart to Rokland in the northwest. Intuiting that this was the last time they would meet before the war began, Kalajesh and Paseid shared a long handshake.

After seeing Kalajesh out, Paseid washed himself and headed to the hydrangea garden. Though he was not too hung up on what Kalajesh had said, it was true that he was reflecting on his own shortcomings with the war now at his doorstep.

War.

Recalling that oddly calmed his heart and made it pound at the same time.

Instead of sitting down at the table Halman prepared for him and spending the time in meditation, Paseid stood in front of the white wall. His rough hands uncovered the fabric laid on the frame. Soon, his black eyes gazed at the faded, odd texture of the portrait.

Something odd gushed up in his chest. A frustrating memory popped up with it.

Recently, he'd committed the rude act of grabbing Elhien's wrist without her permission for showing interest in this. Then, he had discourteously sent the startled girl back home, like he was banishing her. It might have created a bigger bruise in her fragile heart. Furthermore, he hadn't even apologized because he completely erased her from his mind with the excuse that he was busy. That was probably the reason Elhien was even more upset.

Because of this.

Regardless of his mood, the woman smiling most elegantly looked at him from inside the frame. The years had weathered off the paint and now he could only barely make out what each color was supposed to be, but her figure was still clear as day.

The woman in the portrait was truly beautiful, and that in turn made his mood fall even faster. But a tumult hindered Paseid's quiet rumination.

"My lady, my lady! You cannot go in there without permission...!"

He heard the voice of a young girl he hadn't permitted to enter. Elhien almost threw open the unlocked doors of the Garden of Hydrangea, rushed in, panting, and then stopped not far away from Paseid.

"I met big Sir Chesa. I heard that you were here, Your Grace... No, first, I apologize. Forgive me for visiting you right away upon hearing that you have returned, for I did not know your where-abouts for a long time."

Paseid slowly turned around. Halman had followed behind and was looking nervously back and forth between Elhien and Paseid. Paseid saw her bruised wrist.

"It's fine," he told Halman. "Leave us."

Halman saw the exposed portrait and stepped out, unable to hide his anxiety.

Elhien, who had her eyes fixed on Paseid, took the time to catch her breath, then asked, "Um, are you—are you going to that big war?"

Paseid recalled the officially announced appointment from that afternoon and nodded. She must have just found out.

"Yes."

"I heard you volun—volunteered. Why did you…without even letting me know? I know that you are an extremely busy person, but am I really that much of a bother to you?" She stuttered as she continued, like she was about to burst into tears. Elhien's eyes welled up, then suddenly shot beyond Paseid's shoulder. "Oh."

Instead of saying something, Paseid simply turned his head to look back at the woman nailed on the wall.

The eyes of the woman in the portrait sitting with the blue flowerbed as its altar were filled with all kinds of affection and confidence. Elhien quietly studied the portrait of the mature woman and pitifully closed her lips.

She recalled Paseid not wanting to show her this painting the last time she visited the mansion.

Gazing at her face changing its color every moment, Paseid shook his head. "Please do not think that."

"No, I mean…"

"This portrait is of Swan Sekalrid Rarkalia, the last queen of the Rarkalia Dynasty. You would know if you've heard the rumor, but this is the last legacy of Belbarote Paseid Brionake."

Last legacy. Reluctantly enunciating those words, Paseid suddenly turned his head toward the portrait to hide his emotions. Elhien's eyes opened as wide as walnut shells.

"The queen of Rarkalia. That—that is a worship of Rarkalia…" She jumped and covered her mouth with her hand. "I'm sorry."

Paseid gazed at the smiling woman in the portrait without looking offended. "His Majesty is aware of this portrait's existence as well. It is an heirloom passed down from generation to generation. I'm sure you've heard the rumor. The keepsake of the first Brionake in this garden. The reason the Garden of Hydrangea is not open to the public is because I do not enjoy outsiders seeing this and misunderstanding its meaning, like you have done."

"I was just taken aback."

"I apologize for my previous impudence and for surprising you because I did not notify you beforehand. I was swept up in the situation because it was a rather sudden appointment to me as well. It truly was not because I consider you bothersome or because I am avoiding you. Please do not think that."

Paseid approached Elhien and lightly kissed the back of her hand. She snapped back to herself and spoke in a small voice, trying to suppress a sob. "The empire...I heard my father speaking with Count Chesa. You are already toiling away at Rokland. So, why did you bother to volunteer for such a big war? You said you dislike quarrels, Your Grace. There's already enough knights in Rarke who live off the country's money doing nothing like ne'er-do-wells, knights who just fool around every day like Jacalrin rather than..."

"My lady, do not speak so."

"Do you have to go?"

Paseid turned his gaze to the portrait.

"Your Grace, a war against Morgana is...it's different than battles at the border. We don't know how much longer it will take, and it'll be far more dangerous..." Elhien, who was biting her lower lip, carefully but sternly asserted.

Paseid smiled affectionately. "I will return as soon as possible."

"But that's not up to you. I'm not that much of a foolish child." The end of Elhien's sentence shook like she was crying. But she opened her eyes even wider and continued, "If you must go, promise me you will safely return and come to me before anyone else and ask for my hand."

"I have never even thought of marrying anyone else than you, my lady. Truly."

"And when that time comes, see me as a woman, not a sister."

"I already love you, my lady."

Elhien's eyes revealed a hint of disappointment for a moment at the answer that was the same as always. Paseid knew that, but remained silent because he could not find anything else to say. She soon straightened her body, painfully lowered her reddened eyes, and pulled up her lips. "It's all right. I'll...I'll leave for now."

Paseid smiled bitterly. "I'll walk you out."

"No, no. It's all right. I have brought my own people."

Elhien stared back at the portrait for the last time, then hastily shook her hand and turned around. At her firm refusal, Paseid lowered his hand that awkwardly reached out to her. The back of the little girl briskly walking like she was almost running away disappeared into a dot.

After standing motionlessly for a long time, he bent down to pick up the fabric lying on the platform. Then, sensing a gaze from his periphery, he stopped.

With deep blue eyes that did not reveal anything inside and arched supple lips where the red paint faintly remained, she was truly a beautiful woman who seemed somehow stubborn but generous in spite of that. The stone statue by Aletar Dalte was already destroyed, and most of the artifacts related to the last queen were discarded and disappeared into history after the collapse of the Rarkalia Dynasty. So, it would not be wrong to call this the last portrait of the queen.

Swan Sekalrid Rarkalia. The last queen of the Rarkalia Dynasty.

When his grandfather Jegrat, a man who worshipped the founder, was still alive, Paseid grew up hearing praises of the founder more than enough. It was his grandfather's doing that his name was Paseid.

Become a great Brionake like the great Belbarote Paseid Brionake.

But sadly, Paseid could not admire Belbarote like his grandfather Jegrat. Even if he was living with the name he'd inherited from him.

Paseid's fingertips caressed the surface of the cotton of the portrait covered with lint. Like he had explained to Elhien, this portrait was the legacy of Belbarote, the founder who was widely praised to be a wise ruler, said to have been drawn by Belbarote himself. It was an object of incalculable value just because of the fact that it was created at the touch of Belbarote's brushes, but it was also something that could not be shown to others.

When he was young, Belbarote had been the proxy of a tyrant who was seduced by this woman's beauty. But in the end, he had left and executed the queen who lost her virtues as a monarch to open a new era. Though it was true that he had signed an unconditional ceasefire treaty with Morgana to quiet the turmoil within Rarke and that that grudge had been passed down all the way to today, no one could blame him. The descendants knew that it had been the best choice both politically and historically.

According to Rarkian history, Belbarote had bequeathed the throne to the eldest prince in the eighth year the Brionake Dynasty was founded, when Rarke had recovered from the aftermath of the war. It was before he was even fifty years of age.

Tales about Belbarote after he descended the throne only existed in the unofficial history passed down in the family. Everyone had been sorry to see Belbarote resign so suddenly. The man who bore everyone's grief could not leave Muiyadro and had ended up renovating this mansion that was said to be the mansion of another dukedom named Yeigan. He had secluded himself inside it. Then, he was said to have busied himself with the work of a mere gardener.

Belbarote had built a greenhouse in a way that allowed it to be warm all year long in the cold north. Then, he had planted the blue hydrangeas he obtained from the western nomads and taken care of the garden until he died of old age.

That place was this place.

Paseid approached the frame with the fabric, then stopped upon finding the characters of Rarkalia faintly engraved on the wall next to the frame. They were so worn that he wouldn't have seen them unless he carefully scrutinized it.

Shol Lasina, Noyabantjan.
   Forgive me, my queen.

Paseid had grown up looking at the woman in the portrait.

He'd learned who that woman was as he got older. And that she was a tyrant. Only after the queen looking down at him in the painting looked into his eyes at the same level did Paseid realize that the meaning of that engraving was bone deep.

So, he always felt eerie whenever he looked into the queen's face. What sin of the man who had saved the kingdom from its doom was so terrible that he'd dedicated his entire life to seek forgiveness from the queen who'd nearly driven a country into doom with brutal warfare?

The faded lips of the woman looking into him seemed like they were about to say something.

Will you walk the same path as I did?

Suddenly, an ineffable sensation of discomfort stirred him from head to toe.

A war between Morgana and Rarke was once again upon them. Paseid tightly clamped his lips.

No, this is different. The latter generation will not repeat your history. He covered the frame with the fabric. Then he turned around to coldly gaze at the blue hydrangeas filling his entire sight. They were truly blinding waves.

Paseid could not admire the great king who was Belbarote Paseid Brionake. He was a sinner. He was the hero who had protected Rarke, but he'd lived until his last day yearning for a wicked woman, so he remained a sinner.

Paseid slowly walked over and plucked a flower emitting its intense fragrance. How deep did a love have to be to bloom its blue atonement that did not fade for two hundred years? He couldn't even fathom it. He shook off that thought and walked past the blue hydrangeas outside.

And four months later, he led twenty thousand advance forces to the border.

∽

The queen stopped on the marble floor covered with a red carpet. Then she slowly turned around and smiled.

"*Do not answer so seriously. It was a joke. Of course, I like flowers, but I like blue things better.*"

What did that mean?

The tranquil voice resounded in the hall like a lullaby.

"*But I have never in my life seen a blue flower. I have seen butterflies, though. Everywhere I set foot is covered in red, so why not the thing I like be blue?*"

But do butterflies not wander indefinitely, for they cannot plant their roots anywhere? *thought the man. But he swallowed the words as always.*

"*So, I regarded a blue butterfly as myself.*"

"*If there is a flower...*"

"*It would not be bad to regard myself a flower too.*"

The man looked up at the blue sky across the large window at her muttering.

"*Then, will you allow me?*"

"*What?*"

"*If there is a flower.*"

"Sometimes, I really cannot figure out what you are thinking. I sometimes am suspicious of your true intentions of following me."

"Swan."

"Can you not tell it is a joke?"

The man's face sullenly stiffened at her mischievous reply. The queen gazed at him like she would a child, then suddenly grabbed his hand. The middle finger and the wrist of the man who once was a warrior were hardened with callouses from holding a pen. If one studied more deeply, one could even see the dark stains of ink seeped into his skin.

"Yes."

The man's eyes slid along, following the ends of her hand.

A quiet gratitude resounded in his ears.

"Thank you, for everything. Thank you for protecting my Rarke, Belbi."

Belbarote drew a bitter smile, swallowing all the words rushing up his throat as always.

> Forgive me, my queen.
> The honorless wolf bows down and dares to call for you.
> Each day I gained with the peace and dishonor I gained by
>   paying the price that is you.
> Stories I cannot offer you pile up in yearning.
> My beloved, do not forgive me.
> The one who wished to be your flower
> But was a sinner without the courage to dare to ask.
> I, who resent their happiness earned in exchange for
>   betraying you.

RARKE

The north is comprised of Rarke, the Principality of Illaren, and other small self-governing lands of their own. It was divided into more than ten big and small countries, but during the era of the queen's conquest for the grand union, the patriotism and identities of a specific groups were clearly established, and now it's tied together by the cultural similarity and loyalty. Lords pay taxes every year at their own will and swear to strive for the peace of the entire north. Currently, the entirety of the people who accept that the ruler of the north is the son of the wolf is called *Rarke*.

Symbol: white wolf on a peach or gold background

System

Rarke established a two-party system with the Palan party and the Bant party under Brionake's rule, after the collapse of the Rarkalia Dynasty. It has been about two hundred years since ten-something countries with different cultures gathered to become one country. Because its history is short, unlike the empire with a thousand years of history, each region still retains its quirks.

There are a lot of people practicing the customs of Gideraka in the east, and there is a place where Ardonis's custom of husbands living with their wives' families still remains in the west. A vestige of countries that previously existed, like Rayn and the former Esenbark (now Esland), still exists in the south.

State autonomy follows the same lines. The biggest example is the Alliance of Galabua in the southern part of Rarke that has been granted a right to autonomy to a certain extent. As the descendants of the Ailmare Kingdom, their nobles have a strong say and have a relatively lax regulation of the establishment of private armies, for they need strong men due to the characteristics of the land. Apart from the titles limited to single generations according to the king's decrees, most of the land permanently belongs to each house.

The Rarkian royal family usually let the disputes between houses resolve on their own unless they affect the country as a whole.

Taxes

Because the soil in the north varies greatly according to fertile regions and barren regions, a tax is determined not by the size of the land but the headcount of the castle's residents. They often accept fabric, grains, livestock, and fruits of agriculture in the place of gold and silver, but they also replace it at times with labor for constructions led by the royal family.

Race

70% of the north is composed of Temereans. Sichinites are Temereans as well. Temereans are tall and have strong bone structures, sharp noses, and strong jaws. The closer to the Galiau Mountains, the paler the skin, and the farther south, the yellower or more peach the skin. The colors of hair and eyes greatly vary in the range of blond, red, brown, black, and such. But light colors are more common. The northerners tend to admire dark colors because they idealize strong features.

The remaining 30% is composed of large, giant-like people of the east, with blunt faces and aggressive features. Their body hair is pitch black or gray. Darak and descendants of Gideraka are like this.

Marriage and Feminism

Various marital practices exist in the north, such as marrying a sister-in-law if the brother dies, marrying the mother if the father dies, marriage by capture, proxy marriage, and husbands living with wives' families, but now most only remain as vestiges and the most prevalent practice is monogamy.

This is because of the customs from the times when the people had to farm frozen land or could only feed a fixed number with only hunting and gathering. The northerners had a querulous history where they always stole and were stolen from, and hence lived lives very intimate with death. Some scholars speculate that was the reason the *Doctrines of Nuadism* of utopia were created.

They hold the matter of manners regarding women to great account, and this is said to have originated from warriors who did not know when their last days would be asking their great women not to discard their child after their deaths. Some claim that it originated from asking not to harass or discard husbands who return with injuries. In any case, the culture of monogamy that has existed for a long time has become a moral custom.

Also, the biggest difference between the north and the south is the attitude toward bastards and children born out of wedlock. Divorcing a woman is not a fault in the north, but having a child with another woman without divorcing the wife is greatly frowned upon. This applies to the nobles of a lower status, regardless of the rank of their positions, but it becomes more and more apparent the higher the positions.

The funny thing here is that that frown stops at the man and woman who engaged in the affair. According to the pure logic of *the blame is on the sinners and cannot be passed down. Hence, the child bears no sin,* the treatment of the bastard can equal that of a true-born. Of course, that depends on their parents' decisions. Thus, it is known that few suffer because they are born a bastard in the north.

It is said that men and women had similar rights two hundred years ago or so, and there even a feminist religion that worshipped strong women. But since the last conquest queen of the Rarkalia Dynasty, the customs regarding the women in the north regressed. Since the Brionakes' rule began, the northern women believe they must consider humility and obedience their virtues.

Religion

There are countless myths in the north, but most of the Temereans believe in the Myth of the Three Thrones and the Myth of Nuadga. Even if they don't actually believe and worship, they are educated about these myths to the point of brainwashing. They are close to a lullaby for all the children in the north. The northerners, who contemplate about afterlife and their identities after death, proudly carry the phrase *do not fear death* in their hearts. Thus, duels with the risk of lives occasionally occur and many choose the fatal path.

To give a small example, there is a tale told that a young man killed himself by falling down from the top of Mount Gania, a place that is known to be the birthplace of Nuadism, to prove that he did not fear height.

Major Houses

Great Lord of the North – Royal House Brionake of Muiyadro, noble house Brionake of Rokland
    Loem Region (rest omitted) – House Jafein
    Tadilda – House Bolette

Great Lord of the East – Karban (House Winloss extinct)
    Ballaim – House Vinsen
    Garas – House Jizal
    Pansia – the great rich Halipe
    Alliance of Galabua – House Decker of Pasis, House Remli of castle Guiyon, House Rieun of Bandal, House Winger with multiple lands in the east, west, south, and north

Great Lord of the East – the Noble House Brionake
    Erguin of Nortebloom – land of House Brionake
    Baldo, city of horse – of the state

Polbun – former Vannia

South – Esland (former Esenbark, a mountain city most famous for the collection of inkstones)

    Bert, independent city of Rayn

    Briom – land of House Haldroff

MORGANA

The empire of Morgana is composed of Morgana, Angredium, Saligar, Vayn, and other minority groups. It takes about two months to ride across the empire from the eastern end to the western end without obstacles.

Symbol: black lion on a gold or silver background

System

The emperor of Morgana holds absolute power. In the beginning, the royal house practiced nepotism by distributing land to their blood, but as time passed and the kingdom became an empire with an uncontrollably massive land, land distribution based on bloodline was abrogated.

Currently, their system is in the form of long-term lending of the land with titles, and the landlords accumulate their wealth by paying a fixed amount of tax and obtaining the rest. Because there are myriad people, as the land is so massive, they pledge their loyalties for practical benefits and calculated protection of the imperial family rather than for cultural homogeneity or patriotism.

Military System

The establishment of private armies in the lands inland varies greatly according to the size of the land, but it is prescribed that an army must be under five thousand at maximum. But places adjacent to outside forces and a fraction of the great lands where the invasion of the minorities is frequent may accumulate more than that if they register first.

Establishment of more than five thousand private soldiers must be approved by the imperial family through a private agreement, like the former House Mariposa. It is customary that the imperial family mediates and resolves disputes, protects the lords, and reduces their military expenses as the price of the agreement.

When a dispute arises, the black lion army of the imperial family usually forms, and for the events in the east where the archipelago is located, the imperial army (direct imperial guards) residing in the Simore Archipelago resolves it. But if it is far from the archipelago or if it is a dispute at the border or in the inlands, where expected damage is high, or if it is manual labor or construction, the Mariposas of the west are occasionally mobilized.

The guards of the remaining regular lands are mostly composed of mercenaries or a few knights selected from within the land. The commanding knights are mostly from the major central houses, and commoners cannot be ordained higher than a knight-in-training no matter how many contributions they make, with the exception of special situations.

Like during the Great Battle against Rarke, if they are engaging in a relatively large-scale war, they at times recruit soldiers from the nearby nobles in addition to taxes. But the number is limited to two hundred at the least and to five hundred at the most.

Nobility

The central fourteen houses (Hart, Westus, Arsein, Loweia, Vensi, Zordia, Scoza, Ornas, Hower, Zailiar, Denvas, Savos, Telval, Vousis, former Mariposa) are the noble houses that have free access to the Leweife Palace on Simore Archipelago in accordance with the imperial decree. They are the houses that are allowed permanent inheritance of the land and autonomy, and among them is a house that has been allowed to establish a private army of more than five thousand. But in actuality, the significance of their existence is merely an example of a force that has been loyal to the imperial family for a long time, and those with real great military forces are rather rare.

The power and renown of one that has been granted large land by the emperor is great, and merchants are not respected. But it is quite paradoxical that the wealthiest houses are Zordia, which does not have any land, and Savos, a usurer house of Ebloom.

Race

60% of the south is composed of Rotoreans. Many have tanned or yellow skin due to the strong sun, and the color brown is the most prevalent for hair and eye color. Though they do not look very different from the Temereans in the north, Rotoreans have smaller bone structures in general and have smoother jaws. The remaining are minorities that are hard to name, Temereans who migrated from the north, and various mixtures of all of them.

Marriage and Feminism

The virtues of the Morganaan women are wisdom and confidence. Women are permitted to be politically active to a certain extent, if they are smart. Morganaan women have more rights than the northern women, but polygamy is implicitly allowed. Sex business is well developed as well.

Under the permission that those who already have a lot can have more, many men have more than two wives or bring mistresses around publicly. But this also applies to women, though with the implied rule that women must engage with men of a higher status than their husbands. This is to prevent a fight related to love arising or an accident happening.

But because they have a strong sense of class, the differentiation between bastards and true-borns, and the discrimination against bastards, is very prominent, unlike in the north. Bastards cannot appeal even if they are treated like second citizens. There was a case where a noble man claimed he would not consider the child his wife gave birth to, after a public affair, as his own and won even without physical evidence. Not only that, but many bastards are abandoned because no one is sure whose child they are.

Religion

Except for those of the minorities who practice shamanism, most are realists who focus on the present life, unlike in the north. Not believing in the afterlife is like a stepping stone for them to increase the quality of their existing life and achieve cultural progression with the excuse that they must enjoy the now. Cultures such as statues and art are well developed, but they are reserved for the nobles. The landscaping business is very well established, and they have a sophisticated view on leisure, as they have well-developed regions for vacation.

Because they have beliefs related to contemplation of life and time that are not necessarily religious, everyone knows the tales of Martina of the Morning and Noche of the Night. Also, the southern myth of the lion god, which is the myth of the foundation of Morgana, the country that exercised absolute power over the southern continent for over a thousand years, is widely spread. The lion god myth is said to be intimately related to Noche of the Night.

ABOUT THE AUTHOR

Y. R. Shin is a bestselling author in Korea with the Mariposa series and other works including Misa, Barayeon, Water Trumpet Flower, The Castle where Thorn Trees Weep, Tracing the Shadows of Water, and more.

CPSIA information can be obtained
at www.ICGtesting.com
Printed in the USA
LVHW042302201020
669275LV00005B/111

.